Justice

Laurann Dohner

ELLORA'S CAVE
ROMANTICA®
ELLORASCAVE.COM

An Ellora's Cave Publication

www.ellorascave.com

Justice

ISBN 9781419967054
ALL RIGHTS RESERVED.
Justice Copyright © 2011 Laurann Dohner
Edited by Pamela Campbell.
Design and Photography by Syneca.
Model: Nick

Electronic book publication November 2011
Trade paperback publication 2012

With the exception of quotes used in reviews, this book may not be reproduced or used in whole or in part by any means existing without written permission from the publisher, Ellora's Cave Publishing, Inc.® 1056 Home Avenue, Akron OH 44310-3502.

Warning: The unauthorized reproduction or distribution of this copyrighted work is illegal. Criminal copyright infringement, including infringement without monetary gain, is investigated by the FBI and is punishable by up to 5 years in federal prison and a fine of $250,000. (http://www.fbi.gov/ipr/)

This book is a work of fiction and any resemblance to persons, living or dead, or places, events or locales is purely coincidental. The characters are productions of the author's imagination and used fictitiously.

The publisher and author(s) acknowledge the trademark status and trademark ownership of all trademarks, service marks and word marks mentioned in this book.

The publisher does not have any control over and does not assume any responsibility for author or third-party Web sites or their content.

Dedication

ହଚ

To my wonderful Mr. Laurann, who has always shown me that love is possible and true love is lasting.

Chapter One

✖

Jessie watched Justice North from the far corner of the room and bit her lip. She really wanted to work up the nerve to approach him. He'd been on the news often but he appeared even taller and better-looking in person.

Not too many people intimidated her but the man who had been appointed the leader of the New Species Organization by his own people was one of those rare few. She respected strength and courage, something he seemed to have in abundance.

She debated the wisdom of having a conversation with him. Justice gave orders to her bosses and held the power to change some of the task-force policies that she didn't agree with. The chance of finding another opportunity to have a chat with him was slim to none. She wasn't allowed to attend briefings her team leader held with the tall Species leader. Her opinion was irrelevant to him but the issues were important.

She hesitated, considering the ramifications. Tim Oberto would haul her ass into his office if he found out she'd gone over his head. He'd be his normal loud self and tear her to verbal shreds.

Her gaze swept the room, studying the New Species. They were brave for all they'd endured, every single one of them a victim of big business screwing them over.

A pharmaceutical company, Mercile Industries, had created genetically altered humans using animal DNA, had reared them inside secret facilities and forced them to endure decades of horrendous testing on their tortured bodies. They'd done it to make money and worse, they'd been funded in part by the government.

My tax dollars, she grimly acknowledged and clenched her teeth over how deeply that pissed her off. Mercile had pitched proposals to come up with miracle drugs that would help injured US soldiers heal faster, become physically stronger and enhance their reflexes. Those idiots in DC had eaten it up and signed the checks to pay for the research but later denied having knowledge that live test subjects were involved.

She gave them some credit for acting immediately to discover the truth when rumors surfaced of the illegal practices. Once officials had proof, military and police forces had worked together to rescue any survivors imprisoned by Mercile Industries. New Species were created with US tax dollars and born on American soil, which made them citizens.

The first facility had been raided and the survivors had been rescued—freed. Locations of three more hellish places were discovered after employees were interrogated. The teams had hit them hard and fast, rescued more victims and all hell had broken loose. Hundreds of victims needed to be housed. They'd been placed in secure locations and the blame game began. The US had given the New Species a newly built military base, which they turned in to Homeland, a Species-run community to keep them safe from the outside world. Under pressure from the government, Mercile Industries was quickly settling claims brought by New Species. With some of that money they'd bought a second large section of land they named Reservation.

A big body bumped Jessie, drew her from her grim thoughts and she smiled up at the male. New Species were easily identified by their animallike features. They weren't completely human but weren't all genetically altered with the same genes either and dubbing them with that title spanned all the differences. Some had been mixed with large-feline DNA, some with canine and some with primate.

"Sorry," he grumbled as she peered into a pretty set of catlike eyes.

Feline, she silently identified his mixed species. "No problem."

He moved on and she sighed in disappointment. Not many of them wanted to talk to humans. She couldn't blame them after all they'd been through. Mercile Industries had labeled each one with a number and called them experimental prototypes. The staff had treated the children as if they were subhuman, lab rats, without souls. They'd led cold, harsh lives, only leaving their cells for training or testing.

The new race they'd created wasn't docile as Mercile had projected in their grand scheme. Some of the growing Species rebelled and killed the humans who had spent years harming and torturing them. Instead of lab rats, the company had hundreds of angry, bitter, really strong prisoners who'd had enough of their shit. That fact made Jessie smile. *Good for them. I hope they took out a bunch of those bastards.*

Mercile decided to see if they could produce children from the males and females. It was a faster process for a female to give birth to another altered child than it was to spend millions of dollars to replicate the procedure that created them. Mercile had wanted to be rid of the originals, start over and learn from their mistakes. Their attempts to breed the unfortunate victims were unsuccessful. The males and females were unable to procreate.

That's when Mercile started selling the other experiments they'd created. Jessie felt rage thinking about the Gift Females the drug company used to lure in more investors. They purposely made smaller females with nonaggressive-animal DNA and used drugs to control their growth rate to make certain the females never reached over five foot four. The board members of Mercile Industries and all the rich contributors to the secret projects were given Gift Females when enough money exchanged hands. Jessie wondered if that was why the original scientist walked out on Mercile. The doctor who had designed the New Species had destroyed her research and disappeared, taking the knowledge with her. It was bad enough they'd created people as test subjects but to hand them over to sadistic perverts seemed a hundred times worse.

Gift Females were sold into sexual slavery. They'd been locked up, hidden away and grossly abused. Those were the females that Jessie helped recover and the ones that kept her up at night, unable to sleep.

She pulled her thoughts back to the present and stared at Justice North across the room, deciding she could do her job better if she could get him to hear her out. *Tim can be pissed but this is about making it easier for those poor women.*

She'd never seen Justice in jeans and a tank top before. He usually wore business suits at his press conferences. His bare arms revealed thickly muscled biceps, golden skin and he stood with a relaxed ease that made him more approachable. She took a deep breath, blew it out and advanced.

More tiny details became apparent as she drew closer to the tall leader of the New Species. His hair was auburn with streaks of blond. On television and in pictures it seemed a dull, universal brown color. His catlike eyes were exotic and darker, almost black. He possessed the distinctive wide cheekbones that jutted outward more than a typical human's and his nose flattened, seeming more animal than not. It always fascinated her that so few of them had facial hair and she wondered if they shaved to fit in more.

Her breath caught when he suddenly laughed and it was a husky, sexy sound. His full lips were the kissable kind that she enjoyed nibbling on. That realization brought her to halt. *Bad, Jessie. Don't go there. He's the boss of your boss and off limits. I totally need to find a man. I'm to the point where I'm fantasizing about guys I work with. Big mistake.*

She took note of his perfectly white, straight teeth, which were revealed when he laughed. She didn't see any fangs but it was possible he was one of the rare few who didn't have them. Of course, she also noticed he smiled with his lips close together. Mr. North might have trained himself to hide them since he dealt with the public. She'd overheard Tim say some of them did that and he'd know since he spoke to so many of the Species males on a daily basis.

Justice spoke to another Species male who was a few inches shorter and their conversation seemed intense since he never glanced her way. After a quick assessment of the Species leader, she pegged him at about six foot four. *Tall.* She had nearly reached his side when a rough hand gripped her forearm and jerked her to a standstill.

Jessie masked her alarm as her gaze dropped to the big hand on her arm, his hold nearly painful and lifted her chin to peer up. She wondered if he was one of the guards who protected Justice. She'd learned to hide her fear of the New Species when she came into contact with the fierce-looking guys. All of them were big, muscular and scary. This one was no exception.

It was the animal facial features that made them seem so frightening...and their sharp teeth and ability to make threatening sounds. He growled deep within his throat while his green eyes narrowed to glare at her. His jet-black hair fell past his shoulders and his clothes were so new they hadn't been washed.

Shit. Jessie knew hatred when she saw it in his glare. The night before a fifth testing facility had been raided and approximately ninety prisoners had been freed from their hellish existences. She had a pretty good idea this was one of them. He looked too rough around the edges to have calmed from his experience. He obviously hated anyone human and that spelled trouble for her.

She quickly assessed the situation, knowing it had the potential to turn into a nightmare. He was a big bastard, obviously super irate and while his hold on her arm wasn't too painful, the look he gave her seemed deadly. He had issues with her kind and she was the one in front of him. *Not good.*

"Please release me," she softly ordered.

"Human." He snarled.

Jessie tried to tug her wrist out of his hold but his fingers only tightened until the bone threatened to break. She didn't gasp aloud from the intense agony of being squeezed, fought that reaction and instead allowed her training to take over before he snapped her arm. He could easily if he applied more pressure. He didn't seem reasonable and she didn't want to wear a cast for weeks.

She quickly stepped into his body, almost touched his chest and jerked her arm hard downward. He had no choice but to release her or it would have twisted his wrist painfully. Jessie jumped back, put space between them and tensed. He would either attack or stay in place.

Being smaller helped. At five foot four Jessie had the advantage as she tucked her body when her attacker sprang at her with an enraged snarl. He hadn't expected that move and his hands only grasped air when his fingers grabbed where she'd been. She spun to the side, straightened and kicked out with her boot.

She caught the off-balance man in his hip and he crashed to the floor, sprawled on his side. Jessie backed up to put more space between them. The Species male jerked his head up, gaped at her with astonishment and used his arms to launch to his feet. He opened his mouth and growled inhumanly, revealing some sharp, lethal teeth. He lunged again, this time faster.

Jessie thought one word before she dived to the side to avoid his clawed fingers. *FUCK!* She tucked into a ball, rolled on the floor and came up on her feet the way she'd been trained to do. She needed to stay out of his reach and knew it would be over if he got his hands on her. They were physically no match if it came down to hand-to-hand combat. He'd pulverize her.

She caught him lunging at her again out of the corner of her eye. She kicked out, bent to press her hands on the floor to brace and caught the man with a violent up-kick. The impact of her boot with his body hurt her leg but it had to be more painful for him.

He staggered back with a loud gasp and it sank in that she'd managed to catch him in the groin. She twisted around after straightening to her feet, watched him grip the front of his jeans and double over. Jessie winced.

She hadn't meant to kick him in the balls but it was effective. She'd been aiming for his stomach but the guy was too tall and her legs weren't long enough. His head snapped up and she had no doubt he wanted her dead. Pure rage was displayed on his harsh features.

"Calm down," Jessie demanded, trying to sound composed when she wasn't. "I wouldn't have done that if you'd kept your hands and temper to yourself. I won't hurt you if you don't try to hurt me."

Jessie knew all hell broke loose around her. She didn't dare take her attention away from the large male who glared at her, still bent over, gripping his injured crotch. It was only luck that she heard a warning growl and twisted her head to check out the new threat.

Another large Species male sporting new clothes, shoved other males out of his way who were frozen in stunned shock. The new threat stormed toward her and she only had seconds to assess the situation. A few Species snapped out of their stupor and tried to stop him but he easily shoved them to the side. No one was able to prevent him from reaching her.

"Shit," Jessie gasped as his fist launched at her face.

Instinct alone shot her arm up to knock his fist to the side and deflect a direct punch that would have been dead center to her face. His knuckles brushed her ear and pain shot through the side of her head. He gripped her shirt with his other hand. She hadn't seen that move coming. Her sole priority had been avoiding the fist. He jerked her off her feet as if she weighed nothing and terror struck. He would probably either throw her into something or smash her bones by slamming her down onto something hard. Either way, it would be very painful.

Two hands gripped Jessie's hips firmly from behind. *Shit. I'm so screwed.* Two of them had her. She could only hope that some of the Species would come to her aid before the males turned her into a wishbone. Though she was human, she doubted they would allow her to be killed before they stepped in. How hurt she got before being rescued was anyone's guess.

The hands on her hips yanked hard. She was torn away from the one in front of her and the sound of tearing material registered. She'd seen him haul back his fist to attempt to nail her again but now she was out of his range.

Her back slammed into a rigid body and the large male — she assumed it was one — twisted away from her attacker. He put his body between her and the incoming fist, taking the punch himself. Jessie felt the impact through the man holding her and it sent both of them flying forward. She saw the wall coming and turned her head away, guessing it was going to hurt when they hit. He'd squish her between it and his body.

The male holding Jessie twisted again at the last second and his shoulder and hip slammed brutally into the wall instead of her. He dropped her onto her feet, moved lightning fast to position her against the wall gently and she bumped the plaster. It left her gawking at the wide back of the Species male who'd come to her rescue. He braced, his body tense as a loud snarl tore from his throat.

He's protecting me. Jessie relaxed instantly. The guy was huge and stood between her and anyone who wanted to do harm. *Who says chivalry is dead?*

"Back off," her protector roared — a harsh, brutal sound. Jessie carefully studied his back and it sank in that he wore jeans with a black tank top. His muscular arms were well displayed and his fingers curled into fists, lifted at his sides to fight. Her gaze roamed higher to the back of his head and identified the auburn hair with blond streaks. It hit her then that Justice North was the male who'd saved her ass.

"She's human," another voice barked.

"That doesn't give anyone the right to attack. She is a guest here." Justice snarled the words in obvious anger. "We are friends with humans and don't attack them. We especially," he shouted now, "don't attack females."

"I'm sorry, Justice," a new male voice panted. "We should have had more officers present."

"I want every one of the new ones rounded up and taken into the cafeteria immediately." Justice gave the order with harsh authority. "This is going to be settled immediately. This is the second attack on a human female since this morning and there won't be a third." Justice growled those words.

"Even the new females?" The out of breath male spoke.

"No. Just the males. The females seem to know better. I want to see every new male inside that cafeteria in ten minutes."

"We're on it," another man stated firmly.

Jessie stood perfectly still and waited for the tension to ease. Justice still appeared ready to do battle since he didn't budge from his position in front of her. She heard movement in the room, soft voices, a few growls and finally silence. Justice relaxed his stance. His arms lowered to his sides, his fists unfurled and he slowly turned.

Jessie stared up into Justice's handsome face. *Breathtaking fits him,* she thought, as she realized she'd stopped breathing. She sucked air into her lungs and met a pair of furious cat eyes framed with long, black eyelashes. They were a huge contrast to his blond-streaked auburn hair. On television and in photos his hair appeared much lighter and the camera didn't begin to capture his beautiful eyes. They were so exotic that they were probably the most beautiful sight she'd ever seen.

"Who are you?" he growled softly. "How did you get past security?"

Jessie frowned. He should have known who she was and why she was there. She took a deep breath. "I'm Jessie Dupree and I work for the task force assigned to the NSO. I'm their female ambassador to your retrieved Gift Females. Last night I was on the raid in Colorado and I came here with the females who were recovered."

She paused and watched his intense eyes. It was amazing to see them transform. The color changed as his anger dissipated. There was some blue in those dark depths. For a moment she was so distracted, she forgot she'd been talking.

"Tiger gave me permission to be here. I rode in on the helicopter with your females and have been assigned a room on the third floor of the hotel. Tammy invited me to her wedding so here I am. Didn't you see me during their ceremony?"

"No. I was distracted by a long voice message from the president. I had an earphone — was listening to it — and I had to text my reply to him." He took a deep breath and held out his hand. It was a big one with long, strong fingers and those nifty calluses covered both his fingertips and his palm. "I'm Justice North. It is a pleasure to meet you, Ms. Dupree."

She placed her smaller hand inside his. Heat from his hot skin jolted her. His large hand clasped hers but instead of shaking it, his fingers curled around her smaller ones, holding them. His gaze lowered to stare at their joined hands. Jessie couldn't take her attention from his face though. He finally looked up when he released her.

"I apologize for the attack. They are new and have a lot to learn. I'm going to teach them some valuable lessons about manners in a few moments. We won't tolerate that kind of behavior."

She shrugged. "I understand why they hate my kind. They have their reasons. I appreciate you coming to the rescue. I can keep someone off me for a little while but when they gang up, it's not usually a painless or healthy outcome for me."

His gaze lowered from her face down her body. His eyes widened and his breathing changed slightly, increased to a faster pace. His nostrils flared and a soft sound came from deep within throat. Jessie grinned.

"Did you just purr?"

His gaze lifted. "I don't purr." He gripped his tank top at his waist, quickly tugged it up his impressive torso and over his head. He offered it to her. "Put this over your shirt."

Jessie glanced down at her chest and noticed her shirt had been torn in the melee. She studied her black lace bra, grateful not to be wearing the white one she'd worn yesterday — the ugly, full-support bra. The black push-up cupped her breasts and flattered her size 34-D chest. She flinched over how pale her skin appeared against the black and hoped he wasn't blinded by the sight. Jessie didn't tan, she burned so she avoided the sun.

"Thanks but I can hold this together until I reach my room. One of your women, Breeze, set me up with some clothes since I didn't pack for a trip. I was called to the Colorado raid too fast to do that."

Jessie avoided his gaze by examining her shirt as she spoke, sorry he'd seen so much of her breasts. A few buttons were missing and the tear started at a buttonhole and ended under her breasts to fully expose her cleavage. She gripped the fabric together over her breasts to hide them and the cups of her bra. *So much for a first impression. Tim is going to chew my ass big-time and blame me for starting a fight with a Species.*

Her gaze lifted. Jessie examined Justice's bare chest and her attention snagged on a few sections of his naked skin. She would have started drooling but she knew it was extremely rude and unprofessional. The guy was tan, and firm muscles ripped his lean torso. His nipples were slightly darker than his coppery skin and they were hard at that moment. She had the urge to lick him to see if he tasted as good as he looked. *BAD JESSIE!* her mind screamed. She forced her gaze higher to discover he silently watched her.

17

"You should put that shirt back on, Mr. North. You have a chill."

He blinked. "I don't."

Her focus flicked to his nipples, still hard pebbles. "Your chest seems to disagree and it's difficult for me not to stare at you. You must work out a lot to look that good."

I said that aloud. Shit! I didn't mean to.

Another soft sound came from his throat and Jessie smiled, quickly over her slip of the lips. *That was definitely a purr. He's so hot. Tall, good-looking, can fight, stands up for women and makes that sexy sound. Oh yeah, don't forget he's off limits!*

Justice shifted his stance and cleared his throat. "I'm not cold."

She let that one slide, knew she'd said more than enough to get her yelled at by the task-force leader and pressed her lips firmly together. Justice put his shirt back on and she wished it were a crime for him to cover up that wonderful, sexy view of muscled masculinity.

With his chest covered again, her focus remained on his face and she didn't miss when his nostrils flared as he inhaled deeply, taking in her scent. She was glad she had showered recently and wore deodorant. She kept her smile in place as he tucked his tank top into the waistband of his jeans. Just a few feet separated them. He inhaled again and his nose twitched. It was as cute as hell but she worried he found her offensive.

"I hope I don't smell bad. I used stuff from the room when I took a quick shower before the wedding. The shampoo the hotel carries isn't bad but it's kind of generic. Do I pass muster?"

His gaze met hers. "I'm sorry. You smell nice. It's a natural instinct we have."

"It's all right." Jessie leaned forward a little and inhaled deeply. Her eyes remained locked on his. "You smell nice too. I like your cologne. It's kind of woodsy and masculine."

He softly purred and cleared his throat again. "Thank you."

"Are you all right? Did that guy hit you in the throat?" She started to worry he might be hurt with the way he kept making noises.

Justice North blushed. It stunned her a tiny bit and made her like him more.

"I'm fine." He paused. "It was nice to meet you and I'm sorry for the attack. I should go to the cafeteria since I did call for the meeting. I need to yell at my new males and throw in some threats for good measure to be certain they learn good behavior."

He turned and took a few steps away from her before Jessie's mind started to fully function again. Justice was walking away from her and she couldn't stand the idea of never seeing him again.

"Wait!"

Chapter Two

ശ

Justice froze and turned. His dark gaze met Jessie's. "Yes, Ms. Dupree?"

"I wanted to know if you had any free time soon. I hoped we could talk about your females. There are some policies I'd love to discuss with you that need to be changed. I've brought it up with Tim Oberto but he isn't exactly sensitive to female needs. Is there any possibility that you have some time to listen to my ideas? I think they are valid ones."

He seemed to ponder it. "How long will you be at Reservation?"

"A few days, if that's all right. I thought I'd stick around to help the new females adjust to outside life unless I get a call from the task force. I have a lot of free time between recoveries."

He bit his lip. "Why don't you come to the cafeteria with me if you are staying? I'd like them to know you on sight to make certain something like this doesn't happen again. We could share dinner afterward. It's the only time I have free. You can talk to me while we eat. After dinner I have to prepare for a press conference being held outside the gates at ten o'clock regarding last night's activities."

"That would be great." She remembered her torn shirt. "Do I have time to change?" She smiled. "Although if I didn't, I'm betting none of them would forget how I look if I released my shirt. I'm not sure they'd remember my face but it might do something for boosting human relations with your men if they saw me in a bra."

His entire body shook with laughter. *Justice is scorching hot,* Jessie decided. His eyes sparkled and his generous mouth widened to reveal white teeth. She saw a flash of points along his bottom lip. *He has the Species fangs after all.* She felt her body respond. She'd not only have to change her shirt but her thong too if she didn't get a grip. She wondered what his teeth would feel like against her skin if he nipped her with them.

"Down girl," she muttered.

His laughter died. "Excuse me?"

He'd heard her speak. She'd forgotten that Species had enhanced hearing. "It was nothing." She smiled again. "So, do I change or go as I am?"

"Why don't you exchange shirts? I'll talk to them while we wait for you and I'll introduce you when you arrive. Do you know where the cafeteria is?"

"I ate breakfast there with Breeze this morning."

"I'll see you when you return." He turned and walked away.

Jessie watched him move out of sight. The man fit a pair of jeans better than any guy she'd ever seen. He had long muscular legs that stretched the denim around his thighs and his rounded ass. He wore black high tops. They had Velcro strap closures. *They would be fast to take off.*

She grinned over her wayward libido, moving quickly toward the elevator. She appreciated a man who wore things that were fast and easy to get off. She shook her head at her reflection inside the elevator as she rode it up. *He's Justice North, a New Species and you know you can't ever go there. It would cost my job. Tim would not only kick my ass but he'd boot it from the task force.*

Jessie leaned forward, peered at her reflection in the mirror and winced. She could use some makeup but she rarely bothered unless she had to. She'd done all that for her first husband and it had been a waste of time. He'd expected her to primp for him or he'd been insulting. Her need to please had died when her marriage had. The bastard had an affair with a fellow soldier while on training exercises. She backed up and

21

ran her fingers through her hair. It was really bright red, a mess and she couldn't look worse if she tried. She might be attracted to the sexy Species but he wouldn't feel the same about her.

The elevator doors opened and she practically ran down the hall. She wasn't sure what had gotten in to her since meeting Justice but the man turned her on. It had been a long time since she'd met anyone who attracted her. He definitely made her heart race and wild thoughts filled her head. Two years had passed since her bitter divorce and she hadn't been interested in men.

Well, there was that one guy, she remembered, *but does a one-night stand after drinking too much count?* She decided not to ponder that one. That had been a rough night and she'd needed the comfort of another person. It was right after the first time she'd retrieved the body of a New Species female.

The bastard who'd murdered her had buried her small, broken body under the basement floor of the cell he'd kept her in for years. The sight of watching the body unearthed had driven Jessie straight to the nearest bar and right into the arms of the first man who looked good. She'd wanted to forget the pain of knowing what had been done to that poor victim and how they'd been too late to save her. The one-night stand had been a dud. He had talked a good game but once he'd hit the field, he hadn't pitched worth a damn.

She entered her room and grabbed the first shirt lying on the bed, a blue tank top. It was big on her but she wasn't surprised since all the New Species females living at Reservation were experimental prototype females for the drugs they'd used to make them so big and strong. The smallest one she'd ever seen stood about five foot ten. The tallest had to be about six foot three. They were sturdily built women who could bench-press the average male if need be. The supply store carried spare clothes for the residents at Reservation and probably didn't order a size small or medium in anything.

Jessie rushed out of the room, shoving her room key back inside her jeans. The only pants they'd given her were sweats. She didn't like them. That left her living in the pair of black jeans she'd been wearing when she arrived. She wasn't one to use a purse and if something didn't fit inside a pocket or could be strapped somewhere on her body, she didn't see the need to carry it. She stepped back on the elevator and checked her reflection again. Her long hair hung past her ass. It was a brassy, bright red, the color created from two boxes of hair dye.

She'd found the courage to break out of the mold working for New Species. They were different, special and made their own places in life. Jessie had changed her hair to the bright, flashy color in defiance of the norm. She knew she probably should glow in the dark from the luminosity of her hair but she loved it. It really set her dark-blue eyes off and was a drastic contrast to her naturally almost-milk-white skin. She would never tan and didn't care.

The elevator doors opened and she strode toward the cafeteria. The double doors were wide open and two New Species uniformed officers stood guard. She slowed her pace and studied the men, wondering if Justice had informed them that she'd been invited to the meeting.

They moved out of the way. Jessie flashed each man a smile and walked inside the large room, only to stop a few feet past the door. She spotted Justice right off, not being able to miss him towering over everyone, standing on a tabletop on the other side of the room by the long buffet island. He naturally drew attention anyway but elevated he seemed to be larger than life.

"Humans are not our enemies. Not most of them." Justice looked annoyed and his face scrunched a little. "There are good humans and some bad ones like those we were exposed to at Mercile. The bad ones are a minority. Am I making myself clear? Good humans freed us and fought to give us rights and privileges. We are equal in all ways because of them. They are not the ones who enslaved and tortured us. They didn't know what was being done to us but when they found out, they have done everything possible to help us get where we are today. Every one of you sits here because of those good humans."

A male stood. "Are we supposed to trust them now? It is hard, Justice."

Justice relaxed, his features smoothing. "I understand your hesitancy but we must change with the times. Yesterday you were locked inside a cell but today you are free. Yesterday the humans you dealt with were evil monsters but today you are dealing with good humans who would be horrified if they realized what had been done to us by their own people. They want those people punished as much as we do."

A few men in the back suddenly turned their heads to stare at Jessie. She kept her smile in place and figured her scent had reached them. It had only taken about fifteen seconds for everyone to realize she had entered the cafeteria. She stayed put by the door and watched the men, spotting anger on a few faces.

"This is Jessie Dupree," Justice stated loudly. "She's a good human. No one is to attack her again. Her job is to help locate New Species who are still imprisoned. She goes in with a team of trained human males who fight for our freedom and could easily die to save us. Her job is taking care of our retrieved females. She was there when you were freed last night and risks her life to go in and take our females to safety. Her life is devoted to us but she was attacked by a few of you in the lobby." Justice paused, his stern gaze drifting across each man before he spoke again. "It is unacceptable what happened to her. We don't attack humans unless we are attacked first."

"She attacked me," a male growled.

Justice arched his eyebrow and crossed his arms over his chest, a look of anger returning as he zeroed in on the speaker. "Really? How did she attack you?"

Jessie bit her lip to keep her mouth shut. She waited silently until the man finally spoke.

"She offended me and tried to break my wrist."

Justice took a menacing step forward on the table but stopped at the edge. "Did you touch her first?"

"Her arm."

"You grabbed her. I saw marks on her wrist and you put them there. You attacked her first. She defended herself by trying to get free of you." Justice paused. "Quite well too."

The male growled in protest and Jessie's gaze wandered until she found him. It was the guy she'd kicked in the balls who made the angry sound. She tried not to smirk. He had totally deserved it but still, she had meant to catch him with her heel in his stomach. She was short, he was a tall guy and shit happened.

"Any human at Reservation is invited, is here with our blessing and welcome. They are under our protection and you won't attack one. You won't be rude to one either. You will also never attack a female human under any circumstances. Their women are not as strong as ours and weren't raised our way. They don't posses our fighting skills or strength. I swear that you will be dealt with extremely harshly if you attack a human female here. Some of them live with our males as mates. They have committed to each other, mated for life. Those males will kill any one of you who touches his female and it would be his right to do so."

Justice paused and took deep breaths before he began speaking again. "Those are our laws. You are to never attack the officers you see in black uniforms either. They are to be respected and listened to. Their word is law as if I have spoken. Our females are off limits unless they consent to being touched. I hope I shouldn't even have to mention that but I wasn't raised in the same testing facility as you. We treat our females with respect and never share sex with them unless they initiate it. You will know punishment if any of you refuse to live by these rules. I hate to stress this but these are laws that are never to be broken. You will find yourself in lockup if you can't live by them and I promise you won't be set free until you realize we need to have some laws to live in peace together. Am I clear?"

The room remained silent. Justice took the time to meet every man's gaze before he slowly nodded. "Now, dinner will be served. We'll consider this matter closed."

Justice jumped down gracefully from the table to walk directly to Jessie. He looked grim when he paused at her side. "Let's eat."

She wasn't sure what to say to alleviate his bad mood. He offered her his arm. She reached out and her fingers curled around his forearm. Another jolt shot through her body from his hot, firm skin under her fingers. The man was so warm, it almost felt as if he ran a fever.

"We're not eating here?"

"No. I hope you don't mind but we'll dine in the living room of my suite. Do you really want to have a discussion in front of all of them? I don't. They aren't real happy with me right now for laying down the law but it needed to be done."

"I'm probably not their favorite person either. That's fine."

Jessie's heart pounded over the concept of being alone with Justice for dinner. It sounded intimate instead of businesslike. Then again, if he had an office at Reservation, they would be alone if he took her there. The living room of his suite would be larger than an office. Justice led her to the elevators.

Justice refused to look at Jessie once the elevator doors closed, peering everywhere but at her. Jessie didn't release his arm but she had the urge to. Why wouldn't he look at her? He took a deep breath.

"I ordered us dinner. I wasn't sure what you wanted." He paused. "I took the liberty of asking them to bring various dishes. I would have waited to ask you but it would have taken more time. I have a speech to write after dinner and the faster I eat, the faster I can get to it."

"That sounds like a great plan." She smiled. "I'm not real picky about food. I'm happy to eat."

He finally shifted his gaze to hers. "You don't appear as if you eat much. You are small."

She laughed. "Rigorous workouts will do that. My father and brother were both Marines and I married a Navy SEAL." She shrugged. "My mom died when I was five so I've always been around men who stayed fit. That's where I picked up some fighting skills. They wanted to make sure I could take care of myself in any circumstance. I was always mouthy and curious as a child and definitely not the timid type. My Dad said my mouth and my ability to find trouble meant that I needed to be able to defend myself. He was right."

Justice had tensed. His voice was naturally deep but it came out rougher. "Your husband must hate your job if it keeps you away from him."

"Ex-husband. We divorced two years ago."

Justice avoided glancing at her again. She noticed he slowly relaxed as the doors to the third floor opened to allow them to exit the elevator.

"We're staying on the same floor."

Justice didn't say a word as he led her down the hall. It was in the opposite direction of her room. At the end of the hallway he pulled out a key from his front jeans pocket to unlock the door. Jessie had to release him when he opened it and motioned for her to take the lead.

She took note of the nice suite with the spacious living area. A small kitchenette had been built against one wall with a wet bar. The hallway that led to the bedroom was on the other end of the room. Justice motioned toward the couch.

"Please have a seat. Do you mind if I remove my shoes? I don't care how long I wear them, I still can't wait to be barefoot."

"It's your place. Be comfortable."

She sat on his couch. That was another thing about New Species she'd heard from the team. Most of them hated to wear shoes, preferred to go barefoot, since they'd never worn them inside their cells. She knew firsthand the females weren't overly fond of underclothes either. She wondered if it were the same with the males and it caused her to smile. *Is Justice commando under those jeans? Say something*, she ordered her mouth, to get her mind away from that topic.

"I'm not real fond of shoes either. When I'm home, I kick them off the second I walk in the door and I don't put them on again until I leave."

Justice sat a few feet away and removed his shoes. He tore open the Velcro closures, jerked them off and Jessie grinned at seeing his large, bare feet. He must hate socks too since he didn't wear them. Chances were he was naked under those jeans. She'd almost bet on it.

Her attention focused on his lap when he stood but she couldn't tell one way or the other. Her gaze lifted up his body and she blushed slightly. He stared at her with narrowed eyes, obviously catching her eyeing the front of his pants.

"You were staring at me. Did I forget to zip the fly of my jeans?" He reached down to brush his hand over the front of them.

She shook her head, more embarrassed. "No. You didn't forget."

He blinked. "What were you staring at? Is there a stain? Did I drop something on my lap when I had lunch?" He bent forward a little, glanced down, before straightening. "I don't see anything."

She hesitated. New Species liked bluntness. That was one thing she knew about them with certainty. They appreciated honesty. "You don't like shoes or wear socks. I know your females hate underclothing and I was inappropriately wondering if the men felt the same. I was trying to judge if you wore something under your jeans or not. I can't tell. I'm sorry. It was extremely rude of me."

Jessie expected him to be offended or perhaps grow angry. Instead his eyes crinkled and a deep laugh erupted from his throat. It was a nice surprise that he was amused.

"I see. I do wear them. I find jeans are a little harsh on sensitive skin and they can pinch too. I enjoy wearing thick, soft cotton between jeans and my skin."

Jessie wondered how sensitive his skin was where "the thick, soft cotton" covered it. *Is he a boxers or briefs man? Maybe a Speedos guy?* She hoped not. The later were her ex-husband's underwear choice and she would hate to discover Justice had anything in common with Conner.

A doorbell chimed that distracted both of them. Justice walked to the door, his graceful, long legs carrying him there quickly. "That will be our dinner. I don't have a dining table but would you mind eating with me on the coffee table?"

An image flashed of him sprawled out on his back, hopefully naked and her eating food off his muscular body. She shoved it back. *Damn it, stop! He's the boss of my boss. Thoughts like those will get me canned. Stop fantasizing about Justice! Concentrate on something else and answer him.*

He was so thoughtful and polite. It surprised her more than a little, considering the way he'd been raised in the testing facility. "It's perfect. I never use my dining room table at home." She laughed. "I'm one of those people who watch TV while I eat at my coffee table. I know it's a really bad habit to have but I live alone. It beats watching something rather than staring into space."

Jessie couldn't see who Justice spoke softly to but it was a short conversation. Her host pulled a silver cart into the room and closed the door. The cart had four covered plates on top and on the shelf under it were half a dozen various sodas and four small covered containers. Justice pushed the cart across the carpet to the edge of the coffee table.

"You may choose whatever you like. I ordered things I enjoy so I'll eat anything that's left." Justice lifted off lids and tossed them on an overstuffed chair nearby. He had a great aim when each lid landed perfectly on target.

Jessie peered at the four dishes. One plate contained pasta in a white sauce with shrimp and a side of garlic bread. *Good.* There was probably the largest piece of prime rib she's ever seen on the next one with side dishes of a baked potato and some veggies. The third dish almost made her flinch. It was a whole cooked fish, possibly trout and she had flashbacks of her past at the mere sight of it. Her ex ate them constantly and she'd grown to hate the smell. The fourth plate was a stuffed, baked chicken with gravy.

"It all looks good except the fish." She smiled. "You pick."

He hesitated before reaching for the chicken. "I'm partial to chicken. I never had it before we were freed."

"I didn't know that. They didn't feed you chicken?" Jessie reached for the prime rib. She set the plate down on the coffee table carefully. Justice moved across from her and sat opposite her a few feet down so they could both comfortably stretch their legs under the table without touching. She sat on the floor too. Her back settled against the couch, finding it really comfortable.

Justice was nearest to the cart. "What kind of soda do you want? Do you mind soda?"

"The cherry one, please. I love them."

He smiled. "So do we."

"You were never given caffeinated drinks. I knew that one."

"Just water. Sometimes we received juice." He gripped the cherry soda and handed it over. Their fingers brushed.

"Thank you."

They both popped the tabs of their cans and arranged the silverware. Justice dug in to his chicken and Jessie smiled at his amazingly good table manners. It surprised her again. She had eaten with the female Species plenty of times. They ate with their fingers mostly, tearing things apart and swallowed food quickly as if it were about to be snatched away.

Justice cut and chewed his food leisurely. She glanced at the baked chicken. He ate fully cooked meat too, also astonishing her. Maybe men were different from the women and his time away from his cell had changed his eating habits. Jessie knew she thought cooked food tasted a hell of a lot better than raw or almost-raw meat.

Justice's cell phone rang and he sighed. He looked tired to Jessie suddenly as his features seemed to turn haggard. He shifted his body to reach inside his back pocket to dig it out. He glanced at the screen before he met Jessie's curious gaze.

"I'm sorry. I have to take this."

"Go right ahead." She hoped they'd get to talk before he was called away.

He flipped open the phone but kept eating. "What is it?"

Jessie ate as Justice listened to the caller, responded with abrupt answers and kept eating his meal. He looked like a man used to working around a phone since he didn't struggle to eat while holding a conversation. He could juggle the phone and his silverware with practiced ease. He chewed between words. He finally hung up and used his face and shoulder to close the phone. That was talent that drew a smile from her.

Justice lifted his gaze to stare at her while the phone slipped down his chest to perfectly land in his lap. "What is so amusing?"

"You. I've never seen that kind of talent before. You closed your phone without ever having to use your hands and then you wiggled a little so the phone would slide down your chest into your lap. Do you do that often?"

He smiled. "It is a skill I have learned."

The phone rang again and he sighed. He closed his eyes for a second before releasing his fork to reach into his lap. He studied the caller ID and set the phone on the edge of the table. His gaze met Jessie's.

"I can skip that one. It's one of the news stations trying to get an early comment from me."

"Do you ever get days off?"

"Never." He shrugged one shoulder. "I knew it would be a tough responsibility when I was asked to take the lead."

"Take the lead?"

"My people asked me to lead them. I was calmer than most and reasonable. I was the best fighter too and I had the quickest response time adjusting to where they took us after we were freed. I did not try to kill any humans who annoyed us with their way of criticizing everything we did. I was always the cushion between my people and yours. I became the negotiator when there were disagreements between us. The Species were asked to elect a spokesperson to represent them and I was asked by my people to lead. I accepted."

She took a sip of her drink. "You've done an amazing job. My father is Senator Jacob Hills and he always tells me that your job originally was supposed to be limited but you stood up for Species and argued to get them where they are today. He says you are a force of nature that no one should be stupid enough to mess with."

Justice chuckled. "I like him. I didn't realize you were his daughter." His gaze skimmed her. "You look nothing like him."

"I resemble my mother but I barely remember her. She died when I was five years old after a drunk driver hit her car on her way home from the gym. I have a lot of pictures of her though and I definitely take after my mom."

"I'm sorry for your loss. Your father is well liked."

"He likes you too. Not many people realize I'm his daughter and he tries to keep that off the radar. I'm kind of wild." She touched her hair. "He hates the hair."

Justice studied it. "You were not born with that bright hair, correct? I like it but I have never seen that color before and I have seen a lot of people since we were freed."

"It's straight from a bottle. It's not the color he objects to but he does miss seeing it a lot less colorful. It's the length he hates the most. I refused to cut it after an especially bad haircut when I was sixteen that made me look like a boy and it was days before my big sweet-sixteen birthday. That's a big party event and I hated it short. I stopped cutting it after that fiasco. Then my ex-husband demanded I keep it short after our wedding. He said it was too long, always annoying him, and he and my father tried to gang up on me to cut it to my shoulders. 'Responsible people don't have hair to their asses.' That's a quote." Jessie laughed. "I won't cut the hair and Dad gives me some grief about it whenever I see him." She shrugged.

His pretty gaze softened. "It's beautiful. Anyone is foolish who wants you to cut it. I don't know how anyone could find it annoying. I have long hair. It's not nearly as long as yours but long hair for a man isn't fashionable it seems, from what I've been told by our media consultants. I also refused to cut my hair short but I do allow them to keep it at this length. I am responsible and hope humans see me as such. I hope you leave yours flowing down."

He likes long hair. Jessie felt her heart twist. Sexy hot, nice ass, a body that didn't end and he liked her hair. He was nearly perfect. His phone suddenly rang and he reached for it. *Scratch that. A perfect guy wouldn't have an annoying cell phone that kept ringing all the time. He wouldn't be a workaholic.* Justice North lived and breathed work.

"I'm sorry but I have to take this." He flipped open his phone. "Justice here."

Jessie finished her dinner. Justice had finished with his too. Halfway through the conversation he'd shot her an apologetic look and rose to his feet. He walked to his briefcase on a desk by the front door and opened it to leaf through some folders as he spoke quietly. He remained on the phone.

Chapter Three

ℰℭ

Jessie cleaned up their dinner dishes and put them on the bottom empty shelf of the cart. She lifted the lids on the four smaller dishes to identify the desserts when she pulled them out and set them on top. She knew a lot of the Species weren't fond of chocolate and ignored the fudge cake to study the other dishes. One was a mixed-fruit concoction piled on what appeared to be angel food cake. The other two were pieces of apple and pumpkin pie. She glanced at Justice for a moment, trying to decide which one he'd enjoy more. She picked up the fruit and the apple pie and grabbed a spoon before approaching him.

He must have sensed her behind him. He turned and cupped the bottom of the phone to mute his voice. "I'm sorry."

"Which one?" She held them out.

He smiled and accepted the fruit. She had guessed right. She held out the spoon but he didn't have a hand free to take it. She grinned as she dipped it into the dish he held and lifted it toward his lips. He grinned in response and opened his mouth.

She took notice of his fangs as she gently slipped the spoon against his tongue, avoiding the sharp points of his teeth. He sealed his mouth around the spoon and Jessie suddenly became as jealous as hell of that bit of silver with his lips wrapped around it. She pulled it slowly out.

He closed his eyes as he savored the taste, his expression showed the pure pleasure he experienced and he softly groaned. Jessie put the other dish on the table far from his papers and took the dish he held. His eyes opened to stare at her and she kept her smile in place despite the attraction she felt toward him. She dipped the spoon again to offer him another bite.

"You need both hands," she explained softly.

"Thank you," he whispered.

He took another bite, just as seductively as the last, only the second time he kept his gaze on her face. The blue of his eyes showed more and it fascinated her how the color seemed to change with his emotions. The oval-shaped pupils had shrunk a bit, narrowed and more blue spread through his exotically patterned irises. Justice suddenly broke eye contact to search for something. He grabbed a paper and read it. She felt the loss of his attention and disappointment filled her for some odd reason. She'd enjoyed being the sole focus of his attention for those brief moments.

"I see that. It's right in front of me. Tell them that's fine but make them go lower on the price. Just because we won that lawsuit doesn't mean we're stupid enough to spend all of it on high bids." Justice cleared his throat. "Tell them you are calling others to acquire bids on the job. That should make them lower their price. Go with the number we spoke of and if they don't accept it, call others and reopen the bidding. We're set on a budget."

Jessie fed him another bite when the other person on the phone kept talking. She hadn't fed a man…ever. She enjoyed it. He flashed another grateful look, smiling at her. She wondered if a woman had ever fed him, hoped not and wanted him to remember her. She fed him all of the fruit and cake until the plate was empty. She returned the dish to the tray and picked up a few sodas for them to drink. He pointed at the table next to him, grinned his thanks and reached for something in his briefcase. Jessie opened the soda for him and set it down. She went to the couch and ate the apple pie.

"I'm so sorry about that." Justice collapsed on the couch next to her a few minutes later after ending the conversation. Three feet separated them. "Thanks for the fruit. It was really good."

She turned to face him. "I understand."

His phone rang again and his smile faded to a grimace. "I'm not going to look. For a dime I'd toss that thing into a wall and break it."

She touched her front pockets. "Sorry but I don't have any change."

He laughed. "I wish you did."

"Does your phone always ring nonstop?"

"Only when it's on and that's always."

"You should get someone to help you. One man can't possibly do everything."

He shrugged. "I don't know who would do everything that I do."

"I'd train a dozen of them and disappear for a month of vacation. I bet you dream of hiding from cell phones and other people."

"Don't tempt me." A look of longing crossed his features. "Do you think they'd hire me if I ran away to the circus?"

Jessie laughed. "I'm sure they would. I don't think you'd enjoy that job any better though. You wouldn't have calls to deal with but the people factor would be a hell of a lot worse."

He adjusted his big body on the couch, bringing up his foot to rest on the edge of the coffee table. "What did you want to talk about? I would really be interested in hearing your ideas."

Jessie hesitated. "You get this all the time, don't you? People wanting your attention for something?" She felt bad for him. "I'll tell you what. I'll write you a letter, send it to your office and you can look it over when you find some free time. You shouldn't have to deal with work right now. You really need some time to relax."

"You want to leave?" He tensed. "I understand. I'm sorry about dinner getting interrupted. It was rude of me but I really had to take those calls. I swear I will read them if you want to send your ideas by mail. Just put your name in bold black print on the back of the envelope and I'll tell my secretary to bring it to me as soon as it comes in. It will get my full attention."

Jessie stood. "I don't want to leave. You're so stressed out." She peered down at him. "You work more than anyone I've ever met. My father is a workaholic but you make him pale in comparison. Don't worry about dinner or the calls. Do you know what you need?"

He shook his head but curiosity sparked his pretty eyes. Jessie hesitated. *Oh hell, who cares if it is unprofessional? He's stressed out, I want to help him and I'm doing it. It's such a bad, horrible idea but screw it.*

"You need a massage."

His eyebrows lifted. "What?"

His baffled expression was adorable and drew a chuckle from her as she repeated her words. "You need a massage. I can rub your shoulders if you have some lotion around here. I used to do it for my father when he got stressed out. It made him feel better and it will feel nice on top of it."

Justice swallowed hard. "There's some in the bathroom. All the rooms come with those things."

"That way?" She pointed at the hallway.

"Yes."

"I'll go. You relax. Put both of your feet up, get comfortable and don't you dare touch that phone. Let it ring."

Jessie realized she'd lost her mind. Justice could order her boss to fire her ass and Tim would. Justice was the leader of the NSO and she planned to rub the tension out of his thick, broad shoulders. *Oh hell,* she thought as she looked around the bedroom and walked into the bathroom. Justice was a stress case and he needed to unwind. A massage would do him a world of good. She located the lotion and returned to the living room.

Justice had followed her orders by resting his big feet on top of the coffee table. Jessie smiled as she bent, took off her own shoes and met his unsure gaze. He watched her cautiously as if he had no idea what she'd do. She fought back a laugh over his bewilderment. She figured he was probably wondering if she was insane or not.

"I'm going to climb on the back of the couch and sit behind you. Can you take off your shirt?"

He only hesitated for a second before reaching for his waist, leaned forward a little and tugged the tank top higher up his chest to reveal those amazing muscles on his flat stomach again. Jessie stepped onto the couch, sat behind him and planted her feet next to his hips. She flipped open the lotion cap, studying his massive shoulders, understanding how much responsibility rested on them. They were impressive enough that she guessed he was the one man who could handle being the face of Species before the world.

His hair fell in the way and she set the lotion down and reached to her ponytail, pulling out the thong holding it in place. Her fingers dangled it out in front of Justice's face.

"Could you put your hair up on the top of your head to get it out of the way, please?"

He hesitated before accepting it, pulled all his hair up on top and secured the strands. She figured she'd laugh if she saw him from the front. She concentrated on his tempting back instead, longed to touch him and poured lotion into one palm. She set the bottle down and warmed the creamy substance between her hands.

"The trick to relaxing is closing your eyes and letting everything go." She spread the lotion over his shoulders, her fingers gripping the muscle. The tension in him couldn't be denied. His shoulders felt like stone under her fingers and palms. She let her hands glide over his heated skin until the lotion coated the area she intended to massage. "Do you think you can do that?"

"I'll try." His voice came out deep and raspy.

"Good. You just close your eyes and relax."

Jessie dug her fingers into tense muscle. She used her palms to push into his skin to massage deep, knowing she wouldn't hurt him. Her hands weren't strong enough to do that. Enjoyment filled her at touching him, her gaze locked on the tan skin she manipulated and hoped it would work. Justice needed to unwind. He worked way too hard.

He groaned, drawing a grin from Jessie—she hadn't lost her touch. Her hands worked up his neck to knead his muscles before slowly lowering to the tops of his shoulders then back. He groaned and made soft sounds occasionally.

The phone rang a few times but he ignored it. He didn't tense at the disruptions or move under her hands. Jessie's hands started to hurt eventually from the strength she'd used. She stopped.

"Is that better?"

He groaned. "Yes."

"Are you feeling stress free?"

"Yes."

"My mission of relaxation is now complete."

She released his shoulders with regret. It had been a pleasure to have her hands on the tall Species leader. She tried not to allow her thoughts to linger there and knew it was a really bad thing that she was so attracted to him. Her fingers slid the thong free from his hair and she shoved it into her pocket. *Talk about barking up the wrong tree. He's way out of my reach and Tim would kick my ass if he knew I was here.*

Jessie climbed off the back of the couch and studied Justice's handsome features. His dark, sexy gaze met hers. She had to swallow hard over the intense look he concentrated on her, not sure what it meant with him so serious. He was really good at keeping her off balance.

"Is anything wrong? You're staring at me as though you might want to say something."

He slowly rose to his feet and he was so tall her chin had to lift to keep her gaze on his. She held still. He stood nearly a foot taller than her and he was really impressive in size. *Too big.* She let that thought slide. It didn't matter because she didn't feel threatened by him. He continued to watch her intently until he finally spoke.

"Thank you," he rasped.

"You're welcome."

He blinked. "You should probably leave before I do something I'll regret. Thank you for sharing dinner with me and…feeding me the dessert. I especially want to thank you for the massage. It was wonderful and needed."

Jessie's heart rate accelerated a little and curiosity wouldn't be denied. "What are you thinking about doing that you'll regret?"

His gaze searched hers and a long moment passed while he seemed to debate answering. "Touching you."

Her heart did a flip. She identified the look in his eyes now that she had a hint. *Desire.* Justice wanted her as a man wanted a woman. His nostrils flared and he made that soft sound in his throat that did wonderful things to her libido.

"You do purr," she whispered.

Justice ordered his hands not to fist at his sides, worried Jessie might take it as a threat but he longed to touch her so desperately that it became a nearly impossible urge. Having her hands on him, inhaling her feminine scent so close to him while she'd massaged his shoulders, had driven him a little insane.

She was human, worked for the task force assigned under his command and he'd read up on proper human etiquette in the workplace. *Sexual harassment.* Those two words repeated in his head. She wasn't Species, her society's rules were totally different than those in the world he lived in and it wasn't a simple solution of asking her if she wanted to share sex with him. That's what he'd do if she were one of his women. They knew they could freely deny him and he'd respect it. She might be afraid or insulted if he dared utter that question.

He tried to reason with his turned-on body. He couldn't possibly share sex with Jessie Dupree. She wouldn't want him. Her actions were based on kindness and not an invitation to put his hands on her in return. She'd come to discuss work, not end up in his bed.

The image of sweeping her into his arms and carrying her down the hallway to his room filled his head. He'd tear her clothes off, explore her pale skin and run his hands over every inch of her body. His cock responded full force as blood rushed to his groin and the uncomfortable heaviness of the hard-on made him want to adjust his stance since it pressed against the confining denim of his jeans.

Breathe through it, he ordered his body. *Resist. You can't offer her sex. She's human and you're not allowed to have her regardless of how much you want her.* Those thoughts helped him regain some control on his raging need to take her. He'd growl at her if she were Species, show his dominance and offer her his body. He'd strip her in under a minute if she agreed to share sex with him and show her his skill as a lover.

A small trace of uncertainty struck and kept that growl of intent locked within his throat since she wasn't Species. He had no idea if anything he'd learned about humans would apply to her. He swallowed hard, kept silent and hoped he appeared nonthreatening. She was much smaller and weaker than Species women. That was another thing that cooled his heated blood. Jessie appeared frail in comparison and he feared he'd cause her harm in some way if he followed through with his instinct to attempt to get her into his bed.

Jessie stared back into Justice's beautiful gaze while he remained absolutely silent. *I want him*, she silently admitted.

Tim will have my ass, fire me, but oh hell, he's worth the risk. He wants to touch me and I really want him to. Tim doesn't have to know, right? Who would tell? Her gaze broke contact to sweep around the room. *No witnesses, no one to judge and we're both adults.* She peered up at him again, met his intense stare as he continued to regard her, almost as if he waited for unspoken consent.

It could lead to sex if they put their hands on each other. Justice was a big guy, really strong and a Species. She wondered how that would work out between them in bed. She knew that some women had hooked up with them. She had gone to Tammy and Valiant's wedding and Tammy had sure seemed more than happy despite their drastic size difference.

"Have you ever slept with a human?" Those words popped out and couldn't believe she'd said the thought aloud.

"No."

Their gazes remained locked and it encouraged her to keep talking. "I've never been attracted to your kind before but I'm drawn to you in the worst way. Am I being too blunt? I know total honesty is supposed to be normal for Species. Just tell me to shut up if I'm wrong."

"You want me too?" His voice lowered to a raspy growl.

Kinda scary but hot, she decided. His voice change made her heart race faster. Justice moved slowly, leaned his body closer and his hand lifted to cup her face with his big palm. His other hand slid loosely around her waist while he studied her eyes. *Answer him.*

"Yes," she breathed.

"You're so small and I'm afraid I'll bruise or accidentally hurt you."

She grinned, finding his nervousness reassuring. It proved she wasn't the only one on shaky ground and all her doubts about getting involved with him disappeared. "I'm tough and willing to risk it."

"I saw that you were strong in the lobby when you were attacked." He nudged her closer with his hand at her hip until their bodies pressed together. "You turned me on. You were small yet fierce. You fought incredibly well."

"I did?"

"Mmmm," he growled as his face lowered. "Pull your hair back, please. I want access to your neck."

She gripped her long hair without hesitation and shoved it back over her shoulder. She tilted her head to the side to give him open access to her shoulder and throat. He leaned in more and Jessie shivered in anticipation when she felt his hot breath tease her skin below her ear. Justice inhaled slowly and ran his nose from that area, as gently as the caress of a breeze, downward to where her shirt started at her bra strap.

"I won't touch you with my teeth. Don't be afraid. I'm aware that sharp canines scare humans."

"I'm not worried about it and you can touch me with your teeth as much as you want." The concept excited her but she did have one exception. "Just try not to break the skin. I'm not into love bites. I'm not a fan of pain."

He purred deeply, a sexy rumble coming from him. Her hand pressed against his chest and she drew closer until her breasts flattened against his big frame. She could feel vibrations when he purred that way. Jessie gasped softly from surprise when his tongue suddenly traced her skin. Jessie turned her head, found her mouth pressed to skin and opened it to lick his nipple. She latched onto it and nipped him gently with her teeth while sucking. The body against hers tensed and he growled, vibrating again.

The annoying shrill of his cell phone interrupted them. The mouth on her neck stopped kissing and Justice uttered a snarled curse. She released his nipple, lifted her chin and met his passion-filled gaze.

"Don't get it. Let it ring." She held her breath, hoping he'd choose her instead of whoever called.

"Let's go into the bedroom away from it."

She pulled air into her lungs, the tension eased from her body and she smiled. That was one way to get her into his room. Of course, she wanted to follow him anywhere at that moment.

He pulled away to put space between their bodies and his eye color appeared noticeably darker. She didn't usually move this fast with someone but she wanted him, he wanted her and she refused to think too deeply about it. He held out his hand and she eagerly placed her smaller one in his. He turned, his focus remaining on her and led her out of the living room.

Justice released her hand when they entered the large master bedroom, reached back and pushed the door closed. A lock clicked into place, the sound easy to identify. "It's not to keep you in but to keep anyone from interrupting us. Sometimes the males assigned to guard me enter my suite and the locked door will keep them from just opening it."

"Okay."

Jessie reached for the front of his jeans and unfastened the top button. She watched his face as she pulled the zipper down, looking for any signs of protest. Passion blazed in his heated stare and she lowered her attention down his body to watch her fingers hook the opening to spread them apart. He wore red flannel boxers.

They looked expensive and were amazingly soft when she brushed her knuckles against them. He hadn't been kidding about liking comfort between his skin and jeans. She shoved the pants down his muscular legs before going for his boxers to remove them too. His hands suddenly gripped hers and Jessie's gaze jerked to meet his.

"Am I going too fast? Do you want to slow down?" She resisted smiling over how amused she was at the thought that a man might resist getting naked as quickly as possible with a willing woman in his bedroom. *He isn't like other guys*, she remembered.

"There are some things you should know first."

Uh-oh. "You have the same parts, right? Male parts?"

He flashed a grin. "Yes."

"Then what else is there to know?"

He hesitated. "We've been told we're larger than typical males."

Larger. She swallowed. "I can deal with that. Larger as in 'just a bit bigger' or as in 'that is never, ever going to fit inside me'?"

A laugh escaped his lips. "Your kind and my kind have shared sex. They didn't seem to have any problems with that."

"That's good to know."

"There's more."

She bit her lip, unsure if she really wanted to know. Some things were best left unsaid but she appreciated him wanting to be totally up front with her. "More than large?"

"I just want you to be aware. Some Species swell even larger at the end of sex. I don't."

She was a little shocked, hearing that Species fact.

"Tammy told Valiant that at the end, his seed is noticeably hot. It doesn't hurt her but she feels warm heat filling her when he spills his seed. I don't have condoms and can't contain my seed if we do this. You will feel it if I come inside you." He took a sharp breath. "I don't have to. I just wanted to give you the option of having me pull out."

"It doesn't hurt her?"

He shook his head. "She seems to enjoy it from what I was told by him. I just wanted to warn you."

"I'm warned. I think I can live with that." Jessie was glad it wasn't something worse. Semen that was warmer than normal wasn't a deal breaker in the bedroom.

He hesitated. "Can you get pregnant? Are you on something to prevent that?"

"I'm on the shot but I know that's not a worry since you can't have children. That's true, right?"

He hesitated. "It is better to be safe. We are all different and therefore it is always within the realm of possibility. I prefer to be safe rather than take a risk."

"I go to the doctor regularly, I'm on the shot and haven't taken anything that will mess with it, so we're good. I don't have any diseases either. They do regular testing at my doctor's office and I haven't had a sexual partner in about a year. I'm sure I'm completely healthy."

Surprise widened his eyes. "A year?"

She shrugged. "What about you?"

"It's been a few months since I shared sex with a female. She was Species and we don't carry your sexually transmitted diseases. I've never been with a human, as I stated."

"So we're good to go. We had the responsible conversation, we're covered on pregnancy and are both disease free." She smiled and gripped the waist of his boxers to push them down his muscular thighs. She couldn't help but look down at the body she revealed and as soon as she freed his cock, she froze. Her fingers clenched around the soft material.

"Jessie?"

She forced her focus off his lower half to meet his concerned gaze. "You weren't kidding about being larger."

"Do you want to stop?" His pretty catlike eyes narrowed, he frowned slightly and worry tensed his features.

She stared at his cock, studied it. He wasn't freakishly endowed but she'd never been with a man his size. "I haven't changed my mind. Just go slow because otherwise that's going to hurt." She released his boxers, allowing them to fall to the floor. Her attention returned to his face. "I still want you."

"I don't have to enter you. We could do other things. I won't hurt you."

Jessie stepped back as Justice kicked free from his clothes. She gripped the waist of her tank top, pulled it over her head and dropped it to the floor. Justice silently watched her as she removed her jeans.

"I'm pretty sure I'm the same as your women. No surprises on body parts."

He purred again. "Your skin is so pale. It's beautiful."

She glanced at her breasts. "I'm glad you think so. Your women are a lot tanner naturally."

"Your skin reminds me of milk. I love milk. The texture and the taste of it when it's warm is my favorite."

He's good. Jessie smiled at his compliment. The best part was she didn't believe it was a guy line that he practiced to use with potential sexual partners. Justice wasn't the average guy who'd grown up dating and learning what worked to pick up chicks. If he said her skin looked like milk that he loved, that's what it looked like. She removed her panties and matching bra, grateful they were nice.

"You're beautiful," Justice growled, staring at her breasts. "And bigger than our women."

She chuckled. "I'm glad something on me is. Your women are pretty impressive."

He moved forward until they nearly touched and his warm hands gently gripped her hips. He just dropped to his knees to kneel in front of her, his face now level with her breasts. Hot breath fanned them and her nipples responded by growing taut. She got to look down at his face for once as their gazes held.

"The last thing I should warn you about is that we're naturally dominating and aggressive. I'd never hurt you during sex but I might make noises you aren't familiar with. I don't want you to be frightened if they sound scary. It's not my intention to be threatening."

"I like it when you purr. You vibrate and it turns me on."

"You are about to become really aroused if you are being honest with me. You have no idea how much I want you, Jessie. I'm battling my urges to come at you full force."

She wondered what kind of urges he resisted. "I'm not fragile or easily frightened, Justice." She lifted her hands and cupped his face, staring into his exotic gaze and the urge to kiss him gripped her. She knew all about keeping in control at that moment. "Don't hold anything back. Be yourself. I want to know you."

He softly growled at her, a deep rumble that had to be the sexiest thing ever. The blue of his eyes really showed at that moment, leaving no doubt the color lurked in those dark depths and she watched something change in his expression.

"You're going to get me."

Chapter Four

℘

Justice opened his mouth and licked the underside of one of her breasts. Jessie gripped his shoulders and lightly raked her nails across his skin. His hands tightened their hold at her waist and he urged her back until she lay flat on her back across his mattress. He bent forward as he tugged her lower until her bottom rested on the edge and his mouth opened over her right breast. His tongue tasted her, teased and played with the tip.

Heat spread through Jessie at the strange texture of his tongue. That was another New Species difference. It was wet, hot and felt a little rough but in the best way. His sharp canines raked her skin, sending a jolt of passion throughout her body.

"That's a talent," she moaned.

He chuckled and released her breast. "I'm just starting."

His hands slid from her hips to the inside of her thighs, spreading them wider apart and pulled her closer to his hips. He snugly fit in the cradle of her legs. His hot, hard cock nudged against her pussy, slid across her clit and Jessie moaned again. She knew she was already wet and prepared to have him inside her. She arched her hips up, rubbed against his shaft and gained more pleasure. He purred in response.

"Easy," he whispered.

Easy? The man knew how to set her on fire. He sucked on her left breast until she wanted to beg him to fuck her but he seemed intent on inflicting torture. He began to lick and kiss his way down her ribs, her belly and the hollow of her hip as he backed away until his cock didn't press against her any longer. She dug her nails into his shoulders, tried to drag him back up but he refused to take the hint.

It sank in that he planned to go down on her when his lips trailed lower and his hands shoved her thighs wider apart to make room for his face. Her breathing increased in anticipation. It had been a really long time since a guy had gone down on her, not that he'd been good at it but she had hope with Justice. She released him when he moved farther down her body, unable to touch him any longer.

The sharp bite of his teeth nipping her inner thigh made her groan. It didn't hurt so much as heighten her need for him to keep going. She locked her hips in place, tried not to move, to encourage him to keep going but when his mouth left her skin, it didn't return. Her eyes opened — she hadn't realized she'd closed them until that second — and lifted her head to peer down.

Hot breath teased her exposed pussy. He was that close, just inches away from the spot that wanted his attention most. He softly growled at her, his eyes narrowed as their gazes met and held. It was the most erotic sight she'd ever seen.

"Your natural color?" He grinned, glanced down and then back up.

She cleared her throat. "I didn't think dying that would be a good idea. I also don't like it totally shaved."

He chuckled. "The heart shape is sexy and your lighter red hair is very attractive. I don't know how you perfectly get that pattern but I appreciate seeing it. Do you want to learn another talent of mine?"

She nodded eagerly. "Definitely."

"Close your eyes and relax, Jessie."

She let her head drop to the bed and smiled, closing her eyes. "Using my own words against me. I like it."

He was way off the mark if he meant to relax her though. Her body tensed as she waited to see what he'd do next. Her fingernails dug into the comforter when his tongue lightly traced her clit. He purred, a deep rumble of sound and his tongue came back to press tighter against the bundle of nerves. The sexy sounds continued and the vibrations it caused made Jessie cry out. Her hips jerked but his hands gripped her tightly, shoved her ass down against the bed and he nuzzled his mouth against her spread pussy. Raw ecstasy hit her as his raspy-textured tongue moved rapidly up and down, sliding against the most sensitive area of her body at that moment.

She thrashed on the bed, clawed at the bedding and panted. Justice showed no mercy despite it being too intense. Her body seemed to turn to stone and every muscle bunched and as he purred louder, snarled, the vibrations grew stronger.

The climax struck her so powerfully she would have sworn she saw the flipside of her head when her eyes rolled back. She couldn't think, couldn't breathe and barely registered the loud noises coming out of her. It only stopped when Justice tore his mouth away. She lay there for seconds, trying to relearn how to breathe again before she was able to open her eyes and peer at him.

His eyes were so blue they stunned her. His mouth seemed fuller, more kissable and he snarled at her before lifting up. She didn't feel fear or threatened in the least, despite his harsh expression. He dropped his upper body over hers, braced most of his weight on his forearms and his lips hovered so close they breathed the same air.

Jessie arched her spine until her breasts pressed against his chest and her arms wrapped around his neck to hug him and allow her fingernails to reach his back. She lightly dragged the tips along his shoulders. Justice arched against her, pressed her tighter into the bed and totally pinned her under him.

The size and strength of him turned her on more. Justice not only had an amazingly talented mouth, his body was perfection and staring into his exotic eyes made her hurt for him again. It stunned her, considering he'd just made her come and she should be sated but the ache to be filled by him remained. Her swollen clit throbbed after the loving attention it had just received and she wanted more. All of him, the way he'd said he'd give her.

Jessie turned her head a little and lifted it, her mouth targeting his neck. Her lips parted and she tasted the skin exposed to her as she brushed his hair back. She'd never been with a man with long hair and she loved the feel of it as her fingers brushed through it. It was silky and soft, wonderful and she trailed kisses down to the top of his shoulder.

"Take me," she demanded.

Justice arched his body a little off hers and one arm moved until he gripped her ass with a big, strong hand. Jessie lifted her legs, wrapped them around his waist and tried to use the strength in them to pull him closer.

The tip of his thick shaft probed the entrance of her pussy, pressed against her wet heat but he didn't enter her. He paused, his body tense and time seemed to stand still. Confused, Jessie stopped kissing him to drop her head to the mattress and stare into his eyes.

"I don't want to hurt you," he rasped softly. "I'm afraid I will."

"I'm tough. I can take you."

His hand released her ass and he pulled away enough that he wasn't pressed against her. His fingers traced the line of her wet pussy and spread it before his finger penetrated. He growled deeply, his chest rumbling as his finger sank deeper. Jessie moaned, arching her hips into his hand at how good it felt, having him finger-fuck her.

"You're so hot and tight," he snarled, his voice a bit scary again but she refused to be afraid. His finger slid in and out of her, slowly torturing her. "You're too small for me."

"Roll over onto your back on the bed. I'll be on top." She lifted her head and nipped his shoulder gently.

He stilled his finger, no longer tormenting her vaginal walls and she could almost sense something change in the room. Jessie released his skin, dropped her head back and discovered him watching her with an angry glare. It stunned her.

"What's wrong? Did I bite too hard?"

"You want me to submit to you?"

"No. I want you to lie on your back if you're afraid you'll hurt me. I'll be on top, can control you entering me and you won't have to worry about going too fast."

He really looked angry, his features hard and it alarmed her enough that her body tensed in response while some of her passion cooled.

"What's wrong?"

He lifted his body away from hers, put space between their chests and backed his hips away. "We don't do that. It is submitting."

"Me riding you is submitting? Haven't you ever had a woman be on top before during sex?"

He shook his head. "Your men do this? They allow their women to dominate and control them? They submit to you?"

Astonishment sliced through her when it dawned on her that he was totally serious. He'd never allowed a woman to be on top. It was about dominance with them and it seemed to anger him that she'd asked to change positions. New Species were known to be aggressive and a bit controlling but she'd never considered the sexual side of it before. It all slammed home that he was honestly insulted by her offer to ride him.

"We should get dressed." All emotion left his face, a mask of control schooled his features and he straightened his arms to totally remove himself from the bed.

"Justice? Wait," Jessie demanded, her hands gripping his shoulders to keep him over her. "I didn't mean to offend you. I didn't realize it was taboo."

He hesitated and something softened in his gaze. "Our cultures are different but I didn't realize how much so until this moment. I'm not offended. I was but not anymore. Having a female dominate a male during sex is a regular occurrence with your males?"

"Yeah. Will you at least try it for a little bit? You can flip me over right away if you don't enjoy it. Please? I really want you, Justice."

His gaze softened more. "I want to you too." He hesitated, indecision clear but then he blew out a deep breath. "We can attempt it."

"Thank you. I'm pretty sure you're really going to like it."

He hesitated. "You don't want to tie me down?"

She shook her head. "I wouldn't do that. I'm familiar with your history, remember? I'd never ask to restrain you in any way. Can we try this? Please?"

He bit his lower lip, uncertainty a cute expression on him. "A test then."

She released him and scooted upward on the bed until she wasn't under him any longer. She sat, inched to the side of the mattress and gave him a smile. "Lie down on your back. Please?"

He remained on all fours on the bed. He was beautiful to Jessie as her gaze soaked in his body. Justice was a breathing work of art with everything sculptured perfectly, his muscles flexed as he rolled over and stretched his tall, big body the length of the mattress. The uncertain look on his face was priceless and absolutely adorable to her. Her attention focused on his thick, full cock and it reaffirmed her conviction that he was perfection.

Jessie pushed forward on her knees next to his stomach to peer into his eyes. "Relax, Justice. I promise this is going to feel good."

He bit his lip again, an obvious sign of uncertainty. "Do you want me to close my eyes?"

"No. I think you'll enjoy watching what I want to do to you."

She swept her hair over one shoulder and leaned over his chest. Her gaze held his to make sure he wasn't alarmed. Tension was there but not anger. She paused right over his nipple before breaking eye contact. He had dusky nipples, they were beaded slightly from cold or desire and the temptation was too much to resist. She sealed her lips over the closest peak, sucked and rubbed the tip of her tongue over him. A deep growl tingled against her lips from the vibrations it caused, tickling slightly but that didn't make her stop.

His hand brushed her thigh closest to him as she used her mouth to play with his body, her hands flattening on his chest and belly, loving the sensation of firm, smooth skin that she explored. The palm on his belly lowered until she brushed his rigid cock and she gently wrapped her fingers around the wide base of it. *Damn, he's big.*

She pushed that fact away, released his nipple with a rake of her teeth and lunged for the other one. His cock twitched in her hold, seemed to swell more, if that were possible and she knew he was enjoying the things she did. It motivated her to release him again and trace wet tongue kisses over his ribs to his tight abs.

He had ridges of firm muscle and she took the time to nibble on them, the taste of his skin wonderful and slightly salty. She moaned when he growled at her, knew it was a good thing and his cock seemed to strain against her palm. She moved lower, kissing her way down his belly.

Jessie paused when she studied the crown of his cock. She wasn't shocked that Species were circumcised since scientists created and raised them but it did stun her that it was noticeably mushroomed at the tip. Her vaginal walls clenched. *I bet that's going to feel good inside me. Easy*, she demanded, her need to straddle him growing stronger as her arousal level shot higher. *I want this to be really good for him too after what he just did to me. It's only fair, so slow down!*

The thoughts calmed her need to climb on his lap. She licked her lips instead and turned her head to glance at his handsome face. The raw hunger that radiated from his beautiful eyes assured her he was totally onboard with anything she wanted to do. His fingers massaged her thigh, kneed it to the point of an almost frantic urge for her to stop tormenting him.

"You aren't going to protest if I lick you here, are you?" She gently squeezed his shaft and ran her thumb pad along the underside of it, stroking the velvety softness of the skin stretched tightly over a hot, steely arousal.

He purred really loudly, his eyes narrowed to slits and his mouth parted to reveal his fangs, which dented his bottom lip as he bit down. He shook his head hastily, denying it would offend him.

She shifted her body a little to hold his gaze, opened her mouth and refused to look away as she stuck her tongue out and traced the rim of the crown. He closed his eyes, his head fell back and the sounds he made turned her on. The guy purred. It was sexy as hell that she could make him respond that way and she took him fully into her mouth, now concentrating on it.

"Jessie," he growled.

She sucked and took more of him between her lips, testing his girth. Her teeth lightly grazed him but it couldn't be avoided. She worked him deeper toward the back of her throat until she knew she'd hit her limit then slowly lifted up, swirling her tongue along the underside while keeping tight suction. He made animalistic noises that she loved to hear. No man had ever responded so strongly to her before. It was flattering and increased her pleasure at making him feel good.

His hand released her thigh and the sound of material ripping reached her ears. She turned her head to peer at him again, saw his head was still thrown back, his fangs sank deeper into his lip and his fingers clawed the bedding. Fluff from inside the comforter showed as more shredding happened. His nails tore the bedding apart.

Jessie eased up on giving him head and slowly released him from her mouth. Justice groaned, his eyes opened and he stared at her with such an intense look it made her pause. He took a few ragged breaths and she knew he was okay but really turned on. She lifted up a thigh, swung it around and straddled his hips. She reached back and gripped his cock. One of her hands flattened on his chest to keep her balance as she guided him right to where she wanted him.

"Can you hold still for me until I adjust to your size? You're really big."

He gave a sharp nod and his hands caressed her hips. A fine sheen of sweat broke out across his tan and muscular body, making him look sexier, as if he'd been oiled down. Jessie was more than ready and aching to feel Justice inside her.

Jessie groaned as she felt her body resist his penetration but she put down more weight. His thick cock breached her and she threw her head back in pleasure as she slowly sank down on him. He filled her deeper, stretched her to the point of near pain but it felt so good. She kept letting her weight take her down as a few more inches entered her. One of his hands left her to reach up to grab at a pillow near his head.

She lifted up and sank down again, taking more of him inside her. It was sheer bliss and she hoped he felt the same. Her ass brushed the top of his thighs and she knew she'd nearly taken all of him. Her body had adjusted faster than she'd thought it would. The sounds of his purrs motivated her to ride him faster. She wasn't sure which one of them was tortured more by her slow movements. She lowered one more time until her ass rested on his hips, the feel of him completely connected to her was pure perfection and she paused to appreciate the feel.

Justice snarled and wood snapped. Her chin jerked up to see what had happened. Justice released the headboard bar he'd broken. He'd grabbed the top piece of wood, his strength too much for the poor thing.

His eyes opened. He met her gaze and Jessie moved, setting a fast pace, riding him hard. She threw back her head, unable to keep eye contact with him anymore. She felt her climax building despite always needing more than just a man inside her to come—but not with Justice. She rode him frantically, burning to come as she ground her hips against him with every downward stroke. Her vaginal muscles clenched hard and pleasure tore through her when the climax hit. She cried out his name.

Justice rolled over, pinned her under his body and drove into her harder and faster. It spiked her pleasure higher, made her keep coming until she was sure her heart might explode. He snarled one final deep time, a vicious sound and began pulsing inside her with the hot spread of his release.

Jessie panted, clung to him and enjoyed the sensation. Whatever slight pain she'd been feeling in the aftermath of slightly rough sex faded. She opened her eyes and met Justice's. He held most of his chest weight off her with his elbows propped on the bed. Her arms were around his neck, hands gripping his shoulder blades and she didn't remember putting them there.

"Did I hurt you?" Concern narrowed his beautiful cat eyes.

"That was amazing."

He smiled. "Yes. It was."

Jessie pulled him closer and brushed her mouth over his. He groaned and forced her lips open to his exploring tongue. She was the one who finally broke the kiss. Their gazes met and held.

"Did my heat bother you?"

"I liked it. I was a little sore for a few seconds but now I'm not. You should bottle that as a miracle cure for soothing a woman after sex." She laughed.

He grinned. "I liked submitting to you."

She glanced up above their heads. "You broke the headboard."

He lifted his chin to peer at the headboard and got a comical expression on his face. Jessie couldn't help but laugh. His gaze met hers.

"I don't remember doing that."

"Then I guess I shouldn't mention the comforter."

He frowned.

Jessie released his back with one hand, reached to the side and grabbed a handful of filling. She showed it to him. "You should cut your nails, honey. You shredded the bed but thank you for letting me go and grabbing it instead. My uninjured thigh really appreciates it."

Justice gawked at the fluff, stunned. "I don't remember doing that either."

"I think you were too focused on me."

"I definitely was that. You're beautiful, Jessie. Did I tell you that?" He stared deeply into her eyes. "You're the most beautiful thing I think I've ever seen when I'm inside you and you are enjoying us being together."

"That's the best thing anyone has ever said to me."

Jessie turned her head to glance at the nightstand clock. "Oh, shit." Her gaze flew to Justice. "It's nine thirty."

"So?"

"Your press conference."

Justice paled and softly cursed. "I forgot."

She grinned. "I take that statement back. That is the best thing anyone has ever said to me. I made the king of workaholics forget about work."

He laughed. "Stay the night with me. I'll grab a shower, go to the gates to talk to the press and come back."

Happiness filled her that he didn't want to end their time together. "I would love to. Do you have any other work tonight?"

He shifted over her and withdrew his still-hard cock. Near regret showed on his features while separating from her body. He lifted up and moved down the bed to the end of it. "The only work I have after talking to the media is topping what we just did. I think I can manage to do that." His gaze traveled her body. "You inspire me to want to get to the gates and back as quickly as possible. I'll hurry through the press conference."

Jessie sat up on the bed, drew her knees up and hugged them. "You never wrote a speech."

He shrugged, turning toward the bathroom and Jessie stared at his ass. He definitely had the finest one she'd ever seen in her entire life, in or out of a pair of jeans.

"I'll wing it." He turned at the bathroom door. "Do you want to come with me to the conference? You need to shower with me if you do. My scent is all over you unless you don't mind all the Species who get close to you knowing what we just did." He chuckled. "I would be happy for you to keep my scent but I know human women can be touchy about revealing those things publicly."

"I think I'll stay here if you don't mind. I'm not a big fan of three-ring circuses with cameras."

He laughed. "Me neither." He disappeared into the bathroom.

Jessie scooted out of bed and studied it. The comforter was history. She tore it from the mattress and bunched it in a pile. She turned, laughed and realized the sheets were damaged too. His nails had pierced the comforter, torn right through it down to the sheets. After removing those, she laughed again. He'd even tagged the mattress. The situation cracked her up and she began to laugh.

"What?"

Jessie had to catch her breath as she turned to him, saw he'd already showered and was impressed he'd managed to do that so fast. "You have connections in this hotel, right?"

"We own it."

"You better make a call. You need all new bedding and maybe a new mattress."

Justice's attention shifted to the bed. He stared at the bare mattress and smiled. "Oh."

"I knew the comforter was history and then discovered the sheets were too." She laughed. "But you took out the mattress. I guess we could flip it over."

"I'll take care of it when I return." His eyes sparkled. "I'll hurry back."

"I can't wait."

He softly purred as he took in her naked body from head to toe. "Nor can I."

"Hold that thought until you return."

"I have to go but I'll hurry."

"Leave already so you can come back faster. I'll shower while you're gone."

"Make yourself at home."

She watched him unlock the bedroom door, exit and close it behind him. She glanced at the bed and started laughing again. She'd heard of breaking a bed during sex but he'd taken out the whole bed. If that wasn't impressive sex, she wasn't sure what would be.

She quickly showered, remembering his statement to make herself at home. She found one of his tank tops in the dresser and put it on, hungry again. She walked to the door to go in search of leftovers from their dinner but a ringing sound came from behind her. Her discarded pants on the floor rang again.

She rushed for her cell. She dug it out on the fourth ring and opened it, reading it was from Tim Oberto. She answered the call with dread. She hoped like hell someone hadn't called him to report that she was spending time with his boss, Justice North. It was going to be pure hell if that were the case and he'd called to fire her.

"What's up, Tim?"

"We got a lead on a possible Gift Female's location. The warrant just came through. I need you now."

Adrenaline hit hard and fast. "When are we moving in?"

"As soon as you get here."

"Uh…"

"I got your message that you were staying at Reservation and sent a chopper that way. It should be landing in ten minutes and your ass needs to be waiting for it at their heliport area." He hung up.

Damn. She closed the phone and stared at the bare mattress. She loved her job but for once she wished she could refuse an assignment. Justice would come back to find her gone and she wouldn't be spending the night with him. Of course he'd understand, one of his Gift Females might be rescued and she had no excuse to stay.

It still saddened her to leave. *I'll probably never see him again and I wanted to sleep in his arms.* Her shoulders slumped but she pushed it back. She had to go. Ten minutes were ticking down.

Chapter Five

ॐ

Justice read the note Jessie had left on the bed. He'd gotten hung up with the press by the reporters but had hurried back to his room looking forward to being with her. He read the note again, understood she'd gotten an emergency call from the task force after they'd gotten a lead on a New Species female and she'd had to leave. Tim Oberto had sent someone to pick her up. He snarled and crumpled up the note in his fist.

Justice pulled out his cell phone and froze. What would he do? Call the head of the task force and complain that he'd ordered Jessie to work when Justice wanted to climb back into bed with her? He cursed and lowered his cell. Jessie would never forgive him if he did that. Human women were private about their sex lives and independent. He doubted she would want the task force and the people she worked for to know she'd been in his bed. She'd also possibly resent him interfering with her job.

What pissed him off the most were her written words. She'd had fun and had thanked him. Worse, she'd told him to relax more and to attempt to work less. A growl of frustration burst forth again, his instincts at odds with his reasoning. She should have promised to come back or given him her number with an invitation to call. *She didn't. She thanked me for a good time.* He clenched his teeth. *She said it was fun. FUN!* Another snarl tore from his throat with his rising anger. *It was more than fun!*

Justice stared at the bed and his temper finally snapped. Jessie should be there waiting for him to touch her again and hold her in his arms while they slept. She made him laugh, the sex had been incredible and he'd been happy for once. His rage at the loss took hold and he lunged forward, his instincts refusing to be denied.

He attacked the mattress with gusto. His nails dug into the material and he ripped it up. When that didn't make him feel better, he lifted the entire mattress and tore it apart. He attacked the box springs next, snapping the wood with his feet and broke the frame apart. The headboard succumbed to his temper tantrum last while he destroyed it. He stood in the middle of his room panting with a mess surrounding him.

He assessed the damage and cursed, half embarrassed at the destruction he'd created. He hadn't allowed his temper to get the best of him once since he'd been freed despite the many times he'd been really angry. He'd lost it now for sure. He studied the damage grimly before storming out of the bedroom. He threw himself onto the couch, taking deep breaths but her faint scent filled his nose. He turned, buried his face against the cushions and inhaled deeply. It helped him remember every detail of them touching, his sense of smell keenly connected to his memories and he groaned. He wanted the real thing, not just sniffing at what he'd had.

What am I doing? He lifted his head with disgust. He was sniffing the couch just to smell Jessie Dupree. He uttered a vicious curse and stood to pace out his frustration. He finally calmed down enough to place a call downstairs. In minutes he'd ordered a new bed and bedding to be brought up. He hung up and closed his eyes. Jessie Dupree had driven him crazy. He was Justice North. He didn't have time to lose his mind or reasoning over a female, not even a hot, little sexy one who made him happy when he wasn't furious that she'd left.

The two Species males who brought up the new bed frowned at Justice when they cleaned up the destroyed bed and headboard. He glared at them, daring them to say a word about the floral stench in his suite. He'd walked into the bathroom and found a can of air freshener under the sink to mask Jessie's scent before they'd arrived. No one would know she'd been in his bed and her female pride would be intact since they were so private.

The men left and Justice opened his phone. He always had work to distract him and he welcomed it suddenly. He dialed his nighttime staff, knew they'd be awake in their suites down the hall from him and ordered coffee. He liked the sweet, hot drink. He avoided the couch by setting up his computer at the bar instead. Half an hour later he was connected to his staff via the interface and immersed in work. He had coffee in front of him and his staff was busy updating him on projects currently underway.

The doorbell rang and hope gripped him for a second that it might be Jessie but Tiger stood there when he yanked open the door. He silently invited him inside by stepping out of the way.

"Are you all right?" Tiger frowned. "As head of security I'm informed of everything. I received a call that you totaled your bedroom. That is unlike you, Justice. They said everything from the bedding to the headboard had to be replaced."

Justice studied Tiger carefully. He was a trusted friend and he wanted to talk to someone. "It was over a female."

"Ah." Tiger grinned. "I hope she's doing better than the things inside the bedroom did?"

"She's fine," Justice growled. "You know I'd never hurt a female."

"It was a bad attempt at a joke. Do you want to talk about it?" Tiger sat on the arm of the couch.

"I wanted her to stay the night but she left while I was at the press conference. I lost my temper. I'm not proud of it but I was looking forward to spending more time with her. The reporters were brutal and wanted every detail about the raid. They didn't appreciate me telling them some things were confidential and I refused to give up numbers. We're dealing with victims after all and they don't care about our privacy.

They also don't seem to understand that every time more of us are rescued that it stirs the pot with the people who hate us. They put me in a bad mood and then I returned to find her gone."

"So you destroyed the bed? I understand. I really do." Tiger looked sympathetic. "Maybe she'll change her mind and knock on your door later."

"She won't."

Tiger cocked his head. "You know our women, Justice. All those years of captivity made them unwilling to be with us for more than a few hours and they get antsy if you hint at anything more than sex. They don't want to commit because they don't want someone trying to tell them what to do. It's in our nature to dominate and we're a bit controlling. They know our flaws as well as we know theirs and that's why they avoid anything beyond a few hours of physical enjoyment with us."

Justice didn't correct Tiger's assumption that it had been a Species female he'd been with. "I wasn't asking her to move in with me. I just wanted her to spend the night."

Tiger grinned. "You could always get another female. You're Justice North. Our females are all a bit enamored of you. You could walk into a room, hold out your arms and one of them would jump into them. You're the ultimate strong male they are attracted to. Not only do you have physical strength but you're viewed as iron willed because of your job."

"They are drawn to me for the wrong reasons. It is because they think they owe me for all that I do. I don't want a female who feels gratitude."

Tiger's grin faded. "You want one to come to you because she likes you for who you are."

"Yes."

"You're lonely, aren't you?"

Justice sighed. "I guess I am. It would be nice to have one person to share everything with. I would enjoy having the same female to go to bed with at night and hold."

"I understand loneliness. I feel it sometimes." He suddenly grinned. "Then I just find someone to come to my bed and feel much better afterward."

Justice laughed, his amusement over his friend's simple fix for what ailed him near comical. "You're so easy."

"It works for me."

"Wait until you meet one that you want to keep longer than a few hours."

Tiger's smile died. "You found one in particular that you want to spend more time with?"

"Yes. Unfortunately. I should have canceled the press conference, broken all the phones and kept her in the bed with me for as long as possible."

"Kept? You had her in your bed?"

Justice sighed. "Yes."

"That good, huh? I'm sure she will come back eventually and spend more time in your bed. You are well liked and respected."

"I don't think she's impressed with me."

"All of our women are."

Justice just nodded. He wasn't about to admit that she wasn't one of their females but it would be a hell of a lot easier if she were. He'd at least have access to her to tempt her back into his bed if she lived at Reservation or Homeland. He had no access to Jessie since she lived in the outside world.

"Stay with me for a while." Justice hated to ask anything from someone else but he despised the idea of being alone even more. The sexy female would haunt him otherwise. "We'll watch some movies Ellie suggested to me recently and I'll order some food."

Tiger stood and gripped his shoulder. "It sounds fun. I'm not sexy, not going to fuck you but I'll spend the night." He chuckled.

Justice laughed. "For that, you can order the food."

* * * * *

Jessie strapped the gun to her thigh and tightened her bulletproof vest as she studied the men around her. They looked tense but she didn't blame them. She'd overheard the team commander going over the security measures they were about to face. The old man who owned the mansion was paranoid and had a thing for hiring mercenaries to guard the grounds.

Tim Oberto walked to Jessie, looking grim. "You stay to the back, do you hear me? Just because your daddy got you a permit to carry a gun doesn't make you a real team member. You're here to hold the woman's hand and prevent the big boys from scaring the piss out of her. This one is going to be dangerous, Jessie. I will personally put you over my knee in front of the entire team and spank your ass if you pull a stunt similar to the one in Mexico five months ago. You remind me of my daughter and I'd do the same to her."

Jessie frowned. "Mexico wasn't my fault."

He snorted. "Bullshit. You heard that woman scream and you didn't wait for the team to clear the scene. You flew in there and the only thing that saved your ass was being short. That bullet missed your head by an inch because he aimed higher, expecting a man when you kicked in that door. You hold back until the scene is cleared and the woman is secured. You can take her in hand then and *only then*."

"The only reason the female in Mexico is alive is because I went in. He planned to set fire to the place with her tied to a bed to destroy the evidence, which was her. A few more minutes and he would have finished the job."

"Your life is more important."

She shook her head. "You and your men risk your lives. Why can't I do the same for the Species?"

"Because I'm in charge and I said so." He smirked. "Another stunt like Mexico and I swear I'll haul your ass in front of the men and whip your ass as if you were my daughter. Then I'll call your father. I bet he'd yank your chain so hard he'd have you at home baking cookies for him in five minutes flat. That's what I'd do."

"You don't know my father." Jessie glared at him. "He raised me and I know him much better than you do. He taught me to be tough and that some things are worth taking chances on. He is with me on this. These Species we save are worth risking our lives for and he knows that as much as I do. If anyone gets their chain yanked it will be yours, so back off from beating your chest and telling me to act more like your version of what a woman should be."

He spun away. She watched him walk to the assault vehicle he'd set up as the command post. "Bitch," he rumbled.

Jessie glanced at her watch, refusing to let him bait her temper. Tim was a dick but he cared about his team, including her. It was two thirty in the morning and the raid would go down soon. She thought of Justice and figured he was definitely asleep at such a late hour. She sighed, wishing she were next to him in his bed, curled up against his side. Of course, wishing didn't do a thing since she was two states away from him.

Jimmy Torres pointed to his watch, held up one finger and jerked his thumb toward one of the black vehicles. She pulled her hair back to secure it tightly at the base of her neck in a ponytail. She clearly wanted to be identified as a woman and her long hair helped. Her all-black, bulky outfit sure didn't look feminine and the bulletproof vest hid her breasts.

She approached her team. Five men waited inside the black SUV parked a block from their target. She sat in the backseat. It was a tight squeeze to close the door and she glanced at the two guys sharing the bench seat with her. The task force was made up of all men who were at least six feet tall and muscularly built. They only hired large, strong men since sometimes they didn't want Species males to noticeably stand out from the humans they worked with. It made them easier targets to pick off if it ever came down to a firefight.

Jessie shivered, thinking about that. So far she'd been lucky. The closest she'd ever come to being shot was the mission in Mexico. Shots had been exchanged but Jessie had stayed away from the fighting until she'd broken ranks.

The men had been pinned down but she'd been able to slip around to enter the back door of that house and go after that poor Gift Female. Tonight they were going in all at once. It was a large estate with three buildings on the grounds. The Species female could be stashed in any of the three locations. *If the rich asshole still has her. If she is still alive and if the jerk who paid Mercile was given one of the women. The chances are good. You know that. Think positive. We don't get called in unless they honestly believe we can recover one of them.*

"What's the word on this one?" Jessie glanced at Jimmy, seated next to her.

"We received a tip from an anonymous caller that this jerk is holding a weird-looking woman on his property and she's being chained up. When the police ran the jerk's background it turns out he has a strong association with Mercile. They called us. A report like that immediately gets flagged. The tipster also implied this rich asswipe is about to move the woman. We knew we had to move on this one tonight. We're hoping he hasn't moved her yet since whoever called said it would go down tomorrow morning."

Jessie felt hope. "It sounds like a hot tip."

"That's what the bosses said." Jimmy grinned. "So when are you going to hole up inside a motel with me so I can have my dirty way with your body?"

She smiled over the conversation they always shared before a raid. She was pretty sure the ex-Marine wasn't seriously hitting on her, that he was just trying to make her laugh by distracting her from becoming too nervous. He was good at doing that.

"When I'm ninety-two. Do you think you'll still want me by then?"

He laughed. "Sure. I'll let you climb on my lap in my wheelchair. I'll pop some blue pills and we'll talk about the first thing that comes up."

Laughter softly floated around the SUV. Jessie smiled, relaxing a little. She liked most of the men on the task force. They teased her but not one of them had ever harassed her.

"It sounds kind of hard." Jessie winked.

More laughter filled the vehicle. The driver and team leader, Trey, suddenly cleared his throat. "Lock and load, boys and girl. Put your ears on. We're about to crash a party."

Jessie shoved her earpiece in and secured it firmly to her ear. She waited. Six seconds later a voice over the com said, "Check." Jessie held up a thumb. The other men did too. Trey nodded.

"We're all good and we can hear you."

"All right, people," Tim said in Jessie's ear device. "We stick to the plan. On my 'go', let's hit this mausoleum and see if we can wake the dead."

Jessie took a deep breath and blew it out. She gripped the door to brace, her boots flattened on the floor and she swallowed while tucking her chin down just a little. She'd been on enough raids to know what to expect.

"Go!" Tim roared. "All go!"

The vehicle shot forward and Jessie's back slammed into the seat from the sudden force but she'd been prepared. She hadn't put on a seat belt. None of them had since they needed to exit the vehicles quickly when they stopped. The SUV picked up speed fast. The gate next to the road was the only thing in the dark she could see until they reached the well-lit area where the gates sat to admit visitors to the estate.

Trey turned the wheel sharply to leave the road for the driveway. An explosion boomed ahead, bright light flashed and the locks on the iron gates blew apart. Their team had determined that blowing the locks on the gate would be the fastest entry and a marksman had nailed it with an explosive charge from across the street. The walls had motion sensors so going in on foot wouldn't have worked. The rich guy also had motion sensors all over the grounds. Speed mattered and they didn't have time to slow down for pesky locks.

Jessie realized they were the lead car as Trey gunned the vehicle straight at the iron gates. They hadn't been blown open but the damage to the locks was clear even from a distance. They hit it hard, sparks flew and the gates parted with a massive noise. Jessie knew alarms had to be sounding inside the mansion. She turned her head, spotted six pairs of headlights right on their ass, driving in pairs.

Trey jerked the wheel hard, left the driveway and bounced over the curb. They'd been assigned to hit the guesthouse. One vehicle followed, still close on their ass. The easiest shortcut to that location was across the personal golf course.

"Avoid the sand," Bob, the team member in the passenger seat, said and chuckled. "It's a trap."

Jessie grinned. She really liked the guys and their smart-ass remarks. It helped keep the terror at bay as long as possible. The vehicle picked up speed.

"Hang on. We're going airborne, kiddies," Trey warned.

Jessie saw the small hill as they hit too fast and gritted her teeth. The nose of the SUV cleared the peak and they were flying. The vehicle slammed down hard when it landed. Trey weaved a little but kept control. The impact would have thrown her forward since she didn't weigh as much as the guys but Jimmy had thrown his arm across her lap when the wheels left the ground. He'd kept her from moving too much.

"There went our stomachs but we'll pick them up on the way back," Bob groaned. "Remind me to buy us all ass donuts for the next time we try that."

Jessie saw a well-lit, two-story structure coming up fast. She reached down and unfastened the strap securing her gun inside the holster on her thigh. Her heart pounded. She knew it could turn really bad but she still hoped for the best. The fear would keep her sharp and alert. Terror was a good thing in a dangerous situation.

They reached the front of the guesthouse and Trey locked up the brakes hard, skidding ass end around a few feet and killed the engine. Jessie threw open the door and jumped out, moving fast toward the front doors. Trey and Bob were already ahead of her. Jimmy, Mike and Shane remained behind her.

Trey held a metal battering ram about three feet long and charged full force with it as he hit the locked double doors dead center. The wood splintered under the assault, popped apart and opened hard. Trey dropped the battering ram, just tossed it aside and grabbed both his guns. He and Bob entered first by throwing themselves to the sides of the door. Jessie slammed into the wall next to the entrance, yanked her gun out and waited.

"Clear," Bob called.

Jessie eased around the broken door. She glanced around the large entryway, took in the curved stairwell, high ceilings and long hallway leading to other parts of the house. Trey and Bob moved door to door, clearing rooms while she stayed put with her gun trained at the top of the stairs to cover Jimmy and Shane as they rushed up them. Mike took position across from Jessie to guard the door. Anyone coming in or out would face off against a heavily armed man. As soon as both men hit the landing above, she lowered her gun and turned to train it on the broken doors.

The waiting was the worst as Jessie stood there. She heard gunfire suddenly erupt from upstairs. *Shit.* Her gaze flew to Mike, met his grim, tense expression and hoped her team was doing the shooting. He jerked his head toward the front door. She moved, followed his silent command and stepped back outside. Her back pressed against the house as more gunfire came from the second floor. A gun battle had started.

"Gunfire inside the guesthouse!" Tim's voice shouted into her ear. "Four armed men. Second floor."

"We'll get them," Jimmy's voice grunted. "One down. Three to go."

Jessie's gaze kept roaming the yard for any motion coming at them. Tim's voice inside her ear kept her informed of what was happening with her team and the others.

"We have eight incoming heat signatures in two cars speeding toward the guesthouse from the south."

Jessie jerked her head in that direction but didn't see anything. In less than ten seconds that changed. Headlights appeared in the distance and approached quickly. She moved, eased inside the house and nodded at Mike.

"I've got your back covered if you can handle the cars." She glanced at his guns. "You have the better toys."

He smirked. "Keep your head down."

"That's not a problem. I'm short, remember?"

"Knock off the chatter," Tim ordered. "Your mics are live since you're under attack, team five."

Great. Jessie rolled her eyes at Mike. He grinned and lunged next to Jessie, closer to the open doors. The sound of tires locking up prompted him to open fire. Jessie threw up her hand to cover her ear nearest to his weapon. She trained her gun toward the stairs to make sure no one tried to seek down them. Trey and Bob cleared the bottom floor and rushed back.

"Jessie, move your ass this way," Trey ordered. "Bob, get upstairs to support Jimmy and Shane. I'm coming up behind you to guard the door, Mike. Don't shoot me."

"I'll try not to," Mike grunted.

Gunfire was deafening. Jessie found herself shoved farther into the house. They wanted her out of the line of fire but it was hard to do with guns being shot from above and outside. Gunfire pelted the front of the house and bullets dug into the wall by the staircase.

"Three of them just darted from the cars to go around the back," Mike hissed. "Find a hole, Jessie. They are going to try to come at us from the back of the house. We're screwed!"

"Fuck," Trey snarled. "We're pinned down! I repeat, we're pinned down!"

Shit. There were windows everywhere past the hallway where a large living room opened up. If three men with guns breached it then she'd be a target no matter where she stood. They'd turn that corner and kill her friends, taking out anyone hiding along the way. She glanced around and lunged toward a doorway to a laundry room. It was the only place she couldn't see a window. She heard glass break not too far from her and listened intently.

"They are breaking through from the living room," Jessie warned softly. "I'll cover your back, guys."

"Damn it, Jessie," Trey hissed. "Stay down and find a hole. I'll try to cover our backs from this location."

He wanted her to hide. If the three men got behind Trey and Mike they would be trapped and without cover in the long entryway despite her team leader's bluff. He knew as well as she did that they were pinned down. He'd admitted it already to everyone.

"I've got your back," she repeated more firmly.

She heard someone step on glass as it crunched loudly. She took deep breaths and jerked around the doorway, stepped into the hallway and crept to the end of it. She paused there, gripped her gun tightly and peeked around the corner into the living room. She raised her gun arm, saw a man stepping through the shattered window, pointed and fired. He screamed, going down. Bullets from his two companions tore up the wall near her. Jessie jerked back and ducked. The other two were already inside.

"One down," she said softly.

"Jessie," Trey hissed, "find a hole."

She ignored the order. She took another deep breath and glanced around the corner, on her knees. One of the men had inched closer to her along the living room wall. His eyes widened when he jerked his chin down to stare at her in surprise. She opened fire and two bullets hit their mark. One found purchase in his chest and the other hit him in the face. She jerked back right as she saw the third man throw himself out from behind the couch to shoot at her.

"Two down," Jessie whispered to her team. "One to go."

Jessie had an idea. "I'm not really shot. I'm going to fake his ass out and have him come to me. Hug the walls and make yourself smaller targets, guys. I'm sure he can't see if you're in the closet area right inside the door. The cabinet should block his view of you."

"Jessie!" Trey hissed. "Don't do it."

"Shut up and hug the damn wall," she hissed back. She made a loud sobbing sound. "I've been shot. Oh My God. I've been shot. I'm dying. I can't move. Someone help me."

She eased back onto her feet to duck walk as far as she could to squeeze behind the dryer. It was a tight fit while she waited. The guy obviously believed he was a better shot than he actually was. He suddenly jumped into the doorway and pointed his gun at the floor where Jessie should have been. Jessie didn't hesitate as the man's gun exploded when he fired at the floor feet from her. She shot him three times in the chest. His gaze widened, his mouth opened and blood poured out before he just collapsed backward.

"Three down," Jessie got out in a shaky voice. "I'm checking vitals."

"Don't move, Jessie!" Tim roared. "Wait for backup."

Oh, he's pissed and I'm in a world of shit. She hadn't really had a choice though. Trey and Mike had their hands full, were pinned and both needed to hold back the jerks outside. They needed that door from the living room to the entryway secure.

That meant someone had to watch their backs. That left Jessie available to watch the living room and she'd done it.

Jimmy's voice sounded. "Four down. I repeat, four down. The second floor is secured. No female here."

Trey and Mike were still exchanging gunfire at the front door until another task-force team arrived to handle the attackers who were pinned without cover. Two of the property's security guards were dead but another three gave up at that point. Jessie walked out from the laundry room into the hallway once an "all clear" was called.

Trey reached her first. He studied her grimly before leaning down to kiss her cheek. "Good job."

"Two are down in the living room but I haven't checked to see if they are still breathing." She avoided looking at the dead guy in front of the laundry room door. "He's definitely dead. I got him square in the face."

Trey glanced down. "Yeah, he's a toe tagger. I'll check vitals on the others." He strode away to do that.

"Someone's gonna be in trouble," Mike called out as he swaggered down the hallway holding his weapon cradled in his arms. "We were pinned down and you did good, kid. Thanks."

Jessie nodded.

Trey returned from the living room. "Make that three toe taggers. You got one in the neck and the other one in the face and chest. I think all that gun-range target practice is paying off, Jessie. The bad news is that there's no female here. The mansion was just cleared by our teams. The garage and staff living quarters were cleared by our teams. They must have moved her before we arrived."

Jessie frowned. "They were guarding this building for a reason."

She spun, nearly ran and searched the lower floor. She glanced at the stairs and headed that way but Trey grabbed her arm. "It's been secured, Jessie. I'm sorry. If she was here she isn't now. I know it's hard to accept but we missed her."

"Did you find a room they would have kept her in?"

"No. None of the team reported that. They would have."

"They were protecting something. It's a guesthouse but it's empty. All those bodies are security. The dead guys have patches. Why station four men at this location for no good reason and then send eight more out here?" She refused to give up hope.

Trey shrugged. "Maybe the four lived here."

Jessie jerked her arm out of his hold. "I'm going to take another look. I don't care if we have to tear it down but they were protecting something that we haven't found yet."

Trey hesitated. "Hurry. Tim is on his way and he's really pissed at you."

She ran up the stairs. *The men were guarding something.* Her gut was screaming it at her. The guy who owned this guesthouse was associated with Mercile Industries. He was obviously a rich bastard and probably not a nice guy if he hired mercenaries to guard his property.

She reached the first room, found no furniture at all and searched the open closet. She used her flashlight to search every inch of room, kicked all the walls and found them solid. She bounced a little on the flooring inside the closet and the room but nothing indicated any loosened floorboards.

The next room had a card table set up and two dead men were sprawled on the floor. The table and four chairs were the only furniture in the room. She went for the closet first, not looking forward to having to roll the dead bodies to test the floors under them. She searched it with the flashlight but saw nothing. She kicked one side and heard a solid sound. She kicked the back wall but it didn't sound right. She frowned and kicked it again. *Hollow.*

Jessie crouched down and used her flashlight to study the floor carefully. She spotted slight scratches a few feet from the molding. Her fingers brushed over it.

"Goddamn it, Jessie! I fucking warned you," Tim yelled from behind her. "I'm going to turn you over my knee."

"Shut up. I found something." She didn't bother to look at her boss, too focused on the wall in front of her.

There was silence behind her. Jessie bit her lip and pushed on the wall but it didn't move. She stood, backed up and studied the wall from a new angle. She glanced back at her team to see that Tim waited in the doorway, glaring at her. Trey and a few of the other guys had followed him up.

Jessie turned, kicking out at the wall hard. Her foot made contact and punched through the plaster a little. The plaster was an inch thick but only darkness appeared in the small hole she'd made instead of wood beams or insulation that should have been behind it. She crouched down and aimed her flashlight into the hole.

"What is it?" Trey was at her side.

"Take it down," Jessie ordered softly. "It's a false wall." She backed up out of his way.

Trey yanked her flashlight out of her hand and crouched to aim the light at the small hole, nodding. "She's right." Trey stood. He shoved her flashlight at her as he took a step back. He kicked the plaster wall. "Back up more."

Jessie gave him room to do his thing. Trey was a big guy, stronger, and he had the kickass military boots on. In minutes he'd destroyed enough plaster to make a hole big enough for a man to crawl through. He reached for his own flashlight clipped to his belt, dropped to his knees and his other hand yanked out his sidearm.

"It's another room," he confirmed, inching closer.

Jessie's heart pounded as Trey disappeared into the hole on his hands and knees. Seconds passed as slowly as if they were minutes. Trey suddenly called out.

"Jessie, get in here. She's alive."

Chapter Six

‰

Justice yawned and glanced at the clock. "It's after three."

"I'm ready to call it a night." Tiger stretched on the couch. "That was a good action film."

"Thanks for staying with me."

"Not a problem. Any time." Tiger met his gaze. "Females are trouble. Never forget that. We're better off without them."

"I'm not sure I agree."

"Do you want me to stay in the guestroom?"

"Do you feel like driving home?"

"Not really." Tiger yawned. "I'm not used to these late nights."

Justice clicked off the TV and the DVD player, rose to his feet and dropped the remotes on the coffee table. "Stay. We'll have breakfast together and discuss the new cameras you want installed at the gates." He withdrew his cell phone and flipped it open.

"Who are you calling at this hour?"

"Homeland. Our human task team went out on a mission and I want to see if they recovered one of our females."

"They'd have called." Sadness filled Tiger's eyes. "You know how these things go. We would have heard if they'd found one. I know they meant to hit the location at two. It must not have been a good lead."

That meant that Jessie had been called away for nothing. It had at least been comforting, thinking he might be without her for the retrieval of one his women. "Right."

"Hopefully next time they'll find one."

"We can hope. Good night."

He spun on his heel, walked quickly down the hallway and closed the door softly behind him. His gaze lingered on the fresh bedding on the new bed they'd put in his room. No trace of Jessie's scent lingered and he had no one to blame but himself for that fact. He'd sprayed the area too damn well with air freshener.

The good news was, Jessie was safe. He began to strip off his clothes, yawned and hoped wherever she was, she thought about him. If she were in his bed she'd be comforted over the failed mission. He'd make damn sure of that.

His cock twitched at the thought of how he'd distract her and he hissed out a curse. He needed to forget about the sexy human. Jessie Dupree wasn't someone he could afford to spend too much time with anyway. He knew the futility of their future.

He paused in front of the mirror over the dresser, stared at his slightly altered features and for once regretted being Species. He was the face of his people, the symbol the world saw and he'd never have the freedom he fought so hard to give his people.

Envy filled him as he thought about Fury, Slade and Valiant. They'd fallen for humans and kept them. The males were loved and got to sleep with their mates. They had the anonymity to do so. Justice North taking a mate would be world news and when he did, it would have to be a Species female. Not only would his people expect it but the entire population of humans would as well.

His shoulders sagged as the turned away, not able to look at his reflection anymore. He avoided contact with human females for a reason. Plenty had hit on him before but none of them had stirred him the way the fiery redhead had. She had the courage to have such bright hair and engage in battle with males. She was fierce, beautiful and off limits.

He leaned down, removed his cell phone from his pants and placed it on the bedside table. He sat hard on the edge of the mattress, thoughts of Jessie still haunting him, and reached for the light. *Forget her. You have no choice. It wasn't meant to be and it's best that she was called away. It would be a disaster if she became too important. It would only hurt worse since there's no way for you to be with her without the world finding out.*

He climbed under the covers and sprawled out on his back. His cock filled with blood as he remembered the last time he was in that position on the bed with Jessie's warm, sexy mouth on his body, her hair tickling his thigh. He groaned and rolled over.

Forget her, damn it. She'll forget about you. It was just a one-night stand and that's all it can ever be.

* * * * *

Jessie didn't hesitate to drop to her knees and crawl into the darkness. She inched toward Trey, about ten feet to her left. He had his light trained on the floor as she moved to his side.

"I didn't want to scare her," he whispered. "She's locked up in the corner but I can't find a light switch." Trey pointed in a direction under his flashlight so Jessie knew where to look.

"Back off," Jessie urged him. "Get a lamp in here. Something."

He backed away and Jessie turned on her flashlight. Jessie slowly lifted the light until she spotted a large dog-sized cage and a thin mattress on the floor of it. A small woman huddled in the corner, wearing a long nightgown that was as dirty and dingy as the mattress cover she sat on. It looked as if neither had been washed for a while. Jessie lifted the light a little more, careful not to flash it in the woman's face.

"My name is Jessie," she stated softly. "We're going to get you out of here and take you somewhere safe. I'm going to come closer to you but don't be afraid. I'd never hurt you, okay?" She shone the beam on her face and allowed the bright light to temporarily blind her to give the confined woman a good look at her. "I'm a woman too. See? We're not here to hurt you."

Jessie lowered the light and waited until the spots cleared then carefully tracked the beam back to where the woman huddled. She took in more of the woman as she raised the light to the woman's legs. She was Species all right. Her hair was black and her features marked her as carrying primate DNA. It was obvious from her delicate features, the more rounded shape of her dark brown eyes and her cute, perky nose.

Jessie crawled closer. "Do you know that there are others like you? I'm going to take you home to them, to your family. They've been looking for you for a long time. Can you tell me your name?"

The woman gripped her knees tighter to her chest and her features showed her terror. Jessie didn't blame her for the fear. "I'm really not going to hurt you. I'm here to take you out of here to somewhere safe. I'm going to take you to your family. They are people just like you, ones who were hurt by others and it's going to be safe for you there. No one is ever going to lock you inside a cage again. I'm Jessie," she repeated. "What's your name?"

The woman opened her mouth and whispered soft words that were hard to catch. "Mud."

Jesus! Rage tore through Jessie at hearing the shitty name her captors had tagged her with but she tried to conceal it. "That isn't really your name. Do you remember what that is? What you were called before you were brought here?"

The woman hesitated. "My name was Monkey."

Jessie counted to ten to cool down her boiling blood. *Son of a bitch. Is there no end to the mean shit people do to these people?*

"I'll tell you what. Why don't we call you Beauty? Do you like that name? I think it fits you much better than those other ones. The men outside with me came to take you away from the men who held you here. I'm going to take you somewhere safe. You can trust me."

Jessie crawled closer when the Species seemed to calm as some of the fear eased from her delicate features. She switched her attention to the cage, noted the lock and the chains that ran through the squares from the woman's ankles to a bolt in the floor feet from the container. The bolt pierced right through the floorboards and no screws showed. It wasn't going to be easy to free this one with those heavy-duty shackles. They usually took them in chains if they weren't able to get them free on site and that floor bolt would be hellish to break.

"May I look at your ankles, please? I'd like to see if I can get those shackles off and looking at the lock will tell me if they are easy to pick or not."

"Okay," she agreed hesitantly.

Jessie reached through the cage to gently grip one of the shackles. There were key holes in each one and the metal was heavy, solid and wouldn't break with what they carried. The locks were complicated and that didn't bode well either.

"Look for keys," she said into her mic. "They have her chained to a bolt that's going to be tough to remove since it's through the floor and picking the locks isn't an option. I could get into the cage they have her in but those shackles are another story."

"I don't know where they are," Beauty whispered.

Jessie set the flashlight down so it gave off enough light for them to see each other as she released her ankle. She reached up and pointed, turned her head to show the other woman. "I have a device inside my ear that lets the people who helped save you hear what I say. I can hear them as well. I was telling them to look for the key. If they can't find it we'll try to cut the chain. We will get you out of here. That's a promise. Okay, Beauty?"

"Yes. You really are going to take me away?"

"I swear to you I'm getting you out."

"I found a set of keys on a dead guy." It was Tim speaking. "We also found an extension cord and a lamp."

"Just get me the keys and send in Trey since she's already seen him. Have him come in slowly." Jessie smiled at Beauty. "That man in here a few minutes ago is going to bring in keys we think are for the locks. Don't be afraid of him. He's my friend and he'd never hurt a woman."

Beauty looked scared but she nodded bravely. Trey crawled into the room and eased down to sit next to Jessie. In his other hand he had four flashlights turned on to light up the room. Jessie flashed him a grateful smile as she accepted the keys. He backed up a few feet.

"Go or stay?" His voice was soft.

Jessie studied the woman who stared at Trey but she didn't seem panicked or terrified. "Stay," Jessie decided.

Trey didn't move as Jessie tried the keys. She unlocked the cage first, eased open the door and hesitated before touching Beauty. The other woman pushed her feet closer to help. Jessie gave her a warm smile and the other woman smiled tightly in return.

"Bingo. We have a winner." Jessie smiled at Beauty as she unlocked the ankle cuff. "See? We found the keys." Jessie unlocked the other ankle. Beauty was free.

"Clear out and give us an open path to a vehicle," Jessie ordered softly. "We're bringing her out."

"You got it," Tim sighed. "Good work, Jessie. We would have missed her if you hadn't found that hidden room. Your ass is still mine when you secure her."

Jessie rolled her eyes but continued to smile at Beauty as she backed up to give the woman room to leave the cage. "Okay. Can you stand?" Jessie rose to her feet slowly and held out her hands to the woman. "You can take my hands and I'll help you."

The woman hesitated before slowly leaning forward, crawled a few feet until she cleared the open door of the cage and reached a trembling, pale hand to Jessie. Jessie gripped her carefully while fighting back tears. This part got to her every time. The fear in their eyes to even hope, to trust and believe someone wasn't just fucking with them always broke her heart. Jessie helped her stand.

"We're on the move," Jessie informed the team. "Are we cleared?"

"Cleared," Tim answered softly. "We have a vehicle right out the front door and we dragged the dead out of sight. Jimmy tore down some curtains to drape over the blood. She'll probably smell it if she inherited the Species sense of smell but she won't be terrified by the sight."

"She's primate," Jessie answered, letting her team know that the freed woman was less likely to pick up the scent of death or spilled blood. The primates didn't have such an acute sense of smell. "Contact Homeland right away and ask where they want her taken so other primates are there when we arrive. She needs to meet her family."

Jessie kept hold of the frightened woman. Beauty only stood about five feet tall and her rail-thin body revealed she'd been half starved. Jessie could have carried her slight body out of the house if the woman couldn't have walked on her own. She fought back more tears as they walked through the house slowly. The woman had been beaten recently and she hadn't been bathed, in Jessie's estimation, for a few days. Her hair was ratted, a little greasy and dirt clung to her legs and arms from the dusty, hidden room.

Trey remained a silent sentry at their back and she knew he'd remain there in case the female Species passed out from her weakened condition. Jessie led Beauty out the front door into the fresh night air and directly to the open back door of the SUV. She smiled at her charge.

"We are going to get inside this thing and then we're going to do something really exciting. We're going to fly in the sky in a bigger thing to get you some medical help and you're going to meet up with your family. They are going to be so happy to see you."

"You won't leave me?" Beauty looked terrified as she clutched at Jessie.

"No, Beauty, I'm not going anywhere. I'm going to hold your hand the entire time." Jessie squeezed her hand tenderly. "I'm not going to let anything happen to you and I'm going to stay with you for as long as you want me to."

Jessie urged her to climb onto the center seat and secured her in a lap belt. Jessie smiled again, to be reassuring. "I'll sit right next to you and Trey here is going to drive us. He's a nice person." She checked the belt again, leaned over to push Beauty's hair behind her ear and gave her a sincere look. "Everything is going to be fine, Beauty. I—"

Pain exploded in Jessie's back. She was thrown forward and her body slumped over Beauty and the seat. The Species woman screamed.

"Sniper!" Trey yelled.

Jessie fought to push herself up despite not being able to draw breath from the pain in her back. Beauty shrieked in terror again and glass exploded from the front passenger window. Jessie found the strength to shove her chest up, shoved Beauty sideways across the seat and threw herself on top of the other woman.

"I've got you," Jessie panted over the screaming female and gunfire.

Pain exploded again in Jessie's back, sent a path of fire from between her shoulder blades to the back of her head. This time the pain was too much. She tried to gasp in air but it wouldn't come. Everything turned dark, the pain faded and Beauty's shrieks were the last thing she heard.

* * * * *

Justice growled as he rolled over in bed and glanced at the clock. It was four thirty in the morning. He fumbled in the dark for his cell phone and yanked it open, pressing it to his ear.

"This better be good," he grunted.

"Justice? I'm sorry about the hour. I truly am. We have an emergency. I needed your permission for a few things."

"What happened, Brass? Permission for what?" He sat up and reached for the light next to the bed, instantly awake.

"We need to send our helicopter from Homeland for an immediate pickup of one of our Gift Females who was retrieved less than an hour ago. We also need permission to bring her to Reservation. They have the better medical facility and this one is coming in rough. She is quite traumatized. They had to sedate her on scene because of the emotional trauma. I thought they'd be able to handle it better at Reservation. Dr. Trisha is still there."

Justice took a deep breath. "Fine. Send the helicopter to pick up our female. Go ahead and send her here. Call Dr. Harris instead of Dr. Trisha. He is on duty and she's on vacation. She isn't to be called in." He didn't mention that she'd just had her baby since the phone lines weren't always secure. "You know that."

"Right. Sorry. I'm frazzled. The task force wanted to put our female on a private plane to send her to us but I told them that took too long. That's when they requested our helicopter from Homeland. You have the Reservation one."

Justice frowned. "Why don't they fly her themselves? Is their helicopter down for repairs? I know they have one. I had to fight to get the funding for the thing."

"It's in use. One of the task force was shot during the extraction. They had to use that helicopter to airlift their injured teammate to the nearest trauma center almost sixty miles away."

"One of them was shot? How bad is the man? Will he live?"

"It wasn't a man. It was the human female ambassador on the team. That's why our female is so traumatized. When the human female was shot it left our female with all men."

Justice's heart dropped. Jessie was the only female who worked with the task force that he knew about. "What happened?"

"Tim Oberto believes our female was the target. The sniper tried to take out our female is what I was told and the human female was shot instead. I don't know how serious it was but it had to have been pretty bad that they felt the need to use the helicopter to airlift her out rather than get our female to us."

"Jessie Dupree was shot?"

Brass hesitated. "I don't know her name."

"Give me the number to Tim Oberto right now," Justice snarled.

"Uh, ready?"

Justice leapt from bed and ran out of the bedroom. "Hang on." He found a pen and grabbed the first folder nearest him on the desk. "Go." He jotted down the number.

"Brass, do what you think is best. You don't need to ask me first. Get our female home, whatever that entails and get her taken care of." Justice hung up and dialed Tim Oberto's number. It rang four times.

"Tim Oberto," a male sighed.

"This is Justice. I just heard the news. Was Jessie Dupree injured?"

"Yes."

Justice wanted to roar from pure rage. "Is she alive?"

"They are working on her in one of the trauma rooms." Tim took a deep breath. "I don't know her condition."

"She was shot?" Justice trembled.

"Yeah. She took one to the back of the head. It looked bad." Tim's voice broke. "A sniper tried to take out the Gift

Female but Jessie was in the way. She threw herself over your female and took three hits covering her. Her vest took two of the rounds but the third hit her."

"Where were your men?" Justice roared. "She's an ambassador. She is supposed to go in when it is safe."

"Don't yell at me," Tim yelled. "We had secured the area before we allowed Jessie to bring your woman out. It was a sniper. We were pinned down until he could be located. I love that girl like she's my daughter. I'm the one who lifted her off your woman and held her in my arms until our helicopter could reach us. I've got her blood all over my clothes and I'm the one who is going to have to notify her father when they tell me she's gone."

Justice collapsed onto the desk hard, sat there stunned and closed his eyes. He couldn't breathe at first, too stricken at the news that the vibrant woman who'd shared his bed had been shot. It took a lot for him to draw in a painful breath.

"You think she's going to die?"

"She was shot in the back of the head. What do you think? She wouldn't wake up and it was bad."

Pain tore through Justice's chest. Jessie was gone to him forever. Her face flashed through his mind, the memory of her lying naked under him with her arms wrapped around his neck, smiling up at him with her pretty blue eyes. Her red hair had been spread out on his bed. More pain tore through his chest.

"Where are you? I'm on my way."

Tim hesitated. "Of course. Policy," he ground out. "It will make a nice photo opportunity, right? You can stand outside the hospital and say some shit in front of the reporters about how brave she was to give her life in the line of duty to save your people. You didn't know her."

Anger tore though Justice. "I know Jessie. Don't you ever accuse me of something that deceptive again. I don't give a damn about getting my picture taken or about what humans think right at this moment. I want to know where she is because I'm coming there to see her."

Tim sighed. "I'm sorry, Justice. I didn't mean that. I know what a good man you are but I'm just totally mind fucked right now. This is tearing me up. Do you understand that? She's like my daughter. I was threatening to turn her over my knee and whip her ass for what she did tonight and ten minutes later I'm holding her in my arms watching her bleed. I've never felt so damn useless in my life and now I'm just so pissed it could happen that I'm tearing into anyone I can."

Anguish. That was the feeling Tim expressed, Justice identified with him and it, since that emotion poured through his own body. "We're fine, Tim. Where is she?"

"We're in Portland, Oregon. It was the nearest trauma center we could fly her to. The takedown happened in Washington State in a remote area." He named the hospital.

"I'm coming. You've got my cell number, correct? If not you should have it now since I just called you. I want you to contact me the second you know anything about her condition."

"I will, Justice. Again, I'm sorry. I didn't mean that shit."

"Don't give it a second thought." He hung up and dialed the control center of Reservation. He arranged for the helicopter to be fueled, the pilots to be woken and a security detail to meet him in five minutes. He remembered Tiger in the guestroom, woke him too and rushed to his room to dress.

He froze, unmoving, when he sat on the bed to jerk on shoes. Jessie's image fixed in his mind caused him to bite back another roar of pain. He'd never get the chance to kiss her again or see her smile. At best he might be able to reach her before she died and get to hold her little pale hand.

Life wasn't fair, he knew that, he'd had a lifetime of shit handed to him but the loss of her would leave emotional scars too. They'd had so few moments together but they were ones he'd never forget. It hurt.

Chapter Seven

১৯

Justice grimly adjusted his tie for the hundredth time as he glanced at his security team. Humans stared at them as they entered the hospital lobby but it wasn't unusual. Six large Species males, all dressed in black uniforms but one who wore a nice business suit, was bound to draw a lot of attention. Justice ran his nervous hands down his dark gray jacket as he paused in front of the nurses' station. The female lifted her chin and her mouth dropped open, nearly competing with her wide-eyed gaze.

He tried not to intimidate the woman by speaking in a soft tone. "We are here to see Jessie Dupree. She was brought in as a shooting victim."

The woman snapped her mouth closed and swallowed hard. "You're New Species, aren't you?"

Justice refrained from growling and flashing fangs. He didn't want to carry on a conversation with the nurse. He didn't want to play twenty questions either. Jessie was still alive as far as he knew and he wanted to reach her side before it was too late. Tiger tensed at his side and reached out to place his hand on the counter.

"This is urgent business," Tiger softly growled. "Answer Mr. North please and remember to be a professional."

Justice normally would have flinched but tonight he didn't mind one of his men being blunt. He wanted the woman's cooperation regardless of how he got it. "Yes. As I said, we're here to see Jessie Dupree."

The nurse glanced at her computer, typed in information and gave them directions down the hall to a waiting room. They didn't make it ten feet from the desk before they heard the woman on the phone telling someone that a group of scary-looking New Species were at the hospital.

"Do you think she's calling the local news stations?" Tiger groaned. "I hate those bastards."

Justice shrugged. "We'll avoid them on the way out."

He didn't really give a damn about the press. *Is Jessie still alive? Will I get to see her before she dies? This is killing me.* He just needed to see her. He wanted to inhale her scent and touch her at least one last time. His chest hurt badly knowing there wouldn't be any hope in his future to spend a night with her.

Tiger walked into the waiting room first, kept his body in front of Justice and made sure there wasn't any form of threat inside the room. Justice immediately spotted Senator Jacob Hills sitting in a chair with his hands covering his face, bent over and softly crying. Justice froze inside at the grief-stricken sound.

He felt his emotions shutting down from the pain of knowing Jessie had already died. His fingers curled into fists though, rage flashed and he swore vengeance. He was going to find out where they held the sniper who'd killed her, if the man was still alive he was going to kill him with his bare hands. He'd tear the son of a bitch apart for killing Jessie, make him scream and suffer greatly before he died. Pure rage and pain battled until he regained control enough to speak.

Tim Oberto shared the room with four other men still dressed in their task-force uniforms. Justice had to keep taking deep breaths to stop himself from losing the shaky control he had found. The animal urges inside him pushed forward strongly, he wanted to tear the room apart and go insane from the knowledge that Jessie was gone.

Senator Hills glanced up, his hands dropped and his tear-filled gaze discovered Justice. He looked surprised to see the Species and stood on unsteady feet. "Justice, what are you doing here?"

Justice swallowed hard. "I heard about Jessie and flew here right away."

The senator blinked back more tears and approached. He wiped his hand on his slacks and held it out. "Thank you. I never expected any of you to come here but it means the world to me."

They shook hands. "The doctor was just in here." The senator smiled. "I'm sorry for the show of tears but I thought my daughter was dying." More tears flooded his eyes. "She's going to be fine though."

Immense relief tore through Justice, followed by a sense of need to find Jessie. "Where is she?"

"They are cleaning her up." The senator laughed. "I always said she had a thick head. The bullet grazed her skull but it didn't penetrate."

Justice closed his eyes to hide his raging emotions. Jessie was going to live and a graze meant she wasn't seriously wounded as long as there was no brain trauma caused by the impact. He opened his eyes and took calming breaths. He needed to stay in control. What he really wanted to do was tear apart the hospital until he found Jessie. He wanted to bury his face against her neck and breathe her in. He didn't move though, afraid he wouldn't stop there.

"She's pissed about her hair." The senator wiped at more tears, laughing. "Can you believe my daughter? She could have died and she's upset that they had to shave her hair from the back of her head."

"They shaved her head?" Justice growled. He took a deep breath. It was only her hair she'd lost instead of her life. It would grow back. The senator tensed, eyeing him, stunned.

"We're weird about head shaving," Tiger stated, stepping forward to include himself in the conversation. He shot Justice a worried look but forced a smile. "We're grateful that your female will live."

Justice nodded. "I apologize. I'm upset that Jessie was harmed." He forced himself to go into Justice North mode, the male who represented all of New Species. "We wanted to show our support."

The senator smiled. "I knew you were a good man, Justice. My daughter would love to meet you. Would you mind hanging around for a little while? You did fly all this way and she would be tickled pink to get to meet the man I've told her so much about."

"I've met her," Justice informed him. "I would like to see her."

The senator appeared surprised. "You met Jessie?"

"Yes. She brought a group of our females to Reservation and stayed there until last night."

"Your daughter can be quite persistent." Tiger chuckled. "I thought she was going to shoot me if I told her she couldn't escort our females and help them settle in at Reservation after the raid in Colorado."

The senator laughed. "That's my girl. I raised her not to take no for an answer. She's a tough little shit. She took after her mother and it scared me because she was always so small but with such a big personality. You'd think she was a seven-foot linebacker with her attitude." He showed fatherly pride. "She can be a handful."

"Yeah," Tim chuckled. "She is. Last night I was going to put her over my knee and spank her ass."

The senator gasped. "You were going to what?"

Tim sobered. "She reminds me of my daughter. We had a situation where the Gift Female was being held. Two of our men were pinned down and three assailants broke into the back of the house. Jessie was ordered to stay out of it but refused to listen. She killed three of the bastards and kept them off my guys. Then when we couldn't find the female she went looking and damned if she didn't find her. We would have

missed the female if Jessie hadn't been so sure there was a Species there."

One of the task team members stepped closer. "I'm Trey Roberts, Jessie's team leader. She saved my ass and Mike's." He jerked his head to the other man standing next to him. "We were pinned down and those assholes could have picked us off since we couldn't retreat. We were under fire. Jessie shot all three of them."

"She faked one out," Mike chuckled. "She pretended to be shot and dying to get the son of a bitch to come finish her off. She took him down in a snap."

The senator's mouth hung open. "She killed three men? No one told me that."

Tim paled. "I would have but you just arrived. I ordered her to find a hole, sir. She should have hidden until we could reach her but she refused to listen to me. That's why I was going to put her over my knee."

"She isn't supposed to be in danger." The senator gasped again. "You aren't supposed to send her in until it's safe for her to make contact with the New Species."

"You're the one who gave her a gun," Tim grunted. "She thinks she's part of the team because you keep telling her she is. You know how stubborn she can be. I tell her what to do but she doesn't listen. If she did then she would have waited outside but hell no. Not your daughter. She demanded to go in with the men so she could be right on the spot for the woman if we found one. She would have probably stolen a car and rammed the gates on her own if I hadn't put her with a team."

The senator took deep breaths to calm himself but still appeared angry. "You're right. That's Jessie." His mouth tensed. "She's fired. I never thought it would be so dangerous that she'd have to kill three men or get shot. She's not going back. I'll find a replacement on the team immediately but it won't be her anymore." His gaze turned to Justice. "I'd like to request one of your people to take her place temporarily until

we can find someone trustworthy. I don't care if it's a male or a female but the team needs someone your women won't be terrified of. Who better to tend to any of them than one of your own?"

Justice didn't want Jessie going back to work either considering the males on her teams had allowed her to be nearly killed. "I'll find a replacement." He studied the men inside the room who belonged to Jessie's team until he stared at her team leader, Trey Roberts. "Which would work better with your team? One of our males or a female?" He paused. "Keep in mind our females would get testy if any of your men harassed them or sexually bothered them."

Trey blinked. "Definitely male. We tease Jessie all the time but she knows we're kidding. It's a stress breaker. I don't know if one of your women would understand the jokes and one of my guys might slip."

"Done. I'll ask for a volunteer and have him contact you within the next few days." Justice gave his attention to the senator. "We'll have to sort out where he lives and what would be safest. I won't put any of my men out in the open to be targeted by hate groups. He has to have secure living arrangements."

"Done."

The door opened to admit a nurse. She gawked at the New Species. Long seconds ticked into a full minute. The senator moved forward, drawing the woman's attention.

"Yes?"

She forced her gaze to him. "Uh, your, uh, daughter. She is ready to leave. Her tests all look good and she refuses to stay for observation. They are…" She turned her head to gape at Tiger.

"They are what?" The senator snapped.

The nurse's attention flew back to him. "She is leaving AMA. They're releasing her as soon as she's dressed." The woman spun and fled.

"Should I carry pictures of us and just pass them out?" Tiger chuckled. "That way they could stare as long as they want."

"I doubt that would work. They would only want you to autograph them." Justice smiled to soften his words.

Tiger flinched. "I say I don't know how to write my name when they ask me to do that. A lot of humans figure we can't read so they buy it."

Trey laughed. "You get that often, huh?"

Tiger nodded. "Yes. We were invited to the Governor's Mansion two weeks ago and had to deal with a lot of humans at the event. They wanted us to sign things, kept trying to touch us and asked us to pose with them for pictures. Women passed their numbers into my palm when we shook hands."

Mike laughed. "Man, I wish women would give me their numbers. It doesn't sound so bad."

"You wouldn't wish it if you lived it," Justice stated softly. "You are no longer a person but are viewed as a thing. An object. Something not sentient."

"But the women..." Mike winked.

Tiger grinned. "They are too fragile."

Mike openly studied Tiger from head to foot before glancing down at his own body. "We're about the same."

"No. We're not. I'm stronger." Tiger laughed, flashing his fangs at Bob. "I have sharp teeth. Your women are too fragile."

"Oh. Your women enjoy sharp teeth? Wow. That's kind of cool. Yeah. I can see where you couldn't do that with ours. I nipped one on the ass once and she dumped me, claiming I was a freak." Mike showed his teeth. "Mine are smooth and straight and for the two grand I paid the dentist they'd better be. She did have a mighty fine ass though. That was one to sink your teeth into."

Justice sighed, sending the senator an apologetic look. The senator smiled in return, both of them seeming to understand sometimes their men had conversations that they probably shouldn't. Justice ignored Tiger and the team member's conversation. He really wanted to leave and go find Jessie.

"Stay and talk to your new friend, Tiger. I'll be outside the door," Justice stated, moving toward it.

"Don't forget me," Tiger joked.

Justice glanced around the hallway as he stepped out with his other male guards. The senator stayed next to him. Justice's mind worked overtime as he realized seeing Jessie might not be the best thing at that moment. Humans were watching, gathered in groups up and down the hallway to stare at him. Some withdrew cell phones to snap pictures, not bothering to hide their intent.

Anger gripped him strongly when he realized the danger it posed to Jessie. Any photograph or video clip of him reacting strongly to her would be sold to the local news stations. By midnight it would hit every media outlet worldwide, gossips would speculate that they might be dating and she'd become a target for reporters and New Species' enemies.

They weren't dating—that implied she wanted to ever see him again and he wasn't sure that was the case. He hoped she did but that didn't make it fact. He might do something foolish, probably would if he had the chance to touch her and he needed to avoid that. His desire to talk to Jessie though wouldn't be denied. One way or another, he wanted to get access to her face to face but under safer conditions. He refused to put her in danger. He met the senator's gaze, a solution snapping into place.

"Jessie needs a job and I have a safe one to offer her. It is the least I can do since she was harmed rescuing one of our females. She can still work with them but under stable conditions."

The senator smiled. "That would be great, Justice. To be honest, she's going to be pissed as hell when she finds out I fired her. You'd be saving my ass. My daughter has a temper. What kind of job is it?"

Justice hesitated. He was making it up as he went. "She will live at Homeland. It is secure and safe for her there. We have a segregated dorm where we are housing our females. Jessie would be wonderful for them to have around and I'm sure she'd be a tremendous help."

The senator nodded. "It sounds good."

"She can start as soon as she's well." Justice had to smother a grin. He would get to see Jessie often if she lived at Homeland. Hell, he could get as much access to her as it took to persuade her to return to his bed. The thought helped ease his urge to see her immediately. "We'd be lucky to have her."

I'd be damn lucky to have her. An image of her under him on his bed the night before flashed but he pushed it back before he was tempted to storm down the corridors to locate Jessie and throw her over his shoulder. *Don't do it. Too many damn humans, the press has probably already arrived and you can't let your people down. You're the face of New Species. You'll see her soon. Very soon.*

"That would probably be today, knowing my daughter."

Today. Justice couldn't stop the smile that spread across his face. "I'll make all the arrangements immediately."

Justice's cell phone rang. "Excuse me. I have to take this."

The senator spoke. "I understand."

Justice walked off, taking the call. It was about the new female Jessie had rescued. He listened. "Keep her sedated. I want her moved to Homeland immediately."

Justice walked back to the senator. "I must leave. It's the female that Jessie rescued. She is in bad shape inside her mind. She just woke, refuses to be calmed and the medical staff had to sedate her again when she tried to flee from them. When Jessie wants to work we'll have her help us with that female first. You give me a call and we'll arrange transport for Jessie to Homeland."

"I have it. I'll bring her myself. I've got a private plane at my disposal."

Justice held out his hand. "I'm grateful she is well."

"Thank you for coming."

In minutes Justice and his men left the hospital. News vans waited outside and Justice sighed in frustration as reporters rushed at them and yelled questions but he still heard Tiger's grunted curse.

"Our lives suck sometimes."

Justice nodded in agreement. He'd done the right thing by leaving, despite the gnawing regret that twisted his gut at not being able to make sure Jessie was truly all right. As much as he wanted to hold her, to assure himself she lived, he wouldn't destroy her life in the process.

Jessie resisted the urge to cry. She touched the bandage on the back of her head, winced and hated that they'd shaved part of her hair. The nurse gave her a sympathetic look.

"No one will know if you pull it into in a ponytail or leave it down. It's at the back of your head so someone will only see it if you part your hair or wear pigtails. It will grow back in time but with that length, I know it's rough. Once it grows out some it will mingle with the rest of your hair and be harder to see. You need to keep those stitches dry."

"I know." Jessie let the woman help her out of the hospital bed. She curled her lip at the sweats she'd been handed. Her father had bought them in the gift shop and they beat scrubs, her other option. She hated sweats in general but the fact they were stamped with the hospital's name and logo made it worse. "I have the paperwork telling me how to care for them."

"You have to sit in the wheelchair. It's hospital policy for an orderly to escort you to the front door."

"Great," Jessie snorted, keeping her comment clean since the nurse had been kind. She sat and meekly allowed the woman to push her out of the room after setting her bag of bloodied clothes on her lap.

Jessie spotted her father and Tim as soon as they entered the hallway. Some of the team had shown up too. Mike, Trey, Jimmy and Bob leaned against the wall watching her with grins. Shane was the only absent member of her team.

Senator Jacob Hills grinned when he spotted her, cutting off his conversation with Tim and rushed down the hallway. "How is my baby?"

"Yeah," Trey grinned, leading everyone closer. "How are you, baby?"

Jessie's finger itched to flip him the bird but she forced a smile instead. "I'm great. I'm ready to go home." Her gaze met Tim's, not a good sign that he grimly held her glare. It meant he was still mad at her for not following orders. "How is Beauty? I was told she wasn't hurt. Did she make it where they wanted her sent all right?"

Tim hesitated. "We had to tranquilize her, Jessie. She was hysterical after you were shot and couldn't be calmed. We called the NSO right off the bat after you were taken care of. Shane stayed back with her since he said you'd want one of your team with her until she was dropped off. The NSO sent a helicopter to pick her up and he transported with her to Reservation personally but he's on his way home now. They have her safe and she was sleeping like a baby last time he saw her."

Bob chuckled. "Shane filled out her paperwork and put Beauty for her name. We thought you'd be pissed if he wrote down Mud or Monkey."

The senator gasped, shooting a glare at Bob. "You called her those names?"

Bob's smile died. "No. That's what they called her. Jessie renamed her Beauty."

"Oh." The senator relaxed. "I thought I was going to have a nightmare on my hands. You never call them derogatory names. I'll fire you if you ever do. You always treat them with respect, as though they are family."

Jessie smirked. "You mean like how I call Jake a butthead and ass breath? That's what you call family. You might want to tell them to treat them like anyone but family."

The senator grinned. "Your brother hates those names, Jess. If he were here instead of in Afghanistan, he'd tell you himself."

"Jessie," she corrected, smiling. "I'm glad you came, Dad. I'm ready to go home and get back to work."

Tim cleared his throat and jerked his thumb at the men. Jessie frowned as the team quickly walked away, leaving her with her father. He looked grim when she stared at him, confused.

"About that." His blue eyes narrowed. "You're fired."

"What?" she yelled.

"Quiet, Jessica Marlee Dupree," he ordered in a stern voice. It was the same tone he'd used all her life when she was in deep shit. "You disobeyed orders last night and killed three men. You did the right thing, protected your fellow team members and I know that. But you killed three men." His voice broke and tears flooded his eyes. "You're lucky to have your brains intact. Do you know how I felt when I got the call that you'd been shot?" He took a shaky breath. "You are fired. I love you but I can't live with knowing I'm putting you in a position to have to kill more men or have them kill you. You have a new job so listen to me before you lose your temper."

Jessie was in shock. Her father was more upset than she could ever recall seeing him except once. He'd cried when her mother had died and had never fully recovered from the loss. She eased back into the wheelchair, her tense body relaxed and guilt ate at her as she stared at him. He'd gone through hell over her getting shot and she knew it. It hurt to lose her job but she loved her dad more.

"What new job?"

He hesitated. "No screaming and telling me I can't fire you?"

She shook her head. "You're crying. I'm sorry, Dad. You lost Mom and she meant the world to you. You almost lost me and I get it. I hate it because I love this job and I love those guys on the task force but I do understand the hellish position you're in. What's the new job and forget about it if you tell me you're sticking me in an office."

He leaned down and grabbed Jessie hard, hugging her. She hugged him back and wished she could breathe. She wiggled in his arms and he finally let go. He straightened, wiping at tears. He smiled at her though and it made it all worth losing the job and almost turning blue from lack of oxygen.

"I got you a job at the NSO Homeland, Jessie. How is that for a consolation prize for losing your job with the task force? You're going to be working directly with the New Species Organization still but at a safer location." He grinned. "Justice North flew here to make sure you were fine and he offered the job himself!"

Shock tore through Jessie. "Justice is here?" Her head turned, searching for him.

"He received an emergency call regarding the woman you saved last night. He had to leave but he said you could start at any time you're ready. I knew you'd want to get right back to work." He laughed. "I know my girl and you'd want the job so I hope you don't mind but I sent someone to your apartment. It's being packed up as we speak, just your belongings will be sent and all your furniture will be stored. The guys I ordered to pack your stuff are going to ship everything to you there. It might take a few days but it will come pretty fast."

"Thanks. That was great thinking." She forced a smile to hide her surprise at the drastic changes in her life. "You know I want that job."

Justice had come and gone but he hadn't seen her. She masked her emotions from her father, afraid he'd be confused by the sadness that she felt knowing that Justice had come but he hadn't stayed long enough to see her. She felt a little anger too but let it go.

He had flown all the way from California to come to the hospital. *That has to mean something, right? He could have stayed and said hello. Maybe made sure I was fine.* She sighed.

"What about my Gift Female? What was the emergency?"

"I don't know but when you get to NSO Homeland I'm sure you'll find out. He ordered her moved there and said that would be your first job."

Jessie pondered that. Justice might be angry at her for leaving, a reason why he hadn't stayed. She'd split on him. It was work though and she'd had to leave. He should understand that. *Well, to be fair,* she thought, *he'd had to leave for work too.*

"I'd like to say goodbye to my team."

"You do that. They are in the waiting room. I have a car waiting outside to drive us to the airport. We'll stop and buy you some clothes to last you a few days on the way." He glanced at the sweats. "I know you hate those but it was all they had unless you wanted a summer dress in a bright orange flower print."

She made a face. The senator laughed.

"I know. I haven't seen you in a dress since you graduated high school and had to wear the gown. You wore cut-off jeans and a tank top under it if I remember right."

She grinned. "It wasn't a tank top. It was a sports bra."

He reached out and cupped her face. "That's my girl. You always have to be different."

Justice's image flashed through her mind and she wondered if maybe it was part of the reason she was so drawn to him. She did like different and she liked him a hell of a lot. She only wished he'd stuck around to see her.

Chapter Eight

↬

Jessie was nervous as she stepped out of the cab and lifted the gym bag to her shoulder. The sight of protesters marching near the gate angered her instantly. *Don't they have lives? Something better to do than harass a bunch of people who have never done anything to them?* Jessie paused next to the cab window and handed the driver three twenties.

"Keep the change."

"Thanks." He backed the vehicle away.

Her gaze studied the men and women as she headed for the gates. The NSO Homeland was the main home for New Species and they also had a huge wooded area they'd bought and named Reservation. She'd been here before but she'd never had to walk through the front gates. She'd come in a helicopter, dropped off females and had promptly been flown out, having never stepped past the heliport area. Now she was going to live and work inside Homeland. It was rumored Justice lived there full-time and that meant she'd probably see him sometimes.

"What are you doing here?" It was a guy in his forties who stepped out of line holding a sign that read "Abominations won't be tolerated, Love the Lord."

Jessie stopped, cocked her head and gave him the once-over with a critical eye. "What are you doing here?"

He frowned. "I'm using my right as an American to voice my opinion."

She shrugged. "I'm here because my American ass wants to be."

She advanced another five feet before the jerk moved, jumping in her way. She stopped, her body tensed and she evaluated him as a potential threat. He had about five inches in height on her and wasn't in good shape with his beer gut and flabby arms. He glared at her bag with narrowed eyes.

"Are you staying here?"

"You're really smart. Yes. That's why I have a bag with me."

He frowned, looking more pissed. "You can't go in there. It's a den of evil."

Jessie flat out grinned.

That seemed to make the stranger madder. "Do you doubt me? I have the word of the Lord on my side. He told me to come here and let them know they aren't welcome here in America. We're a God-loving country."

Jessie loved guys like these. He was just making her day as she laughed. "Wow. God talks to you? That's great. Could you tell him that I'd like world peace and Elvis back? I dream about him hooking up with some cool metal band. They could make some kickass music together."

The man gawked at her but finally closed his mouth. His eyes rounded while his face reddened. "You mock me? You mock God?"

"No. I'd never make fun of God. What I mock is that you're an idiot who doesn't seem to know it. Instead of wasting your time here you should be getting your own life together. I wonder what God has to say about judging others? Remember that one? I do, from Bible school. I never once saw a bumper sticker that says Jesus or God loves you unless…fill in the blanks. Get a life and realize that if God were really speaking to you, he'd have better things to tell you to do than wasting your time annoying good people. He's about love and acceptance, not stupidity and hatred." Her attention focused on his sign and then him. "You might want to take some classes too since you don't seem to know that comma should be a period. You might learn something like compassion too while you're at it. I know it's nice to walk outside and take in fresh air but do it in a park, not harassing good people who are trying to better their lives. You should try that sometime. It might make you a decent human being. Currently you are doing a shitty job of that."

Jessie moved around him. He was pissed, sputtering and shocked. Jessie spotted two Species officers grinning from where they guarded the gate entrance. It was clear they'd overheard every word. She kept her hands where they could see them and tried to appear nonthreatening as she approached. They remained on the other side of the gates and were heavily armed.

"Hello. I'm Jessie Dupree. I'm going to reach into my front pocket and pull out my driver's license slowly."

One of them gave her permission. She pulled out her license and handed it through the bars. "Justice North spoke to Senator Jacob Hills early this morning and offered me a job at Homeland. I wasn't expected at any certain time but here I am."

One of them handed back her license. He hesitated before reaching for something on the wall out of her sight. He pulled out a clipboard and ran his finger down it. "Let her in. She's on the list."

The second officer unlocked the gate. Jessie walked inside, paused and watched the gate lock behind her. The first officer gave her a polite smile and indicated she should follow him. Jessie gave the protesters a one-fingered wave before she stepped out of sight. The walls around Homeland were thirty feet high and had walking corridors above where more Species officers patrolled.

"It's standard procedure to check your bag. Everyone has to be searched. We also have to pat you down. I apologize but due to serious threats against the NSO it's necessary. I can call a female officer to pat you down if you are uncomfortable with me touching you. I can have one here in under ten minutes.

We have some bottled water and sodas available so you can comfortably wait. We do have to search your bag now though. We need to make sure there aren't any weapons in it or bombs."

"I understand. I usually carry a gun, I have a permit but I didn't bring it with me. I realize it isn't good here so I left it with my team."

The man blinked. "What team?"

"I worked with the Retrieval Human Task Team to the NSO until this morning."

He smiled. "I didn't know they had any females."

"I was the only one." She turned to face the wall and spread her limbs. "Go ahead and pat me down."

The man was efficient and didn't make Jessie want to punch him. His hands ran over her breasts but they didn't stop, squeeze or grope. He crouched down and started at her ankles and ran his hands all the way up. He used the back of his hand to make sure she wasn't carrying a gun inside her panties. He stood and moved back. Jessie turned and stared up at him.

"Thank you. We have notified the office of your arrival and they are sending a Jeep for you, Miss Dupree."

"It's just Jessie. Thank you."

He smiled. "I'm Flame and my partner over there glaring at the protesters is Slash. Thank you for the amusement when you talked to that man out there. He loves to taunt us."

"My pleasure. When he starts up again just start chanting Elvis and I bet he'll shut up." She winked. "It's the best way to deal with them. It will totally piss him off, he'll know it's an insult but it won't sound that way to anyone but him."

The officer laughed. "I'll remember and pass it on to the others."

"It's only fair you give it back. I'm sure you have to put up with a hell of a lot. May I ask a personal question?"

He shrugged. "Sure."

"Why did you pick Flame for your name? I could see it if you had bright red hair but yours is light red."

He grinned. "I love watching a fire burn and often spend my nights sitting outside in front of a fire pit. The smell of burning wood is pleasant, the flames are beautiful and so lively."

"I always like to ask. You're lucky you get to pick your names. I got stuck with Jessica Marlee Dupree." She shook her head. "My parents said it was pretty. I think they were smoking drugs to rhyme two of my names."

He laughed.

"That's why I insist on being called Jessie. I hear someone call me my full name and just cringe. It sounds like I should be crooning old country songs or something. You have meaning for your name."

"You are a joy to be around." He grinned. "Your parents did something right."

"Thanks."

"You are really going to work here?"

"Yes. I don't know what I'll be doing but I got canned from the team this morning. I was sent here."

His smile slipped. "You mean fired? Why did they fire you?"

"I got shot. It was just a graze, really. I killed three assholes too but they deserved it. It's a long story. It was a good shooting but my dad is Senator Jacob Hills so he freaked out. He fired me to make sure I'm not in danger anymore, or put in a situation where I might have to kill assholes." She smiled to soften her words. "I guess he figured I'd be safer here." She studied the high walls and armed Species officers patrolling above with large guns. "I can see this place is pretty secure."

Flame grinned. "Where did you get shot?"

She turned to show him her back and reached up into her hair. In seconds, she'd parted it to reveal a shaved area about two inches long and an inch wide covered with a bandage. "It was just a graze. The bullet took some scalp but..." she released her hair and turned to face him. "Remember to always wear your vest on duty." She glanced at his. "I took two rounds to mine in the back from a sniper." She pointed to his vest. "They work well. All I have is a few bruises."

"Amazing." He grinned. "Do you have any friends here? Working with the task force must have made you some."

"No. I've met a few people but no one I spent a lot of time with." *Except Justice.* She didn't mention him aloud though.

"Why don't you give me a call when you get settled? We have a bar here. I'd love to buy you a beer and introduce you to everyone. I think you'll make a lot of friends. You are really funny."

"I'd like that. You can never have enough friends."

"We have a phone directory. I'm listed inside. I'm just called Flame. I don't have a last name. I haven't had a reason to choose one yet."

A Jeep being driven by a Species woman approached the gates. She was a big woman, obviously an experimental prototype and not a Gift Female. Jessie didn't have much experience with those females except for the one she'd spent time with at Reservation. She'd liked Breeze a lot.

"There is your ride. I hope you enjoy living and working here, Jessie. It's been a real pleasure meeting you. I hope to buy you a beer soon. Call me." Flame waved.

She gripped her gym bag and waved back. "It was a pleasure meeting you too. I'll be calling about that beer." She headed for the Jeep.

The large Species female scowled. "Human, you are to come with me."

"Hello. I'm Jessie. You're my ride?"

"Yes." She didn't look happy. "I'm Midnight. Please climb in."

Jessie tossed her gym bag into the backseat and sat in the passenger seat. She didn't reach for her belt. There were no seat belt laws on New Species properties. They also didn't have a lot of vehicle traffic or speeding issues. She mainly saw golf carts parked along most of the curbs. The driver turned the Jeep around and glanced at Jessie again, obviously not happy to be assigned to drive her anywhere.

"Do you not like humans in general or is it just me?" Jessie kept her smile in place.

"I don't mean to be rude." She glanced at Jessie with a softer look. "I'm not used to dealing with your kind and my experiences haven't been good."

"I see. Well, I'm a total smartass but I'm always nice to people unless they aren't nice to me first. I don't think you're being rude. I just wish you'd give me a chance before you decide not to like me. I'm open-minded about you."

Midnight smiled. "I see."

Jessie had to learn how to break the ice all of her life. As the daughter of a public figure she'd had to deal with a lot of strangers in different types of scenarios. She could be more open and blunt with New Species than with humans and she liked that. Species didn't play games or lie easily. They were straight up.

"So, are you the one who's going to tell me where I work, what I do, where I'll be sleeping and when I start? I'm kind of in the dark except that I have a job and I'm living here."

Midnight flashed her blue gaze at Jessie. "I'm just supposed to pick you up and take you to one of the cottages. I was told to show you the home, wait around until you're ready and then take you to the medical center. I don't know anything else."

These people need help with their job orientation program, Jessie decided. "Fair enough. Will I have to live with someone or do I get my own room?"

"You will get your own cottage. We don't share living space unless we live at the women's dorm but we all have our own apartments. We just share common areas. It's for New Species only and visiting humans are assigned cottages. They are houses located in secured areas cut off from the rest of the general population."

Jessie grew silent, allowing that information to sink in. Secure areas cut off from general population sounded pretty grim. Midnight wasn't a talker and didn't seem to mind the silence that stretched between them. Jessie glanced around her surroundings. There were a lot of buildings that didn't have names but they did have letters to identify them. She realized she didn't see any numbers at all, on anything. She shrugged it off. They left the buildings and drove through a large park. There were tons of trees and an obviously man-made lake.

"That's really pretty."

Midnight glanced at the water. "I like Reservation better. They have a really large lake and it's pretty. I did four weeks there last month and want to go back."

"What do you do there? Is it better than driving new employees around?" She meant it as a joke.

"Slade, he runs Reservation, requested female help while construction was being done there. He needed help with security so twenty of us lived there. Once everything was done we were brought back here. We missed it. This is nice but Reservation is better. Now we trade off shifts so I go for a month but then we switch. It works well and that way our females are divided equally between the two locations."

"Is being divided equally important?"

Midnight hesitated. "We are a lot fewer than the males and they are protective of us. If something bad ever happens at one place they want to make sure not all of us are killed." She paused. "We get threats all the time by your kind to blow us up and hunt us all down like animals. It makes the men worry about us and they divide our numbers evenly."

"I understand. Humans can be pretty shitty, can't they?"

Midnight shot her a surprised look.

"I know how flawed my people are." Jessie shrugged. "Some of us are good while some of us deserve a bullet to the head."

The Species woman smiled but tried to hide it by turning her head forward to watch the road. "We are also needed here because Justice and the council decided we should take care of all our people. Some of our females weren't living here until recently and they need us stronger females to care for them."

Jessie shifted on her seat. "You mean the Gift Females?"

Midnight's suddenly wary gaze cut to Jessie's and she frowned. "What do you know of them?"

"Actually, a hell of a lot. Until early this morning I was part of the team that retrieved them and helped return them to your people."

The woman hit the brakes hard. Jessie almost slammed into the dash. The woman turned all the way on her seat to face Jessie, studying her hair. "You're her! You're *that* Jessie!" A grin broke out across Midnight's face. "Tiny and Halfpint talk about you all the time! They all do but especially those two."

Jessie recovered from almost being a bug on the inside of the windshield and shoved her ass back against the seat. "Tiny and Halfpint are here? Really? What happened to the women's retreat they were living at?"

"Oh, we don't send them there anymore. It became too dangerous. We didn't want those nice human females or our females hurt. They were getting death threats for harboring Species." Midnight still grinned. "Wait until I tell them you are here. They worship you. Whenever they are feeling frightened and scared, they think of you. You are small like them but they said you are fierce." Midnight glanced at Jessie and her smile slipped. "You don't look fierce. You look small and kind of weak."

Jessie laughed. "I'm stronger and tougher than I look."

Midnight didn't seem convinced. "I will drive you to the cottage and to the medical center. I will tell the females you saved that you are here. They might bake you something. They are learning how and are proud of their skills." Midnight lifted her boot off the brake and punched the gas. "Don't hurt their feelings." It sounded threatening.

Jessie leaned back against her seat. "I wouldn't dream of it. I love baked goods and I'd love to see them."

About two dozen really cute homes sat nestled on the other side of the lake. They were all different colors. Jessie hoped she got one with a view. They were larger than she thought they would be when she'd heard the word cottage. They didn't really resemble cottages but she shrugged that off too. The houses she saw had to be about fifteen hundred square feet. Midnight didn't slow the Jeep as they passed the gate leading to those homes.

"Weren't those the cottages?" Jessie stared behind them.

"Yes. I was told to take you to the other cottages."

"There are more?"

"That was the human area for the humans who work or visit Homeland. You were assigned to the New Species side."

Jessie frowned, turning to stare at Midnight. "New Species side, as in only New Species live there?"

"Yes. I don't know why. I asked but was told do it. I do it."

They came to another gated community. A guard shack with a Species officer in his black uniform waited. Midnight hit the brakes.

"Is this the human female?" The man peered at Jessie curiously.

"Yes," Midnight announced. "It is her."

The officer smiled. "Welcome. Your home has been prepared and I was told to tell you that if you need anything to let me know, Miss Dupree. If not me then whoever is here on duty. One will always be posted at the gates. You just push the button inside the door of your home to reach us. It is labeled clearly. It will let us know you need help." His gaze turned to Midnight. "It is the rose-colored one by the dark blue. It's the highest on top of the hill." He pointed.

"Thank you." Jessie forced a smile. *Why would they put me here?*

The officer opened the gate electronically and it swung wide. Midnight drove her through. Jessie looked at the cottages they passed. They were similar to the cottages they had passed where all humans lived. They were cute, newer homes but looked slightly bigger than the human ones. The community was built on a hill overlooking Homeland.

Midnight drove up the street to the top where one exceptionally large dark blue home sat away from all the other homes but the slightly smaller rose-colored one next to it. Large yard areas were located on each side of the two homes, spacing them from the other houses down the street.

"There it is." Midnight pointed. "It is big for one person."

"Yes." Jessie was in shock. "I expected just being assigned to a room."

Midnight parked in the driveway and climbed out. Jessie got out more slowly. She reached into the back and gripped her gym bag, following Midnight to the front door. A key had been left inserted in the lock. Midnight pulled it out and handed it to Jessie.

"Yours." Midnight pushed on the door and swung it wide.

Jessie stepped inside. The living room was nice sized, fully furnished and had a gray-stone fireplace. It was charming and she loved it. She dropped her bag before turning to face Midnight again.

"Let's go to the medical center."

"Aren't you going to explore?"

"Nope. I'll do that later. I'm dying to know what I do now."

Midnight blinked. "All right."

Jessie locked the door and pocketed the key. She followed Midnight to the Jeep. The officer at the gate stopped them with a deep frown.

"Is something wrong?"

Midnight shrugged. "She said she'd look at it later. She wants to go to work."

He reached over and punched in a code to open the electric gate. "Have a good day."

The medical center was located near the front gates. It was a single-story building with a glass front. It looked deserted as Midnight parked the Jeep at the curb. No one was on the street either. Jessie climbed out.

"This is where I leave." Midnight gave her a nod. "Enjoy your work, whatever it may be."

"Thank you." Jessie hesitated. "How do I get home later?"

Midnight shrugged. "I don't know. No one told me to pick you up." She waved goodbye and drove off.

Jessie shoved her hands inside her back jeans pockets and watched Midnight disappear in the Jeep around a corner. She sighed. So far, this had to be one of her weirdest days. She turned, studying the medical center and pushed open the glass doors.

Inside were chairs against the window, one long counter and in the back behind the counter were a few exam tables. They were in the open for anyone to see. Jessie's eyebrows rose. She glanced around the room but didn't see anyone. She spotted doors and a few hallways on the other side of the long counter.

"Hello!" Jessie didn't exactly yell but she knew someone had to have heard her.

"Coming," a man shouted from the hallway. He came down it and peered at her. "You must be Miss Dupree. I'm Paul, the nurse here. Dr. Ted Treadmont is in the back with Beauty. We're so glad that you're here. We've hated keeping her out but she was really traumatized by last night. We want to wake her up and let her see you. We think it might calm her to see you at her side. When she woke up this morning after the drugs wore off, she wouldn't stop screaming. We had to put her right back out."

Jessie walked around the counter. "I'll do what I can."

"Thank you. We were relieved to hear you were coming. Trisha, uh, Dr. Norbit, is on vacation and unable to come back to help out. We thought a female would help. We considered bringing other New Species in to sit with her but we didn't want to shock her more. Most of them were too young to remember much and when they see their own kind they have freaked out. Some of them don't know they look different from us. They've only seen humans, so seeing a Species scares the shit out of them."

Jessie blinked. "I never thought of that. I've yet to find a woman who had a mirror in whatever prison she'd been confined in."

"Yeah. It's a learning process. I'll be glad when Trisha comes back. They've needed her at Reservation for some months now."

Paul led her down a hall. The last bed in the corner was Beauty's. Jessie studied the older man with white hair who sat on a chair with a laptop on his lap. He wore glasses and smiled at Jessie.

"You must be Miss Dupree. Thank you so much for coming. I was informed of what happened last night." His smile died. "Are you dizzy? Experiencing nausea? Headaches?"

"I'm good." Her focus slid to Beauty.

Jessie noticed they'd bathed the frail female. Her hair was now a beautiful, shiny brown. It hung long, flowing down over her shoulders and she looked peaceful in her sleep. The bedding this time was clean and she wore a pretty flower-print nightgown. Jessie winced over the material. It was pretty in the "I'm eighty years old and it's cool to want to resemble a florist shop" kind of pretty but the last thing Beauty needed to worry about was having fashion sense.

Jessie stepped forward. "I thought the bruising would be worse."

"Most of it was dirt." Paul shook his head. "I heard she was really in bad shape when she came in."

Jessie gave him a sharp look. "You didn't clean her?" She glanced at the doctor, deciding he looked a little frail to handle that kind of job.

"Some of the women from the dorm came." Paul hesitated. "Men aren't allowed to touch one of them without their clothing on unless it's life or death. I think they are afraid." He cleared his throat. "You know." He jerked his head. "See the camera? They installed it to watch her."

"They are worried one of you will molest her?" Jessie turned, saw the camera and gave a wave. She turned her back on it. "Can you blame them? I'm sure you're trusted but these women have been through the worst abuse."

Paul nodded. "They said that most of it was dirt."

"She's in good health besides the extremely poor diet and some abuse she suffered." Dr. Treadmont sighed. "They allowed me to examine her with four of their women present." He met Jessie's eyes. "She's been badly abused for years. She's also been starved."

She understood what he wasn't saying aloud. "I haven't found one yet who hasn't been abused or starved." She moved closer to the bed and lifted Beauty's hand to hold it. It felt delicate and small inside her gentle grip. "Do you know what my job is exactly?" She glanced at the doctor.

He shrugged. "What job? I was told you were here to talk with her when she wakes." The man glanced at his watch. "Which should be soon." He stood. "I'll be in my office. One of us is supposed to stay with her at all times."

Paul met Jessie's gaze. "Just give a yell if you need help." He pulled the vacant chair to the bed so Jessie could sit and still hold Beauty's hand. "I was told it's better if men aren't around when you talk to her. Good luck."

"Wait. Do you know what my job is?"

He hesitated. "Just to be here for her. When you've talked to her and get her settled, I know they wanted you to introduce her to a few of the females. They just need to get her not to be afraid of them first. When she's more stable medically she'll be moved into the women's dorm."

Great. "So you'll call someone to let them know when she's ready to be introduced to some of the women?"

He pointed to the camera. "It's got sound and they are monitoring. Talk to the camera and let them know what you need." He fled.

Jessie studied Beauty closely. She looked young but they were usually older than they appeared. She'd guess the woman was probably in her late twenties. Usually she had time to study the male kidnappers involved to profile what kind of monster had victimized the women but not this time. She wondered what kind of monster had locked Beauty up. She was going into this blind. What mattered the most was getting Beauty through the shock of her drastic life change.

Beauty stirred and Jessie stood, gripping the woman's hand a little tighter. Brown eyes flicked open and Jessie smiled.

"Hi, Beauty. It's Jessie. Do you remember me? I'm fine. How are you doing?"

Fear was instant. The woman tensed and gripped Jessie's hand hard. She stared up at Jessie with wide, alarmed eyes, before she appeared to calm. "I thought you died."

"No. I just had a head wound. I'm fine. How are you feeling?"

The woman hesitated. "I'm scared."

Jessie kept talking to her, soothing her, until the woman's fear eased. She learned that Beauty had been with her captor for a long time. She couldn't remember the testing facility and she had no clue what she was.

Jessie was going to have to explain it to her but didn't know where to start. She didn't want to tell her all the horrors about Mercile Industries and what they'd done. That was a story for another time when the woman was stronger. Instead she gently explained that there were some physical differences between them and then started to tell her that people like Beauty wanted to meet her.

"Remember what I said last night? That I was going to get you home to your family and you'd be safe? Well, you're here." Jessie shot a look at the camera. "I want you to meet some of them. Some really nice women like you. They are going to come soon and meet you." She gave her full attention back to the woman on the bed.

Beauty looked afraid again and Jessie tried to soothe her. "They aren't going to hurt you. You were afraid of me when we met but you're not anymore, are you?"

"No. You are nice."

Jessie smiled. "So are they. They've been looking for you." Jessie heard a soft sound and turned her head toward the door. She smiled at Halfpint, realized they'd probably been waiting in the hallway.

Jessie waved her in and studied Beauty. "This is Halfpint. She was just like you, Beauty. She was locked up and hurt." Jessie's voice softened. "She's really nice and she knows how you're feeling right now. She's been where you are."

Beauty looked at the short woman who timidly stepped into the hospital room and gasped. Halfpint lifted a foot to step back but Jessie gestured for her to stay. Beauty released Jessie's hand and both of her hands lifted to her own face. Jessie understood.

"Isn't Halfpint beautiful? Just like you are," Jessie said softly. "I told you that you have family here."

Beauty stared at Jessie with dawning understanding. "I resemble her and not you?"

"Yes. You're far prettier than I could ever be. I envy you. I'd love to have your cheekbones and your beautiful eyes."

Beauty smiled. "Really?"

"Yes. Why do you think I named you Beauty? You're beautiful."

Beauty glanced shyly at Halfpint. "You're like me? You were locked up too by mean people?"

Halfpint blinked back tears. "Yes, I was. Jessie found me too and brought me home. I've been free for a while and I'm so happy here. Can I touch you? I would like to hold you."

Beauty's gaze flew to Jessie. Jessie nodded as she eased back and switched places with Halfpint. In minutes the women were hugging and talking. Jessie eventually eased out of the room and spotted Tiny lurking in the hallway.

"Jessie!"

Jessie hugged her hard. Tiny was another woman she'd saved who looked a hundred percent healthy and happy these days.

* * * * *

Justice turned his focus away from the camera and found Tiger standing behind him grinning. "I like the human. She's really good with our kind."

"Yes," Justice agreed softly. "Jessie is."

Tiger's grin faded. "Are you sure you want her living in our area? We've never had a human stay there."

"I swore to her father that I'd keep an eye on her and that she'd be safe. She can't be more protected than by living where she is."

Tiger didn't look thrilled. "I'm glad I live a few houses down from her. I hope she doesn't have any weird habits."

Justice studied his friend. "What kind of habits?"

"I don't know. Maybe she cooks bad-smelling food or worse, she could listen to loud music that I hate."

Justice glanced back at the security screen. Jessie remained out of camera range now that she'd left the room Beauty was being kept in but he really wished she'd return. He longed to look at her, hear her voice, and wanted to see her in person.

"Send someone to pick her up and take her home. She's had a long day. Tell her to go back to the medical center in the morning. Tomorrow she can move Beauty into the dorm if Ted clears it. Have whoever picks her up take her dinner. She shouldn't cook tonight after the past twelve hours she's endured. She likes prime rib."

Tiger's eyebrows lifted. "How do you know that?"

Justice inwardly winced over revealing too much. "I just do. Make sure she's taken care of and fed well. I have to go make some calls. The governor is demanding we go to a charity event next month and I'm going to accept. It's for animal rights and it would be bad publicity if we refused, so get ready to be annoyed."

"Shit," Tiger groaned. "Take Brass."

"He's going too but I want you there." Humor curved Justice's lips. "If I have to suffer, you should too. The governor's wife found you especially charming."

"She patted my ass!"

"See? She's Species friendly."

Justice laughed, exited the security building quickly and hoped to clear his busy schedule as quickly as possible. Jessie was at Homeland and he wanted to talk to her.

Chapter Nine

∽

Jessie closed the door and held the large bag of takeout food from the NSO cafeteria. She hadn't eaten all day and the smell of dinner made her stomach rumble. She turned on lights to study the living room, debating whether to eat or explore. Her stomach rumbled again, settling the debate.

The couch was plush and comfy as she sat, settled the bag on the table before her and opened it. The scent of prime rib made her groan. Justice had to have ordered it for her since they hadn't asked her what she wanted. At least she hoped he'd done something that thoughtful. For all she knew, prime rib could have been the day's special.

She'd gotten to spend time with Tiny and Halfpint again. That had been great. She'd always believed her job rewarding since joining the task force but nothing reaffirmed that more than seeing the changes in the two. They'd been frightened, injured, abused women who were shells when they'd been rescued. Now they were secure, thriving individuals who had found happiness.

The cafeteria had sent everything from silverware to napkins and two types of sodas. She ate—almost inhaled the food—and enjoyed every bite. She ignored the television across the room, a large plasma screen that hung over a fireplace, and gawked a little at how nice her quarters were. It was a big house, fully furnished and new.

Her attention finally settled on the bag she'd brought and knew she'd have to unpack. She wanted her clothes from home but had to settle for the ones her father had bought at a large retail store. He'd tried to find high-end stores but Jessie had refused. Her father could be worse than her female friends when it came to picking out clothes. He couldn't just sit back quietly while she shopped but instead had to make comments, especially when he didn't agree with her choices.

She gripped the handle of the bag, stood and walked down the hallway. The first bedroom was generic, nice. She moved on to the second one. It was a big room, the master, and she grinned.

"I can get used to this," she muttered. The height of the king-size bed lifted her eyebrows. "I'll probably need a stepstool to climb on to that." The room had a massive nine-drawer dresser and a flat-screen TV was sitting on it. It was probably a forty-inch TV. *Cool.* She grinned. Two nightstands finished off the furniture. She spun away, saw an open walk-in closet and a dark doorway.

The bathroom was huge. She gawked at the Jacuzzi tub taking up an entire corner and dropped her bag. She didn't resist the urge to climb inside, sit and chuckle. Four people could fit in the thing. It had jets and she decided she'd take a bath instead of a shower.

"I need to get undressed first." She didn't want to move. It had been a really long day and her headache threatened to return when she felt a slight throbbing at her temples.

She lifted up a hand to gently touch the back of her head, found the bandage there and sighed loudly. Her life had changed because she'd been shot. Her job with the task force was history. She had a new home yet absolutely no idea what to expect. What she needed, she realized, was to at least get acquainted with her surroundings, starting with the rest of the house.

Jessie forced her body upright, decided it was time to explore her cottage and climbed out of the tub. There was a nice kitchen and open dining room near the living room. She eased open cupboards and drawers, learning everything from silverware to dishes had been supplied. A gasp passed her parted lips when she opened the fridge to discover it had been stocked with enough food to feed a family of eight for a week, at least. The freezer was packed too with everything from ice cream to frozen meat.

* * * * *

Jessie cleaned up her dinner mess quickly and took one of the pain pills her doctor had prescribed. That bathtub was calling to her. She unpacked and grabbed a pair of boxers and a half shirt before returning to the bathroom. It didn't take long at all to fill the big tub, strip and sink slowly into the warm wonderfulness of the bubbling Jacuzzi. The jets against her back were heavenly and she raised her feet, shoving them over two more jets opposite where she sat. The headache slowly faded as she tilted her head gently on the rim, her body relaxed and she released all her pent up stress.

"Oh, I'm never leaving," she whispered aloud, her eyes closing. "This is the life."

* * * * *

Justice glanced at his watch, impatient to leave the office but he'd been informed that a situation needed to be dealt with. He rubbed the back of his neck and thought of Jessie. She'd been dropped off at her home and by now she'd had time to get settled. He wanted to see her more than anything, including addressing whatever trouble had arisen.

A knock sounded at his door, it immediately opened and Fury and Tiger sauntered in. Both males appeared stressed and irritated as the door slammed—further proof of their bad moods. They collapsed into the chairs across from him.

"What's going on?" He glanced at them.

"The usual," Tiger muttered. "Death threats and we were served with a summons to appear in court."

Fury snarled, a vicious sound, and pure rage darkened his features. "Ellie's father is demanding she appear before a judge for mental competency."

Disbelief gripped Justice. "What?"

"She had to cancel his visit. He's angry and believes I want her cut off from her family."

"Competency hearing? That implies they believe she's not of sound mind, correct?" Justice's anger spiked. "Is he accusing her of insanity for loving you?"

"Yes." Fury's hands gripped the chair tightly enough to make the wood groan. "She's carrying our child and it's obvious enough with her morning sickness that he would notice if he stayed with us for a few days. And they say she is being abused by me. She doesn't need to be upset but I have to tell her about this. She will be angry and that will make me furious."

Tiger shot him a glance and his eyebrows rose. "You? Angry? Unbelievable."

Justice smothered a grin at the joke and relaxed. "Don't tell her, Fury. There's no need."

"She has to be told. They delivered a summons to the gate in her name and I always share everything with her."

"She's your mate, living at Homeland. That makes her Species." Justice leaned forward and crossed his arms to rest them on his desk. "Their laws don't apply to us. They have no jurisdiction and they can't enforce it."

Hope filled Fury's worried gaze. "Are you certain?"

"Yes. Don't upset your mate."

"It's her father. I'm sure he might mention it when she talks to him on the phone."

"You're right. Inform her there's nothing the outside world can do. They can't enter Homeland and it's a tactic to cause anxiety. It will blow over once her father calms down. Tell her those things before you give her the news about him being difficult."

"I wish the outside world had never found out about Ellie and me." Fury softly growled. "It's caused so much grief. Everyone believes I'm harming her or that she shouldn't be with me. Why can't they leave us alone?"

"You two belong together." Tiger shrugged. "Your love for each other is clear and perhaps they are jealous. Plus, humans can be really stupid when it comes to us."

Justice grimly agreed. "Your mate and unborn child are safe, Fury. No one can take them from you or enter our gates to take her away. Care for her, love her and be there for her."

"Always." Fury rose to his feet. "I still wish the outside world had never learned about us. I watch it cause her pain sometimes and it tears me apart inside. I want to protect her but this is the man who helped give her life. I understand his disappointment but to accuse me of harming her or her being insane to love me is frustrating." He glared at each man. "If you ever mate a human, protect her better than I have my Ellie. I'm going home now. I hate leaving her for more than a few hours." He stomped out of the office.

"Shit." Tiger sighed, slumping in his chair. "I don't envy him the conversation they are about to have. This is why I swore off women from the outside. They come with nosy families who seem to cause more trouble than having those associations are worth. It makes me feel lucky that we don't have parents."

The thought of Jessie flashed through Justice's mind. Her father was the senator who spoke at meetings for Species and fought in Washington for the rights they had. Worry began to surface. Would Jessie's father have an adverse reaction if he knew his daughter had allowed him to touch her? How much trouble could he cause them if he did? He had real power, was not just some human who wanted to protest outside the gates or send them nasty messages. He slumped in his chair as he leaned back.

"We're lucky to be single."

Justice met Tiger's steady gaze. "Are we? I think Fury would disagree. His Ellie is worth it to him. Their love is true."

"Yeah. You have a point but so do I." Tiger grinned. "Let's make a pact. We won't tell anyone if we ever fall for a woman from the outside. Between humans thinking we're twisted bastards who brainwash women into being with us and our own kind watching us to see what happens when we are with humans, let's skip it and keep it on the down-low."

"The what?"

"It's a term I've learned from a human. It means keep it secret. It's no one's business and therefore they can't start any trouble if they disagree with the relationship. The male said he did that with an undesirable female." His face grew solemn. "He laughed when I commented that her looks should be irrelevant if she made him happy. I wasn't sure how to take that but I think he cares too much for appearances. The term is the same though. It means being with someone and no one knows."

Justice stood. "I don't like that term. Anyone who would dismiss a person because of how they look isn't someone intelligent enough to learn from."

"You going home?" Tiger glanced at the clock on the wall before giving him a curious stare. "Are you not feeling well? You never leave this early."

"I'm tired. I didn't get much sleep." It was partially true. He hadn't slept much but he wanted to see Jessie. "Don't stay too late."

"Sure." Tiger shrugged. "I still have some paperwork to do but I'm going home afterward."

Justice hurried out of the room, thoughts of Jessie distracting him. He wanted to protect her and avoid trouble with her father but that would mean not being with her at all. His teeth clenched in anger. It might not be an issue. She might have only wanted to share sex with him once.

* * * * *

Jessie jumped when the doorbell rang and realized she'd dozed off. She sat up and gripped the side of the tub to haul her sluggish body out and grabbed a towel. The doorbell buzzed again. Jessie cursed, dried and put on her boxers and half shirt. She ran for the front door. The doorbell sounded a third time.

"I'm coming," she called out. She hoped whoever was there wouldn't leave. She yanked open the door.

Justice wore a navy suit with a light-gray tie. His hair had been pulled back into a ponytail, away from his handsome features. His intense, dark gaze slowly lowered down her body to take in her damp skin, her attire. It hesitated over her breasts. Jessie glanced down to see what held his attention— her nipples were hard. She hadn't dried off well so her clothes clung to her in places. She crossed her arms over her chest and tried not to blush.

"Hello, Justice. I was in the bath. How are you? I didn't expect anyone to come by or I'd have grabbed different clothes. How have you been?" *Is that me babbling?* Jessie wanted to kick herself. Justice was on her doorstep and he looked good enough to attack. She closed her mouth, took a breath and forced a smile. "Would you like to come inside?"

His gaze lowered further and a smile tugged at his lips. "Are those men's boxers?"

She looked down again. "I steal them from my older brother when we stay at my dad's at the same time." She laughed, peering up at his face. "The fly is sewn shut and they are comfortable to sleep in. Dad had them in his plane with some of my stuff he brought to give to me the next time we saw each other."

Justice stepped inside the entryway and closed the door softly behind him. Jessie noticed how much taller he was since she was barefoot. Her boots gave her a few inches of height. It made him appear bigger than life in her opinion.

"I came to welcome you to Homeland and see how you are doing." His focus trained on her hair. "Are you in pain?"

"Not anymore. I took a pain pill not long ago."

He hesitated. "May I see your injury?"

"Sure. There's really nothing to see except a bandage." She turned, presented him with her back and reached up to her hair to pull out the pins.

Justice's fingers brushed hers, stilling them. "Allow me." His voice came out barely a whisper.

Jessie's heart pounded at the husky shift of his voice. It sounded pretty sexy to her. She inhaled and nearly groaned aloud. He smelled so good it made her want to turn and bury her nose in his shirt. Whatever cologne he used was money well spent. It reminded her vividly of the night before when they'd been naked and touching. An image of sinking down on his cock flashed through her memory and heat spread between her thighs. She started to ache.

Stop it, she ordered. *He came to check on me and welcome me to Homeland.* If she didn't get a grip she was afraid she'd turn back around when he finished looking at her head, tear open his clothes and run her tongue over any interesting body parts she came across. With Justice that meant every darn inch of his skin.

Justice pulled the pins one by one from her hair. Her body responded to his soft touch when he freed her hair and used his fingers to brush through it. Jessie clenched her teeth, fighting to hold back a moan.

"It's not so bad. Just a flesh wound. It was a few stitches but I can't take the bandage off for two days. They need me to keep it dry."

"They had to cut off some of your beautiful hair," he growled.

Jessie turned her head to look at him, wondering why he suddenly sounded angry. The look in his eyes was one she'd seen before, the one he'd given her when she'd impaled herself on his cock. She inhaled sharply when his hands suddenly gripped her hips from behind and slowly pulled her against his big body.

"I was worried about you. I thought you would die." He took a breath. "I was certain I'd never get to touch you again." He inhaled deeply while a purr vibrated his chest. "I about went crazy, Jessie. Let me stay with you. You owe me a night in bed."

There was no way she wanted to deny either of them more time together, especially when her body ached for him. He purred again when he turned her around to face him. Strong arms lifted her higher until her feet left the floor and she wrapped her legs around his waist. One of his arms hooked under her ass to support her as his mouth found hers.

Jessie moaned against his tongue, which delved inside her mouth, and wound her arms around his neck. She grabbed the tie in his hair and tugged it free until his hair spilled down his back. The silky texture of it was something she couldn't get enough of, just like his passionate kiss. She ground her hips against the hard arousal nestled against the vee of her shorts. Justice growled against her mouth. He broke the seal of their lips and pulled his face back as his gaze traveled behind her.

Justice stalked through her living room in the direction of the hallway and she knew where he carried her. Jessie's mouth brushed across his neck, placing open-mouth kisses on the hot skin she encountered. She laughed as she nipped his skin lightly and licked his ear when he stumbled.

"You think that's funny?" He chuckled. "You distract me from everything when you use your teeth and tongue."

He entered the master bedroom and eased her down on the tall bed. She hated letting him go but knew it was the only way to undress. Her arms and legs released him with regret, loving being wrapped around him a little too much. She watched as he stepped back, reached for his tie and roughly jerked on it until he pulled it over his head. His jacket hit the floor next and she leaned back on the mattress, using her elbows to hold her up. He unbuttoned his shirt in record time, yanked it off and threw it down. The shoes were kicked off quickly and she grinned, noticing he wasn't wearing socks again.

"What is amusing to you?" His hands paused at the waist of his dress pants.

"You don't ever wear socks, do you?"

"Never. I don't own a single pair." He tore open his pants. "Why am I the only one undressing?"

"Because I love to watch you take your clothes off. You're going to wrinkle your suit and it looks expensive. Do you want a hanger?"

Justice shoved his pants and boxers down his body. He stepped out of them to stand naked at the side of the bed. "I don't care about the suit. I just want you, Jessie."

Jessie pushed to an upright position and pulled her shirt over her head. She tossed it away before dropping flat on her back. She gripped the waist of her boxers, lifted her hips and slid them down enough to kick away.

"Are you going to shred my comforter?" She chuckled, appreciating every bare inch of Justice as he stood over her. She scooted to the center of the bed, never taking her eyes off him. Her gaze roamed his broad shoulders, his muscular arms and his pebbled nipples. Her focus lowered to savor the sight of his fully aroused state.

"Is all that for me?"

Justice growled in response as he lunged forward, got on the bed and crawled to her on his hands and knees, looking carnal and hungry. He stopped, braced his weight and grabbed both her ankles to push her legs apart. He released them and climbed higher over her until they were chest to chest. His big body pinned hers to the bed and his exotic gaze narrowed as he stared deeply into her eyes.

"Don't ever die on me, Jessie. Ever." His hand brushed her face in a gentle caress. "I can't wait. I have to have you. I need to be inside you."

Stunned a little at the raw emotion she saw in his eyes and heard in his voice, she nodded. No man had ever wanted or needed her so strongly before. Justice lowered his mouth, brushing his lips over hers, and she opened her mouth for the kiss. He purred deeply, his chest vibrated powerfully and there was no tenderness or playfulness in the kiss. Justice came at her like a man starved and she was his last meal.

Jessie moaned as her fingers dug into his shoulders. His kiss made her so hot she burned with desire, pressed tighter against him and arched her hips against the hard, hot press of his dick trapped between the bedding and her thigh. Justice shifted and his hand drove between their bodies. Jessie tore her mouth from his to cry out when his finger breached her pussy without warning.

It felt so incredible that she couldn't catch her breath as he nearly withdrew it completely from her welcoming body then pushed in deeper, stretching her with a thick digit. He moved it faster, fucking her hard and fast and snarled at her.

"You're so hot and wet for me. So damn tight." He snarled again, a really scary sound and yanked his finger from her pussy. His body tensed and he shoved up from the bed, rolling away from her. "Damn it!" He yelled those last words as he sat up on the edge of the bed, his back to her.

Jessie lay there stunned, wondering why he'd stopped and what was wrong. It took her a few seconds to move, to sit up and gawk at him. She noticed then that she'd scratched his back—red bloody marks from the tips of her fingernails—and her mouth dropped open.

"I'm so sorry. I didn't mean to draw blood."

Justice's head snapped in her direction to stare at her over his shoulder. The look on his face frightened her. He looked completely enraged and she forgot to breathe. He turned to face her, his hands were balled into fists and he snarled again.

"Justice?" Her voice came out barely a whisper. "I'm sorry. I didn't mean to hurt you."

He flinched and his chin lifted until his face was directed at the ceiling and he no longer held her gaze. He breathed hard and fast, panting. "I'm the one who is sorry, Jessie. I could have hurt you." His breathing slowed. "I wouldn't have meant to but I nearly lost control."

"How?" She was baffled. "Justice?"

Justice refused to look at Jessie, afraid he'd see fear in her expressive eyes again. That's what he'd seen when he'd snarled at her. His eyes closed as he tried to calm his erratic heartbeat and raging body. His cock throbbed, hurt, and his fists clenched tighter until his nails bit into his palms.

He'd lost every ounce of his reserve when she'd wrapped around him while they'd been kissing. She was not a Species female but he'd forgotten that huge fact until he'd felt how incredibly tight her muscles squeezed around his finger. She wasn't designed sturdily enough to handle a male in full-blown lust and that's exactly how he'd gone at her. He had wanted to flip her over, shove her ass in the air and fuck her into oblivion.

Just the realization of how painful that would have been for her made him tremble with fear. He'd have left bruises on her hips while holding her still to keep her where he'd wanted, might have made her bleed from his rough entry when he began to fuck her and he wouldn't have been able to stop once he'd started. Memories of how good she felt assured that.

"Justice?"

Her timid, unsure voice tore at him and he opened his eyes, gazed at the high ceiling of the bedroom and knew he should leave. He owed her an explanation at the very least. He lowered his head and met her concerned stare.

"I'm so sorry I scratched you. Your back is bleeding."

"It's not that."

His voice came out too gruff, with a harsh edge in it that he wished he could remove but his emotions were too close to the surface. That other side of him that he tried to keep in check wasn't about to be leashed behind the facade he showed the world outside the walls of Reservation and Homeland. He was a Species male at that moment, one with feelings for a woman he knew he couldn't have and it tore him up inside.

She huddled in the middle of the bed, appearing smaller than normal, pale, her bright red hair spilling down her chest, hiding her breasts. She looked like a nymph—so innocent, completely the image of a female who never should be at his mercy in a bedroom.

"What's wrong? Why did you stop? I'm still on the shot. I'm not taking anything that will mess it up. I was sure to ask that at the hospital before they released me."

She remembered that he'd worried about pregnancy and that made him hate himself a little more. Jessie took everything into consideration, remembered the little things about him that caused him concern, yet he hadn't managed to remind his raging hormones to play nice with her delicate body when he'd had her trapped under him. She wouldn't have been able to stop him and had zero chance of fighting back when the pain began. He rated even higher on his bastard scale.

"The truth is, I nearly harmed you, Jessie. I wanted you too much, too strongly, but thankfully I pulled it together enough to release you before it was too late."

He faced her, knew his dick still strained upward with need. She noticed too—her gaze dropped there before she met his eyes again. Fear didn't show on her features at the sight of how much she affected him but Jessie Dupree was a brave woman. Between her job and the way she'd handled the attack by the Species male, he admired her courage. Another woman would have run screaming away from him by now but she held still.

"Desire isn't a bad thing and I'm totally onboard with it." She dropped her arms from hugging her legs and leaned forward, her hands flattened on the bed and she exposed her lovely, rounded breasts to him. "You appreciate bluntness so that's exactly what I'm going to be. Inhale and you'll know how much I want you if feeling how wet I am wasn't enough to convince you. Use that enhanced sense of smell of yours if your sense of touch didn't convince you."

"I came at you without regard to your fragility."

To his amazement, she grinned and her blue eyes sparkled with humor. "I've been described as a lot of things in my lifetime but that term isn't used often. At least not more than once because I usually take down guys who pull that crap. I'll make an exception for you because you're as cute as can be and you're different from other men. I don't think I could take you down in a sparring match, not with your reflexes and strength. You aren't going to break me in bed though."

"I forgot you were human," he admitted.

"Is there a difference?"

"Yes." He closed his mouth, not wishing to speak more on the matter.

"I'm smaller than your women, not as strong or as buff. It doesn't mean I'm less tough though. I can promise you that."

His body wanted to believe her but his mind was in charge. "I could have harmed you severely. You need to understand that."

"Okay. I do but you stopped whatever you thought would hurt me."

She lowered her chin a little and her blue eyes tracked him as she crawled a little closer. He couldn't help but react to the incredibly sexy picture she made on her hands and knees, coming at him. His heart hammered, his cock jerked in response to the need to take her and he resisted the urge to tackle her flat and fuck her.

"We'll work through this, take it slow, so you don't get scared." Her smile widened. "We did this once and I want to do it again."

"Jessie," he growled in warning. "Stop. I touch you and have a difficult time keeping in control of my urges."

"Your urges felt pretty fantastic until you stopped." She halted and sat up, her legs parted and her hands gripped her inner thighs.

His breathing increased to a pant, his gaze lowered and a purr tore from his throat. It alarmed him that he couldn't stop doing that with her, embarrassed him slightly, but the scent of her need drove him insane. He wanted to shove her onto her back, bury his face between those lovely thighs and taste her.

"You want me," she whispered. "I want you. What's the problem?"

"You have no idea." He trembled again and knew he should leave. His body didn't respond to the demand to stand though and his gaze refused to budge from the sight of her tempting strip of paler red hair, which barely concealed where he wanted to put his mouth. "I'm dangerous."

"I'm an adrenaline junkie and you're extremely sexy, Justice. We're both adults and naked in my room. Do you need more incentive?"

He nearly lost his mind when her hand released her thigh, slid closer to her body and her finger slid over the slit of her pussy. She pulled it away, glistening with her honey and he lost the ability to think.

Chapter Ten

ஐ

Jessie knew she pushed Justice to the breaking point when his catlike eyes fixed on her every movement as though she was the most fascinating thing in the world to him. His breathing grew erratic. The soft sounds he made were purely animalistic and turned her on further.

He had admitted to being dangerous but she didn't believe for a second that he'd hurt her. It might be nuts but her instincts were always something she counted on. No alarms were triggered when it came to the New Species leader. Her attraction to him wasn't the smartest thing she'd ever felt but she refused to deny it. She wanted him enough to fight for him. That meant being provocative in bed and making him break his iron control.

He grabbed her finger without warning and pulled it to his lips. Jessie was stunned when it disappeared into his mouth, he snarled, and he sucked. It was erotic watching his reaction. The need tightened his features and pure desire shone in his gaze as he stared at her. He eased his tight hold with his lips and tongue on her finger, slowly pulled it out and glanced down at his lap. Her gaze followed his to appreciate the rock-hard condition of his sex.

He moved suddenly and his hand shot out to grip her shoulder but his hold was gentle. He pushed against her skin, urging her back and disappointment hit. He was refusing her again. She didn't need the words to know this was one battle of wills she'd lost. She sat back on her ass on the bed, ready to draw her knees up to her chest to cover her body since he didn't seem to want to see it any longer.

He released her shoulder and both of his hands gripped her calves. She was too shocked to do anything but fall back. Her legs fell open when he yanked her flat, dragged her toward him a good foot and spread her knees farther apart.

Jessie gasped when Justice leaned forward to bury his face in her lap. He nuzzled in tightly and purred loudly. He released her legs to grab her inner thighs, spreading her open for his tongue to brush over her clit. He lapped at the bundle of nerves in a rapid lash of his strong, raspy tongue and she cried out at the instant pleasure.

Her fingers grabbed for the bedding near her hips, dug into the comforter for something to cling to. The urge to grab his head wasn't easy to resist but she clutched the soft material instead of grabbing fistfuls of his hair.

"Oh God," she panted, hearing how loud her voice sounded but couldn't have cared less. Justice felt too good. She couldn't think and didn't want to. "Yes!"

He was relentless, finding the exact spot that made her gasp, groan and grind her pussy against his mouth. She wanted to come and knew she was about to. Her body tensed, every muscle tightened. Her back arched off the mattress as the pleasure turned to near pain, the climax building to the point of no return.

He stopped and she cried out in protest. She had been so close. His tongue lowered instead and drove into her pussy before she could utter real words to convey that she didn't want him to stop tormenting her clit. The sensation made her throw her head back and a different kind of pleasure tore through her body. No guy had ever done that before, fucked her with his mouth and she realized she'd been missing out on a lot. He slid his tongue a little deeper, moving in and out of her slowly and his nose nudged against her clit.

"Justice," she moaned. "Please?" She wasn't above begging. She just wanted to come, needed to. Her body burned. "Please, baby?"

His tongue withdrew and his lips nibbled higher, sealed around her swollen clit. His tongue pressed down against it and he purred loudly. The vibrations and manipulation of her sensitive nub as he began to suck on her drove Jessie insane. It felt too good, too intense and she couldn't take it. She whimpered and moaned. Panted. Her body bowed and she sucked in air as ecstasy struck with blinding intensity.

"Justice!" Her body jerked hard.

His mouth tore away from her clit while she shook, reeling from the strongest climax she'd ever experienced in her life. It barely registered to her blown mind when his hands released her inner thighs and one dug under her ass to cup a butt cheek in his big hand while his other one curved around her hip. Jessie didn't have the strength to express her surprise when Justice flipped her over onto her stomach. His hands adjusted, gripped her hips and her body slid down the bed as he pulled her closer to him. She didn't care why he did it or what his intent was. Her body was still tingling with pleasure from his amazing tongue skills. The mattress moved when his weight left it as he slid off the end of the bed.

Justice pulled her until her legs were off the bed, made her stand and leaned forward to keep her bent over the mattress. One of his feet hooked around her ankle, spread her legs and the crown of his cock pressed against her pussy.

Pleasure filled her as his thick shaft slowly penetrated her from behind. Jessie moaned as he stretched her vaginal walls. He pushed in deeper, going so slowly that it almost felt like torture. The sexy sounds he made matched hers as she urged him on, her fingers fisting the bed to brace. He withdrew a little and slowly began to rock in and out of her. Loud purrs filled her ears when his hips thrust faster. Jessie wanted more. She could sense he was holding back and she didn't want him to.

"Faster. Justice, you feel so good," she panted. "More. Give it all to me."

His face buried in her neck and it muffled the snarl as he seemed to give up whatever restraint he had. He drove into her deeper, his hips slapped against her ass and the rapid drag of his cock against her nerve endings sent her to heaven. It swamped her senses, her body tensed again and she cried out when a second climax struck. She bucked under him, her muscles clamped down tightly around his sex and sharp teeth bit down on her skin at the top of her shoulder. He groaned loudly and jerked against her, his cock going deep and staying there as she felt the warmth of his semen bathing her inside.

Jessie couldn't move. She was so sated she didn't know if her body was flesh and bone anymore or pudding. Justice's body kept her from sliding off the edge of the bed to collapse into a limp mess on the floor since her legs wouldn't have held her up for anything. They panted, his teeth eased away and hot breath fanned her skin while they recovered. It was apparent that he kept his weight from totally crushing her, allowing her to catch her breath.

The haze of sexual bliss cleared, normal function returned and she grinned, wishing she could see his face. She said the first thing that came to mind. "That was a fifteen on the one-to-ten-wow-factor scale."

"I'm so sorry, Jessie. I never meant to lose control. You're so small but I wanted you to the point that I couldn't think. Can you forgive me?"

She laughed. "You're apologizing to me? Seriously? There's nothing to forgive." She turned her head just enough to meet his concerned gaze and kept the smile in place. "That was perfect, amazing and wonderful."

He broke eye contact, lowered his face and brushed a kiss on the back of her neck. "You are delicate and just don't seem to know it. I could have really caused damage to your body."

"I'm small, I can't dispute that, but your version of thoughtlessness was mind blowing."

Justice breathed on her neck, keeping his face where she couldn't see it. "You need to trust me when I say that you are fragile compared to me. Are you sore? Was I too rough?" His voice softened. "Do you need me to call the doctor?"

"I don't need a doctor. You're making too much out of this." She wanted to laugh again at his overblown concern—it bordered on ridiculous—but she didn't want to risk hurting his feelings. It touched her deeply that he'd be so anxious over her well-being.

A growl rumbled from his chest. "I took you like you were one of our women but you're not. Thankfully I didn't lose all control." Justice moved back from her, withdrawing his weight completely. "I don't know what is wrong with me when it comes to you. I'm not myself."

Jessie rolled over to stare up at him, admiring the view of tan, tall and sexy. She just knew the sight of his sculptured muscles and strong build would always affect her.

"Maybe that's the problem. You took on this big responsibility of becoming the face of New Species." She sat up, comfortable in her nakedness and peered at him with compassion. "I know what it's like to pretend to be someone you're not. My father is a senator. I was raised around politicians and other idiots and had to don this perfect image my father demanded." She shrugged. "The truth is, I'm not really that polite. I'm a tomboy more than a lady and what I really wanted to do was smack most of the people I was forced to carry on polite conversations with."

Justice sat down on the edge of the bed, turned his body sideways, and watched her, a little confused. "I don't understand."

"You stand before those cameras, the reporters, and the world pretending to be totally human but you're not. You can just be yourself with me, Justice. I accept you for who and what you are. You're the guy who purrs and growls, gets a little out of control when we kiss and there's nothing wrong with that." She pushed forward, her hands flattened on the bed and she rose to her knees. Her gaze held his as she tried to show him she meant every word. "There's nothing wrong with you, Justice North. I think you're amazing and I don't want you holding back with me. I want to get to know the real you, not some image you've tried to perfect for your job. You're off the clock and it's playtime. I'm going to teach you how to have fun and tear down those walls you've built. I'm safe, Justice."

Justice wanted to reach out, pull Jessie into his arms and hold her. She offered him acceptance, understanding and the opportunity to be the male he'd been before he'd volunteered to represent his people. Longing gripped him to the point of pain and he knew in that instant what had to be done. A sharp jab stabbed his heart but he'd made a promise, sworn to do the job and too many were counting on him for him to follow his heart.

Clarity hurt more. He was falling in love with Jessie Dupree, probably had been since the moment he'd torn her from the arms of another male, shielded her with his body and she'd smiled. She believed she embodied safety to him but she couldn't be more wrong. The adorable redhead with her quick smile, generous heart and welcoming arms had to be the most dangerous yet beautiful temptation that had ever crossed his path.

"Are you hungry? Did you eat? I could make you something."

He took another hit to his heart. She wanted to feed him a meal, cared that he might be hungry and was nurturing. It also reminded him that she definitely wasn't Species—their females preferred that the males totally tended to them after sex.

"Hello? You're staring at me but you're not answering." She leaned closer. "Are you tired? I have to warn you that I like to sleep skin to skin. I plan to wrap around you and get close."

He was going to snap again, lose control and kiss her soft mouth. The urge to knock her flat on her back and make love to her raged through his veins again. His fists clenched as he fought the desire to return to her heavenly embrace. It wasn't just his own life he needed to remember but what being with him would do to hers as well. He blurted out words that would make her withdraw.

"My kind bite during sex and it would hurt since you are much less tolerant to pain. I had the urge to sink my teeth into your skin until I tasted your blood, Jessie. I don't want to scare you but you wanted honesty. I'm really strong and you wouldn't stand a chance against me if I ever lost control. I could accidentally break your bones or I might not stop if I get out of hand. I'm dangerous."

"You're not going to hurt me." No fear showed in her blue eyes and she didn't jerk away. "I'm not into pain but I'm not afraid of your teeth either. You won't bite me hard enough to break my skin. I refuse to believe you'd do any of those things. You'll totally get that after a few nights with me."

He needed to leave, to get away from her, before he gave in to his desire to be selfish. His people depended on him to be strong, expected it, and he'd made the promise to do so. Nothing good would come of them being together for Jessie either. Her kind wouldn't understand and her father wouldn't support the NSO anymore. Everyone would suffer.

She'll grow to resent you when she's stuck living at Homeland after the hate groups target her. Don't forget about Valiant telling you how Tammy's best friend cut ties when she refused to leave him. Who will Jessie lose? How long will it take before she hates me? It's better to give her up now, before either of us get hurt more.

"There will never be another night of us being together. I'm sorry but we can't do this again."

Her shocked expression made him wince.

"What?" The surprise quickly turned to anger as her gaze narrowed and her nose flared. "No way. You're attracted to me and I feel the same. You're being paranoid."

"It's for the best. We were drawn to each other but it must end."

She withdrew finally to collapse on her ass on the bed. Her chin lifted and she stared at him. "You just wanted a two-night stand. Got it. I read things wrong by thinking there was something between us but obviously there's not. I read you loud and clear now."

He'd hurt her and knew it. She tried to hide the pain but her expressive eyes gave the emotion away. She mistook his words to mean that what he wanted from her had just been a passing flare of lust. A smart man would have allowed her to believe it but his heart had other priorities. He'd rather be honest than leave her feeling rejected.

"I don't trust myself with you and you scare me, Jessie. I'm always in control but I wasn't tonight. The other part of me wanted to posses you in every sense. I wanted your scent and your...feel. I—" He took a deep breath. "I don't know how to explain it but damn it, I lost control and I'd rather never touch you again than risk hurting you."

Her gaze softened and her tense shoulders relaxed. "You won't hurt me."

"I don't know that and neither do you, Jessie."

"I'm really trying to be patient with you but you're starting to make me mad. I'm a big girl, an adult, and if it's risky, I'm willing to deal with the consequences. I trust you and that's the bottom line."

"You're human." He welcomed anger over the sadness of giving her up. "This is why I never got involved with one." He ran his fingers through his hair, clenched his teeth together and tried to center his thoughts. "It's best if we end this before it begins."

"You're honestly frightened." She suddenly smiled. "Of me. That's kind of funny." Her gaze raked down his body before returning to his eyes. "We said we'd sleep together and

I'm holding you to it." She patted the bed. "What side do you prefer?"

He wanted to stay, to hold her and to know what it would be like for the first time in his life not to sleep alone. His females never wanted to be held for longer than necessary. He wavered on his need to leave and his desire to spend more time with Jessie. Desire won out. It was one night, the last they'd ever share and he refused to deny himself that pleasure.

"I'll lock up and get the lights. I'll hurry."

She grinned. "I'll turn down the bed."

He fled before he could reconsider his decision. He secured her house, turned off everything and briskly strode back to her bedroom.

Jessie watched him go and her smile faded the second he left her sight. Justice was stubborn, paranoid and incredibly cute. His reasons for calling it quits before anything could develop between them were valid ones but she wasn't one to shy away from a challenge. They had a good time together, she'd missed him and he had invaded her thoughts ever since they'd talked.

She climbed off the bed, dragged down the bedding and hopped back onto the tall mattress. He hadn't told her what side he wanted so she lay down in the middle, her ears straining to hear his approach but she shouldn't have bothered. Justice moved with stealth as he sauntered back into the room. A grin threatened to surface again. Did he have any idea how sexy he looked when he walked with that graceful, fluid motion, stark naked? She doubted it. She enjoyed the view of muscles and bare skin before blackness enveloped the room with the flick of the light switch under his finger.

The bed dipped as his weight settled to her right. She turned, blindly reaching for him and her fingertips encountered hot skin. There was no hesitation as she scooted closer, threw one leg over his and pressed herself along his length. He rested flat on his back while she lay on her side. Her head adjusted until his chest pillowed her cheek, his heartbeat a steady throb in her ear. She smiled in the darkness.

"I want to hold you in a different way. Would you mind?"

It was cute how gruffly he spoke. "Sure. How do you like to sleep?"

"Roll over. I want to curl against your back."

She hated to release him but did as he'd asked. His arm slid under her head to cushion it, the other arm wrapped around her waist and he dragged her flush against his body until they were firmly spooned.

"I like this," she admitted.

"Are you cold? Should I cover us with the sheet?"

"It's a nice night and you put off a lot of heat. I'm comfortable. Are you?"

"Very." He breathed on her neck and nuzzled her bare shoulder. "I enjoy this."

"Me too. That's why I vote we do this again in the near future."

His arm around her waist tensed. "It's best for both of us if we don't, Jessie. I don't trust myself with you. You make me go a little crazy from wanting you. I would scare you if I let go of my inhibitions completely and acted on how you make me feel."

She frowned, wishing he would give up his iron control. "I don't want to fight with you but you're being way too protective. Nothing you've said so far is making me leery unless there's something else you're not saying."

"When I come inside you, I want to shout out. It was so hard to fight the urge this time."

"People make sounds when they have sex." She grinned. "I make lots of them if you'll remember. I happen to like the ones you make."

Jessie suddenly turned in his arms to twist onto her back and hooked her legs over his curved thighs. Her palm found and caressed the side of his face before running her fingernails through his hair to massage his scalp. A soft purr filled the room.

"Yeah. I like the sounds you make. That's sexy to me. You have to see me sometimes since I'm working and living at Homeland, right? I'm warning you now that I'm not going to let this go, Justice. It would be another story if I didn't believe that you were really attracted to me and that this could possibly go somewhere. That's not the case though. You're spooked and it's because you care, isn't it?"

His body tensed and the purr deepened into a slight growl.

"Yeah. That's what I thought.

"Jessie," he rasped, "I'm sorry but this is the last night we can spend together. I have a long list of reasons in my head besides the ones I've mentioned."

She bit her lip and sighed. "You're just upset right now. You'll change your mind, and when you do, you know where I am."

"You would face danger being associated with me. We can't do this again."

She wiggled her ass against his thighs, could feel his cock respond by hardening, growing thicker. She smiled into the darkness. His mouth might say one thing but his body and hers were right in tune.

"Okay," she said to placate him. He was a big ole worrier but she'd deal with that later. Her immediate goal was to make love to him. Maybe after a few dozen times he'd get over his me-big-strong-Species-you-fragile-human-woman bullshit. She managed not to laugh at that analysis. "We'll talk later."

Her other hand opened on his belly. She wished he was flat on his back and she could touch more of his body. She traced his bellybutton, dipped her fingers lower and used her nails to lightly scratch him. Justice growled.

She turned to her side, ground her ass against him and pressed her back to his chest until no space remained between them. She loved the heat he put off. With his body wrapped around hers and his arm firmly around her waist it had never felt more right to be in someone's arms.

She inhaled the wonderful scent that was Justice and listened to him purr. *I'm falling in love*, she admitted. *Hard and fast*. The memory of skydiving flashed in her mind. The fear of stepping out of the plane had been overwhelming but she'd wanted to fly. She'd taken the plunge then spread her arms and dived headfirst without hesitation. Justice beat that experience any day and she wanted to take the plunge again. A broken heart had to be a better risk to take than a chute not opening, and far less dangerous.

The twitch of the hard length of his cock that was trapped between them pulled her away from her thoughts. The decision wasn't difficult to make—it was that simple. She ran her hand down to his hip, slid it back and cupped his firm ass. He purred before softly cursing.

"Damn it, female. Stop doing that."

She wiggled, suggestively rolled her hips and gripped his wrist. He didn't resist when she lifted it and laid it over her breast. Her hand slid up, covered the back of his and squeezed, forcing his fingers to close around the mound. Jessie ground her ass against his now-straining cock, turned her head to expose her neck to his mouth and licked her lips to wet them. Her body didn't need any foreplay. She was primed to go and ached to have him inside her again. The memory of his tongue doing wonderful things to her clit and the way he'd felt fucking her was enough to take her there already.

"Take me again," she whispered. "I need you, Justice. Don't deny me this."

His hand massaged her breast without her help this time. "Damn it, Jessie." His lips brushed her exposed throat and his hips moved, rocking slowly against hers.

"Yes," she moaned.

"Hold still. We'll go slow."

Jessie spread her thighs and refused to obey his order or to take it slow. He was too careful, thought too damn much, and she wanted him to let go. She wanted the real Justice, the man who growled and snarled, who wanted to get loud during sex. She released the back of his hand, reached between her legs and wrapped her fingers around his rigid shaft.

"Jessie," he growled.

"Fuck me, baby. Hard, fast. Give it to me."

She used her leg hooked over his thigh to tilt her hips, guided the crown of his cock to rub along the seam of her pussy, rolled her hips as she found the right spot and used the leverage she had to join them. The feel of being stretched, taken by him, spiked her desire.

Teeth suddenly gripped the top of her shoulder when Justice bit down on her skin hard enough to send a jolt straight to her groin. He didn't break the skin but it was a fine line between pleasure and pain. Jessie moaned louder but the sharp points jerked away as he released her with his fangs.

"Hold still," he snarled.

"No." She used her free hand to grab the arm pillowing her head to gain traction and bucked her hips frantically, forcing him to move inside her. She increased the pace and pulled with her hand on his ass to take his cock deeper. "Don't torture me," she panted. "Forget slow."

Justice made a scary sound—a deep, vicious snarl—and his teeth clamped down on her shoulder again. The feel of his bite didn't hurt but it amped her passion higher. Pleasure shot through her body and his hand gripped her hip in a tight hold. She thought he might use his grip to still her hips but she was never happier to be wrong.

Justice drove his cock into her deeply, his hips rocked faster and pounded against her ass hard enough to shake the bed and slam the headboard into the wall. Jessie couldn't think. She was too caught up in ecstasy and the erotic feel of him keeping hold of her shoulder with his teeth. He didn't slow, didn't stop and her muscles tightened in anticipation of the pending climax.

Justice drove into her over and over — fast, hard, deep. He angled his dick a little, hit a spot that made her see stars and he seemed to know it. He kept dragging the crown of his cock against it, not going as deep as before and that did it. Jessie threw her head back against his shoulder and came hard. Her lips parted and she barely registered that she'd screamed.

His teeth tore away from her skin, the hold on her hip tightened and he followed her over. Hot jets of semen filled her. She could feel every drop as her vaginal muscles milked him. A thunderous roar nearly deafened her, her ear too close to his mouth.

They panted in the aftermath, his hold on her eased and his fingers massaged her hip. Jessie wanted to laugh but couldn't muster the strength. That was the Justice she'd wanted to see. Her hearing might not ever be the same in that ear but it was worth it. She grinned.

A hot, wet tongue licked her shoulder and she opened her eyes to stare into the dark room. He was so sweet. First he was rubbing the slightly sore spot from where he'd kept hold of her and now he was using his mouth to soothe the area he'd clamped his teeth over. It was a bit weird but not unpleasant. She could get used to it.

"That was the best sex ever," she murmured. "I like you licking me but if you want to take requests for locations where I'd enjoy that tongue more, just let me know."

He stopped lapping her skin and his breathing had slowed. "I'm cleaning your wound. Damn it, Jessie, this is why we can't be together. It was the best sex, ever but I've hurt you."

"What wound?" She turned her head but couldn't see a thing.

"I bit into your shoulder." He sounded sad. "I'm sorry, honey. Doesn't it hurt?"

"No. It can't be too bad. Don't worry about it." She could live with a little love bite. She'd enjoyed it.

He tensed. "Don't worry about it? I bit you, damn it. I drew blood."

Loud alarms sounded in the distance and Justice cursed.

"It's okay," she murmured, a little surprised that she was bleeding but it didn't hurt. "It's probably just a car alarm."

"It's not." He withdrew his still-hard cock from her body and rolled her onto her stomach to free his arm from under her head so quickly that she gasped. The bed moved as his weight left it. "They heard us at the security gate."

Light blinded her when he turned on the lamp on the nightstand. She waited for her vision to adjust. She could only stare as Justice jerked his boxers up his hips, bent and came up with his belongings clutched in his hand.

Anger radiated off him. "Jump into the shower right now or they'll smell me all over you."

Jessie sat up. "I don't care if someone knows."

"I do. Don't allow them into your room when they come to the door or they'll smell me in here too. Tell them you were in the shower and didn't hear anything when they ask you questions. Move it, damn it. You have about three minutes or less before they arrive. They have master keys to all the homes and will come in if you don't get the door."

He walked to her window and yanked it open. Jessie watched him in astonishment while he shoved at the screen with an elbow to force it out of the way and stepped over the windowsill. He reached back inside, pulled the window closed and pushed the screen back into place hard enough that it made the window rattle. He stepped away from the window and disappeared into the darkness. Her mind shifted into gear.

"Damn it," Jessie hissed, nearly falling out of the bed in her haste to rush to the bathroom. She tried real hard not to feel hurt.

Oh, it hurts so don't bother to deny it. It was clear he didn't want anyone to know about them. Was he embarrassed by her? She flipped on the light, lunged for the shower stall and didn't bother to adjust the temperature as she stepped under the strong spray of icy water.

"Son of a bitch," she hissed, grabbed the bottle of body wash and dumped out nearly half of it to rub furiously on her skin. "Men! I can't believe this. What an ass."

She paused, wondering why she was doing what he'd asked. He might have a problem with people knowing they'd slept together but she didn't. The cold water beat down on her, she shivered and cursed again.

A burning sensation made her wince and she twisted her head enough to locate the source. Red from the noticeable bite marks mingled with the water. She could see the punctures from his fangs and a red outline of his front, flatter teeth. She turned her shoulder into the water, washed off the soap irritating it and the burning stopped.

Maybe that's why he didn't want anyone to know they'd slept together. Justice North, the mighty face of New Species, had lost his composure enough to sink his teeth into one human. The press would run with a story that big, make it in to some kind of nasty, twisted scenario the way they usually did and there would be hell to pay.

"Shit!" She turned off the water, stepped out and grabbed a towel to dry off as fast as possible.

A bottle of perfume she'd unpacked sat on the counter and caught her attention. She never worn the stuff, her father had handed it to the checker while they'd been paying for her new clothes. Maybe it wasn't as useless as she'd thought. New Species hated artificial smells and it would mask Justice's scent. She dropped the towel, grabbed the box and tore it open as she rushed into her bedroom.

She gagged a little as she heavily sprayed the floral perfume into the air around her, closed her eyes and stepped into it so it misted down her body. She couldn't get her bandage wet and the Species had amazing noses. They might pick something up from her hair but now they'd just pick up the scent of gardenias.

"Yuk. If that doesn't mask his scent, nothing will."

She tossed the bottle on the bed, quickly dressed in the clothes she'd taken off earlier and remembered to snatch the bottle up as she ran out of her room when a pounding sounded at the front of the house.

Jessie sprayed perfume as she rushed toward the door then chucked the bottle toward the couch. She waved her arms wildly to spread the horrible smell, smoothed down her half shirt to make sure her breasts weren't showing and unlocked the front door.

Two New Species officers stood there looking grim. Jessie kept back to put as much distance as possible between them and her. Both males were gripping their sidearms, their gazes on her before they swept the room behind her and one of them took a step to enter her house. She opened her arms, gripped the doorframe and blocked it.

"What is going on? What is that, a car alarm?"

The one who wanted in her house had to step back so they didn't touch. "Did you scream?"

"No. I was in the shower and I only heard that racket when I turned off the water. If it's not a car alarm, is there a fire?"

The two men glanced at each other and then stared at her. The second one took a deep breath, sniffed and grimaced. A hand shot up to his face to cover his nose and he took a huge step back. The other did the same. She didn't have their enhanced sense of smell and the reek of gardenias almost made her eyes water.

"Can we search your house?"

"No one is here but me. Do you think I screamed? I didn't. Nothing is wrong except someone's alarm is going off. Maybe the wind set off a car alarm. It happens."

They seemed unsure what to do but they backed up, probably not enjoying what they were smelling. "All right. We are glad you are safe. Lock your doors. If you hear or see anything, hit the alarm." He pointed to the wall.

"Sure. Not a problem. Thanks!" Jessie closed the door and locked it. She leaned against the wood, her tense body going lax and closed her eyes.

She took a deep breath, grimaced and jerked away from the door. She needed to air out the house to get rid of the stink and shower again.

* * * * *

Justice swam another lap in the pool until he heard a squeak and stopped, treading water. He inhaled and turned, locating two security officers approaching from the side yard. They'd used the gate there to find him instead of entering his house.

"What is going on? What activated the alarm? I heard it going off a little while ago. Is everything all right?" Guilt ate at him a little for lying, something he hated to do but he needed to protect Jessie. He doubted they would tell anyone but some of his people were friendly with human employees. One slip and it would reach the wrong ears. He wouldn't take that chance with her. "Do we have a security breach?"

One of them shrugged. "We heard a scream and a roar."

Justice had practiced his story. "I roared but I didn't hear a scream." He pointed to his clothes by the back door. "I tripped over that chair when I came out here to swim after a long, rough day. It hurt my toe and I was mad. I roared, took off my clothes and have been swimming to work away my anger."

The second one shifted, frowning. "You didn't hear a scream?"

"No. Maybe you mistook the chair hitting the wall as a scream. I broke it when I tripped on it."

"We're sorry we disturbed you, Justice. We thought maybe the human had been attacked."

"Jessie Dupree? Is she all right?"

"She's fine. We went to her home first but she wouldn't let us search her house."

"She smells," the other one cursed. "Like bad flowers."

"Perfume," the other one growled. "You should make it a law that they don't wear it here, Justice. My nose still burns."

Justice hid a smile over Jessie knowing that trick. Strong perfume irritated their noses and confused their sense of smell. She had worked for Tim Oberto on the task force and was bound to pick up Species facts from the team members who worked so closely with his males.

"I'll send her a memo."

Both men looked confused. "Maybe someone was watching a horror movie. Human females in those scream all the time. We'll have to ask everyone if they were playing one of those to track the source of the disturbance."

"Don't bother anyone else. The only female alone here is Jessie Dupree and you said she is fine."

"Did you hurt yourself when you broke the chair, Justice? I could call for someone to come look at it."

Justice shook his head, swimming toward the side of the pool. "I'm fine. It just pissed me off."

The men hesitated. Justice climbed out of the pool and walked to a towel he'd thrown over a lounge chair days before. He wrapped it around his hips and arched an eyebrow when he faced them.

"Is there anything else?"

"Why is a human female living here? We don't question your judgment but we are curious, Justice."

"This is the most secure area of Homeland. Her father is someone who watches out for us and works through legal issues on our behalf. I gave my word to him that she would be kept safe. She's also saved our females and brought them to us as her last job. Jessie Dupree is a trusted friend."

One of them spoke. "We understand. Thank you for explaining it."

Justice waited until they were gone before he shook his wet hair, trying to dry off some. He turned to peer over the wall to the house next door. Jessie's bedroom light remained on. He longed to hop the wall and knock on her window.

Frustration gripped him as he turned away. Wanting and doing had to be different things in her case. He'd lost control, drawn blood sharing sex and had attracted attention to them being together by roaring out his pleasure. That disturbed him deeply, it was something he'd never done before with a female. She brought out sides of him that he couldn't allow free. Period.

He needed to think, to clear his head and stay away from her until he could figure out how to leash the frightening emotions she stirred in him. He only knew one thing for certain…

Jessie Dupree was driving him insane.

Chapter Eleven

ಐ

"Breeze!" Jessie grinned. "You're here at the women's dorm! Why aren't you still at Reservation?"

The six-foot-plus woman grinned. "I arrived early this morning. My best friend Ellie wanted me to come home to share some news and I'll be here for a while. She is human and married Fury, who is Species."

"I've heard of them—on TV when they got married. I hope it was good news?"

"The best. I'm sorry but I can't share what it is. All I can say is her and her husband wanted something since they found love together and they finally accomplished it."

"That is good news."

"What are you doing here? Are you checking up on the woman you brought to us? They are still at Reservation and are doing fine. They have settled well. It was decided they should stay there instead of being brought here since they are enjoying the trees and the miles of land to roam."

"Actually, I work here now. It's a long story."

Breeze's eyes widened. "Truly? Doing what?"

Jessie turned her head to glance at Beauty. She'd spent the morning and most of the afternoon helping her get settled in the women's dorm. She'd taken the move well for the most part.

Tiny and Halfpint were Beauty's constant companions, which helped. The only bump in the nearly smooth transition had been when Beauty had seen the much taller, strongly built females. They had frightened her, but she currently sat in the living room talking with half a dozen of them without fear.

"That's Beauty. We recovered her night before last from an estate up in Washington. I don't know all that my new job entails but for right now it's helping her to adjust to her new life. She's taking it well."

"I like her name. It fits. She chose well." Breeze smiled and gave her attention back to Jessie.

"Actually, I chose it. I keep telling her that she can change it at any time and I'm hoping she will. I feel kind of weird naming an adult." Jessie shrugged. "I needed to make up one fast and that's all that came to mind."

"Why did you need to name her?"

Jessie clenched her teeth. "Because the only two names she could remember being called pissed me off so bad I refused to let anyone else ever call her that. We have to do paperwork and it will stick with her on record. I refused to record those names."

Breeze's face hardened. "What did they call her?"

Jessie stared at the taller woman. "I really don't think you want to know."

"Tell me."

Jessie sighed, figuring Breeze had a right to know. "They were calling her Mud and I guess tagged her with Monkey when she was younger. Those were the only two names she could remember."

The tall New Species woman growled and spit out a string of curses that would have made a lifelong sailor blush. Jessie nodded in agreement. The two women stared at each other until Breeze's anger faded.

"Thank you. It is a really good name you chose and it suits her. I think she might keep it and you did her a good favor."

"Thanks." Jessie smiled suddenly. "So, are you looking forward to getting some decent sleep now that you're out of the hotel?"

Breeze laughed. "They sent Tammy and Valiant to his house for good. Justice said they need their privacy since they are married now. He has guards around their property to help Valiant keep her safe. Maybe it's a human and Species thing but no one ever has sex as loudly as those two."

Jessie managed to keep her smile in place—barely—remembering the night before. She and Justice had been so loud they'd set off the security alarm. "Can I ask you something?"

"Sure." Breeze led her into the kitchen to grab sodas from the fridge. She waved Jessie to a barstool. "Hit me! I love that saying."

Jessie took a seat next to her. "The mixed couple that just got married, uh, he's lion, right?"

"We believe so. We mostly guess at what we were mixed with since the records were destroyed. With his coloring and his personality we can assume he was mixed with that DNA. What about him?"

"I met Justice North and he has the same kind of eyes as Valiant. Is he lion?" That would explain the roar after sex.

"His coloring is not right. In my free time I'm studying animals. I wanted to guess better what some of us were changed with." Breeze looked proud. "I think he is perhaps mixed with black leopard—humans call them panthers."

Jessie managed to keep her mouth from falling open despite her shock. "Wouldn't his hair be black? I mean, Valiant has orange-red hair similar to a lion. I met Flame and he has light red hair but he's got the cat eyes. I could see that right off."

Breeze bit her lip. "I can't discuss this with you, Jessie."

"Why not?"

Breeze hesitated again but blew out a breath. "You are a friend to us and save our women. I know you can be trusted. Some of us color our hair. That's all I'm saying."

Justice colors his hair? It explained why he looked different in person than on television and in some of the photos in the paper. He looked different because his hair color varied.

"Why would he...I mean, any of you do that?"

"Some of us need to appear more human but our natural coloring sometimes make that difficult. Please don't repeat this to anyone. I could get in trouble."

"I won't tell a soul. You have my word on that. So as an example, someone with blonde hair could really have black hair?"

"Exactly. It would make one look more human and less threatening."

Someone in the public eye. Someone who deals with humans all the time. Jessie tried to imagine Justice with black hair but it was hard to do. It suddenly explained why his long eyelashes were black. Sometimes she saw a little dark blue in the depths of his eyes but from a distance they appeared the darkest shade of brown ever, bordering on black. *With black hair he would look...* An image flashed inside her head of Justice with black hair. *Frightening. Scary. ferocious.* Justice with light hair did look more human and less likely to scare someone. *It makes sense.*

Jessie had slept with a man changed with panther DNA. It explained the purring, the catlike eyes and his roaring after sex. He'd shredded the bedding and scored the mattress with his nails. *Claws. Panthers were dangerous animals. Maybe he has good reason to fear hurting me.*

"What are you thinking about?"

Jessie pulled her attention from her thoughts to force a smile for Breeze. "A man."

A grin split Breeze's face. "Spill, girlfriend."

Jessie shook her head. "I can't."

"Oh. You are asking about our men for a reason, are you not? I heard that Flame was talking about you. He is feline and that is why you were asking about Valiant, is it not? You did slip and mention his name. I swear I won't say a word to anyone. Flame is attractive and easy on the eyes. He has a good sense of fun too."

Flame? Jessie didn't know if she should be relieved at Breeze's assumption. It beat her correctly guessing that Jessie was thinking about Justice. Jessie just smiled.

"Flame likes you. I heard that you made an impression on him."

"You heard that? He offered to buy me a beer and introduce me around so I could make some friends."

"You should let him."

"There's that whole I'm-human-and-he's-Species thing going on."

The smile on Breeze's lips disappeared. "You would not be with one of my kind?"

"It's not that." She bit her lip, careful of what she said. "I was talking to a few of your males once," she lied, making up a scenario that would fit her real dilemma. "They kind of made it clear that they wouldn't sleep with a human female. He, I mean, they said they wouldn't want to get involved with a human and were adamant about how they'd be too afraid to lose control and hurt her."

"It is a valid fear. Our men are strong and they dominate. Do you know about this?"

"Most men are bossy. That's a universal trait that comes with having a dick."

Breeze didn't laugh at Jessie's attempted humor. "No. Your men tell women what to do because they just want to do it. Our men dominate physically and *need* to do it. There's a big difference."

"Could you explain it to me? I'm really curious."

"When a male and female of our kind share sex they mount us from behind. He will use his teeth at our shoulder to keep us still if he feels his dominance is threatened. Their need to be in control during sex is overpowering. It is hard to describe but there is a spot on either side here…" She reached up and touched her shoulders. "If a male grips us with his teeth it feels really good and doesn't hurt. They never break the skin but we know better than to pull away or accidents could happen."

Jessie had a sinking feeling—she had a bandage hiding under her shirt. "What kind of accidents?"

"Their teeth will sink in just enough to draw blood or they could scar our skin. It is rare but I had a male take my blood once. He killed one of the technicians when he came to remove me from his cell after we shared sex. He did not want to let me go or share me with other males. He was very possessive. He had love for me and I guess he bit me to show dominance and that I was his, perhaps to mark me, because I didn't try to challenge him during sex. He said his insides were screaming that he keep me and they know that we don't want to be kept. It is why we don't have sex with the same male often now that we are free. We want to make sure they remember that we don't want to be kept by them and it lets them know not to feel possessive of us. Our men could be dangerous to your kind."

"Why would any of that be dangerous to humans?"

"When our males clamp their teeth down you don't know not to struggle or jerk away. He could go crazy if you did. We make sure we want to breed together and it has to be totally mutual when we do. If a male was behind you and bit your skin hard, wouldn't that alarm you? You would fight, wouldn't you? Struggle? His teeth are sharp and could tear your skin or his hands could hurt you, trying to hold you still for your own safety. They can be gentle and pleasing but if you were to challenge his dominance during sex, he would feel the uncontrollable urge to prove he is worthy. It is a need. It is what they are. If you let one of our males have sex with you often he might want to keep you if he began to feel possessive. A Species male would not let you go if that happened, would fight to keep you and kill anyone who tried to take you from him. He might feel love if you allow him to know you too well and that is very dangerous in our kind."

"It can't be too dangerous. There are mixed couples."

"Yes, but the males would kill anyone who touched one of their mates. You met Tammy and Valiant. He doesn't like other males to look at her. She willingly submits to him and has given herself to him totally but they share love. Valiant would tear someone apart with his bare hands if he thought she was threatened, Jessie. That is the danger with our men and we had to consider what would happen if one of them had love for a woman who didn't return it. He'd never hurt her but we think any male who tried to touch her would lose a body part. I understand the fear our kind feels for sex with humans and it is reasonable. If you do decide to have sex with Flame, I need to school you first so you know how to handle one of our males safely."

Jessie wasn't sure she wanted the answer but still asked the question. "What would I need to know?"

"Never ask a male to submit to you. They are dominant and it would make them angry and dangerous if you were to do that. To them it would be a challenge. You are questioning their abilities. Males are always in control of sex. Don't struggle during sex if Flame ever grips you with his teeth. It means he is losing control and you need to hold still."

"Is losing control a bad thing?"

"Yes!" Breeze jerked her gaze down Jessie's body, giving her a once-over. "He'd break you. Our males are strong and our idea of foreplay would be rough wrestling to you."

"Okay," she got out, stunned again.

"Never stare into the eyes of an angry male because that is challenging too. Look down and hold still until they have time to calm their anger. Also, never allow him to share sex with you if he is really aroused because they can be aggressive to match their needs. You say no if Flame ever has the desire to bite you and take your blood during sex. It would let him feel he possesses you and you never want that with one of our males unless you are prepared to be stuck with him forever."

"I think I got it. Thanks. Please forget about the name Flame, okay? I'm not considering sleeping with him. I was just curious."

Breeze grinned. "Sure."

The other woman didn't believe her but Jessie let it slide as she stood. "It's been a long day and I'm going home. I'll check on Beauty first and make sure she's all right with me leaving. I'm glad you're here and we'll get to see each other more."

"I will say hello to her and look out for her while you're gone. You can just go and get some rest. Will you be back here tomorrow?"

"Yes."

Jessie left the dorm, her mind dwelling on all she'd learned. According to Breeze's advice on what not to do in bed with a Species male, she'd already really screwed up. She'd asked Justice to let her be on top, which had challenged him. His reaction had been to nearly walk out of the bedroom and end their encounter. Breeze said they'd never allow a woman to dominate the sex in bed but Justice had when she'd gotten to be on top. She had no idea what to make of that except maybe he wasn't as set in his ways as most Species since he had to deal with so many humans daily. Humans worked at Homeland and he had to communicate with the media, her father and a lot of other people who were invested in the well-being of Species.

She'd felt Justice's teeth on her shoulder but she hadn't known what it meant. She'd ignored his plea for her to hold still, unwittingly provoking him try to assert his dominance. She'd moved against him, pushed him to take her the way she wanted and he'd bitten her shoulder hard enough to draw blood. That was another no-no. Of course he didn't want to keep her forever. Nope. He wanted to end their brief relationship before it had a chance to get off the ground.

No wonder he doesn't want to see me again. Depression hit hard as Jessie drove her golf cart home. Earlier that day she'd woken to find one parked in her driveway with a marked map from her home to the women's dorm. The officer posted at the gates to her housing tract had assured her it was for her use. She had a way to get around Homeland but had nowhere to go but to her lonely house.

A new officer manned the security checkpoint but he didn't stop her. He grinned and waved her through as he opened the gates that led into the housing area. Jessie waved back and parked in her driveway. She couldn't get over how deeply she'd managed to screw up with Justice. *Species should come with a handbook titled* Dating for the Clueless *human chicks and fifty things to avoid doing that will insult them.*

She unlocked her front door, glad as she entered that the perfume had finally disappeared. Her gaze darted to the potted plant to her immediate left and she smiled. She'd hidden the bottle there in case she ever needed to mask Justice's scent again. Her mood quickly deflated since she highly doubted he'd be back.

A quick shower, a change into comfortable clothes and an urge to occupy her time in the kitchen helped keep her thoughts off Justice. She enjoyed cooking, it relaxed her and she loved to eat. The only problem was the tri-tip she had put in the rotisserie cooker would feed her for a week in leftover sandwiches. She bit her lip, watched it slowly turn as it dripped juices into the drip pan and decided she could always take sandwiches to the women at the dorm tomorrow.

She was amazed by the amount of her food supply and the huge portion sizes. Of course Species probably ate an eight-pound tri-tip in one sitting but she sure couldn't. She turned away, decided to wash her new clothes before wearing the rest of them and settled on taking a long bath to kill time before dinner was ready.

The jets were wonderful and the water warm. She evaluated her life. Her love life might suck but she was living in a nice place and loved her new job. The doorbell rang, caused her to start but she grinned. It had to be Justice! She toweled off quickly and put her clothes back on, her mind working on a way to talk the thick-headed man into letting down his guard and to come back when the coast was clear. The doorbell rang again and she rushed out of her bathroom.

"I'm coming. Hang on!"

Jessie twisted the locks as her heart raced and she smiled, excited to see him after the night before. Two large Species males stood there instead. Both of them were out of uniform, sporting jeans and T-shirts and they stared at her with a grimness that assured they weren't happy.

The one on the right spoke. "I'm Night. Your belongings were delivered and we were asked to bring them. Do you mind if we unload the Jeep now and carry your boxes inside? We have to inform you that your things were searched by security. It is standard procedure but nothing had to be confiscated."

"Okay. Thanks. Sure," she agreed. "Let me grab my shoes and I'll help."

The Species on the left frowned his displeasure. "No. You are too small and would only slow us down. Just sit and remain calm. We mean you no harm." He took a breath. "I am Sword. You are in no danger."

Amusement sparked at his words, as if he feared she might be terrified of them but their tension forced her to hide it. They really seemed on edge about dealing with her so she lowered her gaze. They were Species and she wanted them to feel at ease with her. Good etiquette went a long way toward gaining that goal.

"Thank you. I'll wait inside and remember I'm not in danger." She backed up.

"Good." Night grunted, spun on his heel and marched down the walkway. The other one followed.

Jessie lifted her gaze to watch them grab boxes from the back of the packed Jeep and finally allowed her chuckle to escape. It was cute how they assumed she'd be terrified of them and sweet that they wanted to assure her they weren't there to murder her. She laughed again, her gaze turning to the living room and spotted an area where they could stack the boxes.

"You can just dump them over there." She pointed, keeping back. "Thank you. I'm sorry there are so many of them. I didn't realize I'd accumulated that much stuff."

An idea formed when one of them sniffed the air, his attention on the open archway to the kitchen and both of them kept doing it as they brought in more boxes. She inhaled the tantalizing aroma of the tri-tip, realized they might be hungry and decided to try to make friends. It beat sitting around all night dwelling on Justice and how to work around the problems they had. The guys finally carried in the last two boxes.

"Thank you so much. I appreciate it. Would you like to stay for dinner? I have plenty and it's a human custom to feed people as a way of showing appreciation."

The men glanced at each other, their apprehension near comical.

"I have tri-tip. It's steak that's thinly sliced and it's got some pinkness to it. It's not as rare as most of you enjoy but I think you'll like it. I'd appreciate the opportunity to make new friends. I just moved here and don't know that many people."

Sword answered for the both of them. "We accept. You should feel welcome by us and friends are important."

"They are." She smiled. "Why don't you have a seat on the couch? You can kick off your shoes, turn on the television and relax while I go slice it up and pop the potatoes in the microwave. It shouldn't be more than fifteen minutes."

They closed the front door and ambled toward the couch. Jessie turned, entered the kitchen and took out the tri-tip fifteen minutes early. It appeared really cooked on the outside but would be rarer than she normally ate it, in other words perfect for her guests. It was quick work to wash three potatoes, jab them with a fork and bake them in the microwave. She cooked up some veggies, chopped some chives for the potatoes and set the table for three.

Excitement gripped her at the prospect of talking to the two males. She was familiar with the females but their counterparts were completely different. She hoped that getting to know them would help her the next time she dealt with Justice. They might be friendly enough to answer any questions she directed their way.

Jessie walked into the living room. "Dinner is ready. Do you want to follow me or I could bring your plates out here if you prefer the coffee table."

Both men stood instantly and cautiously approached as though they feared she might bolt from terror. Sword seemed to be the more talkative of the two as he spoke.

"We'd be honored to eat at your table in the kitchen. Thank you, Ms. Dupree."

"Please just call me Jessie and I'm the one who is honored to have you as guests." She led them into the kitchen and headed for the fridge. After asking what they wanted to drink, she got them sodas and sat down at the table to smile at both males. "Dig in. I'm not formal and don't worry about table manners. Just make yourself at home, okay? There's plenty of food and I hope you can eat it all or I'll have to use the leftovers to make a ton of sandwiches. You'd be saving me the trouble."

Night stabbed a slice of meat, stared at it as if he were afraid to take a bite but then stuffed the entire thing into his mouth. Jessie paused to watch his reaction, hoped he liked it. He grinned as he chewed. His surprise evident as he stared at her until he swallowed.

"This is really good! Thank you, Jessie."

"Yes," Sword agreed, swallowing his first bite. "It's delicious. I didn't know it could taste this way. We just chop them up into big flat slabs and sear them. You should tell us how to cook it this way."

"I'd be happy to write it down for you. It's easy." She pointed to the rotisserie machine. "That does the work. I just season the meat, put it in and wait for it to be done. Anyone can do it."

They ate in silence, the men consuming vast amounts of meat. Jessie resisted the urge to grill them with questions. *At least wait until they are done and full,* she reasoned. Night finally stopped eating, put down his fork and stared at her. She met his gaze.

"Weren't you afraid to invite us to dinner? We are two fierce males in your home that you don't know. We believed you would be terrified."

Sword cleared his throat. "We didn't want to bring your boxes because we thought you might see us and cry." He made a horrible face and shivered. "I can't stand crying."

Jessie fought a laugh but couldn't stop the grin that spread across her face. "I'm used to being around larger men so I'm not easily frightened. Do you know what my last job was?"

Both men shook their heads. Jessie started telling them about her job with the task force, the men she worked with and all the Species she'd met and saved. Both men listened intently with interest. She finished with how she had gotten grazed by a bullet and had ended up at Homeland.

"You know we won't attack you and force shared sex on you?" Sword looked sincere. "One guy said you would probably see us both and think we had come to rape you."

Night laughed. "He said you would hurt our ears with your shrieking as soon as you opened the door."

"And the crying." Sword laughed. "I was hoping you would think I was a rapist and just scream instead of bursting into hysterical sobs. That would hurt my ears less."

Jessie laughed. "Tell your friend I'm sorry to disappoint him."

"He will be disappointed when we tell him about the dinner you fed us." Night grinned. "He was asked to go but I owed him a favor. He told me I had to come in his place to make us even."

Sword laughed again. "You should take him a piece of the steak. I would laugh to see his face when he tastes the meat she fed us."

Jessie stood. "Let me get you a bag and you can take him a few pieces."

"You are a good human, Jessie." Night beamed. "I'm glad that I don't make you scream or cry."

"Me too," Jessie chuckled, placing a few slices of tri-tip into a plastic Baggie before returning to the table.

They were still laughing when a vicious growl jolted all of them from the moment. Jessie spun at the loud, startling sound and gaped at the sight of Justice standing in the open archway between the living room and kitchen. Rage glittered in his narrowed eyes, his fists were clenched at his sides and not even the impeccable, tailored gray suit could soften the dangerous vibes he put off.

He wasn't looking at her but instead seemed solely focused on her dinner guests. The sound of a chair hitting the floor made her head twist in that direction. Both Night and Sword had stood quickly, their heads lowered until their chins nearly touched their chests and their gazes locked on the floor. They stepped back away from the table and fear paled their features.

Jessie frowned as she turned to stare at Justice, then the males, gauging what was going on. Justice was furious for some reason, his men were terrified of his show of temper and she was clueless as to why he was acting so nuts.

"Hello, Mr. North." She refused to call him Justice since he'd made it clear he didn't want anyone to know they had spent time together. "Thank you for having my things delivered. I don't know why you're upset but we were having dinner. You're welcome to take a seat if you're hungry."

Justice's furious dark gaze met hers. He growled at her and his sharp teeth showed. Jessie crossed her arms over her chest while staring right into his eyes. She wanted to ask him what his problem was.

"Leave," Justice growled. "Now."

Both men walked around the edge of the room to keep as far from their leader as possible, hugging the walls and keeping a safe distance. She glanced at the table, spotted the forgotten bag of tri-tip and grabbed it. She stormed after the men. She avoided Justice by walking around him too.

"Wait."

The two men were at the door when she stopped them with her voice and held out the food. "You forgot this for your friend. I don't know what is going on but I'm sorry about that."

Night glanced at her. "Never stare a Species in the eyes when he's growling at you. He's pissed about something." He took the bag. "Thank you, Jessie."

A vicious roar filled the room behind Jessie. Night flinched and both men fled. Jessie ground her teeth and closed her front door slowly. She heard the Jeep pull away and took a few deep, calming breaths before turning to face the pissed-off man behind her.

Justice glared at her from about eight feet away and growled again. His cat eyes flashed with pure rage, his hands were still fisted and he was showing perfect straight teeth and his sharp-looking fangs. Jessie glared back, lost her own temper and no longer had to worry about any witnesses since they were alone.

"What was that?" she yelled. "I invited them to dinner after they carried in all my stuff and I thought it would be nice to make some friends. How dare you just walk into my house and scare them off. I'm not missing the part either about you just inviting yourself into my home. Did you miss the doorbell? Are your hands broken so you couldn't knock?"

Another low growl came from his throat. He reached up, gripped his tie and tore it off. He reached for his jacket next, not bothering to unbutton it, as material tore and buttons rained down on the tile floor. Jessie watched him and her anger faded from the shock.

"You don't allow males inside your house and invite them to stay," he snarled. "They came in here and they stayed too long. I imagined the worst when they didn't leave."

"You were watching my house?"

He kicked off his dress shoes and one of them hit her couch. The other sailed in the air until it hit the wall by the door. He breathed rapidly, all traces of the well-groomed, usually calm man were gone. This was a side of him she'd never seen and had to admit it was scary. She tried bravado since it had always helped her in the past.

"Why are you watching my house? Did you forget that you told me last night you're not coming back here again? I remember that conversation really well. I also remember how you climbed out a window so no one would know the mighty Justice had been in bed with a human. You didn't come back. Does sleeping with me rate right up there with having fleas?"

Justice's eyes narrowed and he growled. "Run," he warned in a deep voice. "You need to get away from me."

"This is my house," she gasped. "You leave. I'm not going to go hide until you get over your temper tantrum."

He lunged. Jessie felt the danger instantly. This wasn't her ex-husband. He'd yelled at her when he got pissed but Justice looked savage as he came at her. This involved more than yelling.

"Shit," she hissed. She tensed and remembered Breeze's words. She put her head down, closed her eyes and froze. Then she started to pray.

He was next to her instantly, breathing heavily. Her heart pounded as she wondered if he were capable of hurting her. She wasn't sure anymore. Seconds ticked slowly by until it felt like an eternity passed. Justice's breathing slowed as he took deep breaths. Relief washed through her as the sense of danger passed. Breeze's advice had been dead-on.

"Jessie?" Justice's voice still came out sounding animalistic but softer and he didn't sound threatening.

She opened her eyes to stare at his chest less than a foot away. "What? Is it safe yet for me to move or are you going to hurt me?"

"Damn it," he hissed, spinning away.

Jessie looked up to see Justice's back to her. She didn't know what was going on or why he had acted that way, not sure at that moment if she wanted to know. She headed to the kitchen, just walked away. Space between them sounded like a really good idea.

She cleared the table and rinsed the dishes to load them into the dishwasher. She put away the small amount of leftovers and dragged her feet to avoid the living room. She hadn't heard the front door open, which meant he was still out there.

"Jessie?"

She turned to find Justice in the kitchen by the door looking normal now, except for his disarrayed clothing and missing shoes. "What was that about?"

"I can't be with you and this is why." His expression was unreadable. "I saw them come in and I thought about one of them touching you when they didn't leave. I lost it. If they had laid a finger on you, I would have killed them." His voice broke and he cleared his throat. "I would have killed my own males. I'm calm now but you're to never let males inside the house again. You are never to be alone with one again. Anywhere."

Jessie stared as his words sank into her stunned brain. He didn't want her but he didn't want anyone else to have her either. *The son of a bitch.*

"Let me tell you how it's going to be, Justice. You don't tell me who I can and can't have inside my house. I work for the NSO but my personal life is my own. You lost the right to give me your *opinion*," she stressed that last word, "about what I do or don't do the second you decided you didn't want to see me anymore. You don't want me so don't you dare tell me I can't spend time with other men."

He moved so fast she didn't have time to try to defend herself. Justice grabbed her, the world turned upside down and shock kept her from fighting back as he stomped toward her bedroom with her thrown over his shoulder. He kicked the door shut behind them hard enough to make it slam and dumped her flat on her back in the center of her bed in a fast movement that left her dizzy for a few seconds.

Justice glared at her. "If you want someone, you'll have me," he snarled. His fingers clawed between the buttons of his expensive dress shirt, tore the thing open and ripped it away from his chest. He hands lowered to his pants. "I'm the only male who touches you."

Jessie was shocked but not fearful. She was breathing hard though, a little angry still but as she assessed her emotions, mostly surprised. Her gaze flicked over Justice as he tore out the thong that held his hair, letting it spill over the tops of his shoulders. The sight he presented was one she'd never forget.

He looked sexy, fierce, primal and every muscle in his body was outlined from the adrenaline he obviously experienced. The pants tore away, he threw them and she had another big clue as to what he was feeling. He was aroused, his cock at full attention and it distracted her enough to miss seeing his hand shoot out and grip her ankle. He yanked her toward him, forced her body to slide on the bedding and his other hand fisted her pants. Material tore and during the seconds she remained in her stunned stupor, he completely ripped them from her body.

Instinct and years of training took over as her foot shot up and slammed hard into his stomach. The impact was enough to break his hold on her ankle and send him stumbling back with a loud grunt of pain. Jessie rolled, landed on her feet on the other side of the bed and glared.

"I'm not going to allow you hurt me." Her voice shook and her arms rose in a defensive posture.

He glared at her, rubbing his stomach. There was a red mark. "I'm not going to hurt you. I'm going to fuck you. You wanted to see the real me." His chin lifted and he spread his arms open. "Here I am, baby."

Chapter Twelve

❧

Oh shit. Well, I said I wanted him to stop holding back. I guess I should have been careful of what I wished for. Jessie pushed back her thoughts, gave him a thorough once-over and arched her eyebrows.

"Nice language. That will put me in the mood. That's sarcasm, if you missed the point. Forget about it, Justice. Why don't you just piss on the corner of the bed to mark your territory?"

He growled but Jessie wasn't afraid anymore. Her shock had worn off and she was prepared for him now. He was jealous. It irritated her more than anything. He didn't want her but he didn't want anyone else to be with her either.

"If you think I'm going to let you come at me that way, think again. You dumped me. You need to leave until you know what you want. Then we'll talk."

Justice stalked around the edge of the bed with his arms still open. He planned to grab her instead of taking off and she backed into the space between a window and the headboard. She wasn't going to dive through glass.

"I know what I want. You."

"Stop."

He halted but didn't look happy about it. His gaze held hers, his nostrils flared and his arms lowered to his sides. "No. Come to me, Jessie."

She shook her head. "I'm not that easy, *baby*." She used his own term to address him. "You climbed out a window last night to hide the fact that we're seeing each other. If that wasn't bad enough, you never came back. I waited up for you and it pisses me off to be treated that way."

He frowned. "I was protecting everyone."

"You were being an ass and you could have slept in my bed but you didn't. No one would have known if you'd sneaked back inside. I covered for you and masked your scent with the officers. They had no idea you'd been here."

"You want to argue right now?" He glanced down at his straining sex and then at her.

She nearly laughed at his frustrated expression. She wanted him, he was naked in her bedroom and they could always talk later. All that arguing, the fear and now the anger made her feel alive. The bottom line was that she wanted him and he wanted her. He wasn't questioning being with her at that moment. She reached for her shirt, saw his eyes widen as he watched her open it and took her sweet time undressing. She was going to make him pay a little for the crap he'd put her through.

She threw her shirt at him and he caught it. Her bra came off next, another item she tossed his way. He inhaled deeply, taking in the scent of her clothing and blindly dropped them on the floor. It was easy to tell he wanted to lunge at her but he held back, fighting for control again. Now that they were on the same page about ending up in bed together, she wanted him to come at her the way he had before she'd kicked him.

Her thumbs hooked her underwear at her hips and she turned a little, kept him in view and slowly wiggled her ass as she lowered them. His gaze fixated there, a purr coming from him and he watched her bend until she stepped out of them. She left them on the floor, her hands gripped the side of the bed and peered over her shoulder.

"What? Do you want a written invitation to join me? Why don't you climb on the bed first and we'll discuss our issues later?"

He moved fast, came at her instead of the bed and his hands gripped her hips. She hadn't expected that or to be lifted, twisted in the air and dumped onto her back on the soft mattress. She bounced once and hands gripped her inner thighs. He spread them far apart, bent them up and totally exposed her pussy. Her gaze lowered and she realized his cock was inches from entering her. She tensed a little, afraid he might just fuck her outright when she really wanted a little foreplay first.

"You invited me to dinner but I just want to eat you," he rasped.

His words sank in as he took a step back, bent over her and his hair fell forward to land on her lower belly. He brushed a kiss on her inner thigh, his hold adjusted on her legs and he feasted on her clit. Jessie threw her head back, fisted the comforter and moaned at the instant pleasure his hot mouth gave her. His tongue rasped over the sensitive bud rapidly, drawing her passion to explosive levels and she released the bedding to cup her own breasts. She squeezed them, adding to the experience and vibrations were added to the mix as a deep purr came from Justice.

"Oh God, I love when you do that," she panted. "I'm so close, baby. Don't stop or slow down."

He vibrated faster, that sexy sound grew louder and Jessie cried out as the climax hit fast and furiously. She bucked her hips but his strong hands held her pinned to the mattress, his mouth released her and he finally let go of her inner thighs. She opened her eyes and watched him climb over her in a way that reminded her that he was part panther. He made her a believer with the way he seemed to gracefully prowl up her body. Their gazes met and his mouth descended to take hers in a kiss that stole her breath.

She hooked her calves over the back of his ass as he drove into her. His cock parted her vaginal walls in one swift thrust. She cried out against his tongue and he snarled, tearing away from the kiss. She had over two hundred forty pounds of unrestrained male fucking her into oblivion as he rode her hard and fast. The ecstasy of being taken that way, of how good he felt, sent her into a second climax.

Justice twisted a little, shoved his face into the bedding next to her and roared out when he followed her as her vaginal walls contracted around his thick shaft. The sound didn't hurt her ears this time, muffled a lot by the covers and she clung to him, only then realizing her arms were wrapped around his shoulders.

She explored his warm back with wandering hands, loved the feel of having him on top of her, inside her. Justice kept his face down against the bedding, his arms braced enough to keep his upper chest from smothering her with his weight and she turned to brush kisses on his neck.

"That was amazing."

He lifted his head, met her gaze and frowned. "I wasn't gentle."

"I'm not complaining. The amazing part was a compliment." She grinned. "The best quickie ever."

A sound rumbled in his throat—a cute one of displeasure—and his face hovered inches above her own. He shifted his weight and one hand cupped the side of her face. His thumb brushed her cheek, caressing it.

"I'm sorry I lost my temper and acted so…"

"Dickish? Anal? Jealous?" She was happy to suggest words when he seemed at a loss.

His exotic gaze narrowed. "Gruff," he decided. "I admit to the jealousy. If you ever allow someone else to touch you, I will kill him, Jessie. I will tear him apart. Do you understand me?"

Her smile faded. "You really mean that, don't you?"

Anger flashed in those beautiful eyes. "Yes. The thought makes me killing mad." His voice deepened. "Just the thought of another male kissing you, putting his hands on you, even—"

"I get it," she cut him off before he really got worked up. "Real bad shit and violence. A coroner will have his level of gross tested." She shifted her hands to press against his chest, her fingers caressing him. "I'll make a deal with you."

"There are no negotiations here."

"Stop telling me it's over, that we can't see each other, and you won't have a reason to feel jealous because I don't cheat." She held his gaze. "I'd have a guy in my life and in my bed. I don't need two. I just want you."

His anger eased. "It's not that simple."

"Nothing in life worth having is."

"I made a commitment to my people and getting involved with you adds to the problems we have." He took a deep breath and his anger faded to be replaced by sadness as he stared into her eyes. "I can think of a thousand reasons why it's a bad idea to be with you but I'm still here. You're my one weakness, Jessie. I want you and it seems logic doesn't help me stay away."

It made her melt a little inside for him to admit that. "What kind of problems do you think being with me is going to cause? Talk to me."

"As soon as it comes out that we're dating, it's just going to drive those hate groups into another frenzy about how we're animals and how wrong it is that we're allowed to live. The religious fanatics are going to scream about the sins of animals having sex with humans." A small smile curved his lips. "It felt sinful, it was that great, but you get the point."

She chuckled. "Yeah. The upside is that most people think those groups are full of idiots and don't listen to them."

"They terrorize the gates, make death threats, and I have other things to consider as well." His humor vanished. "They'll target you. We've learned this firsthand. They don't just come after us but the women we are with. You wouldn't be able to leave Homeland without being in danger."

"I'm good at taking care of myself and I happen to work and live here now. I'm not real worried about that." She ran her hands to his shoulders, massaging the tension there and shrugged her own. "I hate shopping so I sure won't miss the malls and I can buy anything as long as I have the internet. What's next?"

He hesitated and his attention shifted to her hair, spread out over the bed. She knew he was avoiding something and wiggled under him to pull his focus back to her eyes. He met her gaze and she arched her eyebrows.

"What else? Talk to me, damn it. You can totally be honest. Just spill."

"Your father."

The two words had a chilly effect on her. "Right. My dad. Yeah, that could be a problem."

"He might pull his support from our cause and he represents New Species in Washington. We count on him and it would get sticky if he found out about us. Messy. Ugly. It could hurt my people."

"He'll take us being together well. I'm not worried about that at all. He's a public figure though, Mr. Reputation, and there might be a shit storm about his job if his daughter—me—is with you. Some might call for him to resign because he's too emotionally invested, considering." She chewed on her bottom lip.

"He won't accept you being with me."

She relaxed. "He'll be thrilled as long as I'm happy. Trust me on that. I'm more worried about his job than anything else. Representing New Species has become his p—" She halted that line of talk, cut off saying "pet project" since that probably wasn't the best term to use considering Justice might take offense. She cleared her throat. "Passion in life," she substituted.

Justice sighed. "Exactly. Us being together might cause a lot of trouble for everyone and…"

"And what?"

"We're not sure where this is heading."

"Right." She agreed. "We barely know each other."

"That's why I wanted to avoid seeing you," he admitted. "We should really consider this, Jessie."

"I want to be with you and this is where you want to be too. Am I wrong?"

"No."

"Okay." She sighed. "So there're only two reasonable things we can do. It's either stop seeing each other, which we don't want to do, or we could just not mention we're seeing each other to anyone until we're sure there's something to tell them."

He studied her. "You wouldn't be hurt if we kept our relationship a secret? I'm not ashamed to be with you. You accused me of that and it's not true."

"It's just kind of smart right now if we keep things between us, right? I think we both agree it's for the best considering all that's at stake. I really don't want to cause trouble for my dad or get those lunatics at the gates stirred up. Your poor officers already put up with so much harassment from them. I'd hate to add to it."

He frowned. "I don't believe in lying."

"Not telling isn't lying." She smiled. "At least I've been assured of that from my father but he's in politics. Just pretend you're dealing with the press. You've had to learn how to handle them. As long as we're totally honest with each other that is all that should matter." She cupped his face. "So how about it, Justice? Do you want to secretly date? Minus the dating part because that would mean someone would see us together." She chuckled. "I'm not big on going out to dinner or a movie anyway. I like quiet evenings at home."

"You're perfect."

"Oh, I wish that were true. You're staying the night, right? I've yet to get to sleep with you and they say the third time is a charm."

"Try to get me out of your bed." He put more weight down to pin her securely under him.

"I'm too tired and I have no motivation to move you since I like you exactly where you are. I didn't get a lot of sleep last night and I know it's early but I'm tired."

"I didn't either. I wanted to come back but I didn't know if you'd welcome me after I fled to avoid detection. I'm sorry about that. I don't want to hurt you but I have to think about my people and everything I do reflects on them. I've felt so torn."

"I understand that more than you can imagine. My father suffered if my brother or I screwed up while growing up. Everything we do reflects on him and you represent Species to the world. You've got a lot in common with him but not in a creepy, I'm-having-sex-with-someone-like-my-dad way."

He laughed, his body shook over hers and he grinned. "You make me happy, Jessie. I'm so glad you came into my life. You're a breath of sunshine in the dark stillness my life has become."

"You just rock my world and my headboard."

Amusement looked really good on him, she decided, admiring his handsome features. She was pleased he wasn't trying to deny that something was between them anymore. She understood why he'd been reluctant to keep seeing her. Every concern he'd mentioned was valid for both of them. She had become dedicated to protecting and locating Species, not causing them more grief. They'd just keep their involvement private. It would avoid problems and it didn't make sense to stir a hornet's nest until they were sure of where their relationship was headed.

"At least we didn't set off any alarms tonight." He slowly withdrew from her body and rolled onto his side, opened his arms and silently urged her closer.

Jessie didn't hesitate to snuggle into his warm embrace. It felt amazing to be sheltered against him and that feeling of being where she belonged, with whom she belonged, hit her again. She didn't allow it to freak her out since she was too tired to worry about possible future heartbreak. He was worth the risk.

"Sleep, Jessie," he rasped, kissing the top of her head. "I'm here and I'm not leaving."

"This is nice," she admitted. "You should sleep here every night."

Justice's heart squeezed at Jessie's soft invitation to share her bed on a permanent basis. He wanted to. Longing struck hard and fast to do just that. The idea of her belonging to him brought out emotions he'd never experienced before. He closed his eyes, inhaled her scent and his arms tightened around her.

This happiness must be what Fury, Slade and Valiant feel when they hold their mates. That thought jerked his eyes open and his heart raced. The idea of keeping Jessie at his side, in his bed and committing to her in every way didn't strike fear into his heart. It left him feeling achy and his cock hardened in response, wanting to claim her.

Damn. Calm, he silently urged his body. Jessie's breathing had changed, she slept peacefully against him and he refused to wake her to make love to her again so soon. He held back a snort. He had taken her in a way that wouldn't have been considered loving in anyone's book. He'd been too rough, too frenzied to show her he was her male and that only he should be the one in her bed.

The memory of storming into her house shamed him. He would have killed Night or Sword if he'd discovered one of them trying to share sex with his Jessie. The rage lingered, just thinking about another male putting his hands on his woman. *Mine. Yeah. That's how I think of her and I have it bad.* He pulled her flush with his body, held her a little tighter, making sure he didn't crush her. She felt tiny compared to him, fragile, and his protective instincts flared to life as never before.

It wasn't easy to admit he would have killed one of his own males but he didn't shy away from the truth. For Jessie he'd have done it. He would have regretted it later but he'd still have Species blood on his hands. It was unsettling to realize how deeply his feelings had grown in such a short time.

A soft *buzz* drew his attention and he carefully shifted Jessie enough to free his body, careful not to wake her, and roll away. He had to answer his phone or someone would search his home to make sure he was well and discover he wasn't there. It annoyed him as he eased out of bed, grabbed his torn pants and rushed out of her bedroom while he pulled the cell out of the intact pocket.

"Justice here." He hadn't glanced at the caller ID.

"Sorry. Were you eating? In the shower? It took you five rings to answer. I don't want to hear about it if you were in the bathroom doing other things." Tiger chuckled. "This couldn't be put off."

"I ate before I left the office. I was just away from my phone. What is it?"

"Guess who showed up at the gate demanding to see you right away? It's your favorite reporter and she's waiting for a response."

"No." Irritation flashed. "I refuse to talk to that female again."

"She's being adamant. She's threatening to headline the morning's paper with news of a Species getting married to a human at Reservation."

He walked into the living room and paced. "It doesn't matter. Tammy told her friends and it was bound to get out that Valiant married her. They were already photographed together when she was kidnapped and the team tracked her and rescued her. I expected this to happen."

"Okay. Don't you always say it's better to be polite to these vultures than to make them angry enough to shred us in their newspapers?"

"I refuse to allow that female near me again."

Tiger laughed. "She wants a piece of Justice."

He growled in response. "She's a menace who believes I'm too stupid to know she's attempting to seduce me to gain access to classified information. She's not looking for a mate but instead a series of exclusive stories to boost her career."

"She is cute though a bit too talkative."

"I swore I'd never allow her another interview after the last one."

"I wish I could have seen your face when she showed you her boobs." Tiger snorted. "I wouldn't have minded seeing them. How did you get out of that mess?"

"I yelled for my secretary to come into office and chaperone the rest of the interview. You talk to the reporter. She may show her breasts again if she believes you're gullible enough to believe she's sincere in her sexual interest in you and thinks she can sweet-talk information out of you in bed."

"Hell no. I'm avoiding human females. I'm too smart for that."

Justice remained silent, unable to say anything since Jessie slept down the hallway, their mingled scent of passion still teasing his nose and keeping his dick hard from wanting her again.

"I'll deal with the vulture. I'll tell her that you aren't here but had to fly to Reservation for a meeting. Speaking of, Miles Eron called to remind you that you're due at his office at nine in the morning."

"Great." He refrained from snarling, tired of meetings.

"They are worried about our image and that's why we hired him." Tiger paused. "They'll ask you to dye your hair again. It's getting dark. You know how our media consultants are."

"It's torture when they mess with me. That shit stinks."

"That's why I'm glad I'm not you. I'll deal with the booby flasher and you get back to whatever you were doing."

Justice hesitated. "Can I ask you a favor?"

"Of course."

"I'm tired, Tiger. I'd like one night of uninterrupted sleep. Can you just handle anything that arises and make sure I'm not disturbed?"

Sympathy welled in the other male's tone. "Of course. You deserve that and so much more. I'll take care of anything that comes up. Sleep and rest. That meeting in the morning is going to be hell and we both know they are going to have that woman at the office waiting to dye your hair. I'll stay at the office and route all calls here for that reason alone."

"Thank you."

"Get some sleep and don't worry. I've got everything handled and I'll call the officers to make sure they steer clear of your house. I don't want them patrolling too close and waking you."

"That isn't necessary. I already told them to avoid my home."

"They worry about you and want to make certain you are safe. We can't allow anything to happen to you." Tiger laughed. "Nobody else wants your job. Everyone needs you too badly because there's not one of us who could keep so calm regardless of what the humans say or do. You're the most tolerant, well mannered of us all. We'd be in a world of shit if you were killed because no one else could hold it all together."

Justice's shoulders slumped. "I don't think that's true."

"It is." All humor left Tiger's voice. "That's why I'm going to make damn sure you get some sleep. We're screwed without you. Sleep deep, my man." He hung up.

Justice closed his phone, gripped it in his fist and barely avoided crushing the thing. He stared down the hallway toward where Jessie slept. He'd never imagined wanting anything more than caring for his people and making sure they succeeded in merging with the world outside the testing facilities. One sexy, fiery redhead had changed his life. He wanted her but he doubted he could have both.

He left his phone on the table in the hallway, closed her bedroom door and glanced at the clock. It was early to go to bed but he was tired of his life, exhausted from shouldering so much responsibility and heartsick that one day soon he'd have to give up Jessie for the good of his people.

He crawled into her bed, inhaled her scent and pulled her into his arms. She murmured his name in her sleep, brushed a kiss on his chest when her face nuzzled against him and he wrapped his arms tighter around her.

Being Justice North sucked but for now he was going to have the one thing he wanted most. He closed his eyes, determined to enjoy every second he could spend with Jessie.

Chapter Thirteen

೫

"So when do we get to sleep in your bed?"

Jessie put the last dish in the dishwasher and turned. Justice sat at the table with his laptop open. He'd slept every night at her house for the past four days but in the evenings he still had hours of work to complete. In the mornings he was gone before she woke and stayed gone all day. He left the office in time to share dinner with her and she appreciated it, knowing he was a workaholic. Her father hadn't ever been that considerate when she'd lived with him and Justice obviously made the effort to spend time with her.

He didn't look up. "We can't."

She frowned. "I haven't seen your house yet and I'd like to."

He finally glanced up from his screen. "Jessie, I have too many people visiting my house. They are always dropping by for one reason or another and I have a Species male who cleans my home. You can't go visit or sleep there."

"Why not?"

"Anyone who entered my house would scent you and know you'd been there. The male who cleans my bedroom would definitely know we were sharing sex when he changed my bedding or grow suspicious if I began washing them myself." He gave her an apologetic look before dropping his attention back to his computer. "No one has any reason to come here and it's safe."

She watched him type until his cell phone rang. He blindly reached for it and answered. He spoke softly to someone about a banquet dinner and the security arrangements for about ten minutes. The phone rang a few minutes later—someone trying to set an appointment with Justice for an interview from what she could determine from his part of the conversations.

Jessie left the kitchen while he dealt with them and sank onto her couch. She tried not to feel a little self-pity. He'd be on the phone and his computer until at least ten o'clock the last few nights. He used her dining room table for his home office and she sighed when memories of her childhood surfaced. She'd sworn she'd never fall in love with a man who was obsessed with his work the way her father was but Justice made all other workaholics pale in comparison. It was ironic as hell and she hated irony.

She smirked. At least workaholics who had girlfriends could give valid reasons for taking a night off. Justice couldn't allow anyone to find out about Jessie. She couldn't see his house or spend one night in his bed. It had been her brainchild to stealth date but the reality of it sucked.

It will get better, she consoled herself. *He's used to living alone, maybe he's catching up on some of his workload to take a full night off again…and you're so full of shit. He's not going to change and if anyone knows it, it should be me.*

She stood, stretched and strolled to the sliding-glass door. There was a slight breeze as she slid it open and stepped into the backyard. Her gaze lifted to the starry sky, the nearly full moon and she crossed her arms over her chest.

Relationships were hard, she knew that, and she'd fallen for a guy with a lot of responsibilities. It was part of the reason she loved him and it made him who he was. To expect him to drastically change would be wrong. She'd learned that firsthand with her marriage to Conner. He'd married the daughter of a senator—the image—but the real person hadn't been quite to his liking. He'd bugged her to be more similar to the public figure she'd had to be for her father's benefit until their relationship fell apart.

"Jessie?"

She turned to watch Justice step outside, frowning. He was off the phone and away from his computer. She smiled. "Hi."

"Dinner was great. I loved it. Thank you."

"I figured you did since you ate all of it and when I filled your plate again, you polished that off too."

"I'm sorry I was on the phone the entire time but it was an important call. We're trying to buy some property in New Mexico. It's never simple for us. We not only have to buy the land but we have to win local support and make sure the state is willing to work with us before we buy it. That's why, so far, the only two properties we own are in California. We're having issues with some states."

"It sounds like a big hassle."

"You have no idea. Why are you outside?"

"I'm hot. Maybe I'll go soak in the tub."

Justice closed the distance between them, smiled and grabbed her hand. "Come with me." He walked her deeper into the backyard toward the wall of the house next door.

"Where are we going?"

He chuckled. "Next door."

She stared up. "Why?"

"There's a pool and you said you were hot."

Jessie laughed. "Um, Justice? I think someone would mind us using their pool."

He turned and released her hand. "I'm going to lift you up. Straddle the wall. I'll hop over first and I'll lift you down. Ready?"

"We're going to get caught." Jessie warned.

"Are you ready?"

She grinned, thrilled that he was doing something so spontaneous and risky to spend time with her. He gripped her hips and lifted her easily to set her on the wall. She threw her leg over and watched Justice remove his dress shirt after unbuttoning it. His tie and jacket were in her dining room, along with his shoes, which he always removed as soon as he came home. His swift, graceful leap over the wall took her breath away, impressed her deeply and she grinned when he lifted his arms to her.

He gripped her hips, she leaned over to brace her hands on his shoulders, and he lifted her off the wall to slowly drag her body down his tall frame. It was sexy, so was he, and her libido instantly fired into overdrive. He wasn't all business now and attached to his laptop or phone. He was the man who looked at her as if he wanted to ravish her, get her naked in a pool behind a dark house and she hoped he wanted to have his way with her.

"We'll go swimming." He eased his hold. "Nice cool water awaits us."

She wouldn't mind forgoing the pool to kiss him. A grin formed at the prospect of him naked and wet. The kiss could wait until then. "Don't blame me when we get busted for trespassing if the owner comes home. You're springing for bail money," she teased.

"I'm Justice North. Who'd arrest me at Homeland?" He chuckled.

She lifted her arms when he gripped the bottom of her shirt and tugged it over her head. Jessie laughed and helped him get her out of her clothes. He discarded his pants and boxers, bent and swept her into his arms. She knew what he was going to do, grabbed her nose as he hesitated at the edge and met her gaze.

She nodded and he stepped into the deep end. Cool water submerged them and he released her so they could swim to the surface. She laughed, throwing her hair back from her face and the moon shone enough to make it easy to see him. She treaded closer until he wrapped an arm around her waist, towing her toward the shallow end where he could stand. He held Jessie a foot from him with his hands on her hips.

"Cooler now?"

She smiled. "Nope. I'm hotter."

"Hotter?"

Jessie reached between their bodies until she cupped his cock. She massaged it until it grew thick and hard. He closed his eyes in pleasure and a purr rumbled from his throat. Jessie twined her arm around his neck and wrapped her legs loosely around his hips and kept stroking him.

"You make me hot," Jessie whispered.

Gorgeous eyes opened to stare at her. "You make me burn."

Her hand gripping his shaft positioned him under her and she used her legs to adjust her body. Justice threw back his head as Jessie took him inside her. He purred softly as she tightened her thighs around his hips, taking him deeper inside her pussy.

"Just looking at you makes me wet. Feel?"

"Yes." Justice walked backward as Jessie moved on him, using her hold on his shoulders and hips as leverage to slowly fuck him. She moaned, moving faster and marveled over how good he felt driving in and out of her, hitting all those nerve endings. He felt hard and large inside her. Justice growled softly. He suddenly grabbed her and unwrapped her legs from around his waist. Jessie protested with a groan as Justice withdrew his cock. Her eyes flew open.

"What's wrong?"

He flashed his teeth as he grinned and sat down on the stairs in the water. He turned Jessie in his arms until her back pressed against his chest. He eased her down on his lap slowly. Jessie moaned as he slid inside her again. Justice spread his thighs, forcing hers open wide since they were on the outside of his. Strong hands gripped the insides of her thighs from around her waist. Justice thrust upward. Jessie threw her head back against his shoulder.

"Yes!"

One hand slid lower and Justice brushed his finger over her clit from the front. He thrust upward at a faster pace, pressing against her bundle of nerves harder and moans tore from her lips. Justice purred from behind her, his hot breath fanning her shoulder as he lowered his head and bit her shoulder. Jessie came screaming when the sharp nip of pain sent her over the edge. Justice tore his mouth away and roared out his own release.

Justice's hands wrapped around her waist, hugged her tightly and nuzzled her neck. His sharp teeth scraped her shoulder and his tongue lapped at her skin. She smiled, glad he held her or she'd probably have melted right off his lap into the pool from how relaxed her body grew.

"Did you make me bleed again?" She didn't care if he had. "It's okay if you did. It felt good."

"I didn't break the skin," he answered softly. "But I'm certain security will be knocking at your door again." He grew solemn. "I think we were too loud. We need to get you back inside your house before they check on you. Leave the back slider unlocked for me and I'll—"

Something squeaked loudly and Justice tensed. His reflexes were quick as he jerked her off his lap, spun her in his arms and dragged her into deeper water. Her back hit the side of the pool, his big body pinned her there and he leaned in close, shielding her.

"Get out," Justice growled.

"We heard a disturbance," a man spoke from the other side of the yard.

"Leave now." Justice sounded furious.

"But we heard you, Justice. Is everything all right? We heard a female scream."

"I'm not alone. Now leave," Justice snarled.

The gate slammed and Justice softly cursed. He sank lower into the water, allowing her to breathe more easily, and hung his head. She worried. He'd admitted to being with a woman in someone's pool, to trespassing, but he'd kept the officers from hanging around.

"Tomorrow I'm going to talk to them about the difference between doing their jobs and being annoying. I won't have them rushing to find me every time I roar."

She hesitated. "Do you think he saw me?"

"No. We are upwind and got lucky. The two males didn't know it was you, Jessie. They will assume I drove one of our females through the back entrance to avoid them seeing her. I have a private way into the community."

"Look at the bright side. We aren't in trouble for trespassing since we're not under arrest."

"It's my house and pool." He suddenly grinned. "We were never in any danger of that."

Surprised, Jessie stared up at him. Her gaze shifted to the large, dark house. It was the largest one in the community and she felt a little dense for not guessing who it belonged to. Of course it would be his.

"You moved me in next door to you?"

"I wanted you close to protect."

She studied his face as he peered at her until he grinned. "I was hoping that you'd want me back in your bed. You have to admit this makes it easier for us to be together without anyone knowing. The cottage nearest to you is empty and nothing is on the other side of my house. It was designed this way for privacy for these two homes."

Jessie wrapped her arms around his neck and smiled. "Why is there a house right next to yours if you were so concerned with not having a neighbor on the other side?"

His smile faded. "I wanted a mate eventually and knew a female wouldn't live in a home with me. I had the cottage built to house my mate when I decide to take one. Women need their space and freedom. I just hope that she won't have a problem being this close to me but I'd want her near enough to protect."

Jessie felt pain stab her heart. He'd moved her into a house that one day his wife would live in. She knew exactly why a female would want her own home and the freedom to live away from Justice. He was counting on his mate being Species. She'd caught the way he'd worded his last sentences—the source of her heartbreak. He had said hope, as in still wanted it. He'd never consider Jessie as someone to keep around. She was just sex to him.

Jessie released his shoulders. "I'm tired and need to get home." She pulled away from him to wade through the water toward the stairs.

"Jessie? Is something wrong?"

Besides you being a bastard? She wanted to say that aloud but didn't, too afraid she'd reveal how much his words wounded her. "What could be wrong?" Pain twisted at her as she trudged up the steps. The air seemed chilly as she left the heated pool and rushed to her discarded clothing.

"Jessie? What is wrong?" Justice sloshed out of the pool.

She assessed the wall as she jerked on her shirt and pants, shoving her underwear into a pocket. It was too high to climb so she turned and spotted the lawn chairs. She lifted one, carried it to the wall and easily climbed it. Pain shot through her ankles a little when she landed on the soft grass in her yard and rushed to get inside, away from him.

Justice easily leaped over the wall after her. "Jessie? Damn it, what is wrong?"

She glanced over her shoulder. "What could be wrong?"

She stepped through the still-open sliding-glass door and headed toward the dining room. A naked Justice followed closely behind, dripping water on her carpet but she barely noticed as she focused on her target. She closed his laptop, leaned down to grab the handle of his briefcase and laid it open on the table.

"What are you doing?" Justice sounded irritated and confused.

Jessie ignored him to slide his laptop inside his briefcase and carefully picked up the folders spread on the table. She shoved his cell phone in last and closed the case. She gripped the handle, spun around and lifted it toward him as her gaze finally met his.

"Take your work and go home."

"Jessie?"

She stared into his beautiful, confused eyes. He had no idea why she was upset or why she wanted him to leave, that was as clear as the frown on his face. That was the problem. She shoved the case at him again.

"Take it or I drop it."

He gripped it from the bottom. "What is wrong?"

She fought tears while glaring up at him. She was really hurt and worse, really mad. She shouldn't have to explain it to him but she saw that he wouldn't understand unless she did. She released his briefcase to place her hands on her hips, ready to tell him exactly what the problem was.

"I'm done, Justice. You didn't want anyone to know about us because you knew we wouldn't last. You said it was to protect everyone but I assumed that was for only as long as we were still getting to know each other. How naive of me to honestly think you wanted to see if we had a future. You moved me into the house of your future mate and you just made it very clear you're set on a Species woman. Well, guess what? Fuck you, Justice. I have feelings. Do you get that?" She yelled the last part.

His eyes narrowed. He still appeared baffled by her outburst.

"Don't look at me that way. There's not a thing wrong with me. You're the problem. This unworthy-of-you human female is fed up. You'll sleep with me, make love to me, have me fix you dinner and yet you hide the fact that we're together."

"We discussed this and you know it's to protect—"

"Bullshit!" She didn't let him finish. "Yes, I get why we should hide our relationship but I thought once we grew closer, maybe realized this was long-term, that it would change. It's never going to until you dump me when you decide to take a mate. Would *you* ever be with someone who refused to acknowledge you in public? How about this one? Would you be with a woman who told you she was going to toss you aside the second she found a man she'd take seriously and made it clear that would never be you because she's ashamed of being with you? Well, I won't. Get the fuck out now."

Jessie turned, stomped around him and out of the kitchen.

"Jessie! Wait. I'm not ashamed of you."

She snorted as she spun to face him. "Right. That's why I can't sleep in your bed, or hell, even go in your house. Someone might find out you're doing me. Isn't that what you said?"

"I didn't put it that crudely," he growled. "We agreed to keep our relationship private. You said—"

"I don't give a damn what I said. I didn't know you planned to use and toss me aside regardless of whatever feelings we might share. That's the bottom line. You don't want anyone to find out the great leader of the NSO prefers climbing into bed with a human but only a Species is going to be your mate." She glared. "Get out and don't come back. I'm not doing this anymore, Justice."

He followed when she entered the bedroom. She turned, saw him coming and tried to slam the door in his face. His hand shot out and his open palm hit it to prevent the door from closing. He shoved it back open.

"I'm not ashamed of you, Jessie. It's just that I'm the person who is the face of New Species. What would that say if I let it be known I preferred a human? I'm risking a hell of a lot to be with you because I want you that much. I hadn't even met you when I had the house plans drawn up. You can't hold that against me. I put you here so we could be together."

"You said you hope she doesn't have a problem living this close to you. You HOPE! Not hoped. HOPE! Present tense instead of past tense. I caught that. Now get out and go find yourself a Species woman to be with. Someone you want everyone to know about. Leave."

Justice growled. "Damn it, Jessie. You're missing the point. I'm risking a hell of a lot to be here."

"Big deal. It's not a risk when you know there's not much of a chance of anyone finding out. That's why you had me live next door to you. You can just hop the back wall the way you did the other night when your men came to the door. That's what you did, isn't it? Just jumped the wall and you probably answered your own door when they checked on you. I can't do this, and more importantly, I won't unless you're willing to tell everyone we're together. Otherwise, I don't want to be with you again. Prove to me that I mean more to you than just someone to sleep with while you bide your time, waiting to take a wife."

"I can't go public with our relationship, Jessie. Not even for you." His gaze darkened, anger tightened his features and a soft growl passed his parted lips. "I have an entire race of people who look up to me and who count on me to take care of them. I have to do what's best for them and giving fanatics a reason to target us isn't going to help them one bit. Those humans really hate it when they find out one of us is with a human female. You'd be in danger. You couldn't leave Homeland without being harassed at best, killed at worst. Think of your father too."

"Get out."

Justice shook his head. "We're going to talk about this. You need to see reason."

Jessie counted to ten but it barely calmed her. "I'm getting a drink."

"Let's talk first. I want to work this out. You mean a lot to me, Jessie."

"Do I mean enough for you to let people know we're together? Do you care enough to risk getting some hate mail over our relationship?"

"You do mean that much to me but I just can't do it. I've thought about it often and there's no way I can let it be known we're a couple. You'd be in danger and it would cause too many problems. We're happy right now. No one needs to know we share a bed at night. I have no plans to take a mate any time soon and you're reading too much into what I said."

The pain was sharp to Jessie's heart. He was never going to admit to being with her and just because he didn't want to get married to someone else right away didn't ease the burn of knowing it would never be her he planned a future with.

"I'm thirsty. Do you want a soda?"

"No." He was irritated.

"I'm getting one."

She walked around him and as soon as she reached the hallway, sprinted toward the living room at a dead run. Justice cursed loudly when he realized she planned to flee and she barely made it to the front door before he grabbed her arm. Her hand hit the button, it lit up and an alarm shrieked outside. She met his stunned, wide gaze.

"Why did you do that?"

She raised her chin. "You better grab your things and run, Justice. I'm going to let them inside and they'll find you naked if you don't leave. Try explaining that one to your officers."

A snarl tore from his throat. He released her and grabbed his briefcase and jacket. He remembered his shoes and tie and retrieved them before he fled out the open sliding door. Jessie ran for it and locked it behind him. She checked the windows and made sure they were locked too, until the doorbell rang.

Jessie grabbed the perfume bottle hidden inside the planter by the door and sprayed heavily. She coughed and made a face at the strong aroma of flowers as she tossed it out of sight and yanked open the door. Two officers stood there gripping guns. It was obvious from their heavy breathing that they'd rushed to her home.

"I'm so sorry! I accidentally hit it and didn't know how to turn it off."

One of the Species officers frowned. He inhaled and jumped back with a sneeze. "How did you accidentally set it off?" He reached inside, pushed the button and the alarm silenced.

"I stepped outside to get something from my golf cart that I forgot and came back in. I hit it instead of the light switch. I'm really sorry." She suffered a twinge of guilt for using them to get Justice to leave but he might have talked her into giving him another chance. She deserved more than being someone's temporary bed mate. "It won't happen again."

"Are you sure you are fine?"

"Yes. I'm really sorry for causing a disturbance."

He hesitated. "You might want not to use so much…" He made a face. "What is that smell?"

"Scented candles," she lied. "You don't like them?"

He sneezed again and backed up. "I think we're allergic. Please find something else to use if you want to change the scent of your home."

"I will. Thank you. I'm sorry about hitting the wrong button and making you sneeze from my candles." She closed and locked the door.

Five minutes later she heard tapping on the glass slider and walked into the living room. Justice had put on jeans and a tank top. He silently stood on the other side of the glass and pointed to the lock. She shook her head and turned off the living room lights, not willing to discuss it anymore. She entered her bedroom.

"Jessie?" He was outside her bedroom window. "Let me in."

"I'm calling security again if you don't leave. Go away!"
She pulled the curtains closed and turned off the lights.

He cursed but it grew silent. She waited a long time but
he didn't try to get her attention. She climbed into bed, tugged
her underwear from her pocket and tossed them toward the
floor. Tears filled her eyes and slid down her cheeks. She'd
fallen in love with a man who would never allow himself to
love her back. His job and people came first and always
would. It really hurt.

Justice punched the wall and snarled. His knuckles split
from the force as they drove through plaster. Jessie was
hurting, she refused to speak to him and he had no one to
blame but himself. He'd spoken without thought, mentioned
the original plans he'd had and screwed up by answering her
questions.

He yanked his fist back, studied the blood and pressed his
other hand over it. The torn skin burned, ached and he
relished the pain. He deserved it and so much more. The
memory of his Jessie's pain had been so clear in her eyes that it
haunted him. The urge to go to her, to hold her in his arms,
became a physical need.

"Damn," he rasped as he turned and leaned against the
damaged wall of his home office.

It's for the best, the logical side of him reasoned. The other
side of him protested loudly when his body tensed, the urge to
roar gripped him and he had to take deep breaths through his
nose until it passed. Jessie was stubborn. She wouldn't see him
again unless he made their relationship public knowledge and
she'd made valid points when she'd yelled at him.

He battled the desire to storm out of his house, leap the
wall and tear through the slider to reach his Jessie. He'd do it if
he believed he could seduce her into allowing him to sleep in
her bed but she'd hate him in the morning. She'd made up her
mind not to see him secretly anymore.

"Damn!" He snarled, closed his eyes and leaned his head back against the wall.

He wanted her, needed to be with Jessie as much as his next breath, but his people would suffer. She would suffer. He'd dealt with the hate groups and the press for far too long to be naive about how it would unfold. Reporters would run with the story, it would be worldwide news that Justice North was dating a human and there would be hell to pay.

Her image would be plastered on every newspaper and news station. They'd dig into her past, leaving no stone unturned to rip her life apart and offer it for public consumption. She'd then become a target of anyone who believed it was vile for a human to sleep with a Species, be labeled horrible names by them and some lunatics would wish her dead. She'd grow to hate him for the chaos her life became.

The senator would possibly lose his position or worse, keep it to rally against the NSO if he were upset his daughter had preferred a Species male over a human one. The support they still received from Washington would dry up. Money was coming in from the lawsuits against Mercile Industries but it was slow going and it might be years before they were a hundred-percent financially solvent. Their government contacts had assigned the human task force to help them recover captive Species and gave them access to track all the corporate financial records of the pharmaceutical company's investors.

Species would die, never to be found, wherever they were being held if they lost the task-force teams. The Mercile employees who had avoided arrest would never be brought to justice if the teams stopped hunting them down. It would be a disaster, lives would be lost and he'd sworn to do everything he could for his people. Loving Jessie risked all that.

His knees buckled and he slid down the wall until he sat on the floor. He'd thought surviving the years in the testing facility would be the most painful heartache he ever suffered.

He'd had no hope, no future to look forward to, but now he'd had something wonderful.

The loss of happiness left a bitter taste in his mouth. He just couldn't keep Jessie. It would cost too much and the price wouldn't just be his to pay. He'd die for her but it wasn't just his life on the line.

Her father might accept you, his inner voice whispered. *It might not be so bad. You could have her and keep the task teams. She might not care what happens in the outside world if she's here where the ugliness can't touch her.* His eyes opened and he stared at the wall across the room. It was a risk, a huge one and he just couldn't take the chance. Not for his people and definitely not with Jessie's life.

Pain ripped through his heart and he knew it was best if he didn't take the chance. He'd rather lose Jessie than have her hate him when everything around her was touched by the ugliness the outside world could become. He'd rather she hurt a little than watch her suffer through losing all she held dear. He bent his knee, rested his arm there and dropped his forehead against it. He refused to allow the tears that filled his eyes to fall.

He'd found love but he couldn't have her. It had to be enough to watch her from afar, his only comfort.

Chapter Fourteen

ဆ

Justice slammed his fist on the desk and glared at the phone he'd just hung up. Some new hate church had taken to the airwaves to rant about how New Species were animals, not people, and referred to the NSO as nothing more than a private zoo. It made his blood boil.

No Species had asked to be genetically altered with animal DNA, it hadn't been a choice they were given, and their only so-called crime had been to survive year after year of abuse at the hands of scientists, doctors, and researchers who used their bodies to create drugs to help humans. Not that they got much appreciation for any medical advancements their suffering had provided.

The door opened and Tiger popped his head in cautiously. "I could hear you snarling from next door." He edged inside and closed the door. "Are you all right?"

"It's just a bad day."

"That's not uncommon. Has something happened that is unusually bad?"

"We just have a new group of people to contend with."

"We always do." Tiger took a seat, crossed his arms over his chest and frowned. "You look like hell. Did you sleep at all last night?" His gaze lowered to Justice's hand. "I hope whatever you punched looks worse than your hand."

Broad shoulders shrugged. "I lost my temper."

"That's unlike you. You need to take a break."

"I know but when do I have time?"

"How goes the building of your house on Reservation? I plan to come visit you and sit on that covered porch I saw in

211

the blueprints. It looks nice and the view of the lake should be a great one. We can go fishing."

"It's about three weeks from being completed and I'm getting a headache just thinking about it. The inhabitants aren't happy to have work crews in their territory. Slade is ready to shoot me for making him deal with more humans." Justice raised a hand and tore his hair free of the thong holding it in a ponytail, shook his fingers through the strands and leaned back in his chair. "Not that I will ever have the time to enjoy it."

"We're working on it. The council is ready to take over some of your responsibilities. You have me, Slade, and Brass too. We'd do anything for you."

"I know that and appreciate it."

"What the hell is up with you, my man? Honestly, all day you've been terrorizing anyone who comes near you. You're acting more like a bear than a leader. It's out of character."

"You sit in my chair and then we'll see how amiable you are every day."

Tiger blinked a few times and allowed the silence to grow uncomfortable before he spoke again.

"Whatever is wrong, you need to find a way to work through it. Everyone has noticed your anger. Are you growing to resent us? I've had seven of our males walk up to me in the past few hours to ask me that question. Is the stress getting to you?"

Justice sighed. "I'm having a bad day. Everyone has those."

"You don't. You are the most even-tempered male I know, and you keep your sense of humor. You only show this side to our enemies when you need to remind them we are not to be messed with. Do you want to fight?"

Surprise flickered through Justice. "What?"

Tiger dropped his arms, gripped the arms of the chair and leaned forward. "Fight. Do you need to get out some aggression? It feels good and you haven't done it in a while." He rose to his feet. "Let's go."

Justice hesitated.

"Now," Tiger growled. "Take off the mask and remember who you really are."

He stood slowly and stepped around his desk. Tiger yanked open the door and walked through the reception area. Justice glanced at his receptionist. "I'm taking a break."

She nodded. "I'll hold your calls." She refused to meet his eyes.

Guilt gripped him that he might have frightened the female with his gruffness. "Thank you," he responded sincerely. "I appreciate you."

"Let's go."

Tiger opened the outer door into the main part of the NSO building and they walked side by side out into the sunshine. Brass sat in a Jeep at the curb. It surprised Justice to see him there but the male only gave him a grim nod. Tiger waved Justice to the passenger seat then gripped the roll bar, jumped up and collapsed into the backseat. Justice sat, pulled his feet inside and the engine started.

They drove to the main security building and entered the training room they used to keep in shape. Tiger glanced at the Species inside.

"Everyone out. No one comes near the door. Brass and I are going to show Justice a few new training techniques and if he likes them, you'll be learning some new skills soon."

Faces glanced their way but all eight of their people left quietly. Tiger locked the door and Brass crossed the room to lock the second door. There were no windows in the large room, only mats on the floor and a bunch of exercise equipment set up along one wall. Justice hesitated.

Tiger returned, bent down and tore off his boots. He lifted his head, stood and began removing his weapons. Movement to his left drew Justice's attention to Brass. The male also removed his boots and weapons.

"Should I be worried?" He kept his tone calm. "Two against one?"

Brass flashed him a grin. "Remove the suit. We'd hate to mess it up." His gaze ran down the length of it. "It's nice. We're not. We'll avoid your face. You have to look pretty for the cameras."

Justice narrowed his gaze as he reached for his tie. "Pretty?"

Tiger chuckled. "Pretty. We love the hair too. Any female would be proud to have such a nice color. They did a good dye job."

Anger tingled through Justice. "Do you know how much I hate the stink of it?"

Tiger walked onto the largest mat, faced him and tore his shirt over his head. He tossed it far enough to hit the floor at the edge of the training area. "Tell us about it. We have to smell you for days."

Brass removed his shirt and stepped onto the mat. "He's sure pretty though. Did you see the cover of that fitness magazine they put him on? I was impressed." He chuckled. "That suit covers his muscles though, doesn't it? It didn't make him look in shape unless sitting behind a desk is a strong workout."

Anger burned brighter at their teasing as Justice dropped the tie, removed his jacket and his shirt. He added to the pile of clothing until he stood in his boxer briefs. "I didn't model for that. They took a picture of me at the charity event and slapped it on there." He took a menacing step toward them. "You really want to do this?" His fists clenched.

"You should hang your suit over the barbells over there. It will wrinkle." Brass snorted. "It would be on the evening news if you wore clothes with creases that weren't put there by an iron. It would make us look bad."

A snarl tore from Justice and Tiger threw the first punch. His blow hit Justice in the shoulder and he reacted by kicking out, hitting his friend in the hip and sending him flying to land on his ass. Brass growled, crouched low and Justice lunged. Their bodies tangled, hit the floor and the fight was on. They exchanged some body blows from forearms, threw each other around and Justice finally tossed Brass away from him. Brass rolled on the mat and Tiger dived at Justice. He rolled out of the way, shoved up to his feet and turned in time to punch Brass as he came at him too.

The three of them fought, returned blow for blow, avoiding each other's faces, and mixed it up with some kick-boxing and wrestling. Brass dropped out first after Justice put him on his ass. Panting, he held up his arms, done. Tiger snarled and launched at Justice but he was ready for the move. He sidestepped, ducked and threw out an arm to nail the male who had missed him by inches. Tiger hit the mat on his back, groaned and stared up at him.

"I give," Tiger said and lifted his hands.

Sweat poured off Justice as he stood there, stared down at his friends and realized he'd carry some bruises for days. The pain was good, he felt alive and some of his anger was gone.

Tiger turned his head to glance at Brass. "See why I told you to come with," he rasped. "I could never beat him."

Brass groaned, rubbed one of his shoulders and nodded. "He might look civilized but he's got a vicious fighting ability."

Tiger met Justice's stare. "Feel better?"

He did. "Yeah."

"Do we have to do this every day?"

"Shit," Brass muttered, "I hope not."

Tiger chuckled. "Me too. It's easy to forget he's more than a pretty face."

Justice shook his head. "You're trying to anger me again."

"No, I'm teasing. It's what friends do."

"I thought we were getting our asses handed to us so he gets out his aggression." Brass got to his knees, lifted up and stood. "That's what friends do." He walked closer and gripped Justice's arm. "Don't hold that shit inside. We're here for you. We'll do this daily if you need to beat on someone."

"Speak for yourself. I was kidding." Tiger rolled, got to his feet and stretched, grimacing a little. "I need a hot bath and a female to kiss my bruises." He turned to Justice and his smile faded. "Whatever is getting to you, either talk it out with us or deal with it. You aren't yourself lately, you've kept things in and we're a family. Are you ready to share what is going on?"

Justice clamped his mouth closed. Jessie wasn't up for discussion.

"That's what I thought." Tiger stepped in front of him and held his gaze. "I guess we'll do this again tomorrow if you are in a bad mood. And the next day. However long it takes. Go home and quit scaring everyone. Take the rest of the day off."

"Thank you." Justice meant it, glancing at them both. "I needed this."

"We know." Brass dropped his arm. "Take the Jeep. The keys are over there near my boots."

Justice showered quickly in the locker room, dressed and waved to his friends as he left. He grabbed the keys but knew returning to his office wasn't going to happen. The fighting had helped but rage still burned in his soul. He was angry at life, angry that Jessie had thrown him out and that he'd lost her.

He took the private road to his house because he didn't want to deal with questions from the officers at the entrance to the Species section of why he was home midday. As he parked the borrowed vehicle in his driveway a sound made him turn and he watched with narrowed eyes as Jessie drove up the street, parked next door and avoided even glancing his way.

She ignored him and it pissed him off. He hesitated and glanced around. No one was within sight. He turned back to watch her saunter toward her door. He moved fast, kept his pace light and she never saw him as he came up behind her. She unlocked her door, opened it and stepped inside. She turned then, saw him and her eyes widened.

He stepped inside before she could react, his hand shot out to close the door and he kept his body between her and the alarm that would alert the officers to rush to her home. She wouldn't be rid of him that easily again.

"We need to talk."

Her blue eyes flashed astonishment but narrowed with anger quickly. He was glad he didn't frighten her—that was not his intention—and stepped closer to invade her personal space. Her scent tortured him. Her lips parted and his gaze fell there. The urge to kiss her gripped him strongly and he fisted his hands to prevent them from cupping her face.

"Don't you have some Species woman to woo into being your mate? Should I pack my stuff soon so she can move in instead?"

"I'm not looking for a mate." His anger intensified. "I tried to tell you this last night."

"Do you want to take me out to dinner somewhere not private?"

She was baiting him.

"You know that isn't going to happen. We've been over this. It is dangerous for—"

"Your future Species mate to find out about us? Would that hurt your chances of her accepting a home where your past lover lived?"

"Jessie," he growled. "Stop."

She suddenly reached up, flattened her hands on his shirt and pushed. "Leave."

He pressed back, his body trapped her against the wall and his palms landed flat on the surface next to her, keeping her there. "I miss you. I didn't sleep last night. Can't we discuss this reasonably?"

"No." She licked her lips, drawing his attention again. "We can't."

Frustration, anger and regret flashed through him hotly and he reacted. His head lowered, his lips sealed over hers and when she gasped, his tongue took advantage. She tasted of sweet coffee and chocolate as he kissed her. She tensed and tried to turn away from his hungry mouth but he cupped her face to hold her still.

Her hands fisted on his shirt but she didn't shove. She responded and he growled as passion replaced everything else. Jessie was his for the taking and his cock filled with blood. His need to show her how much she meant overrode all else and he let go of her face to remove his jacket. Material tore but he didn't give a damn.

Jessie helped as buttons popped off his shirt to ping on the tile entryway. She spread his shirt with force, not taking the time to unbutton it. His hands slid between them, grasped her shirt and it easily shredded.

She whimpered against his tongue, kissed him wildly and her hands rubbed his bare chest. He cupped her breasts, tore at the bra that kept him from feeling their softness and jerked the cups down enough to free her nipples. His fingers and thumbs found the taut tips, pinched them gently and she moaned.

He let go, frantically worked open the front of her pants and hooked his thumbs in the waistband, catching hold of the thin straps of her panties. He broke the kiss when he slid to his knees, kissing his way down her throat to her chest and sucked a nipple inside his mouth. Her fingers slid into his wet hair, held him tightly and he just jerked her clothing, freeing her of everything from the waist down. His knee moved, pressed down to hold them and she jerked her feet out of the tangle of fabric.

The scent of her arousal drove him insane. He wanted her and judging by the heavy musk of desire, she wanted him just as much. He couldn't wait anymore. His hands located the front of his pants, just ripped them open, and freed his aching cock. He tore his mouth away and grabbed her hips as he stood.

Jessie knew she should stop this madness but she was lost. Her feet left the floor as Justice's big body pressed her tightly to the wall, pinned her there, and her legs lifted to wrap around his waist. She couldn't find purchase at first—his damn clothes were in the way but a few wiggles slid them lower. Her thighs gripped skin as his hips were bared.

He shifted his hips, the crown of his cock nudged her pussy, found the right angle and she cried out as he drove into her in one fluid thrust that almost made her climax. She was burning alive, so turned-on that she wondered if she'd totally lost her mind but the feel of him was incredible.

He withdrew, nearly left her body and his mouth crushed down on hers. His tongue drove inside to meet hers as his hips slammed upward to bury his thick shaft inside her to the hilt and his hands gripped her ass to grind her pelvis against him. She cried out from the sheer pleasure but his kiss captured the sound, muffled it, and he pressed her tighter to the wall.

Their bodies rubbed as he took her against the cool, smooth wall and powered in and out of her body at a fast rate that drove her into a haze of bliss. He shifted his hold to hook his arm under her ass. His other hand wiggled between them, his thumb pressed against her clit and he fucked her even harder.

She gripped his shoulders, tore her mouth away before she bit him and buried her face against his neck. Their shirts were still on but parted enough that her nipples rubbed his skin as they rocked together and she inhaled the smell of soap and shampoo coming off him. He rolled his hips, found that certain spot with his cock that made her gasp in wonderment and he kept hitting it as if he could read her mind.

"Yes," she panted. "Don't stop."

"Never," he snarled.

Her vaginal walls clenched tightly, her body trembled and her belly quivered. She was pinned, couldn't move with the way he held her and could just feel as he manipulated her body. His thumb caressed her clit, revving her passion higher and she cried out when the climax struck, tearing through her.

"Jessie," he groaned, his hips jerked hard and hot semen bathed her deep inside as he started to come.

He lowered his head, buried his face against her shoulder and groaned louder. He stroked her more slowly with his thick shaft, drew out the ending of their lovemaking and finally just held her as they tried to catch their breaths.

Reality sank in slowly. She'd just had mind-blowing sex with someone she'd sworn off. She could blame the anger, it definitely had played a part in her going from cold to hot in a flash but mostly she had to admit it was because she loved him.

He wanted sex from her—the only thing he would accept—and she'd given in to him. He was just too sexy, his kisses were too irresistible and that mouth of his should come with a warning label, in her opinion. One kiss and he could make a woman lose her head and her panties.

Justice brushed a kiss on her throat as he turned his head a little and his hot, heavy breath tickled her neck as he shifted his hold again by pulling his hand out from between their bodies to cup her ass with both hands.

"Hold on to me. I'm carrying you to bed. We'll eat later. I want you again."

The sad part was she wanted to let him take her there. Spending hours touching and losing herself in his arms was so tempting it hurt to resist. She didn't want to be a doormat, the woman he slept with until he decided he wanted to settle down—she had to take a stand. She wouldn't be used by any man.

"Put me down."

"You're not heavy." He pulled away from the wall and she had to grip his shoulders to remain upright and not fall back against it as he took her with him.

She wiggled frantically, lifted up by pressing her arms on his shoulders and squeezed her vaginal muscles. It forced his still-hard cock to slide out of her. The second they parted, she let her legs drop away from his waist and shoved.

He stumbled but didn't drop her. Instead he growled as she yanked her head back to stare into his surprised eyes.

"Jessie?"

"Let go."

Confusion came next, an emotion she related to. He made her feel that way so it was only fair he suffered it too. He lowered her but didn't release her entirely. "What is wrong?"

She would have laughed if it wasn't so sad. "This doesn't change anything. It was just breakup sex."

"What?" He gaped at her.

"Breakup sex," she repeated. She released his shoulders to shove at his chest. "It happens. We have something between us but it's not meant to be. You have your plans and I'm not part of them."

Justice was quick to growl. "It was no such thing. We are not breaking up. We're going to bed and talk." He tried to pull her closer. "We are happy together."

"Do I look happy?" She stared up into his face. "I want more than to just be the woman you spend your nights with. I'd like to be there during the days too. I want to meet your friends and maybe even see your office. I want to go with you if you have to go to Reservation to stay for a few days so we don't have to be apart. The works. That's what I want, Justice. Full-fledged girlfriend rights."

Another growl rumbled from him. "It's not safe. We have been over this."

"Yes, we have. You have your mind made up and so do I. Do you know what that's called?"

"Stubbornness on your part not to see logical reasons why it would be bad if anyone knew we were together?"

She wished she could smile but it hurt too much. "Let me go, Justice."

His fingers flexed but he eased his hold until his hands dropped to his sides. "There. I'm not touching you."

"I mean let *me* go. You don't want to hurt me, right? You're so paranoid about doing that. Being with you the way we are doesn't work for me anymore. You can't or won't give me what I need. That's hurting me." Tears filled her eyes. "You're hurting me."

He shook his head. "No."

"Yes." She yanked her torn shirt together to cover her breasts, wished it were longer because she felt too exposed at that moment, both physically and emotionally. "Please leave, Justice. If you care about me at all you'll grab your clothes, jump the wall and go." She turned away, couldn't stand the tortured look on his face, and walked to the back slider. She unlocked it and shoved it open, refusing to look at him again. "Go. Please? We can't do this again. It's too painful."

"Did I hurt you? Was I too rough?" He rasped the words, sounding as tormented as he'd appeared. "Jessie? Look at me."

She refused. "Go, Justice. Just…go."

"I can't," he whispered. "I think about you. I…"

Justice was at a loss for words. It tore him apart, seeing how dejected Jessie appeared. Her shoulders slumped and she hugged her torn shirt as if it comforted her from something sorrowful. Why couldn't he find the right words to make her understand how much she mattered to him? He wrote speeches to address the world of humans often but he failed to come up with a way to express his feelings to the only one of them who had won his heart.

"Go," she whispered, the sound of tears in her voice. "Don't make me scream or push that damn alarm again. It makes me look like an idiot when they show up here and I have to pretend I did it by accident. I need space. If you care, prove it. Leave."

Agony tore through him as he turned on numb legs, collected his clothing and hesitated at her side. "Jessie? Please talk to me. Don't make me go. I want to stay with you." He was tempted to grab her, throw her over his shoulder and tie her to the bed. He could make her see that they belonged together but her pain stopped him. Seeing her that way tore him up inside. "Jessie, I—"

"It's over."

"I don't accept that." Anger stirred. It wasn't over. He wouldn't accept that.

She turned and rushed for the front door. The sudden movement surprised him and he was slow to react until she spun, her back hit the wall and her hand lifted to hover over the alarm button. She met his gaze then, her eyes filled with tears.

"Do I really have to press this thing again? Really? Go."

"Don't."

Her finger tapped it lightly. "I'm not spraying perfume this time to cover your scent. They'll all know about us if I press it. I'm not screwing with you." Her chin lifted in defiance, anger flashed in her eyes. "Don't come back unless it's to ask me out on a date, in public. That's the last thing I have to say except you've got five seconds to be gone."

"Jessie, don't do this."

"One."

"Damn it, female. We can work this out."

"Two." Her back stiffened and she sucked in air.

Anger gripped him. "I won't be threatened."

"Three and I mean it, Justice. On five I'm pressing this thing and letting them inside the house. You won't have a choice after that. Everyone will be talking about us and it will probably even find its way to the press. You know they love juicy rumors and run with them."

She'd be in danger. He snarled.

"Four."

He spun, stormed out of her house, and leapt over the wall. He wanted to roar. He wanted to tear something apart. *She will calm down. She'll miss me as much as I will her. She just needs time.* That reasoning helped as he entered his back door and threw himself on the nearest chair. He tossed his clothes to the floor and closed his eyes. Rage and sadness battled in his heart and mind.

Chapter Fifteen

∞

Two weeks of misery had passed since she'd kicked Justice out of her house. He'd left her alone, had managed to avoid her completely. She forced her attention on Breeze. The big building loomed behind the Species woman and excitement shone from her eyes.

"This is it. You're going to have fun, Jessie."

"This is your big hangout, huh?"

"Yes. It's a bar and a dance club rolled into one. This is where we hang out with friends or hook up with a male if we would like to share sex. I will introduce you and you will make new friends. The dancing is fun and we are getting good at it. Ellie loves to dance and she taught us how. It will be good for you to do more than work or stay inside your home."

"I love Ellie," Jessie admitted. She'd met the woman who ran the women's dorm, had instantly hit it off with her and become fast friends. Ellie was the first human woman to marry a Species male. She only worked a few hours a day at the dorm but she ran it smoothly. Jessie spent all her time at the dorm when she wasn't sulking at her house. It seemed her NSO job consisted of hanging out with the women and being their friend.

"I love Ellie too," Breeze admitted.

"She's fun but I hope she feels better soon. That stomach flu thing worries me. She threw up again today."

"She is under a doctor's care and will be fine." Breeze changed the subject. "Do you see why she is my best friend?"

"I do."

Loud music blasted from the interior of the building before they reached the double doors. Breeze opened one side and waved Jessie in, her grin wide at sharing the Species club. It highly amused Jessie, who secretly figured it would probably be the lamest bar and dance club ever because these people were new to the party scene but she swore she'd try to have fun.

The room was large, open and dimly lit. They had a bar running along one wall near the front door and tables set up in the same area. Pool tables and pinball machines had been added. At the back of the building, down some steps, a dance floor filled with moving bodies drew her attention.

It stunned her to see dozens of women from the dorm there along with even more men. There had to be over a hundred and their ability to dance seemed pretty advanced. She watched them swaying gracefully, their movements sexy and not dorky at all. Her eyebrows lifted but she kept her smile in place as the door closed behind them and Breeze gripped her hand, tugging her toward the bar.

"We love to dance," Breeze shouted over the music. "Let's get a drink."

Jessie ordered a mixed drink, wanting to get a little buzzed after the weeks she'd had, but noticed most of the patrons were sipping sodas straight from cans. They took seats at the bar. Breeze twisted in her seat sipping her soda and stared with longing at the dancers.

"Go dance, Breeze. I can tell you want to."

Breeze glanced at her. "You come with me."

"I will in a bit but I want to finish my drink first."

"Just come out and find me when you are done. Our males are polite and won't attack you. You have to tell them you want to share sex with them if you want to take one home with you. I love to dance!" Breeze shot off her seat, leaving her soda, and nearly ran toward the dance floor.

Jessie was glad she hadn't been swallowing her drink when she'd heard the other woman's parting words. *Share sex? Take someone home? Shit!* She took a gulp of her drink, hoping her new friend didn't expect her to hook up with some guy for a one-night stand. She'd had plenty of talks with the women, knew they did that often but she hadn't expected Breeze to think she might enjoy that pastime. She finished her drink with that grim thought hanging in her head.

The bartender was a female Species named Christmas. She was a naturally happy person and smiled all the time. She walked up to Jessie with another drink then walked away. Jessie shrugged and took a sip, admiring their customer service. They didn't exchange money, obviously they didn't wait for someone to reorder a drink and they made sure their patrons were never thirsty.

Jessie turned on her seat, studied the dancers and spotted Breeze dancing with a tall Species male near the front. The grin was instant. The couple moved together, chest to chest and they flirted outrageously. She could almost imagine them having sex as the tall woman turned in the taller guy's arms, shoved her ass against the front of his jeans and wiggled in his arms. Jessie took another sip of her drink, realized she'd probably be driving herself home since Breeze had found a hook up and decided to quit at the second drink. She didn't want to drink and drive, even if it was just a golf cart.

She finished her second drink and Christmas met her eyes. Jessie shook her head no. The bartender moved on and Jessie faced the dance floor again. Breeze and the male had danced four songs together, the music all fast paced but when the song ended, the next one was a slower melody, geared for slow dancing.

Quite a few of the dancers left the dance floor to head toward the bar. She could attest after watching them dance that they had to be thirsty. As the bodies thinned a couple dancing caught Jessie's eye. The smile slipped from her face and pain shot through her heart.

Justice danced with Kit, a female Species she'd talked to often at the women's dorm. Her light red hair fell to her shoulders. She stood about six feet tall and had beautiful catlike eyes. She wore a black leather miniskirt and a half shirt to reveal her taut belly. Jessie spied shapely legs that seemed to go on forever down to her sexy spiked heels. It probably accounted for why she appeared to be almost as tall as the man who held her tightly in his embrace as they moved together.

Justice was a great dancer. *He's a panther*, Jessie remaindered herself. They were graceful animals and it showed in the seductive way he moved. His muscular arms were exposed since he wore a tank top and tight, formfitting, faded blue jeans. His hair was down, not bound in his usual ponytail and he looked sexy as hell.

Kit moved closer to him and turned until her back pressed against Justice's front. Justice reached out and grabbed her hips, moving erotically against her as if they were making love. Kit turned her head, peered back at Justice and smiled. They looked like the perfect pair and Kit was some mix of cat, just like Justice. There was his ideal mate.

Jessie's stomach heaved at the realization that Kit might be the one he moved into her house one day. Jessie fought back the tears that filled her eyes but she refused to cry over the asshole and clenched her teeth to fight it. The image of them in bed together was vivid as their bodies moved to the music, touching, with Justice's hands on Kit's hips. One of his arms slid around her waist to tug her closer and Kit laughed. The woman turned, wrapped her arms loosely around his neck and rubbed her body along the front of his with their lips nearly touching.

Jessie turned away, hooked her feet on the bottom of the barstool and lifted up from her seat to lean forward. She frantically peered down the bar and caught Christmas' attention. She mouthed *one more please*. Christmas waved.

Jessie sat back on the stool and turned her head, unable to look away from the train wreck of her shattered heart. Justice still danced with Kit clinging to him. As Jessie watched, the woman lowered her body, rubbing against Justice's front and his hands splayed on her bare belly. Jessie forced herself to turn away, finding it too painful to watch, just in time for Christmas to drop off her drink. Jessie forced a smile to thank her, waited long enough for the bartender to move on and downed the thing in a few big gulps.

"Jessie!"

Flame stepped to her side, grinning. "You are here."

"I am. How are you?" She ran her gaze over him, happy he blocked her view of the dance floor with his big body. He wore a tank top like most of the men there and black slacks. His hair was pulled back in a ponytail.

"I'm great. You never called."

She hadn't. "I'm sorry. This is the first night I've come here. Breeze brought me."

He sat down on the barstool next to her. "How is your job?"

"It's easy. I sit around all day talking to women and getting them to open up to me. I've taught a few cooking classes and showed them how to use the internet." She shrugged. "I like it."

"Have you made friends?"

"I have." She meant that. She'd made a lot of female friends. Not that she could tell them her problems since her main one was Justice North. "How is your job going?"

He grinned. "We started harassing the protesters back and they don't like it. Some of them have left."

She laughed, more than a little tipsy and happy to latch onto another topic that would keep her from glancing over her shoulder to see what Justice did with Kit. "That's great."

"Dance with me." He held out his hand. "Don't be afraid. If you can't dance it won't matter. Half of us can't but we enjoy having fun."

Jessie hesitated. Her gaze shifted to the dance floor with dread but Justice wasn't there anymore. He'd left with Kit, a sweeping glance around didn't find him and she realized he'd left the bar entirely. If he was gone she wouldn't have to worry about running into him. Maybe dancing would take her mind off wondering what he was doing with the tall, sexy feline female. She put her hand in Flame's larger one. His skin was hot, reminding her of Justice. She pushed that thought away, not wanting to burst into tears.

Jessie realized she was the shortest person on the dance floor as it dawned how much taller all the people around her were. Flame grinned and started to dance, better at it than he'd implied. She let go of everything but the music and just felt the beat. The alcohol helped and when Flame moved in, she didn't hesitate to dance against him.

Justice left the bathroom and walked to the bar where Kit had said she'd meet him after she used the women's room. She'd ordered him juice and waved to a few people. He sensed someone coming up behind him and turned to welcome Breeze.

"Hi, Justice. How are you tonight? You are taking a night off work for a change?"

He smiled. "Everyone should have a night off."

"Have you heard from Tammy and Valiant? How are they doing?"

"They are good, Breeze. I'm happy to say they no longer terrorize anyone's sleeping habits."

Breeze grinned and turned, watching the dance floor. She laughed. "Good. She's having fun dancing. She does it really well too."

Justice took a sip of the drink Christmas handed to him. "Who is? Did you bring the new one here?"

"Kind of." Breeze laughed. "She's new but it's not Beauty. I brought Jessie Dupree."

Justice nearly dropped his glass. He twisted on his seat and scanned the dance floor, not having to look hard to find Jessie. She danced with Flame at the outside edge of the group. Justice's eyes locked on the pair. Jessie's hair was down, brushing against a tight pair of jeans that hugged her ass and the black, low-cut, tight shirt displayed a lot of creamy cleavage.

She danced so well that jealous rage filled him instantly as he watched Jessie wiggle her ass and move her arms above her head. Flame grabbed Jessie's hand and spun her in his arms until she fell against his chest, her hand gripped his shoulder and Flame dared to dip her. The sight of the male bending his female back and pressing tightly to her, tore a growl from his throat. He shot to his feet so fast the barstool hit the floor.

Breeze and Kit jerked their heads toward him. Breeze spoke first.

"What is it? What's wrong?"

He glared at Breeze. "You brought a human in here?"

She looked shocked. "It's Jessie. Nobody would bother her."

"She's safe here," Kit confirmed. "Everyone loves her. The males will behave."

"She shouldn't be here." He managed to leash his temper enough not to snarl at both women. His furious gaze returned to Jessie in time to see more of her breasts than he wanted anyone else to view. "Get her out of here now."

Breeze gasped. "But Justice, I swear no one will hurt her."

He snapped his head in her direction and glowered. "She's human and under our protection. Not all of us like humans. Get her home now where she will be safe."

"She's with Flame. No one will dare go near her with him. He'll defend her in the off chance there is a problem." Breeze bit her lip. "She's safe with me and she's safe with him. Flame would never allow anything to happen to Jessie. He likes her."

Kit snorted. "Flame likes Jessie? That's putting it mildly. She is all he asks about when I see him. He talks about her endlessly. You don't need to worry, Justice. I would bet, if Flame gets his way, he will guard her body all night long in every conceivable way. The only thing he would let touch her tonight is himself."

Justice saw red and stormed toward the dance floor. Flame had released Jessie but they still danced too closely together. Justice watched Jessie and the way she moved reminded him of her the first night they had been together when she'd climbed on top of him when he was buried inside her.

Justice reached the dance floor when Jessie's back was turned toward him. She put her hands above her head, her wrists together and wiggled her body. Justice's gaze locked on her shapely ass and he wanted her so badly his pants grew painfully tight. His heart raced, blood rushed to his ears and he knew at that moment if Flame reached for his woman the damn male would lose his hand.

Jessie was having a good time. Flame was a great dancer. He'd dipped her a few times and spun her again. Jessie loved the song playing, it was one of her favorites, and she put her hands up to sway to the beat.

A large hand suddenly clamped around both Jessie's wrists over her head. She gasped as strong fingers shackled them and she couldn't pull her arms down. She wrenched her head around and was stunned by Justice's enraged features.

Jessie was shaken to discover him still in the bar. She'd been certain he'd left with Kit. He stepped around to her front, kept her arms pinned above her and continued to glare. Rage poured from his gaze, which seemed darker than normal— none of the usual blue hints showed. She sobered fast.

"Hi, Justice." Flame yelled to be heard. "Is there a problem?"

Justice finally shifted his gaze from hers to address Flame. Dark eyes narrowed, his nose flared and a snarl came out instead of words when his lips parted. Flame paled and stepped back. Justice ignored him to stare at Jessie again.

"You need to go home. This is not a safe place for a human." His voice came out harsh, gruff and not quite human.

She gritted her teeth as her own anger rose. Justice was just pissed that she was there and dancing with another man. She didn't have to read minds to know where his thoughts lay—his body language screamed jealous outburst. The son of a bitch was a hypocrite.

"Bullshit. I'm having fun with my friends and I'm dancing."

"You're leaving now." Justice's nose flared.

Jessie hated him at that moment. She really did. He was there with another woman, one she'd had to watch him rub against and yet he had the nerve to order her to leave.

"I'm sorry, Mr. North," Jessie defiantly stated. "I would have asked your permission but I saw you dancing with Kit. I didn't want to interrupt you with the way you two were touching and rubbing against each other."

Justice paled slightly and something in his eyes changed, softened. His hold on her wrists eased and she jerked them down, took a step back and put space between them.

"We'll discuss this later. Go home."

"Actually, we don't have anything to discuss. Trust me. I came here and I totally learned my lesson. I will never make this mistake again." She fought tears. "You have a good night with Kit. You look so…picture perfect together."

Justice stared into her eyes and took a hesitant step closer. Jessie blinked rapidly at the tears that filled her eyes and spun away, totally ready to fall apart in her inebriated state but too proud to do it. She'd only gotten a few steps when a big, warm hand halted her by gripping her upper arm. She peered up at Justice.

"I'm sorry for tonight but it's the way it has to be. There are times when we must do certain things for the good of all."

What did that mean? She got the sorry part. The rest of it was Greek to Jessie. She didn't understand a word.

"I didn't get that last part."

He watched her for long seconds and his fingers let go. "We'll discuss this tomorrow."

Tomorrow. He wasn't going to his house or he was going to have company that would keep him from talking to her that night. Pain tore through her at those implications. Kit and Breeze headed their way. Kit stopped next to Justice and put her hand on his arm.

"Justice, she was just having fun. Leave her alone and come dance with me."

Breeze stared. "I swear if you let her stay I will help Flame guard her."

Flame hurried to jump on that. "I will protect her with my life, Justice."

Justice addressed Breeze. "Take her home now."

Flame held his hand out to Jessie. "I'll take you home."

Jessie saw Justice's nose flare and he glared at her. Her gaze lowered when Kit's hand massaged his biceps and he didn't pull away from her touch.

That's how it is. He is allowed to sleep with Kit but I can't talk to other men. Jessie forced a smile as pain ripped through her. "I'd love for you to take me home, Flame. Thank you." She gripped his hand and turned her back on Justice. "I drank too much and shouldn't drive."

"Jessie?" Justice snarled.

She glanced over her shoulder.

"Do you remember what I said about interaction with Species males? I had that talk with you. You better remember what I said carefully."

She gaped, released Flame and slowly turned to face the man she loved. She remembered how he'd sworn to kill any man she let touch her. Kit pressed her body against his side, ran her fingers down his arm to rest on his stomach, rubbing him just above the waistband of his jeans. It was a familiar thing to do.

"Calm down, Justice," Kit purred. "You worry about her because she's under your protection but Flame wouldn't hurt her."

"Breeze, take her home. Flame, stay here." It was an order given harshly in a no-nonsense, threatening tone.

Anger flared in Jessie. *The bastard!* "Mr. North, I'm a big girl and I'm single. I don't have anyone to answer to, especially someone I don't know. I had an ex-husband but he was a cheating bastard who didn't know how to be loyal. He slept around but expected me to sit home all alone. I divorced him because it doesn't work that way and it never will with me. When a man cheats with someone else he has no right to get mad if I have sex with someone else. I'll go home now but thank you for your..." She hesitated, knew she'd said too much but didn't care. "Concern." Jessie turned away. "Let's go, Flame. I'll give you a tour of my house since you're being nice enough to drive me home."

They got a few feet when she realized she wasn't too steady on her feet and Flame gripped her arm, laughing. "You drank too much, little Jessie."

"Probably. I had three and I'm not much of a drinker."

"When is the last time you drank?"

"Oh, about a year ago. It was the first—"

An arm hooked around her waist, jerked her right off her feet and she slammed into a warm, hard body. She was too stunned to do more than gasp as her feet touched the floor again. Strong arms held her pinned and unable to move. A loud snarl deafened her in one ear, the one closest to Justice's mouth, and Flame spun to see what had happened to her.

"She's drunk and you aren't taking her anywhere." Justice snarled again. "Go, Flame. I'm protecting her and it's not up for discussion. Her father would be furious if anyone touched her while she wasn't in her right mind from drinks."

Flame backed away, looking shocked and rushed away without another word. Jessie drew in a deep breath, her stunned brain trying to take in what had just happened but hot breath fanned her skin as Justice lowered his head to whisper in her ear.

"I will kill him, Jessie. Is that what you want? To see me rip Flame apart, limb by limb? Think before you speak or act. I'm not fucking Kit. I haven't shared sex with anyone but you since we met. It was for appearances only, to make my people feel confident and believe everything is well." His arms loosened. "Go home. I have a helicopter to catch in an hour and must attend a meeting at Reservation first thing in the morning. We'll finish this discussion after I fly home in the afternoon." His big body trembled behind her. "Be happy I must leave because you don't want to talk to me right now anyway. I'm dangerous. I'd teach you why you'll never accept any male but me."

He released her as swiftly as he'd grabbed her, backed up and shot a glare at Breeze. "Take her home and keep her away from all males. She's had alcohol, needs to be protected and isn't sober. Smell her and you'll understand. If anything happens to her it's your ass." He stormed toward the front door.

"Justice?" Kit cursed. "Damn!" She approached Jessie and put her hands on her hips. "You made him mad," she pouted. "We were having fun and I don't like your father if he puts such worry in Justice over your safety."

Breeze came forward, looking confused. "Let's go, Jessie." She sniffed. "How many drinks did you have?"

Talk, she ordered her reeling mind. "Um, a few." She closed her mouth.

Breeze led her outside to the golf cart and drove her home. The silence stretched between them. Jessie still felt hurt over Justice's dancing date, humiliated by the scene he'd created and really drunk. She shouldn't have had that third drink.

"I'll walk you inside." The other woman studied her. "Species rarely drink alcoholic beverages. They taste and smell bad."

"You're politely saying I stink, aren't you?"

A laugh answered her and Breeze helped her stand. The world swayed a little for Jessie and she remembered she didn't drink often for a reason. Lightweight. The hand tightened on her arm and steadied her.

"You are small and shouldn't drink that awful stuff, Jessie. You're smart and don't need it. You should see how uncoordinated you are and your eyes are all shiny."

"Not a good look for me, huh?"

"No."

Jessie laughed, loving how blunt Species were. She tried to unlock the door but the darn keyhole kept moving. Breeze softly growled, jerked the key out of her hand and opened it. She turned the lights on.

"I'll help you get into bed."

"I can do it myself. This isn't my first drunken rodeo."

"What does that mean? We didn't have any bulls at the bar."

Another chuckle came from Jessie as she peered up at the tall woman. "It's a saying. I've gotten shitfaced before. Thank you for bringing me home but I can handle it from here."

"Are you sure?"

"Positive. Thank you." She spun, stumbled and focused on putting one foot in front of the other. The door closed loudly behind her, assuring her that her friend had left. Depression hit hard.

Justice and Kit had looked good together and he might not have slept with her recently but the familiar way the Species woman had touched him left no doubt they'd been lovers in the past. He'd probably been living it up and flirting with other women while Jessie had been staying home, miserable. It made her mad and worse, really hurt. She wasn't sure if he'd told her the truth. For all she knew he could be banging the hell out of every Species woman at Homeland.

Hot tears filled her eyes and she regretted getting drunk since it made her more hormonal and less rational. Justice was a jerk but he'd been a hot one. She'd loved being in his arms and the guy could make her come screaming. There was the part about her falling in love with him too but she snorted over that.

"I have bad taste in men," she sniffed. The sound of her broken voice and the pain in it shattered the last bit of bravado she had as the sobs hit. She staggered to her bed, climbed on it, curled up and pulled her knees up.

She had fallen in love with a workaholic guy, the leader of New Species, her boss. It had spelled disaster from the moment she'd seen him looking so sexy in his tank top. The tight jeans hadn't helped either. A woman would have to be blind and dead not to notice Justice.

"Jessie?" Bright light flooded the bedroom as Breeze rushed into the room. "Did you fall? Are you harmed?"

Shit! She wiped at her face, sniffed and forced her body to move. She sat up but refused to glance in the direction of the door. "I'm fine. I cry when I drink. It's just a human thing," she lied. "I thought you left."

"I know some people get sick and throw up when they drink. I'm your friend and I was left in charge of you by Justice."

Hearing his name only hurt more and sobs racked her body. She shoved her hands over her face, swore to never drink ever again and tried to talk.

"I'm fine. Just go home, Breeze. I'll be great in the morning."

"What is it, Jessie? You are always so happy and now you are red, wet and sad." Breeze gripped her shoulder and forced her hands down by shoving at them to search Jessie's gaze. Breeze softly cursed. "I see pain. Who has caused it?"

"It's nothing. No one hurt me."

"You just glanced away from me," Breeze accused. "You're lying. Don't do that. We're friends but I refuse to have a dishonest person around me. You must be honest."

Guilt ate at Jessie hard. Breeze had been nothing but honest and kind to her. She'd shared secrets about Species, had trusted her, and she wanted to do the same but this was too big to tell. "I wish I could blurt it all out but I just can't."

Anger suddenly filled Breeze's face. "Did Flame cause you pain? Did he touch you in a bad place? Was he coming on too strong at the bar? I will cause him such great pain he will—"

"No," Jessie shook her head. "He was a total gentleman while we danced."

Breeze was baffled. "What has caused you pain? Are you ill? Do you need a doctor?"

"You have no idea how much I need someone to talk to but I just can't."

"I understand. It is classified. We have these things too."

Jessie cried harder. That fit her and Justice's relationship all right. No one was ever supposed to know. Breeze said soft, soothing words and put her arms around Jessie. She patted her awkwardly on the back as she hugged her. Eventually Jessie stopped crying.

"I'm sorry I fell apart. I shouldn't drink. Usually I can control myself when I'm like this."

"It's fine, Jessie. We all have moments when we cry."

"You cry?" Jessie studied her.

Breeze hesitated. "I did when I was young but I learned that tears don't ease the pain or change the reasons for it. I do envy you the ability to release some of that hurt through the physical exertion of crying. You should be tired now and will sleep after that much crying. I will tuck you in and stay with you until you fall asleep. Our females who you bring to us enjoy having that done. It makes them know we care and I care about you, Jessie. You are my friend."

"Thank you. You're my friend too. I appreciate you letting me fall apart on you the way I did. It really helped not to be alone."

"Any time." Breeze hesitated. "Just try to give me warning next time you feel this way. I will wear a thicker shirt so your tears don't soak my skin."

A laugh burst out of Jessie. "I apologize for getting your skin wet. I promise, I will tell you immediately if I feel advance warning the next time I cry."

"Thank you." Breeze winked at her.

Breeze pulled back the covers and Jessie climbed in. Breeze disappeared into Jessie's bathroom and came out moments later with a hairbrush and tissue. She handed the tissue to Jessie.

"Blow your nose."

"Thanks, Mom."

Breeze laughed and pointed to Jessie's hair. "I will brush it. It will soothe you and everyone enjoys having it done."

"That's so nice. I appreciate it."

Jessie relaxed as the other woman draped her hair down her back, applied the brush at the bottom and slowly worked out all the tangles. It did feel nice. Her body relaxed and she yawned. The brush paused and the bed dipped as Breeze shifted. One of her hands shifted Jessie's hair to lay it over her shoulder and a soft growl tore from her.

"Who did this to you?"

Confused, Jessie turned her head to frown at her. "Did what?"

Breeze gripped her shoulder, shoved the shirt out of the way and revealed more of her skin. She glanced down, saw the almost-healed red marks that remained from when Justice had bitten her hard enough to break the skin and knew the color drained from her face. There would probably be a faint scar there for the rest of her life once the redness faded.

"Jessie? Who did this? This is from one of our males." Breeze uttered a foul word. "There are only two ways for a male to bite like this. He either mounted you from behind and you fought so he bit into you to force you to stay under him or one of my kind mounted you and is going around biting humans. Some of humans who have slept with Species beg our men to bite them. They think it would be a turn-on but it is strictly forbidden for our males."

"Leave it alone," Jessie urged softly.

Breeze released Jessie's shoulder, stood and glared at her. "You've been mounted by a Species male. It was either by force or one is biting females for the novelty of it. That wound isn't that old. Is this why you were crying? I want a name now."

"Please, Breeze. It's not that way. You need to drop it."

"I'm calling for officers. You don't understand the seriousness of this. If one of our males is forcing your females into sex or biting them for fun, they need to be stopped immediately." Breeze spun for the door.

"Stop!"

Breeze turned and Jessie gave her a pleading look, panicked at the idea of her friend making that call. "It's not that way."

A growl tore from Breeze. "How is it? I'm calling the officers."

Justice would be furious. Their secret would be out if the officers were involved. Every bit of pain she'd gone through would have been for nothing and he'd think she'd done it out of revenge. She wasn't that petty. "If I tell you the truth will you swear to me that you will never repeat any of it to anyone?"

Breeze looked uncertain. "I won't be silent if a male is harming females."

"That's not what happened. It wasn't forced and…" She touched the bite mark. "It wasn't just one of your men going around biting my kind for the hell of it."

Breeze sat on the bed. "I give you my word. Talk."

She bit her lip. "The day that Tammy and Valiant got married I met one of your males. I was attacked by a newly freed male and a guy protected me. We had dinner together and one thing led to another. It was mutual."

"His name?"

She hoped to avoid answering. "We had consensual sex."

"He bit you?" Breeze grimly frowned. "Did you change your mind during sex and he tried to force you to stay under him? They don't have much control once they start. I'm sorry, Jessie. Did he hurt you bad?"

"He didn't hurt me at all."

"You saw him again. Here?" Her gaze fixed on the mark on her shoulder. "It's barely healed. You have been here about three weeks, right?"

"It was here."

"How did the bite happen?"

"We were having sex." She paused. "He gripped me with his teeth. He told me to hold still. Do I really need to say this out loud?"

"You will if you don't want to explain it to our officers. Spill."

Jessie's cheeks warmed. "He was trying to be really slow and gentle with me so he didn't risk hurting me but I wanted him not to be. I kind of forced the issue and he bit me. It's that simple. It didn't hurt and he was sorry but it wasn't to hurt me."

Breeze kept staring at her, silent, and kept the frown in place.

"What?"

"Why were you crying before? Does he live at Reservation and had to go back? I know some of our men from there were here a few weeks ago. Tell me his name I will get him back here. You obviously miss him to shed tears at his absence."

"We're not seeing each other anymore. I broke it off with him."

"Why are you crying? Did you change your mind and want him back?"

"I wish it were that simple." More tears threatened to spill. "I need your promise you won't say anything to anyone. I really need a friend right now, Breeze. I need someone to talk to. Someone I can trust."

"You can trust me. What secret is making you cry? I won't drop this."

"I had to break it off with him because he doesn't want anyone to know he would sleep with me." Hot tears fell down her face. "He slept in my bed night after night but during the day if I had passed by him he probably wouldn't have spared a glance. I'm so in love with him that it makes me sick. He has it set in his head that one day he's going to get a Species woman as his mate. That's his big plan and I'm not in it."

Breeze softly cursed. "He is stupid. You are a fine female, Jessie. Any of our men should be proud to claim you. How long were you together?"

"He slept in my bed for four nights straight and he would probably still be in it if I hadn't told him I couldn't do this secret-lovers thing anymore. I just can't live that way, Breeze. It hurts that he's never going to openly acknowledge me."

"He is stupid. Some of our men have mated with your kind and are happy. I have a plan. I will pretend to know nothing and make him spend time around Ellie and Fury. He will see how happy they are and learn it can work between you. Tell me his name and I will do this." Breeze grinned. "We will fix this."

"He already knows them."

That wiped the grin from Breeze's face. "What is the problem? Everyone can see how happy they are. He should embrace the happiness he can have with you."

Jessie's heart pounded as she hesitated. "The problem is, he believes he'll be letting your people down if he's with me. He's worried about hate groups going crazy, my dad pulling his support from the Species issues in Washington and that all hell will break loose. I think he's also worried that he'll be setting a bad example to your people if he picks me over one of your women."

Breeze frowned. "No one has that much influence on all of us or your father."

"There is one," Jessie whispered.

The color slowly drained from Breeze's face. "Justice."

Jessie burst into tears and Breeze softly cursed.

Chapter Sixteen

ဢ

Breeze paced the bedroom, shooting glances at Jessie and clenched her fists. "It makes more sense now. Justice is very smart." She paused. "Now I see it. He moved you into this house to keep you next door to him. Everyone wondered why he would put a human here. They only live in the human village except for Ellie who lives with Fury. We were told it was because Justice is close with your father and he wanted you in the safest place at Homeland. These homes are guarded and secured more than any others."

"I know."

"He lives next door and can come in here without anyone knowing."

Jessie nodded. "I know."

Breeze gaped at her. "He is so smart. Tonight…" Breeze threw her hand over her mouth before dropping it to her side. "He wasn't worried about your safety or you being in a bar with our kind. He was jealous. He was so enraged over you being there and you were dancing with Flame."

"I know that too."

Breeze's gaze narrowed. "He was so enraged, Jessie. You could have gotten Flame killed when you agreed to dance with him and that's why he stopped him from taking you home. Possessiveness in one of our males is dangerous but I warned you of that."

"Justice was out with Kit. We don't have commitments. I stopped seeing him two weeks ago."

"Did you see his rage?"

"Did you see his hands all over Kit and the way she was touching him?"

"Good point." Breeze sat down. "Poor Jessie."

"You won't tell anyone, will you? Please don't."

"I won't ever do anything to harm Justice. Now it all makes sense. He is not stupid. He is Justice North."

"So a name makes him smarter?" Jessie smirked.

Breeze's mouth softened into a smile. "No. It just makes sense why he wouldn't claim you and would hide being with you. He represents us to your world and we all look up to him. He is respected greatly and appreciated for all he does." Breeze's smile faded and sadness filled her gaze. "Being with a human could harm him in many ways, Jessie."

Her shoulders slumped. "I know. I get it. I do. I remember the press went crazy when Ellie and Fury were married. It was a circus and all those hate groups were popping up on talk shows ranting about how wrong it was for them to be together. Fury and Ellie are just regular people no one knew about until then. Justice is…"

"Justice North. Everyone knows his face and name." Breeze reached over and squeezed Jessie's knee in support. "It will be big news when he takes a mate, no matter who it is. It would be more accepted in both our worlds if she were one of my kind. It's expected."

"I know." Fresh tears filled her eyes. "You're not saying anything that shocks me."

Breeze hesitated. "You told me your secrets. Can I tell you one of ours? You have to swear on your life to never tell, Jessie. This is very serious. You are in so much pain but you need to know another reason why Justice would be so set in taking one of my kind as a mate instead of you."

"I swear. What is it?"

"You know a lot about us but do you know that we can't have children?"

"Yes. I don't care about that. I'd willingly give up having a family to be with him."

"Jessie, if Justice were to take you as a mate he would have to worry about something happening that could reveal one of our most feared secrets. We have to protect ourselves from certain things getting out there. Justice is in the public eye all the time and you would be too as his mate. There would be no hiding that secret forever with the two of you. Our other mixed couples can be hidden away and no one would ask questions in your world. It will be harder with Ellie and Fury but the news of them has died down enough since they married. They also never leave Homeland or have to talk to any humans if they don't wish to."

"I don't understand. Why would the mixed couples have to be hidden?"

Breeze locked gazes with Jessie's. "Swear on your life that you will never reveal what I'm about to say. It would put many lives in danger."

"I swear."

Breeze shifted on the bed. "Remember when I said I came home because Ellie had news to share with me?"

"Yes."

"She's pregnant."

Shock tore through Jessie. "How?"

"She had sex with her mate after having a surgery to fix a blocked fallopian tube. It kept them from a successful pregnancy but now everything worked."

"But—"

"Human females and Species males can conceive a baby together. We discovered this by accident when one of your females got pregnant by one of our males. We've hidden it from humans but that baby has been born already. Our mutated genes are dominant and the infant appears fully Species. We think all the children born to mixed couples will be. If your world found out—"

"Oh God." Jessie reeled from shock. "Those hate group fanatics would go crazy. They are sure that one day you will all grow old and die off. They have bets going on when the last of you will die, like those death pools some sickos make on celebrities. They are such assholes."

"Yes. If Justice were to take a human mate that secret would come out if you were to get pregnant." Breeze hesitated. "Our doctors are working on finding out why we can't get pregnant—it's a female problem, obviously not with our males. The female reproductive system is far more complicated and we're not sure if they'll ever figure it out. We hope one day it's possible since we all want children. He would want a child too if Justice were to take you for his mate. He would have the choice. It would be hard for me to resist having a child if I could. He couldn't conceal you or that child because, as his mate, everyone would notice if you were not at his side. We hope with time that the hate groups will disband and everyone will accept our existence but right now would be a bad time to let the world know there are infant Species. We're terrified they'll become targets and we must protect them at all cost. They are our future."

Jessie closed her eyes, pain seared through her and the magnitude of Justice's position had never been clearer. "I get it. He can't ever be with me."

"He'd risk too much. It would not only put your life in danger but his own and those babies. All of your kind who mated or could mate with our males would represent the possibility of creating more of us. The hate groups would stop at nothing to prevent that."

"I get it." Her heart was breaking. She'd had hope that he'd miss her, he'd change his mind, but now that was dashed to bits. He wasn't paranoid. He'd understated the danger if anything. "It's really over between us."

"Do you want to move into the women's dorm, Jessie? Is being next door to him too hard?"

"I have to think about it."

"I have never been in love but it must be torture."

A laugh bubbled up from Jessie. "Yes. That's a perfect word to describe it."

"Justice is not serious about Kit. Sometimes he will take a female dancing or share sex if they are both interested. He never sees anyone more than once in a while. Does that help you? If he mounts Kit tonight it will just be sex. You are the female he put close to his house and slept with in a bed. He never has asked a female to do that before. I would have heard about it, and to be honest, they would have agreed to allow Justice to constrict some of their freedom. He's well respected and any female would be honored if he wanted them close to him. He feels for you. Know that and be comforted by it."

All Jessie felt was raw, horrible, gut-wrenching pain. "I need another drink."

"I will join you. I hate alcohol but we will suffer together."

"You're a great friend. Thank you."

"I'm just sorry you fell for Justice. Flame would have been a better choice and you could have had him as your mate."

* * * * *

Justice paced the living room at Reservation. Memories of Jessie haunted him. He was always given the same hotel suite when he visited, it was considered his second home and his gaze lingered on the couch where she'd given him a massage.

He missed her. It was a constant ache that never faded, a pain that made his heart hurt and a deep sadness that wouldn't leave him. Jessie Dupree had changed his life and attempting to forget her seemed impossible. He cursed, ran his fingers through his hair and hated life.

The computer screen beckoned him and he sat on the edge of the couch, close to the exact spot he'd been in when Jessie had put her hands on him. He clenched his teeth. The news had run with the story about a Species male marrying a human. They didn't know Valiant or Tammy's names but it hadn't stopped the press from going to print or television.

He read report after report of incoming phone death threats, a few copies of gate incident reports at both Homeland and Reservation when the protesters grew rowdy after hearing about the wedding and finally the assessment level the human task-force team had sent. They were at high alert for an attack.

The cell phone rang and he snatched it up, flipped it open and pressed it to his ear. "Justice here."

"Sorry to call so late," Brass said and sighed. "Were you sleeping yet? I know you just arrived an hour ago and have a meeting first thing in the morning."

"I'm still awake. What is wrong?"

The hesitation on the part of the other male made him tense. It had to be pretty bad for Brass not to want to share the information or to call him at that late hour.

"Tell me. I'll imagine far worse."

"I doubt it. Your meeting has been moved and they are coming here to your office instead of you going to them. Miles Eron called, their offices were broken into and though they didn't get access to our files, it was clearly their intent."

A headache formed and Justice leaned back, his free hand rubbing his forehead. "How do they know that? Maybe it was just a human crime."

"Miles said he keeps all our information locked in a safe and they weren't able to break into it but they spray-painted graffiti on the walls. It was geared against us."

"What did it say?"

"Just the general stuff and how they are angry that Miles and his company work for us. He said the damage was minimal but he's afraid you coming there would be a risk to your safety. He's driving here instead."

"Damn."

"They are either humans who hate us or it was vultures looking for the names of Valiant and Tammy. Some of our officers have reported that some paparazzi have come to the gates to offer them money for information on the couple. They have been heavily harassed by them all day and evening. It's ongoing. I wouldn't put it past them to break into Miles' offices and make it appear as if a hate group did it. He agreed with me and so did the police investigating since the damage wasn't bad and nothing was stolen. They targeted the safe as if they knew where to look."

"Just what we needed."

"I also have another issue."

"Terrific. What else is wrong?"

"We had two breaches at Reservation. They were caught before they cleared the walls but they did reach the top before they were apprehended. One of them had a camera and is known from his police record for trespassing to take photos of celebrities to sell to the tabloids. The second male was armed and ranting about killing the woman who would dishonor herself by allowing a minister to marry her before God. We had them both transferred to the local sheriff. One is going to jail while the other is being sent to a hospital for a mental evaluation."

"Is that all?"

"Yes."

Justice sighed loudly, thinking of Jessie again. That man with a gun could come after her if anyone found out they'd been seeing each other. It just proved being with him put her in too much danger. He might miss her and it tore him up but she was safe at least.

"Justice?"

"I'm here."

"Miles will meet you in your office here at nine o'clock. I'm sorry for disturbing you."

"It's my job."

"Good night and try to get some sleep."

"You too."

He hung up and stared at the spot where Jessie had sat on the back of the couch. His eyes closed and he allowed the pain to grip him. His fingers curled tighter around the phone. The desire to call her house was so strong he nearly gave in to it but it would only make things harder. He would talk to her tomorrow after he returned to Homeland. He'd do it before the event at the bar tomorrow night, which had been planned to help Species relations with humans.

A decision had to be made about whether he should have her continue to live in the house next to his. It was too tempting to be so close to her but the idea of Jessie anywhere else was just too hard to consider. He might not be able to be with her but knowing she was so close would have to do.

He rose to his feet, turned everything off and headed to bed. He doubted he'd sleep. His thoughts were too fractured between the safety of his people and the fact that he wished a long-haired redhead waited between his sheets.

Images filled his head of what he'd do to Jessie if she were there. He'd touch and kiss every inch of her body. His cock twitched just considering the possibility. He swore he could almost smell her. He sniffed the room, sure her real scent had long faded. No trace lingered. It was all in his head.

Some males who had mated reported being obsessed with the need to be close to their mates. It stopped him cold on his way to the bathroom. *Oh God. She's not my mate. Stop it! Don't go there! It's bad enough already without those crazy thoughts.*

He walked into the bathroom, flipped on the light and gripped the counter to lean forward. He peered deeply into his own eyes, their appearance so different from humans and a constant reminder that life had handed him difficult challenges.

If any other male had wanted to take a human for a mate he'd strongly back them on it. He'd happily deal with whatever headaches arose from the fallout. They'd plot the best way to deal with whatever threats arose and handle them. They didn't mind challenges—life would be simpler without them but they didn't shy away from battles.

Of course it hadn't been his female who'd been put in danger. Jessie would be the one with a target on her back, he'd be putting everyone out, and he'd sworn to do everything in his power to make life easier for Species. Anger tightened his hold on the edge of the counter and it cracked under his strong hands. He glanced down, saw the damage, softly cursed and released it.

Everything he touched seemed to break when it came to Jessie. His jaw clenched and a growl threatened to rise. "Not her, not for me. I won't put the woman I love in danger."

* * * * *

Three beers later Jessie knew she's passed well beyond drunk to flat-out bombed. Breeze had taken down a six-pack of beer by herself and drank most of a bottle of wine she'd found buried at the bottom of the fridge. Breeze studied Jessie.

"I've been thinking."

"I can't stand up."

Breeze laughed. "Lightweight. Justice deserves you. You are wonderful and you deserve a good male as your mate. He should take a chance and so should you. Maybe your world won't be as opposed to the idea as Justice thinks. For the most part they took it well when Ellie and Fury married. It was bumpy at first but it seemed your kind loved them after Fury nearly died protecting Ellie. Maybe they will one day find out about our children and not be disagreeable. Who really could hate a cute little baby? You and Justice deserve to be together and be happy."

"He won't think so and I don't like the part about Fury nearly dying. I don't want Justice to be shot."

"Our males are stubborn sometimes and set in their ways. They won't see reason when they should. We should make him see that he should be with you despite causing some trouble."

Breeze blurred as Jessie watched her, pretty sure it was her eyesight and not the woman melting. "I don't think that's going to happen. He doesn't listen well."

"There is a party tomorrow night at the bar we went to tonight. I'm going to get you invited, Jessie. You are going to get dressed up and show Justice that he can't ignore you."

Jessie laughed and nearly fell out of the chair. She gripped the table to keep upright. One hand missed and she hit her thigh.

"Jessie? Look at me."

Jessie did. "Which one of you? There are two."

Breeze shook with laughter. It made Jessie feel motion sick and she groaned.

"Don't worry. I will take care of all of it. We will make Justice realize you are the female for him. You won't cry anymore."

"What does that mean?"

Breeze looked thoughtful. "I hope you are not shy."

"Shy?" Jessie suffered a bout of lightheadedness. She tried to shift on her seat but slumped over.

Breeze laughed as she caught Jessie before she hit the floor. "Lightweight," she chuckled, lifting her and tossing her over her shoulder. Breeze carried her into her bedroom and dumped her on the bed. "Now let's see if you own anything sexy." She approached the closet, a determined look on her face.

Chapter Seventeen

ε

"My head," Jessie groaned.

Breeze laughed, making her head hurt worse. She'd swallowed two aspirin and prayed desperately they would work soon. It felt as if someone were using a jackhammer behind her forehead.

"You should never drink." Breeze chuckled.

"Stop laughing. Please? It hurts."

"I had to carry you to bed."

"I don't remember anything past the second beer. How many did I have?"

"Many more but I drank three times what you did. I didn't pass out. I tried to get you to drink wine after the beer was gone but you just said there were two of me."

"Thanks for putting me in bed."

"I brought you something."

"What? Hopefully it's a shot to knock me back out."

Breeze walked out of the bathroom where Jessie soaked in the tub and returned carrying a dress bag in her arms. "It's a dress and everything that goes with it. Ellie helped me find you something pretty to wear. You are her size but your boobs are larger. This will fit."

"I don't wear dresses but thank you. Was I rambling about the damn things last night or something?"

"You will wear this tonight."

Jessie frowned. "Why? What is tonight?"

"You are going to a party with me. Don't you remember?"

Jessie shook her head and regretted it immediately. Movement was bad. "What party?"

Breeze grinned. "This is going to really be good. You don't remember us talking about it." Her laugh sounded again. "You are going to a Species party as my guest. Other humans will be there and it will be fun."

"I don't think so, Breeze. Justice was pretty clear that I'm banned from Species social gatherings and my head hurts so bad I just want to climb back into bed until next week."

"I have made all the arrangements and you're going. It is a done deal."

"Did I mention I don't wear dresses? My father is a senator and he dragged me to so many benefits growing up that I can't stand the sight of them." Some of the pain in her skull eased, a sign the pills were working and she peered at Breeze warily. "Plus, you know someone is going to mention to Justice at some point that I went to that party. I don't want to fight with him. When we talk I don't want there to be yelling involved."

Breeze sat on the counter. "This one you will go to and you will wear a dress. I want you to put on makeup the way your women do and we'll have fun. It is settled and I'll howl if you argue. I'm mixed with canine and have been practicing." She grinned, obviously proud of that. "It's loud enough to make your ears want to bleed, so shut up, my friend. Now I will wash your hair for you and you will get out of the tub before your skin wrinkles. We only have a few hours to get ready since you slept all day."

"What time is it?"

"Four in the afternoon."

Jessie groaned. "It can't be. I had to work today."

"I told Ellie you would not be in today. She went on the internet, sent a human to pick up the things she chose from the outside and they delivered it all to the gate. She bought you everything for tonight. I had to come get one of your shoes and look at your bra to get your sizes. I hope you don't mind but I borrowed your key to the front door. We went to a lot of trouble so don't argue, Jessie. You are going to that party if I have to carry you. I did it last night and I'll do it again. Now, scoot away from the edge and let's wash your hair."

Two hours later Jessie felt a hundred times better. The aspirin had fully kicked in, the bath had helped and the headache was just a memory. Breeze had gotten ready with Jessie for the party, almost fearful she'd bolt. She admitted she might have been tempted if the taller woman hadn't kept her within eyesight at all times.

Jessie gawked at her reflection and tried to hide her dismay. Breeze preened from her side, happy as could be by the look of it. The dress was too tight, revealed way too much cleavage with the plunging neckline and the handkerchief skirt flashed too much leg.

"Ellie picked out this dress?" She glanced at Breeze for confirmation.

"I told her I wanted you to look very sexy and nice. She said that dress would make every male notice you. I think it's perfect but I wish you'd put your hair up in one of those nice buns your women wear. I see them do that on television when they go to nice parties." She stepped closer. "The makeup hid the marks Justice left on you so there's no reason to have your hair fall over your shoulders."

"I like it down. It's long enough that it gives me a headache if I put it on top of my head for more than a few hours."

"You look good." Breeze shot her a grin. "Everyone will think so."

Or they'll mistake me for a hooker. She refrained from saying that aloud, not wanting to explain the definition to Breeze or hurt her feelings. The party seemed to mean a lot to her friend and for that alone she'd put up and shut up.

"I hope there's no dancing." Jessie looked down at her exposed cleavage. "This dress wouldn't survive anything other than slow dancing without getting me arrested for indecent exposure. I'm afraid to take a deep breath in case my breasts spill out. I think I have another bra that isn't a push-up."

"You're not changing a thing that Ellie picked for you to wear. She knows what she is doing and she went to a lot of trouble for us. There will be dancing but no one said you had to participate. You have a great body and you look wonderful. You don't have our muscles and you're pale but you have nothing to hide away, Jessie. What is that saying? If you have it, flaunt it? You have it, wear it proudly."

Jessie suddenly frowned, studying Breeze. Her inner alarms warned her that something was up. "What are you plotting? You're too pleased with yourself and you have this glint in your eyes."

"Nothing." Breeze glanced away, looked everywhere but at Jessie and fidgeted with her hands.

"Is Justice going to be there?" It was the worst scenario she could think of. "I was told he is at Reservation by his secretary when she called here to explain that our meeting was canceled. He must have told her we had one because he sure wouldn't have mentioned he was coming here to yell at me over last night."

"He was delayed by some issue at Reservation." Breeze met her gaze and held it. "It would be interesting if he had been able to attend. Every male will be looking at you and will want to mount you."

Jessie sighed. "I don't want a repeat of last night ever again. It was embarrassing to be treated like a five-year-old being sent to her room. He caused a scene on the dance floor with Flame when he prevented me from leaving with him."

That mischievous gleam returned to Breeze's dark eyes. "That won't happen tonight. Justice won't be able to yell if males dance with you and wish you'd share sex with them."

"Breeze, you had Ellie pick this dress on purpose just to piss Justice off if men hit on me, didn't you? He'll hear about it and hit the roof."

Breeze wouldn't look at her but her grin widened.

"Breeze!"

"It will be good for him. He made you cry. You will make him angry and he won't be able to do a thing about it tonight. The Council and all our people except those working security will be there and he has no logical reason to say you shouldn't go to the party. This is your night to get even, Jessie. Justice will have to hold his temper in check even if it kills him when he discovers you're there. You can flirt and dance with all the males you want and he'll suffer wondering if one of them will win your attention. It will be good for him to learn what it is like when he finds out how attractive you are to our males. Think of how you felt, knowing he took Kit dancing. I bet after tonight he will learn to never go out with other females again. For that reason alone you should do this, Jessie."

Jessie sighed. "I don't want him to get really upset."

"Our men don't get upset. They get angry, blow up, but they recover from it quickly. The way to get even with one of our males is to piss him off and do it when he can't retaliate. He will learn this way and remember."

"You mean he can't retaliate tonight. What about tomorrow? His secretary said he'd be back in the morning."

"You are sleeping in the women's dorm tonight. I'm not stupid. I thought of this. We are having a slumber party in the library of the dorm and you have been invited. It will last for days. I packed your pajamas in the bag already. By the time you come home, he will have cooled down and learned his lesson."

Jessie chewed on her bottom lip, considering it. "Are you sure?"

259

She had to admit it was tempting. Justice would blow a fuse when he got the call that she was at the party and had disobeyed his orders. He did deserve a little grief.

Breeze smiled. "Don't worry about Justice. I promise one way or another, he will have cooled off by the time he gets you alone. Our men don't stay angry for long. Let's go. I don't want to be late." She gripped her arm and tugged. "I'm driving."

Breeze parked down the street from the bar. Jessie climbed out of the golf cart and met Breeze on the sidewalk. "The party is being held at the bar?"

"It is where all of our social gatherings are held."

"What's the occasion? I forgot to ask."

"We do this every once in a while. It is good for us to mingle with each other and humans. It is one of the things that Ellie thought up to help bridge the gap between our differences and it has gone over well. We have had two of them in the last year. They are fun and liked by the humans we associate with and our people." She hesitated. "I'm surprised you haven't been to one. You worked with the human task force and they are invited."

"My boss never told me. Tim kind of babied me."

"What does that mean?"

"He's protective and treats me like I'm his daughter. He probably didn't invite me, thinking men would hit on me."

"Oh. That's valid." Breeze walked faster toward the door. "Hurry up. Some Species come from Reservation too, just to attend. They don't have the large building at Reservation to do this. We have the sleeping dorms and can always fit more people here comfortably. They can stay for days. Some of the males and females you helped rescue in Colorado will be here too. We wanted them to share the joy of freedom with us."

The part about the freed Species from the Colorado testing facility filled Jessie with a little dread, remembering her attack but she figured it would be fine. Other humans would be there which meant they were prepared to deal nicely with them. Breeze waved her inside.

The music pumped loudly through the large area and flashing lights had been turned on over the dance floor. The place was packed with people—the women wore nice dresses and the males sported suits or nice casual slacks with dress shirts.

"The council is here too. I'll introduce you later." Breeze had to yell over the noises. "They are friendly."

Jessie had never met the four male council members. Each one represented one of the testing facilities and the Species who'd been detained inside each of them. Jessie guessed that they would soon have a fifth council member from the newly discovered Colorado facility if they didn't already.

Breeze gripped her hand. "Come. Let's dance!"

She spotted Trey, her old team leader and a few of the task-force members sitting at the bar. "Hang on. I see some friends. Do you want to meet the guys I used to work with?"

"Not now." Breeze tugged on her again. "Let's dance. Say hello to them later when we are thirsty and want a drink. We'll sit and talk."

Jessie sure didn't want to drink after her hellacious hangover. The team would be there for hours, the night was still young and the party had just started. It wasn't as if she had a choice as her friend's grip tightened and Breeze dragged her onto the dance floor into a sea of moving bodies.

Jessie was short but she saw a few shorter women on the dance floor. Tiny and Beauty were sort of dancing together. Beauty grinned, stood on the dance floor as Tiny danced around her and watched everyone else dance. Jessie laughed, happy not to see fear on the other woman's face while in the midst of such a large crowd of people.

A few things became apparent to Jessie about Species as she danced in a group of them. They danced together but not as couples for the most part, just grouped together with everyone. She relaxed more and just went with the music. Breeze leaned in.

"Teach me something sexy."

Jessie stopped swaying to the beat. "Like what?"

"That thing you were doing while you were dancing with Flame the other night." Breeze backed up and held up her arms to wiggle her hips. "This move."

Jessie slid her arms up and showed her. She did a turn and swayed her hips, something she'd learned in a belly dancing class years before. Breeze mimicked her and so did a few of the other women nearby. She showed them what she knew, happy to teach them. Breeze moved closer.

"Do this." Breeze showed her some moves.

Jessie was having the time of her life. She danced from one male to the next, something they all did, as the songs changed. Another song came on and a male gripped her waist from behind. Jessie spun away from the Species she'd just danced with to dance with another one, grateful not to be home dwelling on Justice. Going out seemed to be the perfect solution to getting over the man she loved.

Justice hadn't felt like attending the party but it was expected. Kit had asked to be his date but he'd turned her down. She'd hinted that she would consider being his mate last night when he'd taken her to dinner. She'd made it clear he could share sex with her at the very least and he'd regretted agreeing to take her out. He'd just done it because he'd thought that being with someone to talk to for the evening would distract him from obsessive thoughts about Jessie and ease everyone's worry if he appeared happy. Instead of being a friend, Kit had tried to seduce him.

The four council members sat at a table with him and he studied them. They wanted more control and for him to hand off some of his duties to them. He'd readily agreed to a morning meeting to discuss the matter, looking forward to handing off some of his responsibilities. It would help him by allowing him to work fewer hours and make them feel as if they were doing more for their kind.

His thoughts drifted to Jessie again. Last night he'd barely slept and when he had, it had been to suffer dreams where she was in his bed under him. Waking alone with a raging hard-on hadn't made for a pleasant morning. He'd showered and gone to the office only to get into an argument with Miles.

Miles had brought the woman who dyed Justice's hair and his annoying assistant, Tonya, who had hit on Justice previously. She was an aggressive female who tried to lure Species males into her bed. He always felt hunted when he had to deal with her. He pitied the fool who took that one on. She had a mean heart, cold eyes and calculated her actions as if everything were a game.

"What has that irritated expression on your face?" The deep voice belonged to Jaded.

He lifted his gaze to stare into the bright green eyes of the council member. "Do you see my hair?"

"It's lighter. That shade of brown isn't your color." The other guy grinned and touched his own jet-black strands. "This looks much better on you."

"Stop teasing him," Cedar, the other council member, ordered softly, his voice deceptively cool. "He does a lot for us and I'm sure the stench of whatever they used is bothering him more than us. I can smell it from across the table."

Someone approached and distracted Justice from their teasing. He knew it was to lighten his mood but he doubted anything could. Tim Oberto smiled as he paused by the table.

"Thank you for inviting us, Justice." He glanced at the council members before directing his attention once more on the NSO leader. "You still haven't given me the name of the replacement I need. We have a few leads we're looking into and I want a New Species onboard before we have a retrieval target to locate."

Brawn leaned forward. "Replacement?"

"I'm sorry, Tim." Justice had a lot on his mind. "Tim wants one of our males to join the team that makes first contact if a Gift Female is found." He met the human's gaze. "I promise that tomorrow I'll go over the files, find someone who is good with human interaction and who will volunteer to live on the outside. I assume you have a plan to keep them safe while living there?"

"I do."

"I'll choose someone and he'll contact you by the end of business day tomorrow."

"Good enough." Tim glanced at the council members. "Gentlemen." He fled.

Brawn chuckled. "He doesn't know us or he'd never use that term when referring to anyone at this table but Justice."

Justice's thoughts drifted to Jessie again. After the party he planned to jump the back wall, talk her in to allowing him inside her home and they were going to talk. She would not share sex with anyone but him. That was just how it was going to be or he'd kill the male. He had a plan. They'd swear not to date others. It would keep him from committing murder and he'd never have to see that hurt look in her eyes that he'd seen when she'd realized he'd taken Kit out.

"Speaking of not being gentlemen, I love human women." Jaded chuckled. "There is something that makes me so hard when I see them. I don't know if it is because they are so different from our females or if it is because they are just so different from us."

Cedar laughed. "I am hard right now watching the human I danced with before I came to the table. I'm still having fantasies about her small hands brushing over my body. I know they would feel so good touching me. Her skin was so creamy and while their faces are strange, hers made me think her beautiful."

"I see the one," Bestial said and nodded. "I would like to take that dress off her and see if she is creamy colored everywhere." He growled. "Who is she?" Bestial pointedly stared at Justice. "Who is the human out there? I want her name so when I go after her I have an advantage. I think her thighs would fit perfectly over my shoulders."

The males laughed while Justice shook his head at Bestial, in amusement. "It is probably Ellie you are speaking of. They are here tonight since she's not showing enough for strangers to notice yet. You should stop. She's mated to Fury and he would put your own thighs around your shoulders before he stuffed you into a bag to send you home to Reservation for looking at his female. The only other human female who would be here is the new doctor I hired. She is attractive and single but I don't think she's prepared for you. She's a bit timid."

Bestial pointed. "What is her name? She's going to make me break the zipper of my pants if she keeps shaking that sweet ass much longer."

Justice grinned and turned in his seat enough to follow the direction of the council member's finger. He'd met the new doctor, Allison Baker, a week before. She was sweet, a bit shy and soft spoken. Someone as gruff as Bestial trying to seduce her into sharing sex would be outright funny. He just hoped the poor thing didn't quit her new job out of fear, not realizing she was in no danger.

The human was easy to spot with her shorter, smaller body and shock tore through him when he realized the source of Bestial's erection. Her black dress only enhanced the brightness of her hair that fell to her ass. Her pale skin nearly glowed in comparison to the tanned Species next to her. Jessie was out there and it was her sweet ass Bestial was fantasizing about. Rage tore through him instantly and he couldn't breathe.

She danced between two Species males, too close not to avoid brushing against them, and as he watched, she placed her hands on the chest of the one facing her. Justice drew in air to his starving lungs, a haze of red nearly blinded him and he remained frozen. Humans were present, the entire task team, some of the staff they'd kept on at Homeland and the medical personnel, including the new doctor.

He forced his body to relax. It took every ounce of his control not to lunge out of the chair but he tried to be rational. She was dancing with males, not sharing sex with them. It was a party. She wasn't in danger of going home with one and she sure wouldn't be either. He needed to think of a way to get her home without causing a scene. His gaze darted around, searching for Breeze. He'd have a word with her in private, say Jessie was in danger and order her to escort her home.

"See what I mean?" Cedar chuckled. "I danced with her. She has the smallest and most delicate hands. I'd like her to run them over me. Human hands are soft. They don't have the roughness of calluses. I bet it feels better to be stroked with soft hands."

"I like the way she moves." Bestial growled again. "Imagine having that under you."

Justice didn't have to imagine. He knew what it was like to have Jessie pinned under him. Rage flooded him again and he directed a glare at the four council members. They ignored him to stare at Jessie as though she were a rabbit they wanted to hunt down and eat. He clenched his teeth.

"She's taken. Forget it." Justice managed to keep his tone human.

Bestial glanced at him. "By one of ours?"

Justice said nothing, too busy fighting his rage.

Bestial shrugged, staring toward Jessie again. "I will show her how much better I am than her human lover. He is stupid to allow her to go anywhere without him. I would be dancing with her in my arms, making sure no one else touched her. Her human lover is too dumb to keep her."

Cedar laughed. "What if she is married?"

"They have divorce. Human males are too weak to keep a female." Bestial pointed. "That's a female I would keep."

"You'd mate her?" Cedar glanced at the woman. "Yeah. If I were to mate a human that would be the one. I could spend the rest of my life mounting her."

Jaded spoke low. "Imagine her swollen with a child. Now I'm really hard."

Brawn, the last council member, rumbled, "I would love to possess a woman that fully. I would want to taste her breast milk. Now that you pointed her out, Bestial, thanks. I think I will go see if she finds cats sexy." Brawn stood.

Justice had to keep a tight leash on his rage. "She works and lives here. Sit down."

"Good." Brawn grinned. "She won't have far to move when I take her to my bed. She's a keeper."

"You don't know her. She could be annoying." Justice felt his control slipping.

"I wouldn't care. Look at her." Brawn met Justice's glare. "I'm going to claim her by the end of the night." He flashed his fangs. "I'll take her home, mount her, fuck her until she screams my name and keep doing it until she swells with what's mine."

Justice growled loudly and slowly rose to his feet. His eyes narrowed and every muscle in his body tensed. Brawn continued to smile, seemingly unaware of the danger, but the other three council members stood to put distance between them and the table.

"Is there a problem, Justice?" Brawn arched an eyebrow. "You look upset."

"Don't go near her," Justice snarled.

Brawn cocked his head, still smiling. "Is there a reason I can't?"

"She works here."

Brawn shrugged. "She doesn't belong to any Species and that makes her fair game. It's not like I'm planning on playing with her. You know her father, right?"

"Yes and I swore I'd protect her."

"I'm going to claim her so there's nothing to protect her from. I'll make her mine, fill her with my seed and it will plant there. She'll make an excellent mate and mother to my young."

A roar tore from Justice's throat and he flipped the table over so it wasn't between him and Brawn anymore. The people around them started, stopped talking and quickly backed away from the two tense males. Justice's hands fisted at his sides, his breathing increased to a pant and his fangs were revealed when he sneered at the council member who wanted his woman. Brawn took a cautious step back.

"Brawn," Cedar urged softly "you've gone far enough."

Brawn watched Justice, took another step backward to put more space between them and shifted his gaze to the overturned table. "If not tonight, perhaps another." He lowered his chin to his chest, kept his gaze down and withdrew farther until he spun on his heel and disappeared into the group near the bar.

Justice studied his people after he fought back the urge to track Brawn and beat on him. The verbal claim he'd tried to make on Jessie was enough justification to pound his fists into that smug face. Species stared at him with nervous, confused glances as they watched him silently, refusing to make direct eye contact. It had been apparent he'd almost fought with a council member. No one approached him, his rage still evident and the remaining council members edged farther away.

His gaze turned to the dance floor. Jessie and the other people out there were oblivious to the tense situation, the music having covered the sounds of the altercation. The sight of her body rubbing against a male shot his rage higher. He fought back another roar, panted and stood there until he leashed his inner beast. Otherwise someone would die. He knew how dangerous he was in that condition, not to only his female but his people.

Slow, deep breaths helped. His fingers unfurled and he sealed his lips over his fangs. Jessie needed to leave, to stop allowing other males so close to her or he'd cause a scene worse than the one he just had.

It's going to be a miracle if I can get her out of here before blood is spilled. That possibility helped calm him more.

Chapter Eighteen

℅

Jessie turned when the hand gripped her waist with force. The male was a little aggressive to hold her that tightly while dancing but she knew no one would hurt her. She looked up and gasped. Justice glowered at her. He was at the party and he didn't seem happy to see her, judging by the way rage glinted in his dark eyes. She glanced down when his other hand reached out and both of them locked around her hips. He wore a dark-navy suit, a black, silk tie and appeared civilized from the neck down.

"You need to go home right now."

Jessie met his gaze again, taking in the extent of his anger as she studied his harsh features. *He's livid.* His nose flared, he softly growled and his fingers tightened their hold, to confirm her assessment. She frantically turned her head to search over her shoulder, spotted Breeze and didn't see surprise on her face. She had a sinking feeling that her friend had set her up and had known Justice would be at the party.

"You are leaving," Justice demanded harshly, his voice gravel rough.

Breeze stopped dancing, shook her head and gave her a fist sign. Her dark gaze flicked around the dance floor, and she winked when she glanced back at Jessie. She smiled, almost seeming to want to assure Jessie she was safe.

"Jessie? Did you hear me? Look at me now."

She turned her head back, stared up at Justice and frowned. He wouldn't dare create another scene similar to the last one. Other humans were there and he'd have to back off if she stood up to him. He was mad she'd been dancing. It didn't take a genius to figure out he probably didn't approve of how she was dressed and he wanted her out of the bar.

"No. I'm having fun and I'm not leaving. Humans are welcome at this party and I was invited."

His eyes narrowed and his fingers flexed on her hips. "I won't tell you again. Go home."

Her anger stirred. "Look, if you want to dance, ask me and we'll do that. Otherwise release me so I can have some fun. That's all I'm doing. I came with Breeze and I'm leaving with her." Her voice lowered. "There's no need for this chest-beating routine, so knock it off. It's not as though I'm allowing any of the men to run their hands all over my body the way you let Kit do to yours. None of them are grinding their hips against my ass."

He jerked his hands away from her body as if she'd burned him, backed up and his eyes widened with shock at her refusal to obey or her blatantly calling him out about the previous night. Jessie turned away, presented him with her back and stepped closer to Breeze. It didn't surprise her in the least that he'd refused to dance with her. It was too public, people would see him with his arms around her and that wasn't something he'd do. At least not with a human. She wondered if Kit was around again, to paw him and rub her body against his.

She reached Breeze, frowned and shot her a dirty look. The Species smiled in response but her gaze lifted to stare at something behind Jessie. All the color drained from her face and she nearly stumbled into another dancer in her haste to put space between them.

What the hell? Jessie spun around to see what had obviously frightened Breeze and slammed into a solid body draped in an expensive, soft suit. She glanced down at his hands clenched at his sides, her chin jerked up, and on the journey to peer at his face she noticed his extremely tense stance. Rage showed in his eyes as their gazes met, his lips parted and he flashed the sharp points of his teeth.

"I said go home."

"Stand up for yourself," Breeze called out just loud enough to be heard over the beat of the song. "Don't bully her, Justice."

Yeah. Stand up for yourself. This is bullshit and while he's my boss, I'm off the clock. She straightened her shoulders and didn't look away from his hostile glare.

"Thank you for your concern but I'm safe and having fun with my friends. With your busy schedule, I'm sure you should be doing something besides harassing me. This is a dance floor so dance or leave it. I already know the answer to that so good night, Mr. North."

"Jessie," he snarled, "go home."

Movement from the corner of her eye caught her attention. She flicked her gaze to the right, inwardly winced when she realized that not only were the other people keeping a wide berth but they'd stopped dancing to openly watch her and Justice. She turned her head to the left and found more people staring at them from the bar area.

Jessie stared up at Justice, hated him a little for doing this and realized he wasn't going to stop until she left. It would definitely be as embarrassing as the last time, perhaps even worse, and she felt her temper slipping. She closed her eyes, took deep breaths and counted slowly to ten. *One. Two. Three. Four. Fi –*

"Jessie? Move your ass out the door and go home. Don't come to this bar ever again."

That was it. Jessie's eyes snapped open and she gave up on trying to keep it cool. "I work for you but this is my time off. I know everyone is afraid of you because you're Justice North but guess what? You're not my leader. I quit if this is how you're going to treat me every time I go somewhere. Will that make you happy? I'll go home and pack right now. I don't need this, Mr. North. I'll be off Homeland within the hour and you won't have to watch out for me ever again."

Jessie spun and stomped across the dance floor toward the door. New Species moved far out of her way, making her feel as if she'd suddenly contracted leprosy, the way they cleared a wide path to avoid getting within ten feet of her. She was so enraged that tears threatened to spill but she held them back. She wouldn't give him the satisfaction of seeing how deeply he'd affected her.

Son of a bitch! I just quit my job. I loved working with the women and living in that house. No more soaking in that glorious tub but that's fine. I'll get another job and Justice can go screw himself. He —

"Jessie?" Justice snarled.

She jerked to a halt, shocked at the loudness of his voice and turned. The last bit of her restraint snapped. Anger burned brightly and she was done dealing with his temper tantrum. She loved him but he was being a complete ass. She wasn't taking that shit from any man, even him.

"What?"

He'd followed her and only feet separated them when he paused to glare, seemingly oblivious to the people who gawked. She wished she could forget that probably two hundred Species and dozens of humans were witnessing this argument. The music cut off and the room grew as quiet as a church all of a sudden. *Shit.*

"Come here."

She stared, stunned. "Excuse me?"

"Come here." He pointed to the floor in front of him.

Oh, hell no. She spun and headed for the door again. If he wanted to yell, he could do it without an audience. Maybe it was a Species thing to verbally ream someone's ass in public when they were angry but she wasn't going to walk over to him to take that kind of treatment.

Someone moved into her path and she winced. Tim Oberto looked thunderous as she met his furious gaze, certain he'd shout at her once they were outside for mouthing off to the precious NSO leader. He blocked the door and there wouldn't be a way to avoid him.

Trey stepped next her old boss, gripped him by his arm and hissed something in his ear. Her teammates drew in closer to the two men, shooting nervous glances around them and the tension was clear in their faces. They were expecting trouble and wanted an out from the building. It was standard operating procedure.

Jessie wanted to scream in frustration and anger. *How could my night turn so bad, so fast?* She and Breeze were going to have words. She was sure the woman had meant well but all she'd accomplished was to get Jessie into a ton of trouble. Her father would hear about this and he'd probably lecture her about disrespect, tell her she should have left the first time Justice had asked and she'd just have to silently take it without protesting unless she told her father the truth. That wouldn't go over well. Her dad wouldn't be happy that she'd slept with Justice. He always preferred to pretend she was a little girl instead of a woman with needs.

"Get back here!" Justice roared.

Jessie's heart raced, she halted again and wasn't sure what to do. Everyone in the room had heard him. *Hell, they probably heard him at the front entry gate.* It stunned her that he'd make such a huge spectacle out of their argument. Everyone was going to be talking about it for weeks, if not months. Jessie turned slowly. Justice stood in the same spot as before, he hadn't moved an inch and his finger still pointed at the floor where he wanted her to be.

She took a deep breath and clenched her teeth as she slowly put one foot in front of the other. His finger relaxed, fell to his side and his other hand unclenched from a fist. She paused three feet in front of him to stare up into his exotic eyes.

"What? You're causing a scene. You told me to leave and I am." She kept her voice soft and hoped no one could hear her.

"You never do what I tell you." He didn't lower his voice, spoke loud and clear, and the sound easily carried across the room.

Jessie dropped her gaze to his black tie, remembering to avoid eye contact now that she had calmed a little. She didn't want to challenge him. She doubted it could get any worse but she wasn't about to test that theory.

"I'm doing what you want, leaving. I'm going home to pack." She kept her voice low. "Everyone is staring at us. I wish a hole could open up under me to get me out of here and I refuse to allow you to humiliate me ever again."

Jessie turned and made it three feet before Justice grabbed her. He spun her around by her elbow and his other arm wrapped around her waist. She gasped when he yanked her up against his body. Jessie jerked her head up to stare at him with shocked, wide eyes. He jerked her tighter against his long frame, pinned her flush to him and released her elbow. That hand drove into her hair at the base of her neck, fisted a handful of it and gently pulled until her head tilted back.

"What are you doing?" she hissed. "Have you lost your mind?"

Justice leaned his face closer, peered deeply into her eyes and all the anger faded from his. "I almost lost something. I'm doing what I should have done from the beginning."

Jessie flattened her palms on his chest to gently push away but his arm didn't loosen around her waist. "What are you talking about?"

His voice came out a husky rumble. "I'm claiming you publicly, Jessie. I'm letting everyone know you are mine."

Jessie was glad he held her because her knees gave out under her. His strong arm kept her from collapsing to the floor as she reeled from his words, her mind fumbling with the meaning behind them.

"But…" She couldn't find words.

"I nearly lost you." His voice grew gruff, louder and he rumbled the words, "You're not walking out of my life. You're mine, Jessie. You belong with me."

He ran his tongue over his lips, his gaze dropped to her mouth and she realized he intended to kiss her as he slowly dipped his head closer. She couldn't move, too astonished to do anything more than watch his mouth descend closer to hers.

His lips brushed hers and she closed her eyes, tense. Justice's tongue swept inside, forced her mouth open wider and he growled. The passion he hit her with overwhelmed her in seconds. She melted against him, her fingers gripped the lapels of his jacket and fisted the expensive material just for something to cling to. It had been weeks since he'd touched her, her body remembered and missed his touch and everything faded except Justice.

She kissed him back, meeting his need with her own and moaned against his tongue. The hand gripping her hair loosened to cradle the back of her head and Jessie forgot about the room full of people witnessing them entangled in the middle of the room. She forgot she was mad at him. There was just them, they were together and he didn't want her to leave him. Her hands released his shirt to slide up around his neck and her feet left the floor as Justice lifted her higher up his body.

Justice finally broke the kiss. Dazed, Jessie stared up at him, panting, her body turned-on and then she remembered where they were. A blush heated her cheeks and she didn't dare look away from his sexy gaze as they stared at each other. She wasn't prepared to deal with the reactions of the room. The only thing that mattered was right in front of her, holding her tightly.

Justice looked away from her and adjusted his hold until he swept her up into his arms to cradle her against his chest with her legs hooked over one of his strong arms. She clung to his neck and realized he'd carefully captured her skirt when he'd lifted her legs to keep her from flashing anyone. She braved glancing around to see what he did. Every face, both human and Species, appeared utterly stunned.

"This is Jessie." Justice paused, turned his head and seemed to want to address everyone. "She's human. I know some might have a problem with that. I'm sorry if you do but I won't give her up regardless of your reactions. She's mine and she's going to be my mate."

Jessie was glad he held her. Her arms tightened around his neck and she darted a glance at her old boss. Tim's mouth hung open, his face was red and his eyes were filled with disbelief. She quickly glanced away. Trey still gripped the older man's arm, jerked hard on him to move him away from blocking the door and her old team leader smiled when he caught her eye. He dragged Tim toward the bar, waving the rest of the team back with a jerk of his head.

"I know it's going to cause problems with some humans because of my position." Justice paused and Jessie stared into his eyes. He glanced away. "I'm more than willing to step down if that is what you think should happen. Just let me know tomorrow after you make a decision. Right now I'm taking my mate home to make wedding plans. Have a great party and have fun." He strode for the door.

"Justice?"

Justice stopped walking, his hold on her tightened and he slowly turned to acknowledge the deep male voice that had called out his name. Jessie studied the room, searching all the faces for the speaker. A tall male stepped forward—a big guy with a broad chest and massive arms. His catlike eyes locked on Justice as he lifted a hand to brush back straight black hair from his ear. Justice growled low, a threatening sound, and Jessie didn't need to be told he was ready to fight.

"You may have the job if you want it, Brawn. I won't fight you and put my mate in danger."

"We welcome your mate," Brawn announced loudly. "No one could take your place so don't expect a call tomorrow asking you to step down. She'll make a welcome addition to our family." His cat eyes focused on Jessie. "I don't want to fight him but I do admit to being a little envious. Take care of him, Justice's mate."

Jessie was too stunned to reply but Justice didn't have that problem.

"Thank you."

The man lowered his head and his gaze toward the floor. Justice turned away and strode quickly for the door. An officer rushed to it, smiled and held it open wide to allow him to carry her out into the night air.

"I can't believe you just did that," Jessie whispered.

Justice grinned when he glanced at her. "Me neither, but I'm glad I did. I'm taking you home to pack your belongings. You're moving into my house tonight and you're never leaving." He stopped walking and his gaze held hers. "We're getting married and that isn't up for debate."

"You could ask me." Amusement filled her, and happiness.

He cocked his head. "I could." He looked away, laughed and carried her to his Jeep to deposit her in the passenger seat.

Jessie heard the music start up again inside the bar as the man she loved jumped into the driver's seat. He tore off his tie and turned in his seat to dangle it between them.

"Before you answer, let me tell you a few things. I won't take no for an answer. I will use this to bind you to my bed until you change your mind if you don't answer the way I want you to." He chuckled again. "Will you marry me?"

She grinned. "I don't know." Her attention fixed on the tie for a few seconds before she met his gaze again. "I might be tempted to say no just to get you to tie me to your bed. It sounds fun and kinky."

"Jessie," he purred.

"Yes."

"Yes to your name or yes you will marry me?"

She bit her lip, giving him a teasing look. "I'm still thinking about what you'll do to me when you have me naked and bound on the bed. Give me a minute."

He dropped the tie into his lap and started the Jeep. "We'll settle this at home."

She laughed. "So, if I'm your mate doesn't that mean I get to keep my house? You had it built for whoever that would be. That would make it mine still to live in."

He shook his head. "I had it built for a Species mate. You will live with me and sleep in my bed every night or I'll burn that house down."

"But it's such a beautiful house."

He turned his head to grin at her. "You should hate to see it destroyed. Remember that if you ever think about leaving my bed for your old one."

"I'll marry you."

"I wasn't worried. I was serious about tying you to my bed until you changed your mind. I told you it wasn't up for debate."

* * * * *

Breeze approached the table slowly, glanced at the four males sitting there and put her hands behind her back. She waited until she had their full attention before she spoke.

"Thank you," she said softly, sincerely.

"You said he cared for her," Brawn grumbled. "You didn't tell me he was obsessed to the point of going feral. He nearly took my head off when I told him I planned to claim her."

Cedar laughed. "He might not have overturned the table or wanted to tear your head off if you'd *just* said you were going to claim her. Breeze asked to make him jealous to get him to admit to his feelings for the human. You provoked him into wanting to kill you."

Bestial grinned. "I did like the part about taking her home, mounting her and fucking her until she screamed. Justice sure didn't, but I was amused."

Jaded chuckled. "Yes. Let's not forget that classic line that finally broke his barely contained control. What did you say, Brawn? You were going to fill her with your seed and plant it? That was a nice touch."

Breeze reached out and squeezed Brawn's wide shoulder. "You said all that to him?"

He sipped his juice. "I about lost my head. As your councilperson, I'm here for you always when you need a favor. Next time though, warn me if you might get me killed so I at least see it coming. I expected anger but he honestly wanted to rip me to shreds. Next time you need a favor, I want to be the Species who lies for you and makes the call, pretending to be Justice's secretary."

Breeze stepped closer to his chair. "You're my hero. Would you like to dance? You feel tense and I know how to relieve that."

Brawn's gaze widened and he grinned. "I would love to."

Breeze lifted her fingertips to rub the exposed skin at his neck. "Let's go."

Brawn stood and winked at the other three men. "Risking my ass paid off, so don't laugh too hard. You sit here while I dance with a beautiful female."

"We helped," Bestial said and laughed. "Do you have any friends who want to dance with us?"

Breeze wiggled her finger at them. "It's party night. We're all in the mood to have some fun."

Cedar stood. "Good deeds do pay off."

Jaded finished his drink and stood. "I love party night."

"Me too," Bestial growled. "Let's go have a few hours of fun with our females."

Chapter Nineteen

❧

Jessie zipped her gym bag but Justice took it from her before she could lift it from the bed. She grinned, amused that he'd really driven her straight to the house to pack. He'd helped by bagging everything inside the bathroom and had taken most of it next door already.

"I could have done this tomorrow when you're at work."

"I want it settled tonight." Justice reached up and caressed her cheek with his fingertips. "I don't want you to have a reason to come over here again. You live with me."

His tender words filled her with happiness. He was totally committed to their relationship now, it wasn't a secret anymore and he wasn't hesitant in the least to make it permanent.

"What about all those boxes in the living room? Are we going to move those too?"

"No. I will have someone do that in the morning."

Jessie glanced around the room to make sure she wasn't leaving anything behind. "I'm done. That was the last of it."

"Let's go." Justice dropped his hand to grab a second bag. "Lead the way, mate."

Jessie walked up the front steps to Justice's home, a little nervous since she'd never been inside it before. She hoped she loved it as much as the house she'd just left. She reached for the door handle to open it for him.

"Wait."

She glanced at him, arched an eyebrow and crossed her arms over her chest as he set down her bags. "What? Did you leave it a mess?"

He chuckled. "Stay here. Don't peek." He opened the door, shoved it wide and picked up her bags again. He disappeared inside.

She couldn't see a thing since he didn't turn on lights. He moved around inside. She could hear him but had no clue what he was trying to hide from her. With her luck the guy was a slob, but a sexy one. He had mentioned he had a male who cleaned for him. At least she wouldn't be stuck picking up after him.

He stepped out of the darkness onto the porch and she gasped in surprise as he suddenly bent, his shoulder pressed against her hip and an arm hooked behind her legs. He stood quickly, draped her down his back and flipped on a light inside the door. His other hand massaged her ass as he carried her inside, used his foot to kick the door closed and chuckled.

"Lock the door."

She had to grab her hair with a fist just to see, twisted the bolt near her face and turned her head to get a limited glimpse of a surprisingly neat living room. "Put me down."

"No. I'm not totally clueless about humans. I'm always studying their ways and I'm familiar with carrying a bride over the threshold the first time she enters their shared home. We're mated as far as I'm concerned, the wedding is just paperwork for your world but you're mine, honey. I'm carrying you to bed and showing you the proper respect you deserve by following your valued traditions."

It was so sweet she didn't have the heart to tell him that most guys didn't toss women over their shoulders. She chuckled, released her hair and cupped his muscular ass as he quickly strode through the hallway. He had the best butt and she barely took notice of his room when they entered it as he flipped on the light.

He adjusted her when he bent, easing her to sit on the edge of his mattress and crouched before her. He smiled. "Welcome to our home. Now take off your clothes. I missed you and if I don't make love to you soon I'm going to lose all control." He rose, kicked off his shoes and tore at his jacket. "Hurry," he softly growled.

Jessie watched him strip quickly, enjoying the view of every sexy inch of skin and muscle he revealed. He looked up after he removed his pants, narrowed his eyes and frowned.

"Undress. I mean it, Jessie. It's been two weeks and I would hate to tear it off you. It's a nice dress."

Jessie kicked off her shoes. She reached behind her and unzipped the dress and unhooked her bra. She let them slide down her body as she slid off the bed. Justice purred when she stripped out of her panties. She backed up when he took a step toward her.

"Wait."

Justice froze. "What?"

"We need to talk for a minute."

"I don't want to talk."

"Well, we need to."

He growled. "What about?"

"Did you sleep with Kit?"

He frowned. "No."

She frowned back, closely studying his features for any hint of a lie or guilt. "Really?"

"The only female I want is you. I don't settle for less than what I want."

She nodded, sure he was being sincere. "This whole mate thing, does that mean you won't cheat on me?"

He smiled. "That's what it means. You're it for me and I'm it for you. It's a commitment to only be with each other."

"For life?"

"Forever."

"Okay. Good."

"Are we done talking now?"

She glanced at the bed and smiled. "Just a few more things to go over."

He clenched his hands, his body tensed and his aroused cock twitched visibly, waving a little at her. "What else?"

"Do I get my job back that I quit tonight? I like working with the women over at the dorm."

"You never lost your job. I didn't accept you quitting."

Jessie grinned. "Good."

"Now are we done talking?"

"There's just one more thing to go over."

"What?" He inched closer, looking ready to pounce on her.

Jessie sucked her bottom lip inside her mouth. "You."

He blinked. "What about me?"

"I want you on the bed and I want to be on top."

His eyes narrowed while Jessie held her breath. They stared at each other and he took a step back. "You want to get even for tonight and last night. You want me to submit to you to soothe your injured pride."

"No. I just want to be on top. You liked it last time and so did I."

"You want me to let you be in control of our sex?"

"I like that position and I swear this isn't about getting even or dominance."

He shot her a wary look and climbed up on the bed to flip over onto his back. "Only for you and if you ever tell..." His gaze roamed her body. "I'd have to assert my dominance over you publicly in worse ways than I did at the bar."

"What does that mean?" Jessie leaned against the bed. "Why are these beds so high? I need a stepstool to get up there."

Justice laughed and reached over to grip her wrist and yanked her all the way on the mattress. "We're tall. I'll help you into bed. It's the getting out of bed you'll have a problem with since I'll want to keep you here. I'd have to mount you in front of all of my people if I have to assert my dominance."

Jessie laughed at his joke but he didn't. He arched an eyebrow instead, watching her silently. She stopped laughing, realizing he was serious. It shocked and stunned her.

"Really? That's... If you ever tried to do that to me in front of other people I'd shoot you. You would really have to have sex with me in front of them all? I'm totally not into that whole voyeurism-sex thing."

He suddenly laughed. "No. I just wanted to see your expression."

Jessie relaxed and smiled. "So what would you really do to me if I told someone you let me do this?" Jessie straddled his thighs and lowered her body across his. Her head dipped and her tongue licked his stomach near his bellybutton.

"I'd have to punish you," he softly groaned.

Jessie scooted higher to lick his nipple and sucked the hardening flesh between her teeth. She nipped him and he made a low purring sound. Jessie felt his hard cock trapped between their stomachs jerk in response. She released his nipple and brushed kisses across his chest until her mouth encountered his other nipple to tease.

"How would you punish me, Justice?"

His hands gripped her hips. "I'd torture you, Jessie. You like me to move fast inside you but I'd hold you down and move so slowly you'd beg me to fuck you the way you like. I wouldn't. I'd draw it out until you couldn't take it anymore."

Jessie's entire body responded to his sensual threat. She shifted her hips and lifted up as she pulled away from his nipple and sat up straight. Her fingers curled around the shaft she gripped, stroked the velvety length and brushed her thumb over the crown. Moisture from pre-cum helped her tease the edges as she drew circles.

"You know if you threaten to tease me that I can do the same, baby."

"Jessie," he purred, "it's been weeks. I want it to be good for you but keep that up and I won't last."

Jessie lowered her hips over his, adjusted his cock and rubbed her pussy over it. She moaned softly, enjoying it when it teased her clit, ready to take him inside her. She'd missed him too, knew how good he'd feel and pushed her hips down. Justice threw his head back and released her to claw the bed as she took him inside.

"Nails," she moaned. "You feel so good. Just don't destroy the bed. I'm sleeping in it with you later."

"Fuck the bed," Justice growled.

"Fuck me," Jessie moaned, lowered her chin and stared into his passion-filled gaze.

Jessie closed her eyes, threw her head back and sank down farther, taking more of him, to enjoy him stretching her vaginal walls. The sensation of Justice filling her was the best thing in the world. She pressed down until she knew he was fully, snugly settled and their connection was complete. She moved up and down to adjust, taking it slow at first and it was torture. Her body's desire to come urged her to ride him faster.

Justice purred and growled, making erotic sounds that drove her passion higher. His hand came up, gripping her leg and his thumb slid between her spread thighs. He brushed her clit, drawing circles with just enough pressure to make her vaginal muscles clench around his thick girth. Jessie moaned louder, riding him faster.

Justice suddenly rolled. Jessie gasped in surprise but then moaned when he drove into her deep and fast, trapped her with his weight and she knew he was in control. He looked sexy and fierce as he softly growled at her, showed his teeth when he smiled and braced his arms to pin her tightly under him.

"My turn."

Justice thrust into her fast and hard, not holding back anything and she wrapped around him. Her legs hooked over his ass, her arms wound around his neck. Their bodies moved together perfectly as he thrust inside her, hitting every nerve ending that screamed for release. He drove into her deeper, more forcefully and adjusted his cock to hit a spot that made her cry out his name.

Pleasure crashed through her as Justice moved faster and harder. She screamed his name as the climax hit. Justice threw back his head and a roar tore from his throat. Their bodies jerked and locked together. Jessie relaxed as the last twinge of pleasure washed through her and Justice's body draped over hers.

"You're my mate," Justice whispered against her ear, brushing a kiss on her throat.

"Thank God," she whispered back.

Justice chuckled. "There is one thing I would like to tell you." He lifted his head to make her look him.

"What is it?"

"We discovered it's possible for us to have children when a human became pregnant by one of our males. Their healthy, strong baby was born weeks ago." He cupped her face. "The baby is Species, has our facial traits and resembles his father. I want to have a child with you. Will you think about it?"

Shock hit her—not that they could have kids, something that she already knew but wasn't supposed to, thanks to Breeze trusting her. It was the fact that Justice wanted to have a child with her. He'd gone from fighting them being together to asking her to be the mother of his unborn children. It was a fast switch.

Justice rolled them on their sides, opened a little space between their bodies and cupped her stomach. "I want you to swell with my child and I want you bound to me in every way possible." He stared deeply into her eyes. "I want to do everything to bind you to me in every way. You make me happy." He smiled. "You make my life complete."

Tears filled Jessie's eyes. "You are so good with words."

He frowned. "What does that mean?"

She laughed and wiped her tears away. "It means I'd love to have a baby with you though I'd like to wait a year at least. I want time with you first and you need to take more time off work before we have one. I want us to raise our child or children together, not just me raising our baby while you're gone at work."

"I'm your mate. We'll do everything together."

"Honey, you're a workaholic." She licked her lips. "My dad is one and he wasn't around for me much when I was a kid. My worst fear was growing up and marrying someone like him. Ironic, isn't it? You make him look downright lazy when it comes to the hours you put in but I'm an adult. I get why you work so hard but kids don't understand how important your job is. They just feel abandoned and like they come in second. Do you understand? You need to learn how to relax more before we become parents."

"I'm going to hand over some duties to the council and that will free up a lot of my time. I can wait a year and you'll see that we will have lots of time together. I can relax and you're going to teach me how. I had no life but being the face of my people. That's all changed now, Jessie. I love them but you're my number-one priority." His gaze narrowed. "You're my mate. You come first before all others. I will step down in the morning to show you how much you mean to me. I love you and you're everything to me."

She knew he meant it and her love for him grew stronger. "I don't want you to quit but I do want you to work less hours. What you do is so important and I don't want to change who you are. You're the man I want to be with. I just ask for more of your time. Getting help from your council sounds ideal."

He smiled. "Done. I would like to have more than one child. I would like to keep you pregnant and I could do it."

"We'll talk numbers after we have our first one."

He looked hopeful. "But at least two?"

"I love you with my entire heart and you make me happy too." She grinned. "When you're not pissing me off but I still love you more than I want to kill you. You make my life complete too."

"I was told this next thing is good news. When I get you pregnant what is the worst thing about being pregnant?"

"Getting fat."

He laughed. "Second worst thing?"

"Morning sickness."

"How about nine months of being pregnant?"

"Yeah. That sounds like a pain but it's worth it."

Justice suddenly rolled onto Jessie and pinned her under him. "It's a Species baby you will carry, Jessie. The first baby was born in twenty weeks, healthy and at full term. We heal faster than you and we were designed different. It seems our babies develop faster than yours do. The second human mother-to-be is experiencing the same accelerated pregnancy. We think twenty weeks is the pregnancy length." His gaze searched hers. "Would you still carry my child?"

Jessie was stunned. *Five months?* Justice rolled away and sat up.

"It is too much, isn't it? Are you afraid now to consider having my child?"

Jessie rolled onto her side and propped her head on her bent arm. "No. I'm just trying to process this news. It's stunning."

"Are you repulsed?"

"No. Never. I'd love to carry our baby inside me and it's kind of cool. Hell, I could almost have two of our children in the time it takes my kind to have one baby."

290

Justice

He looked relieved. "So you are agreeing to have at least two. Good."

She inched closer, reached out and rubbed his thigh. "So, any other surprises to throw at me?"

"The doctors have helped Fury's mate, Ellie, get pregnant. She had something called a blocked tube but now they are having a baby. We're planning to move them to Reservation to hide that when she begins to show more. We can't allow your people find out yet. We don't think they are ready to learn of us having children and are worried they will react badly if they knew Species babies exist. Our child won't be alone."

Jessie nodded. "We're going to have to open a school for our children before they are old enough to need one. We sure can't send them to public schools outside the gates. They'd be in too much danger."

Justice covered her hand to hold it. "My mate is smart. What other things are you thinking?"

"I'm thinking we will need to practice getting pregnant. We want to do it right."

He glanced at her and growled. In seconds he had flipped her over and yanked her to her hands and knees. He entered her gently, fucking her deeply and Jessie moaned. Justice thrust into her slowly and steadily until she nearly came. He paused when she was right on the edge.

She turned her head. "Don't stop."

"You have complaints? I need practice?"

He suddenly thrust in hard and fast, curled around her back and his teeth gripped her shoulder. One of his hands left the bed and his finger strummed her clit.

Jessie came screaming and Justice roared his own pleasure from behind her. They collapsed on the bed side by side, still connected and Jessie laughed once she caught her breath. Sometimes him not understanding what she was trying to say wouldn't be a bad thing. He'd mistaken her joke for a complaint. Justice nipped her shoulder and she jerked from the jolt of pleasure. It sent a pulse straight to her clit, reminding her how sensitive it currently was.

His teeth released her. "How was that?"

She turned her head to look into his smug gaze. "It's a human joke. Sorry. I love the way you take me, Justice. You don't do a thing wrong. It's just a saying. It means we should have lots more sex so they say to 'practice getting pregnant' as a joke."

He chuckled. "I see."

"But I'll be sure to say that again. When I do could you forget you know what it really means? I liked this a hell of a lot."

"So you want a lot more sex?"

"I always want you."

He grinned. "We were designed for endurance and strength. Do you know what else?"

"You're wildly handsome and have the best body I've ever seen in my entire life and it makes me want to drool when you take off your clothes?"

He kissed her. "Besides that."

"What?"

"Our recovery time. You want more sex?" He moved inside her slowly. "Did you ever wonder why I always pull out of you after sex? I don't soften if I'm inside you. As long as I'm in you I can go for hours."

Jessie moaned.

"This time we're going slow."

She shook her head. "That's torture."

Justice secured her there while he kept moving inside her. His other hand roamed her belly, her breasts and played with her nipples.

"You're going to love it. I'm going to keep moving in you slowly and steadily while I touch you all over. It's another talent of mine."

"You're going to kill me."

"No. I'm just giving you what you want."

"Faster."

"You're so impatient." His hand left her breast to roam down her stomach and he used his legs to spread her thighs wider apart, pinning them open to touch her exposed clit with taps of his fingertip. "Slow and steady, Jessie."

Jessie almost climaxed from the sensation of the gentle beat that he tattooed over the bundle of nerves. He thrust in slowly, keeping time as he played with her body.

"Do you really love me, Jessie?"

"Yes!"

He stopped tapping on her, his hand twisted and his finger and thumb pinched her clit gently, tugging a little and rubbed. He drove into her steadily but shifted his hips, thrusting into her deeper. In seconds Jessie was screaming his name as she came. Justice threw his head back, arched his spine and roared as he came, filling her with his warm release.

Long minutes later Jessie opened her eyes and twisted her head to smile at Justice. "Maybe slow is nice."

"Nice?" He grinned and arched his eyebrows. "That was just nice?"

"That was amazing."

Justice slowly withdrew from her body and rolled them to their sides, spooning against her back. "I don't want to make you sore. I'll amaze you more later when you've had some rest."

"I love you."

Justice kissed the curve of her shoulder. "I love you too, Jessie. Go to sleep. I want to hold you all night." He reached back and managed to turn off the light on the nightstand.

Jessie curled into him and closed her eyes. She was marrying Justice and he said she was his mate. The sensation of being in his arms, in his bed, was the most right thing she'd ever felt.

Justice heard Jessie's breathing change and knew his mate slept. He pulled her a little tighter against his body, curved his legs to draw her closer and breathed in her alluring feminine scent. She was his forever and he wasn't alone anymore. She was his other half, the softer side he'd never have without her and also his biggest weakness.

He searched his feelings, worried he might resent having that new flaw in his formerly impenetrable armor but instead only felt a sense of peace. There would be hell to pay in the morning when he had to deal with the fallout of publicly claiming her but none of that mattered. Jessie was worth taking on the world if that's what it came down to.

Her father would be upset, probably withdraw his support but he'd find a way to handle that. He'd make sure she remained safe. He'd protect her at all costs and if the danger became too great, he'd step down from his position. They could move to Reservation inside the Wild Zone near Valiant and Tammy. Construction was progressing on his home by the lake, intended as a retreat from the pressures of his life but it could become their full-time home. He'd have his own personal army of near-feral Species to help him keep all danger away from his mate.

He pictured leaving his suits behind for a loincloth, something that some of the males there had reverted to, and grinned. He could possibly talk Jessie into wearing little. They could play all day and all he'd have to concentrate on would be loving her. Things suddenly didn't seem so grim when he pictured their future.

He relaxed and closed his eyes, holding her tightly and knew one way or another it would work out. He wouldn't accept anything less. He had Jessie and that was all that mattered.

Chapter Twenty

Justice awoke to a strange, faint noise, something unfamiliar, and opened his eyes. Jessie remained tucked securely in front of him, their bodies still pressed tightly together and she breathed slowly and steadily, sleeping. Whatever had disturbed his sleep hadn't been her. He listened, putting his senses on alert and picked up the sound of a vehicle approaching.

He turned his head, glanced at the clock and realized there were a few hours before the sun rose. No one should be driving near his home at that time. Security patrolled the grounds but stayed far from his house the way he'd ordered them to do after he'd chewed them out for invading his privacy every time he roared. He carefully eased his hold on his mate and slid from the bed without waking her.

He rushed out of his room, down the hallway and into the living room. The lights were still on from when he'd brought Jessie home so he dashed into his dark office, moved to the front window and shifted the curtain slightly to peer outside. An SUV pulled over and parked down the hill a little, past Tiger's home, in the empty lot next to Jessie's old home, and the engine died.

His heart raced. Something was wrong. They hadn't had the headlights on before they parked and no interior lights came on when the four doors opened. All the NSO vehicles had fully working equipment and that included lights. Someone had removed them to make sure they failed. The five dark figures emerged and left the doors wide open. The only reason to do that was to avoid noise.

His gaze narrowed, fixed on the five. He realized they wore all black from head to foot. Their faces were either covered with dark masks or had been painted to disguise their features. They approached the house next door where Jessie had lived. He studied them long enough to notice the way they moved and used too-familiar hand signals to communicate. They were going to divide up and surround something or someone.

Justice fled the office to rush down the hallway to one of the spare bedrooms where he had a better view after they moved out of sight. He saw one dark figure leap over the gate that led from the front to the backyard of the cottage next door. It was clear their target had to be Jessie.

Rage flashed through every fiber of his body. He dropped the curtain, backed away and yanked up the phone on the nightstand. He punched in Tiger's home number, his mind plotting what to do. It rang until the machine picked it up. He hung up and dialed his cell phone. It rang three times.

"It's four-thirty in the morning," Tiger growled, a little out of breath. "This better be really good to disturb me when I'm busy."

"Five of our males surrounded Jessie's cottage. They came in stealthily, dressed to hide their presence, which means they plan to attack," Justice growled. "Call males you trust and get to my house. Move. They obviously don't approve of my choice in mates."

"Son of a bitch," Tiger snarled. "I'm not at home. I'm at the women's dorm. I'll grab some of the males still here and we're coming. Don't engage them until we arrive. You're outnumbered."

Justice hung up and dialed the gate shack next. It rang six times, no one answered and he clenched his teeth. Either the officer on duty was in on it or the five males next door had done something to him. He had no immediate backup. Justice ran back toward his bedroom.

He reached the bed and lunged for Jessie. One of his hands clamped over her mouth while his other one gripped her hip. He dragged her body from the center of the bed to the side of it, lifted her off the mattress completely and Jessie gasped against his palm. He leaned down to hiss in her ear before she had time to struggle, "Five Species are at your house. Be quiet, get dressed and stay at my side. I can see in the dark well enough to lead you."

Jessie nodded in understanding. He eased his hand from her mouth, lowered her until her feet took her weight and snagged her arm. The closet was close. He opened the door and pulled her inside. The door closed and he flipped on the inner light, momentarily blinding them both.

Jessie grimly studied him with her beautiful blue eyes and pride surfaced that his mate seemed so calm. She wasn't wasting time battering him with questions or reacting with hysterics to what he'd said. He released her, grabbed a shirt and thrust it at her. He tore open a drawer, got them both boxers and dressed next to her in the tight space.

"You said five?" she whispered as she rolled the waist of her borrowed boxers.

"Yes. Species, and I assume they are male."

"Shit."

He couldn't agree more. He allowed his anger to take control and he knew blood would be spilled if the males realized she wasn't home and dared come to his house to search for her. It would be death for them without question. He'd kill or die to protect his mate.

He wanted to flee with her but there could be more of them out there waiting, coming on foot. Inside the house he at least could hold ground until Tiger arrived with reinforcements. He pushed back shock that his own people had come after his mate. It was horrifying and something he'd never considered.

Jessie tried to hide her terror as she yanked on the shirt Justice had given her. She didn't care if was inside out or on backward. The information he'd shared barely registered in her sleep-fogged brain but they were in deep shit, he'd said they were Species and that had to be pretty bad. They wanted her.

She watched Justice face the back of his closet, grab the hanger bar filled with his suits and yank the entire thing out. He released it, everything hit the floor and he pushed on the wall near the top, his fingertips searching for something. There was a click and it sprang open on one side. He grabbed it and the hidden cabinet door opened.

Her lips parted but she pressed them together, not saying a word about the two handguns mounted to the wall and the bags of spare clips next to them. She just watched as he grabbed a bulletproof vest. He spun, shoving it at her.

"Put it on."

"You."

His eyes narrowed. "Do it. We don't have time to hold a debate, Jessie. I heal and move faster than you do. My kind will fight another Species hand to hand but you are human and I'm not sure they'll give you that respect. They might have guns and shoot you. Wear the vest."

He had that determined look that clued her in that arguing with him would be a waste of time. She accepted the heavy vest, put it on and tried to make the too-large garment fit. Justice wasn't strapping on weapons but instead turned, thrusting them at her. His weapons stash was impressive as she glanced at them.

"Nice. I take it you're keeping the shotgun?"

He shook his head. "We don't use weapons on each other, Jessie. We fight with our bodies. You on the other hand are not Species. You would lose to one of our men if it came to that. I won't lose you. You need help surviving if it comes down to it."

"Do you think they'll come here?"

"They will figure out where you must be since you are not next door. They must want you badly to risk so much and I'll assume they'll come here next."

"Shit." Jessie checked the safeties on the guns, made sure they were off and popped the clips, seeing they were fully loaded. "I'm so sorry. This is because of me."

Justice moved lightning fast to grab her chin, forced her head up to meet his gaze, and softly growled in anger. "You didn't do this. Mates are precious, to be protected at all costs and considered Species. Those males are to blame for betraying us." His hand dropped away. "I want you to go sit in the tub in the bathroom. There are only two entries there. Kill anyone who gets past me. It means I'm dead."

Her mouth dropped open. "They wouldn't dare hurt you. You're their leader."

He grabbed four clips for the handguns and shoved them down the front of her vest. "I guess they want to fire me. Move, Jessie." His gaze softened. "Tiger and some men are on the way. Trust him. He'll get you to safety and back to your father if something happens to me."

"You gave me both guns." She offered him one, butt first. "Please take one."

"Species don't use guns to fight each other but you need them. Don't fight them hand to hand. Just pull the trigger before they can attack."

Jessie stared into Justice's dark eyes. "I'm not hiding inside the bathroom while you're facing five of them by yourself. I can shoot and I'm staying by your side. These guns and I can even out the numbers pretty quick."

He suddenly leaned forward to kiss her lips. "I love you." His smile died and his eyes narrowed. "We don't have time to vote on my plan."

An alarm screamed throughout the house and Justice cursed. "They have breached our home. Get inside the bathroom. I can't concentrate if I don't know where you are. Do it or you'll get us both killed."

He flipped off the light, grabbed her arm and shoved open the closet door. She was propelled forward by his strong hold, led into the bedroom where he quickly checked before he left her there.

Son of a bitch. He was going to face off against five Species males alone because she had breasts...or it might be because she was human. She couldn't see him telling any of the muscular Species females to hide in the bathroom while he fought. They were kickass and he'd have kept a Species female at his side to help even out the odds.

Jessie resisted the urge to follow him, knew it would distract him since he seemed certain she needed his protection and hoped that no one would really dare attack Justice. Species adored him and appreciated all the sacrifices he made. It was inconceivable that any of them would wish him harm.

She could barely make out the dim interior of the room, seeing more shadows than anything. Her gaze drifted to the best location to set up an offense—that being the far corner away from the one window and the open door to the bedroom.

The tub was the exact size and model of the one inside her old home. It was perfect, would provide cover and she climbed into the big thing, crouching down to make a smaller target. She shifted the clips inside the large vest so they weren't digging into her breasts and gripped the guns in both hands. Her gaze darted back and forth from the window to the door.

The window was big enough for a person to come through and the open doorway to the bedroom would allow her to keep track of what was going on in the rest of the house. Of course the screaming alarm grated on her nerves. It was muted somewhat in the back of the house but she wished for a com link to Justice. It was a mental "to buy in the future" on her list of things to do.

The alarm cut off and only eerie silence remained. She hoped that was a good thing. Maybe the males had fled when they realized security would hear it and come rushing to Justice's aid. They sure came when he roared so sirens would definitely bring them running.

Time ticked by and not knowing drove her a little insane. She bit her lip, stood and stepped over the edge of tub. She wanted a view outside, a chance to see if anything was going on and hesitantly approached the window. She shoved one gun between her thighs, listened to make sure nothing moved on the other side and felt for the lock. She pushed it down and slid the glass open along the track, breathing in fresh air. Her hand gripped the second gun again, lifted it and felt safe with the weight of both resting against her palms.

Nothing moved in the dark backyard or near the outline of the pool, where the dim glow of lights at the bottom of it provided some sight. She backed away. Her gaze turned to the doorway to make sure nothing crept up on her. She heard a soft thump and her focus jerked back to the open window in time to spot a large figure rush from one side of the yard toward her.

Maybe it's security but what if it's not? Fear had her backing away from the window and hurrying back to the tub where she stepped in and crouched. She aimed the guns at the backyard, held her breath and her heart raced.

A shadow darkened a corner of the window. They sniffed loudly and growled. It was a soft, vicious noise and assured her it wasn't anyone happy to catch her scent. A Species male would smell her since she'd stood there. Her fingers tightened on the triggers while she waited for him to make a move.

Justice heard the faint sound of a footstep on tile and it gave away the location of one male. He was near the end of the hallway that led to the bedrooms. The approaching intruder wore shoes that squeaked, new ones did that sometimes when the soles weren't broken in and it clued him to the fact that these males weren't well trained. None of his officers would make that mistake. They were too skilled in stealth to make noise.

He wondered if he'd made a mistake, judging them to be Species, but no humans could move the way he'd seen the males outside walking. Their grace and fluidness was too animalistic, whereas human men were stiffer and stepped heavier. It confused him since all his males had to undergo training yet these weren't skilled. He leaned against the bedroom wall next to the open door to the hallway. He didn't want to go far from Jessie. The position allowed him to protect the bedroom windows and the entrance from the hall. He glanced at the bathroom door to be assured she was safe so far.

Another sound caught his ear, one he identified as a window sliding open. He gritted his teeth after determining it had come from the bathroom where Jessie hid but gunfire didn't pierce the quiet house. Jessie would have shot anyone trying to breach the house through the smaller room. It must have been another window and he'd misjudged the direction.

He heard another slight sound, wood scraped plaster, and he realized the intruder moved down the hallway closer to the bedroom. A table sat eight feet from his bedroom. He'd obviously bumped into it, once again betraying his lack of training. Rage gripped him as he inhaled, picking up the distinctive Species scent. They were his males coming after his mate. The five males were obviously willing to kill him to get to Jessie. They had to know he would die to protect her from harm.

He picked up the stench of sweat, grease and something metallic. His fingers arced into claws. The Species male had brought a gun or knife to the fight, weapons to be used against Jessie. He sprang from his hiding spot into the hallway. A roar tore from his throat as he grabbed the male, lifted him and slammed the heavy body into the wall. Plaster gave way from the force, the male hissed in surprise and pain and the fight was on.

A punch caught Justice in the jaw, the force enough to make him stagger back and he lost his hold. His opponent hit the floor in a crouch and pounced, slamming into his chest. Justice used his teeth to rip into skin. The male tried to crush his ribs in a bear hold.

The male cried out and Justice grabbed the man's chest, dug in and broke bones. The body was dead under him when they crashed to the floor. Justice pushed up off the body and spit out blood. He tensed, seeing movement at the end of the hall. He roared again and rushed after the retreating shadow.

Jessie heard Justice roar, then a loud hissing noise and a big boom. There was no mistaking the vicious sounds of a fight and she wanted to rush out of the bathroom to jump right into it. She held still though since the dark shape remained at the window. The person still waited to attack and she kept her attention on him. She knew Justice was still alive when he roared out again. The fight seemed over and she could only pray he'd won.

There was movement at the edge of the window. A hand gripped the frame and a large shape filled the space in the blink of an eye. It crouched on the windowsill. The male sniffed and his head seemed to turn to stare directly at her. The menacing shadowy shape didn't appear human or Species. It looked scary as hell and large. Jessie squeezed the trigger on both guns, fired repeatedly and the shadow fell backward after she nailed it with four bullets.

She held her ground, waited to make sure he didn't rise up to attack again but he didn't. Seconds ticked by and the sound of another fight filled her ears. Furniture crashed at the front of the house, animalistic snarls and fists hitting flesh tormented her. She lifted up, stepped over the tub and risked rushing to the window to make sure she'd taken out the threat who'd come after her.

She peered outside, made out the shape of a male and he wasn't moving. She pushed the window closed, locked it with her thumb and ran toward the bedroom. Anyone trying to come through the bathroom window would have to break it to get inside and it would warn her. The need to find and help Justice drove her fear back and made her reckless as she flipped on lights, more worried about being blind in the dark than giving away her location.

Glass broke down the hall as she lunged in that direction, only pausing to flip on a switch to light her way to the living room. The sight that greeted her was shocking and horrifying. A big male lay sprawled on his back, his shirt torn away over his ribs and his skin was torn open. She fought the urge to be sick as she visually examined the dead body. Blood was all over the place—sprayed on the walls and pooled in the carpet. The man on the floor wore black, his face was smeared with black face paint and he had a black cap on his head to hide his hair.

It wasn't Justice so she moved forward. She had to step over the body, her bare foot sank into warm wetness and she knew it was blood. She kept going though. The sound of the fight still raged nearby. She kept her guns trained and ready to fire at anyone who came at her until she reached the large, open, dark area of the living room.

She hit the light switch with her elbow to turn on the lights and gaped at the destroyed room. The couch was knocked over, the glass coffee table shattered, a bookshelf was sprawled facedown to spread a mess of books five feet to her left but what held her attention was the two fighting males who sprang apart in the center of it.

Justice wore boxers, blood smeared over his body and he looked fierce as he snarled at the black-clad male. He didn't spare her a glance as he circled his opponent but she couldn't stop staring at the deep scratches on his back, arms and the damage to one cheek where he'd been struck hard enough to show the forming bruise.

The other man bled heavily from his face—his nose broken, his lip split and one cheekbone damaged. His black outfit hid any other injuries but one arm appeared wet, probably blood, and some skin near his side showed where the material had torn.

"Get back, Jessie," Justice gruffly ordered. "I heard gunshots. Are you harmed?"

Jessie caught movement from the corner of her eye and twisted her head in time to see another attacker rush from the kitchen. She didn't think, just saw the black clothing, the black, paint-smeared face and aimed the guns. He moved faster than a human but her bullets didn't miss. He shrieked loudly, a high-pitched wail of pain and dropped to the floor to land on what used to be the coffee table. He didn't move.

"I'm fine. I've got your back, honey. Do you want me to shoot the bastard near you?" Jessie's voice shook but her hands didn't.

"Stay out of this and there's two more."

"There's only one besides that asshole you're fighting. I killed someone who tried to come in through the bathroom. That's who you heard me shooting at. I don't miss."

Justice growled and Jessie knew he was pissed but she'd deal with his anger later. She shoved the gun in her left hand between her thighs, using the wall to keep her balance and dropped the clip out of the gun in her right hand. She dug out a fresh clip from her vest and popped it in. She grabbed the gun from between her thighs.

"You have your human fight for you?" the man who'd attacked Justice spat. "You are too weak to lead us."

"Who are you?" Justice snarled. "I don't even know you and you dare come after my mate?"

Justice tensed and a roar tore from his throat as he sprang for the other male. He pushed up from a quick crouch and sailed into the air. He had to have strong legs to do that. Seeing it stunned Jessie but she had to admire the beauty of the move. He flew about five feet until his body slammed into the other man.

They went down together in a roll and growls tore from their throats. They fought like animals, slashed with their clawed fingers and bit. Justice used his legs too. He managed to wrap one of them around the other male's thigh and jerked hard. The guy under Justice howled in agony, having his leg bent at the awkward position.

They rolled again until Justice ended up under the male but he pushed hard enough to throw his attacker into a wall. The black-clad figure hit it hard enough to damage plaster. Justice jackknifed his body and ended up in a crouch. He threw his body at the man who was trying to separate himself from the drywall.

They went through the wall and Jessie gaped at the big hole they'd created. She hated to leave the safety of the hallway but she couldn't see Justice anymore. There was an archway to the other room she had never been in. Her house didn't have the same floor plan. She ran for the archway.

It was a home office almost as large as the living room. Justice and the Species were separated, on their feet circling each other, each searching for a weakness. Jessie inched into the room and put her back to the wall. She didn't want someone to creep up behind her but she couldn't go farther into the room. A huge glass slider revealed darkness outside. Someone could come at her that way and it was too risky to get too close.

"We will never be led by a lover of humans," the other man barked. "You shame us."

Justice snarled. "You're from testing facility five, aren't you? You stupid bastard. We built everything when we were freed so we could rescue you. You betray your own kind because of your hatred for humans? Did you not hear what I said to you? Did you not understand what our people have accomplished? We have found peace here."

Testing facility five? Jessie's mouth fell open. That was the one in Colorado she'd helped raid. She stared at the man still circling with Justice and knew his guess had to be correct. The intruder was one of the males she'd help free.

"I am the best and I will win," the man growled. "I will lead our people when your body is cold and I will snap the neck of your human female. I will show our people that is how to deal with humans. Death to them all for they have done."

Justice roared and attacked. He didn't seem to notice when the male grabbed for something behind his back but Jessie did. As Justice reached him, a knife flashed. She tried to yell out a warning but it was too late. Jessie screamed as the male threw Justice away from him. The man she loved hit the floor on his back, groaning and grabbed for his bleeding body.

"Hey!" Jessie yelled, pure rage flowing through her.

The man turned and growled.

"Lead this, fuckhead." She shot him in the face and emptied the clip into his body after he hit the carpet.

Jessie dropped the empty clip from the gun and ran to Justice. He clutched one hand over his hip but blood still soaked his boxers. His gaze locked with hers and she couldn't miss the astonishment on his handsome features.

"He used a knife."

Jessie jerked her head around, expecting the fifth male to attack. Justice bled badly and tears filled her eyes. She pushed his hand away and saw the ragged tear in his boxers. She dropped the guns on her lap, crouched on her knees next to him and tore the material wider apart. There was a jagged wound next to his hipbone that drew a sound of anguish from her. It looked bad.

A loud noise boomed and wood split in the living room. It sounded as if someone had kicked down the front door. She grabbed Justice's hand to shove over his injury. "Press here, hold it tight and don't move. I love you."

She grabbed the empty gun and reached into her shirt. Her hand smeared Justice's blood all over her vest, shirt and breasts as she yanked out the clip. She slammed it into the empty chamber as she rose to her feet. She gripped both guns in her fists and spread her feet apart to plant them on both sides of Justice's hips.

It was a bad place to be as far as tactical advantages went. Windows were all around them — a huge glass slider and the open archway that led to the living room. There was no cover. Justice was too heavy and too hurt to move. The fifth male would strike and she hoped he'd come from the archway since that's where she'd heard the house breached.

Her eyes scanned the room frantically. The second she saw movement she planned to kill the son of a bitch. He wasn't going to get to Justice.

"Jessie, get out of here and find somewhere safe that you can see him coming."

"Shut up. I'm not leaving you."

"Please, Jessie." His hand rubbed her ankle. "Save yourself. I'm fighting to stay here."

Jessie glanced down at her mate's pale face. His naturally tan skin was whiter than she'd ever seen it. Blood spread on the carpet near his hip and his boxers were soaked. He smiled when their gazes met.

"You are so beautiful when you are on top of me." His eyes closed and his smile faded as his head slumped to the side.

"JUSTICE!" Grief made her scream his name.

His chest rose and fell, assuring her he hadn't died but she knew he would soon. Jessie needed to apply pressure to his wound but she'd have to put down the guns to do it, something that would assure both their deaths. She put her bare foot on Justice's bleeding hip and pressed down with as much weight as she thought would help but wouldn't worsen the damage.

"Justice!" A male roared from the living room.

Jessie trained one of the guns at the archway when she saw movement. A familiar face suddenly entered the room and Jessie barely stopped her finger from pulling the trigger. Tiger stared at her while more males filled the space behind him, nine in all. Reinforcements had arrived.

"He's been stabbed." Jessie's voice broke. "Four of those assholes are dead but one is missing. Call an ambulance."

Tiger's stunned gaze dropped to Justice on the floor. Glass suddenly exploded from the right and Jessie jerked in that direction. Something large with a black face came crashing through the slider right at her and Justice. Instinct saved her life. She shot with both guns. A heavy body slammed into hers and threw her onto her back, away from Justice.

Jessie lay there hurting under at least two-hundred-fifty pounds of limp and lifeless Species male. She couldn't breathe—the air had been knocked from her lungs. Forever seemed to pass but it was really only seconds. Suddenly the body was thrown off her and she gasp in air as her gaze locked with Tiger's. He bent and offered her a hand.

"The medics are with me and they'll do everything to save Justice," he promised. "Let me help you up."

Chapter Twenty-One

ᔆᗝ

"Justice is going to be fine." Dr. Treadmont smiled assurances. "He pulled through surgery and we're using drugs to help his healing accelerate."

Jessie closed her eyes and fought tears of relief. "Thank you." She opened her eyes and gave the doctor a grateful look. "Thank you so much."

Tiger cleared his throat and drew her attention. He and about fifty other New Species were crammed inside the medical center reception area with her. Some of them sat in chairs, on the long counter near the front doors and on the floor. She'd taken up residence sitting on a desk she'd pulled next to Justice's room while he'd undergone surgery.

"Can we get you showered and changed now?" Tiger inched closer.

Jessie glanced down, noting she hadn't removed the vest and her bloodied clothes. She shook her head.

Tiger frowned deeply and worry narrowed his catlike gaze. "You know Justice would want us looking after you while he can't. You're in shock and you're covered in blood. Please allow us to care for you, Jessie."

"I won't leave him."

Dr. Treadmont sighed. "You can shower here inside one of the rooms. I'm sure someone can fetch you clean clothes."

Breeze stood from the counter. "I'll have one of the women do that." Her gaze met Jessie's. "Justice will want to see you clean when he wakes." She smiled faintly to soften her words. "You look scary."

Jessie shrugged. "Probably, but I won't leave Justice."

Tiger bit his lip. "Can I have the guns?"

Jessie tightened her hold on them. "No."

"The only New Species allowed access to Medical are those from Justice's testing facility or those he trusts the most, Jessie. He's safe. No one here is going to hurt him and none from testing facility five are here."

"I trust you because Justice does. I trust Breeze because I know she's my friend." Jessie glanced around the room, meeting concerned gazes. "I don't know who else to trust." She stared at Tiger. "I'm not leaving him when he is down."

Tiger backed up. "Okay, Jessie."

Breeze walked closer but paused ten feet back. "How about this plan, Jessie? Tiger and I will sit right there and no one but the doctor and Nurse Paul will go inside the room. We swear we won't let anyone near him. Will you go down the hall to shower? Will you hand me the guns? You're in shock. Justice is safe now but we won't move from his door until you return so you are assured of that."

Jessie blinked at tears. "I let all of these people in because you said they'd never want to hurt him and they had a right to be here too since they love him. Would you shoot any of them if they tried to get past you to his door?"

Long seconds ticked by. Breeze looked stunned.

"That's what I thought. I'll kill anyone who poses a danger to him. I'll sit right here."

Tiger stepped forward again. "I would kill anyone to protect him. Justice is my best friend and a brother to me, Jessie."

Jessie hesitated but Justice had told her to trust Tiger. She slowly moved, slid off the desk and stood on shaky legs. "Okay."

He held out his hand. It was obvious he wanted the guns.

"Do you swear?" She hesitated.

"You have my word, Jessie. No one will get past me. Breeze and I will guard him and I'll shoot anyone but the doctor and nurse if they try to go to Justice."

Jessie slowly placed a gun in Tiger's waiting hand. "Don't budge while I'm gone."

"The other gun, Jessie." Tiger opened his other hand.

She shook her head. "I keep this one."

Halfpint stood and crept slowly around the counter. "Jessie? Why don't you let me help you? I know where a room is close to this one with a shower. I'll walk you there and Tiny will run to the dorm for clothing. Is that all right?"

Jessie allowed Halfpint to lead her down an opposite hallway to an empty room. There was a hospital bed inside and a bathroom tucked into a corner. Halfpint followed her into the small room and closed the door behind them.

Jessie placed the gun on the sink, unfastened her vest, removed the last ammo clip and laid it next to the weapon. Gentle hands helped her strip bare and her friend turned on the shower, adjusting the water. *Justice is going to make it. I'm suffering from severe shock and I want to curl into a ball and sob.* Exhaustion also gripped her, along with guilt. *This wouldn't have happened if I hadn't pushed him into publicly claiming me. It's my fault for not being happy with the nights we spent at my house.*

"Jessie? The water is warm. I'll stay right here." Halfpint rubbed her arm. "You look so sad but it's going to be okay. Justice is a strong male and he'll survive."

She shook her thoughts away to stare at her friend. "Don't touch the gun. I want to keep it and I don't want to risk you accidentally firing it, thinking you're doing me a favor by getting rid of it while I'm in the shower."

Halfpint glanced at the sink, then back at Jessie. "I wouldn't ever. They scare me."

Jessie believed her and stepped into the warm spray of water. She looked down to stare at the water that turned red at her feet from the blood coming off her body. She'd killed

Species. It was their blood going down the drain, along with her future happiness. One night had torn her world apart.

"Jessie? Are you okay? You're not doing anything."

She lifted her head and forced her limbs to move as she accepted the washcloth handed to her. She used lots of soap to scrub her skin, washed her hair and allowed her friend to wash her back where she couldn't reach.

"I'm not glad this happened," the other woman murmured. "But I'm happy I'm here to help you this time. You took care of me when I was rescued. It's going to be fine, Jessie. You said those words to me and I believed them. You were right. It's your turn to listen to me say them and believe me. It's going to be fine."

Jessie knew it couldn't turn out well. Justice had claimed her and some of his people had attempted to kill him. She should have listened to him when he said no one could know about them. She had thought he was being overprotective and paranoid, a mistake on her part, and now Justice lay recovering from surgery. He'd come close to death and the only way to fix the problem would be to leave him. Her heart broke.

She dried off quickly and someone tapped lightly on the door. Tiny opened it and peeked inside, then entered quickly to close it behind her. She studied Jessie as she held out folded clothing. She glanced at Halfpint.

"With her large breasts I didn't think our shirts would fit and I know humans wear bras. We don't have one to give her but I borrowed a shirt from a male outside who had a spare clean shirt inside his Jeep. It will prevent her free breast movement from showing to keep her modesty. The pants should fit. How are we doing?"

Halfpint hesitated. "Good. She's not talking much."

Tiny gave Jessie a weak smile. "Everyone is talking about what you did. You saved Justice. They think you are very brave and you should be an experimental prototype female, which is a compliment. Some of our males said you were guarding Justice with two guns aimed at them when they reached the house and that you killed four males. No one is upset over the deaths. Are you afraid of that? We are not mad. We're grateful."

"I killed four Species males. How can you be grateful?"

"They were wrong to go after you and Justice. Their heads were not right and ones who would turn on their own shouldn't live. They are not safe to be around for anyone. We are grateful you and Justice live and they didn't kill you."

Jessie needed to sit down, not caring that she only wore a towel. She collapsed on the toilet seat. "Not everyone is going to be grateful. That means it's going to piss some Species off and they will try to come after Justice again because of me." Tears slid down her cheeks unheeded. "He told me no one should know about us and that it would be dangerous. I never thought his own people would try to kill him. I've caused a civil war."

Tiny appeared baffled. "Here are the clothes." She left.

"Let's get you dressed," Halfpint urged softly. "Come on, Jessie. It is going to be fine. You want to go back to sit with him, right?"

Jessie put on the pair of borrowed stretch pants and baggy T-shirt that fell to her thighs. She didn't have a bra or panties but didn't care. Her reflection mocked her when she faced the mirror. She was paler than usual and her eyes looked wrong — their blue depths were darker than normal and red rimmed from crying. Her hand closed over the gun blindly and she glanced down at the implement of death.

"I'm ready to go back."

"You don't need the gun, Jessie."

"I'm keeping it." She fisted the spare clip. "This isn't over."

"Okay. Keep it if it makes you feel safe."

They walked back to the main room and she aimed right for Tiger. He stood from sitting on the desk so she could take up her position guarding her mate.

"Jessie? Can I please have the gun?"

She shook her head. "Not until he's up and able to defend himself."

"It could be days," he tried to reason. "They've given him medication to help him heal but it still takes time. It was a bad wound."

"Then you can have it in a few days."

He sighed. "You have to sleep sometime. You might shoot yourself or someone else by accident."

Jessie held his gaze. "Look up civil war, Tiger."

He frowned.

"It's something that has happened a lot. Do you want to know the worst part about history? It repeats itself usually. I'm not giving up the gun and I'm not leaving Justice unless I have to use the bathroom. You can guard him then."

"I know what a civil war is but it won't happen with Species. Those five males who attacked were too new to freedom and didn't understand how things are on the outside. This will never happen again."

"What about the others from that testing facility? You don't know if they'll be a danger to Justice for sure. You weren't subjected to the Mercile staff that made them so hateful of anyone not Species and have no idea what went down inside there. They haven't been freed long enough to know that all humans aren't like the ones they lived with all of their lives. I'm the enemy to them and they accused Justice of betraying them because he claimed me."

The medical center door opened and Jessie tensed. Ellie and her husband Fury came in and approached her.

"Stop," Tiger ordered them. "She's sworn to kill anyone who comes within ten feet of Justice's door." Tiger glanced at

Jessie. "Can they come to you? Ellie is human and Fury is one of Justice's most trusted friends too."

Ellie paled. "Jessie? It's okay. We heard what happened. We'd turned the phone off last night and slept late."

"I trust you." She studied Fury. "You too since you're with her."

Ellie's gaze widened at the sight of the gun in Jessie's hand. She bit her lip and inched closer. "Are you all right?"

Jessie shook her head.

Ellie lifted her hand and held out a travel mug. "I have some coffee. Why don't you drink it? You look as if you could use something warm."

Jessie hesitated but lifted her hand. "Thank you. I'm thirsty."

"She wouldn't take anything to drink or eat from us," Tiger said softly. "She's afraid we'll drug her."

Ellie passed the mug over. "They wouldn't do that to you. We're all on your side. What happened to you and Justice is horrifying. It was a few crazy males who didn't realize how stupid they were being. You know how that is. There's a few of them with every group."

"Thanks." Jessie sipped the coffee. "I know that but I'm not willing to risk Justice's life. This is my fault and I won't chance being wrong a second time. He didn't want anyone to know about us but I thought he was making too big a deal over it." She fought more tears. "He was right."

"No," Ellie shook her head. "You two love each other and no one gives a damn here that I'm full-on human. No one treats me badly, Jessie. They have accepted me with open arms. It was a few bad apples who created this mess. I'd kill and die to protect Fury. I understand why you're so scared though and why you have a gun." Her gaze flickered to it. "Will you please put it down while I talk to you? Just set it next to you? Those things terrify me."

Jessie placed it down on the desk next to her thigh. "I'm sorry."

"It's okay. Are you hungry? I could go home and fix you breakfast. I could bring you back more coffee."

"I would appreciate that but you make it. I should eat to keep up my strength."

Ellie nodded. "Okay, Jessie. Drink that and I'll get you more. I only have the one mug with a lid. What do you want to eat?"

Jessie drank the rest of the coffee and handed the cup back. "Anything easy. It doesn't matter. I don't want…"

Jessie tried to clear the spots that appeared before her eyes. She swallowed, her lips feeling numb and her tongue heavy. She tried to reach up to feel her mouth but her arms refused to lift. The meaning of her symptoms sank in but it was too late. Her eyes widened with shock as she stared at Ellie.

"You drugged me."

Ellie stepped back. "I'm sorry but you're in shock and wouldn't listen to reason. You and Justice are both safe. Just…"

Tiger caught Jessie as her body slumped. He grabbed the gun and handed it to Fury. He lifted her into the cradle of his arms, sat on the desk and held her against his chest.

"Thank you, Ellie. I know it was a lot to ask but I thought if she'd take food or drink from anyone, it would be you because you are human and you love a Species. She knows you can relate to her situation."

"I feel like shit," Ellie admitted. "Did she really kill four of them?"

Tiger nodded. "The son of a bitch leading them used a knife and stabbed Justice with it. When I came in she stood over Justice to protect him with two guns in her hands. She nearly shot us. The remaining son of a bitch decided to make a last-ditch effort to try to kill her or Justice when he threw himself through the slider door. She reacted before any of us could and sank five bullets into the bastard before he plowed into her. He was dead before he ever knew what hit him."

"Jessie is afraid she started a civil war," Halfpint informed them.

Ellie spun. "She said that?"

Tiny bit her lip. "What is it?"

"Not something that will ever happen here," Fury growled. "It's where members of the same group of people turn on each other and fight to the death. It is when one splits into two and fight for dominance."

"That will never happen," Breeze agreed. "We have enough idiots to fight without taking on each other."

Laugher sounded around the room. Tiger didn't laugh.

"We have secured everyone from testing facility five here and at Reservation," Tiger growled. "Jessie doesn't trust them and I have to agree. We can't be sure of what they had to deal with in Colorado. Some of them might attack again."

"Do you want to put her down?" Ellie glanced at Jessie on Tiger's lap.

"I will put her in bed with Justice when the doctor says it is fine. He would want her there and I want to keep her close to him."

"We're going to have to talk to each of the new ones." Fury shifted his stance. "I hate to say it but if they can't be a part of us, I don't want them running around."

"Fury!" Ellie gasped. "Are you saying we should kill them?"

"I said I don't want them running around. Maybe we can contain the dangerous ones until they smarten up."

"Justice will decide. For now," Tiger peered down at Jessie's sleeping form, "we have them separated and accounted for. I have officers talking to all of them to see where their heads are. My main concern is Jessie. She is either going to recover from this or she's going to shoot anyone she doesn't trust who goes near Justice." He suddenly grinned. "Hey, she could shoot reporters. That's a plan."

Fury chuckled. "Don't get excited. I know how great that would be but then Justice would be angry to have a mate locked up at a slammer."

"It's 'in the slammer'. And yes, that would be bad for her to be sent to prison. Of course, as his mate, she's a Species and they can't take her away since their laws don't apply here." Ellie pointed a finger at Tiger. "Don't think about it and wipe that grin off your face. You can't send her after them no matter how much you hate those vultures. Did anyone call her father? Maybe he could help her snap out of this and realize it's not as bad as she thinks."

"No humans," Tiger announced. "Imagine how it would sound if this got out. We're going for the 'we are better people' campaign and now we have five dead Species assassins. It would be a disaster."

"Public relations nightmare all the way," Fury agreed. "Her father isn't going to be called."

The door to Justice's room opened and Nurse Paul stepped out. "He's doing great." Paul glanced at Jessie in Tiger's arms. "Sorry," he whispered. "I didn't know she fell asleep. Justice is going to be fine and should wake soon."

Tiger pushed off from the desk. "Good. Let's go into his room and I'll put her next to him."

Paul shook his head. "She can't be put in bed with him."

Tiger arched his eyebrow. "Really? Stop me from putting her there." He pushed past Paul.

Tiger gently laid Jessie on the bed beside Justice. Both of them slept while he watched them. Pure rage filled him. His best friend and his mate could have been killed. His focus fixed on Jessie and his anger softened. She was tough and she loved Justice. His best friend had chosen his mate well. He backed away from the bed to leave them in peace and go back to sit on the desk.

Chapter Twenty-Two

℘

Justice woke and realized three things instantly. Jessie lay beside him sleeping, he was in pain and Tiger sat in a chair next to him, silently regarding him with a grim expression. He'd survived the attack since he was in Medical.

"How bad are my injuries and did you catch the fifth male?"

"Jessie killed him. You had surgery but you're going to be fine within a few days. I had Dr. Treadmont give you the drugs to help you heal faster so that's the reason if you feel a little aggressive. Please control it."

Justice turned his head to study Jessie. She lay curled on her side facing him, his arm rested under her head and his hand curved around her back. He didn't see a mark on her delicate features, reassuring him she hadn't been harmed. He felt relief. His attention shifted back to Tiger.

"When did she fall asleep?"

"She didn't." Tiger hesitated. "Don't get mad because I can explain. She's drugged. We had no other choice."

"Why?" Justice growled softly. "Was she harmed and needs the rest to heal?"

"She's fine except for the fact that you gave her two loaded guns with spare clips and she stood outside this room threatening to kill any Species besides Breeze or me if they came within ten feet of your door. She meant it. She said she would trust me since you do and she trusts Breeze because she's her friend."

"She doesn't know who to trust after the males came after us." He smiled. "She defied my orders to remain in the bathroom and saved my life. She is battleworthy, Tiger. You should have seen her."

"I did. We arrived and found her planted protectively over you and holding two guns. I'm lucky to be here because she pointed them right at me. The fifth male was outside the back slider of your office. He must have realized when we arrived that he had one last opportunity to kill both of you. He launched himself through the glass. She turned both guns on him, didn't miss once and he was dead before he ever touched either of you. She reacted before I could. We had to drug her, Justice. She was in shock and told Halfpint and Tiny that she thought we were going to suffer a civil war. She was ready to kill any of us who got near you, thinking we'd split loyalties. She's very protective of you."

Justice grinned and his arm tightened around her. "She's a perfect mate."

Tiger laughed. "I'd say so. Remind me to never piss you off. She'll hurt me."

"I'll explain things to her when the drugs wear off." Justice paused. "We need to weed out the new ones to make sure none of them want to come after Jessie or me. I won't allow that to happen."

"I thought of that already and ordered all of the new ones, including the females, to be detained for questioning. Our officers are talking to each of them to see if we have any more problems." He paused. "We will deal with them if there are more of them who hate humans enough to turn on their own people. We can't allow them to endanger any of us if they are unstable."

"I know." Justice sighed. "Did you ever think we'd be discussing this?"

"Never. It must be done though."

"Yes."

"The council is in the waiting room. They wanted to ask you to give permission for them to take over your duties while you are healing. They asked me to tell you that if you need to take some time to," Tiger's gaze drifted to Jessie, "calm your female, please take as many weeks away as you need." A grin suddenly split his face. "Everyone is requesting you hide your weapons from her in the future."

"She can keep them after she realizes this won't happen again." Justice suddenly laughed. It hurt and he groaned. "I would feel safer at night knowing she has access to a gun. She can protect me but I'll hide them when I make her angry."

Tiger laughed. "Should I tell everyone that is the reason why you won't take her guns away? They might believe it and not know you are teasing."

"No." Justice laughed. "Just tell them I'll think about it." His smile suddenly died. He glanced at Jessie and then Tiger. "Did she say anything about me?"

"She was worried and she cried when we thought you weren't going to make it."

"I meant about how I tore apart the first male who came at our bedroom? Was she horrified? Upset? Sickened? I never wanted her to see that side of me."

"She never said a word but I saw the body. She walked through his blood and had to have known how you killed him. It was obvious. Didn't you tell her we don't use weapons against one another? That it is our way? Didn't you tell her that we were sure it would result in death if our males ever fought when it comes to protecting a mate?"

"I never explained it clearly, in enough detail."

"You are afraid she won't be able to look at you again and not remember? I'm sure she'll still love you."

"I 'm worried she will fear me."

"You are her male, Justice. Her mate. You tore your bed apart at Reservation, over a female. She was the one, wasn't she? She was there that night but had to leave suddenly for her job. I had to allow their helicopter to land to pick her up during your press conference with the reporters outside the gates. I should have put it together but I assumed the female was one of ours."

"I should have told you but you know how you are when it comes to our males and humans. You'd have worried. She is all I've wanted since I first touched her and all I could think about."

"She will get over it if it bothers her, Justice. She is not new to you. She knows you and still put herself in your bed. That is trust that you would never cause her harm. She killed to protect you and sat out there on the other side of the door pointing two guns at council members." Tiger laughed. "She thought she was protecting you."

Justice groaned. "She didn't."

"She certainly did. They were amused but they stayed more than ten feet back. Well, except for Brawn. He walked closer. You know how he loves to push things."

"What happened?"

"She pointed one of her guns at the front of his jeans and told him unless he wanted neutered he should step back. He backed up."

Justice chuckled. "I wish I could have seen that."

Tiger grinned. "I did and I'll have many laughs over the memory. Speaking of Brawn, they realized you hadn't chosen anyone to take Jessie's place on the task team and they knew you had a meeting with Tim this morning. Brawn met with him instead and volunteered for the job. He left half an hour ago."

Justice tensed. "The task force?"

A grin split Tiger's face. "Won't they be in for a treat?"

"You should have stopped him."

Tiger laughed harder. "You are the one who agreed they could help you make decisions and take on some of your responsibilities."

Justice relaxed and smiled. "I wish I could see him interact with humans. What a nightmare. He would have been my last choice. I was thinking Flame would have been perfect since he enjoys spending time with humans."

"Yeah." Tiger chuckled. "I agree but they got Brawn instead. Poor Tim."

Jessie suddenly stirred next to Justice. He turned to her, ignoring Tiger. Jessie's eyes flickered open and he smiled at her, cupping her face. "Hi, Jessie."

Jessie smiled in return but memory returned as her eyes widened with alarm. She tried to jerk up in the bed but Justice held her down by tightening his hold on her. "It's over. We're safe. Calm down, honey."

Jessie flashed her gaze around the room and found Tiger. She glared. "You had Ellie drug me."

"I did. You wouldn't listen so I thought you would listen to Justice." He stood and walked out of the room.

Jessie was furious. "He had me drugged."

Justice grinned. "He was probably afraid my mate was going to kill him. I'm proud of you but..." His smile disappeared. "I'm going to punish you for disobedience. You should have stayed inside the bathroom."

"I saved your ass."

"I know. Thank you. You still need to be punished and I decided the best way to teach you a lesson."

She was pissed off. "You can't be serious? I saved your life, Justice. Just because I'm a human doesn't mean I had to hide inside the bathroom. You never would have asked one of your women to do that. You —"

Justice kissed her. Jessie groaned against his mouth, happy to feel his lips on hers, thrilled that he felt well enough to do it. Her hands reached for his chest to assure his heart beat strongly. He pulled away and stared deeply into her eyes.

"Will you at least listen to what kind of punishment you are getting before you start yelling?"

"Fine. Tell me and I'll tell you if you can or not."

A growl sounded in the back of his throat while his eyes narrowed. "I'm sending you to Reservation. I decided the best way to teach you to listen to me is for you to spend at least two weeks out there."

"You're sending me away?" She was stunned and hurt. "But—"

"I wasn't finished." He smiled. "I'm going to personally give you lots of orders and you will learn to follow every one of them." He pulled her closer. "I'm going to demand you take off your clothes and climb into bed with me. So, do you think this is fitting punishment?"

She grinned. "I have been very bad."

His lips brushed hers. "You need to learn how to take orders. Should we start right now?"

Her eyes darted down to the bandage on his hip. "You're hurt."

"I'm alive and you are in my arms. I always want you."

Jessie suddenly grinned. "All that movement can't be good for you. Do you know what that means?"

He arched his eyebrow at her.

"I should do all the work." She pushed him onto his back. "You should lie back and let me take care of you."

He growled but stayed flat. Jessie sat up and leaned over him. Her tongue circled his nipple and she sucked it into her mouth. Justice's fingers dug into her hair and a purr rumbled from his throat. She teased and taunted his nipple until the hold on her hair became too tight. She laughed and released his nipple.

"Slow and steady, right?"

"They gave me drugs to help me heal," he said through clenched teeth. "I have no patience. I'm feeling extremely basic."

"What does that mean?"

His eyes narrowed and his nose flared. "I'm super horny and aggressive so don't tease me for long. I can't take it in this state of limited control. I don't want to hurt you and if you tease me too long I might in my need to be inside you."

Jessie climbed off the bed, glanced at the door and shoved off the borrowed pants. She climbed back on the bed and looked down at the sheet covering Justice. She grinned.

"You made a tent."

He chuckled and lifted the sheet. "Do you want to climb in here with me?"

Jessie glanced at his hip. If she were really careful she could sit on him and not touch the wound. "I don't want to climb in. I want to climb on." She gripped the sheet and lifted it enough to swing her knee over him carefully. She stood on her knees straddling his hips and reached between them. Her hand wrapped around his hot, rigid shaft, stroking it. He purred and closed his eyes.

Jessie slowly guided Justice's cock to the entrance of her pussy and eased down on him. His hands were suddenly gripping her hips and his eyes snapped open to meet her gaze. He tried to move her on him with his hands but she swatted them away.

"Hold still," she ordered softly. "Your stitches."

He snarled and his hands tightened. His impatience and aggressiveness turned her on more. He hadn't been understating it. She eased her body lower, letting him sink deeper inside her. He groaned.

"Fast and hard, Jessie."

She hesitated. "Don't move. We're going slow and steady."

"You are going to kill me."

"No, I'm going to make you test the glass windows to see if they are roar proof. Your injury is going to kill you if you don't hold still. We shouldn't be doing this at all but I want you as much as you want me."

"I do," he agreed.

The door suddenly banged open behind them. Justice jerked into a sitting position and wrapped his arms around Jessie protectively, while she gasped.

Tiger stepped inside the room and closed the door behind him. He spun, presenting his back to them. "Sorry!"

"Get out," Justice snarled.

Jessie was horrified. She was straddling Justice and Tiger had walked in on them having sex. She would have jumped off his lap but he held her down so tightly she was impaled on him.

"I'm sorry," Tiger repeated, sidestepped to the corner and his arm rose.

Jessie gawked at the camera as Tiger tore it off the wall. Her face dropped to Justice's shoulder, remembering the camera that had been in Beauty's room had sound too. That meant if there was a camera watching Justice for security purposes, not only had they just seen everything but they'd heard too.

"Sorry. No one else is getting in and I'll, uh, burn the tape." He fled.

Justice laughed so hard he shook Jessie's body on his. She lifted her head to glare. "What is so funny? Did you know it was there?"

He sobered. "I never thought about it. We keep them for females so they are safe. Who besides you would attack me sexually?" He eased back on the bed. "That is always welcome." He caressed her hips.

"Who watches that camera? Did he say tape? Was that recorded?"

"The entire security room watches." He licked his lips. "Well, I have good news and bad news."

She frowned. "What?"

"The bad news is that now my males know that Justice North submits in bed to his mate. The good news is that I guess my threat to mount you in public isn't credible since everyone will hear about this." He grinned.

She fought the urge to laugh. "I'm going to go hide now."

Justice thrust up into her. "You're staying right here and so am I."

He purred. At Jessie's moan he thrust into her again. Jessie rocked her hips, riding him. She forgot all about her embarrassment and made love to the man she loved.

Chapter Twenty-Three

∞

Jessie stared at her father while Senator Jacob Hills regarded her silently. His blue eyes were unreadable as they remained in Justice's office. Jessie had asked Justice to step out so she could privately talk to her father.

"So," she finished. "I love him and he loves me. We are going to try to keep a lid on this until we get back from Reservation. Justice is taking a few weeks off to give us some time to spend alone."

Jessie searched her father's face for any sign of emotion but couldn't pick up a single one. Whatever he thought or felt, he kept it to himself. The man was a master at doing that. It's why he was so good at his job.

"Say something."

"Are you sure about this?"

She frowned. "I called you to come here because I want you to give me away at my wedding. I'm marrying him, Dad. I love him and he's everything to me. I've never been surer of anything in my life. Say so now if you don't want to do it because I'm getting married in ten minutes. Justice was adamant about marrying me before the honeymoon." She smiled. "I didn't give a damn myself, being with him is enough but he wants to do this right."

A smile cracked Senator Jacob Hill's lips and his gaze softened. "I'm glad to hear that. I'd be honored to have him for a son and be proud to walk you down the aisle."

Jessie threw herself at her dad. They hugged tightly, him more so than her.

"Can't. Breathe. Need air," she hissed.

He released her, chuckling. "Sorry. Where is Justice?"

"He wanted to tell you about the two of us himself but I kind of threatened to buy him socks if he didn't let me do it alone."

Her father laughed. "That's an effective threat?"

She laughed. "The man doesn't own socks and hates them."

"Let me go shake his hand and welcome to the family. Ten minutes, huh?" He glanced at his watch. "You could have at least given me a little hint that there was going to be a wedding. I would have dressed better." His gaze roamed over her. "Jeans, Jess? You're really getting married in jeans?"

"Justice loves me. I asked nicely and he agreed we could get married in them."

Jacob laughed. "You got him out of a suit and tie? He's marrying you in jeans?"

She grabbed his hand. "Come on. He's been worried that you'll try to talk me out of it. He's afraid I'll change my mind. I told him that wasn't going to happen but he's still learning that I stick to my guns."

Justice waited down the hall, looking tense. Jessie winked. Justice visibly relaxed. He pulled his hands out of the front pockets of his jeans. Jessie noticed the jeans and black tank top he wore. It was the outfit she'd met him in. He looked so hot and sexy in those clothes with his hair down that she licked her lips. The urge to drool was there.

The two men shook hands and her father gripped his shoulder. "Welcome to the family, Justice. You are going to have your hands full with this one." He released him.

Justice chuckled. "I look forward to it every day."

Jessie laughed at seeing that aroused glint in Justice's eyes, knowing his thoughts had turned to sex. They exchanged the joke when their gazes met. Justice reached out and pulled Jessie into his arms to tuck her in front of his body.

Tiger stepped out into the hallway and peered at the three of them. He blew out air loudly and smiled. "So everything is good?"

Jessie's father laughed. "I'm happy that Jessie and Justice are getting married. Was there ever any doubt I would be?"

Tiger nodded. "Hell yes. The minister is here. Are we ready?"

Jessie turned her head and peered at Justice. "I've been ready."

"Me too." He hugged her before reluctantly releasing his hold. He looked at his soon-to-be father-in-law. "We're honeymooning at Reservation for two weeks but plan to have a more public wedding soon. We realize this is going to be a press nightmare. We wanted to do this small, private one right now and go away together before having to deal with however your people take it."

"Well, I will be the first one in front of them telling them how happy I am when you do announce it and how I couldn't have picked a better man for my only daughter."

Justice cleared his throat. "Thank you, Jacob. I'm deeply honored and I will kill or die to protect her. She makes my life complete. Her happiness goes before my own, always."

"I know." Jacob Hills blinked at tears. "Damn. Don't make me cry." He laughed. "Let's get you two married so you can leave for the honeymoon."

They all walked outside. Jessie saw that her father was a little confused at the line of golf carts waiting by the doors. He looked to her for an answer.

"Is it an outdoor wedding?"

"There's only one place to party at Homeland. Have you ever been to the bar?"

"No. I haven't."

She grinned. "You're in for a treat then. There is going to be dancing."

His features brightened. "I love that. I learned how to waltz for that ball I was invited to at the White House next month."

Everyone in the golf cart laughed except Jacob Hills. He frowned. "What's so funny?"

"These are actual fun parties, Dad. No politics are allowed and ditch that tie."

"You'll have fun," Justice assured him, taking Jessie's hand and kissing it. "We've planned a nice wedding for everyone to enjoy."

Her father glanced at Justice. "I'm sincerely glad to have you for a son, Justice. Whatever you do, don't take your phone or laptop on your honeymoon." He laughed. "The only work you should be doing is making sure you keep my daughter out of trouble."

Justice grinned "I intend to spend all my time getting to know your daughter extremely well. I swear she's my priority and work is going to scale back so I have plenty of time for us to be together."

Jessie grinned. "I'm going to teach him how to relax and have fun."

He met her gaze, she knew he was remembering the night she gave him a massage on the back of the couch, and he softly purred.

"Did you make that sound?" Jacob gaped at his future son-in-law.

Jessie laughed. "Nope. That was me," she lied. "I do that sometimes because it's fun." She gave him an innocent look. "Come on, you fell for that? My future husband is a total badass, not some kitten."

Her father laughed and turned away, following Tiger to one of the carts.

"Jessie," Justice whispered, making sure no one heard. "Thank you."

She looked up and winked. "You owe me." Her gaze lowered down his body and paused over the front of his jeans before she met his gaze again. "I've always got your back and your front."

Also by Laurann Dohner

❧

eBooks:

Zorn Warriors 3: Tempting Rever
Zorn Warriors 4: Berrr's Vow

Print Books:
Cyborg Seduction 1: Burning Up Flint
Cyborg Seduction 2: Kissing Steel
Cyborg Seduction 3: Melting Iron
Cyborg Seduction 4: Touching Ice
Cyborg Seduction 5: Stealing Coal
Cyborg Seduction 6: Redeeming Zorus
Cyborg Seduction 7: Taunting Krell
Mating Heat 1: Mate Set
New Species 1: Fury
New Species 2: Slade
New Species 3: Valiant
Riding the Raines 1: Propositioning Mr. Raine
Riding the Raines 2: Raine on Me
Something Wicked This Way Comes Volume 1 *(anthology)*
Something Wicked This Way Comes Volume 2 *(anthology)*
Zorn Warriors 1 & 2: Loving Zorn
Zorn Warriors 3: Tempting Rever
Zorn Warriors 4: Berrr's Vow

About Laurann Dohner

❧

I'm a full-time "in-house supervisor" (sounds *much* better than plain ol' housewife), mother and writer. I'm addicted to caramel iced coffee, the occasional candy bar (or two) and trying to get at least five hours of sleep at night.

I love to write all kinds of stories. I think the best part about writing is the fact that real life is always uncertain, always tossing things at us that we have no control over, but when you write, you can make sure there's always a happy ending. I *love* that about writing. I love to sit down at my computer desk, put on my headphones and listen to loud music to block out the world around me, so I can create worlds in front of me.

❧

The author welcomes comments from readers. You can find her website and email address on her author bio page at www.ellorascave.com.

Tell Us What You Think

We appreciate hearing reader opinions about our books. You can email us at Service@ellorascave.com (when contacting Customer Service, be sure to state the book title and author).

Why an electronic book?

We live in the Information Age—an exciting time in the history of human civilization, in which technology rules supreme and continues to progress in leaps and bounds every minute of every day. For a multitude of reasons, more and more avid literary fans are opting to purchase e-books instead of paper books. The question from those not yet initiated into the world of electronic reading is simply: *Why?*

1. *Price.* An electronic title at Ellora's Cave Publishing runs anywhere from 40% to 75% less than the cover price of the exact same title in paperback format. Why? Basic mathematics and cost. It is less expensive to publish an e-book (no paper and printing, no warehousing and shipping) than it is to publish a paperback, so the savings are passed along to the consumer.

2. *Space.* Running out of room in your house for your books? That is one worry you will never have with electronic books. For a low one-time cost, you can purchase a handheld device specifically designed for e-reading. Many e-readers have large, convenient screens for viewing. Better yet, hundreds of titles can be stored within your new library—on a single microchip. There are a variety of e-readers from different manufacturers. You can also read e-books on your PC or laptop computer. (Please note that Ellora's Cave does not endorse any specific brands.

You can check our website at www.ellorascave.com for information we make available to new consumers.)

3. *Mobility.* Because your new e-library consists of only a microchip within a small, easily transportable e-reader, your entire cache of books can be taken with you wherever you go.

4. **Personal Viewing Preferences.** Are the words you are currently reading too small? Too large? Too… ANNOYING? Paperback books cannot be modified according to personal preferences, but e-books can.

5. *Instant Gratification.* Is it the middle of the night and all the bookstores near you are closed? Are you tired of waiting days, sometimes weeks, for bookstores to ship the novels you bought? Ellora's Cave Publishing sells instantaneous downloads twenty-four hours a day, seven days a week, every day of the year. Our webstore is never closed. Our e-book delivery system is 100% automated, meaning your order is filled as soon as you pay for it.

Those are a few of the top reasons why electronic books are replacing paperbacks for many avid readers.

As always, Ellora's Cave welcomes your questions and comments. We invite you to email us at Service@ellorascave.com or write to us directly at Ellora's Cave Publishing Inc., 1056 Home Avenue, Akron, OH 44310-3502.

ELLORA'S CAVE
Romanticon

Annual convention
for women who
refuse to behave

www.JasmineJade.com/Romanticon
For additional info contact: conventions@ellorascave.com

Discover for yourself why readers can't get enough of the multiple award-winning publisher Ellora's Cave. Be sure to visit EC on the web at www.ellorascave.com to find erotic reading experiences that will leave you breathless. You can also find our books at all the major e-tailers (Barnes & Noble, Amazon Kindle, Sony, Kobo, Google, Apple iBookstore, All Romance eBooks, and others).

www.ellorascave.com

CPSIA information can be obtained at www.ICGtesting.com
Printed in the USA
BVOW07s1659260813

329576BV00001B/27/P

9 781419 967054